DARK HUNGER

SARA REINKE

ZEBRA BOOKS
Kensington Publishing Corp.
www.kensingtonbooks.com

ZEBRA BOOKS are published by

Kensington Publishing Corp.
850 Third Avenue
New York, NY 10022

All Kensington titles, imprints, and distributed lines are available at special quantity discounts for bulk purchases for sales promotion, premiums, fund-raising, educational, or institutional use.

Special book excerpts or customized printings can also be created to fit specific needs. For details, write or phone the office of the Kensington Special Sales Manager: Attn. Special Sales Department. Kensington Publishing Corp., 850 Third Avenue, New York, NY 10022. Phone: 1-800-221-2647.

Zebra and the Z logo Reg. U.S. Pat. & TM Off.

ISBN-13: 978-1-4201-0054-9
ISBN-10: 1-4201-0054-8

First Zebra Mass Market Printing: September 2008
10 9 8 7 6 5 4 3 2 1

Printed in the United States of America

ACKNOWLEDGMENTS

Special thanks to Kevin Strasser for letting me pick his brain about life and love as an above-knee amputee. (And to his wife for letting him let me.)

Chapter One

Rene Morin pressed the barrel of the Sig Sauer P228 nine-millimeter pistol against his right temple and looked down at the cell phone in his hand. He'd set it to speaker mode, and listened as the number he'd dialed only moments earlier began to ring. Part of him hoped the woman on the other end of the line wouldn't answer. *But, oh,* mon Dieu, *another part of me hopes like hell that she does.*

He glanced at the digital clock on the small end table beside the couch. It was just after two o'clock in the morning. Considering he was in a motel room just outside of San Antonio, Texas, that made it . . .

What? Midnight in San Francisco? Eleven o'clock?

He never could keep track of changes in time zones. *That's what happens when you live three times the lifespan of a human. Little things like time become irrelevant.*

Rene's mother had been human, but his father had been what horror movies would have called a vampire. Only recently, Rene had discovered that there were others like him, creatures who called themselves the Brethren living tucked away and in secret in Kentucky. Secluded and relatively self-sufficient, the Brethren weren't allowed to leave the compounds that masqueraded as champion Thoroughbred horse farms to the outside world. How Rene's part of the Brethren family tree had managed to escape remained a mystery to him. He'd only just learned of such things from two other recent Brethren escapees—a set of twins who'd brought more questions with them than answers.

Brandon Noble, Rene thought, as the phone he'd dialed rang for the fifth time. *And his stubborn con-nasse of a sister, Tessa Davenant.*

Tessa. If ever a woman had been designed to drive a man to plugging a bullet in his head, Rene figured it was her. Just thinking about what she'd done that afternoon in Thibodaux, Louisiana, was enough to piss him off all over again.

But he didn't want to think about Tessa right now. He wanted to think about the pistol in one hand, the phone in the other, and the terrible, leaden loneliness in his heart that had led him to seek comfort from each.

"Hello?" A woman's voice came through the speaker on his cell phone, hoarse and sleepy, startling him from his thoughts. The barrel of the pistol wavered, then lowered from his face, and Rene let it dangle in his hand, resting against his lap as he blinked at the phone.

Irene.

"Hello?"

Christ, she sounds exactly the same.

He'd kept tabs on her surreptitiously over the years, and knew that she'd called California home for more than two decades. Even so, time and distance hadn't been able to fully strip the lilting Southern drawl from her voice, just as they hadn't from Rene's.

"Hello? Is somebody there?"

His throat had constricted; he couldn't speak, even if he'd wanted to. He stared at the phone, even as the illuminated display went dark, the woman on the line—

Irene—hanging up on him. He was surprised by the sudden warmth in his eyes; they had flooded involuntarily with tears at the sound of her voice.

Viens m'enculer, *I miss you.*

The phone slipped from his hand, falling to the floor between his feet. He left it there, reaching instead for a bottle of Bloodhorse Reserve on the coffee table in front of him. It was practically empty; over the course of the last couple of hours, Rene had downed all but a meager swig. *Liquid courage,* he'd told himself, and he'd needed it. *A man can't just up and call his wife almost forty years after she left him without a little bit of something distilled beneath his belt.*

He swallowed what remained of the bourbon and smacked his lips appreciatively at the bittersweet flavor. That was how the Brethren clans had been able to amass a sizable fortune over the years: bourbon distilling and horse breeding. *Paris Hilton rich,* was how Lina Jones, his former partner on the police force, had described Tessa and her fraternal twin, Brandon. Rene thought that was a pretty accurate assessment. In his estimation, Tessa was as spoiled as Paris Hilton. *And every bit as fucking annoying, too.*

As he set the bottle back on the table, he cut his eyes deliberately away from the faded, creased photograph beside it. Tessa had found it in Thibodaux earlier that day; it had fallen out from among the pages of that damn enormous book she seemed hell-bent on lugging around. *A Tome,* she'd called it, with particular emphasis on the pronunciation of the word to indicate she thought it needed an initial capital letter.

His grandmother had obviously hidden the book. He'd never even seen it before that afternoon. Within its brittle, musty pages, Odette LaCroix had tucked the photo of him and Irene standing side by side in their Sunday bests, Irene with a little pillbox hat on her head, her brow covered by a thin, netted veil, a bouquet of inexpensive flowers clasped between her gloved hands.

Our wedding day, he thought, and he didn't need to see Odette's small, prim handwriting on the back to know the date it had been taken. *May 19, 1970.*

His gaze traveled from the picture to the pistol that he still held in his hand. *You were too good for me, Irene,* he thought. *I never deserved you. Or our baby.*

Still blinking against the dim fog of tears her voice had brought to his eyes, Rene raised the gun again. Once more, he pressed the barrel against his forehead, and closed his eyes, resting his index finger lightly against the trigger.

"I miss you," he whispered aloud, and that was when the door to the adjoining bedroom flew open with a clatter. His startled eyes flew open, and he had about a half second to realize Tessa Davenant was rushing across the room, her mouth open as she yelled at him.

"What are you doing?" She plowed into him, knocking him backward against the sofa, and he felt her paw at the pistol, tearing it away from his grasp. She uttered a sharp, disgusted sound as if she'd just grabbed hold of a live rat, and threw the gun across the room, sending it clattering against the TV stand.

"Have you lost your mind?" she cried, and then she reared back and swung her hand, slapping him across the face. "What the hell is the matter with you?"

When he didn't immediately answer her, she moved to slap him again and he frowned, catching her wrist in his hand. She struggled against him, and he caught her other arm in his free hand. After a momentary tussle—she was a skinny little thing, but surprisingly strong—Rene shoved her onto her back against the couch cushions. He leaned over, using his weight to pin her down and hold her still, despite her best efforts at struggling beneath him.

"Get off me!" she yelled.

"Stop trying to hit me, then," he replied.

At this, twin patches of bright, angry color bloomed in her cheeks and her brows furrowed. "I wasn't trying to hit you. I was trying to keep you from shooting yourself in the head!"

"Well, who the hell asked you to?" he asked, his frown deepening.

Tessa blinked, falling abruptly still. He had to admit that as annoying and infuriating as she could be, she was a damn beautiful girl. Not his type, granted—he preferred his women blond, big-breasted and *quiet*— but striking nonetheless. She had a heart-shaped face with large, dark eyes framed in heavy lashes; a small, delicate nose and lips just curved enough and full enough to make him curious as to what it might be like to kiss them. Her dark hair was cropped at chin length in a sleek, simple bob, with a fringe of thick bangs that fell just above her brow line. Brandon had told Rene that Tessa was a dancer, trained in classical ballet, and her legs were long like a ballerina's, firm and shapely with muscles.

"You're crazy," she said.

I must be if I'm sitting here starting to sport wood thinking about you, pischouette, he thought, shifting his weight to resettle the suddenly strained crotch of his jeans.

"And you're drunk," Tessa said, with a glance at the table and the bottle of bourbon. "Get off me."

"And if I don't?" he asked, raising his brow. She was close enough and he was drunk enough to feel reckless and bold, so he leaned toward her. Tessa squirmed, turning her face away as he drew the tip of his nose against her cheek. "What are you going to do, *pischouette*?" he murmured against her ear, feeling the satiny softness of her hair against his face, the sudden, hammering cadence of her heartbeat through the thin fabric of her nightgown. He could also feel the hardened points of her nipples through this same silken gown, and the realization of this made his growing erection become even more uncomfortable.

"Get off me, Rene," she said again. "I . . . I mean it."

Using the tip of his tongue, he drew the bottom of her earlobe lightly between his lips, and heard her gasp, a sharp, fluttering intake of breath. He slid his hand up her thigh, trailing from her knee to her hip, pushing her robe and gown up and out of his way. He'd started the game just to mess with her; he was indeed drunk, and feeling lonely and vindictive to boot, but now, as his hand moved against her, his fingertips reaching the lace-trimmed edge of her panties, he found himself no longer necessarily playing. His arousal had suddenly grown large enough to press painfully against the seam of his fly.

He raised his head and looked down at her. She was wide-eyed and nearly hiccuping for breath, trembling and tense beneath him, her face filled with simultaneous anticipation and fright.

She looks like a virgin on her wedding night, Rene thought—an impossibility, considering Tessa was four months pregnant. That little physiological technicality was probably the only thing that had kept him from wringing her neck earlier that day, or at least had prevented him from leaving her ass behind in Thibodaux.

"Do you know, *chère,*" he whispered, lowering his face to kiss her, letting his lips brush against her mouth as he spoke, "the things I could do to you right now?"

"You can start"—Tessa's brows narrowed as she locked gazes with him—"by getting off me."

She grabbed him by the hand and hyperextended his thumb and wrist with a single, sudden twist. Shocking pain ripped up his arm, clear through his entire body, like he'd just grabbed hold of a high-voltage power line. The maneuver paralyzed him instantly; he sucked in a sharp breath through gritted teeth, unable to move or pull free without sending more spears of molten agony racking through him. "*Viens m'enculer!*" he gasped. *Fuck me!*

He gasped again as she turned him loose. "Jesus Christ," he growled, wincing as he rubbed his aching wrist and stumbled clumsily upright. *Mental note,* he told himself. *Never fuck with a woman whose brother is a black belt in aikido.* "That hurt, goddamn it."

"Good!" She punted him in the ass. "You want to get wasted and kill yourself? Fine by me. I don't know what I was thinking to have tried to stop you."

"You were thinking you'd be stranded here because you can't drive a stick shift," he offered, which only made her scowl even more. He managed a hoarse laugh, though his wrist was still sore. "Oh, come on, *pischouette.* I was just joking. My car's an automatic."

His bleary gaze had wandered from her face to the creamy margin of flesh visible above the V of her fuschia-trimmed robe. He could just make out the side swells of her admittedly lovely breasts as they came together in a semblance of cleavage, one made all the more apparent as she crossed her arms. When she followed his eyes, she leapt to her feet, snatching the robe in her hands to close it more fully. "You are such an ass," she said as she turned on her heel and marched back toward her bedroom. "And stop calling me *pischouette!*"

She slammed the door behind her, leaving him alone. Rene forked his fingers through his hair, shoving the shaggy mess back from his face. Tessa Davenant was a piece of work like no other he'd ever seen. And he had miles to go before he would be rid of her—clear to Lake Tahoe, California, in fact.

He sighed. "It might be easier to just fucking shoot myself," he muttered.

Chapter Two

I can, too, drive a stick shift, Tessa thought, fuming as she glowered at the closed door now separating her and Rene Morin. *Asshole.*

She couldn't drive one very well, granted, but she could sure as hell get away from him if need be. Brandon had taught her using his tutor Jackson's car, an old, mud-brown Nissan Sentra with threadbare seats, manual transmission and a bumper sticker that proclaimed: *HONK ALL YOU WANT—I CAN'T HEAR YOU!*

Like Jackson, Brandon was deaf. He was also mute, both conditions the result of injuries he'd suffered as a young child during a botched robbery at the great house. Three farm workers had snuck inside in the wee hours of the night and tried to burglarize the Nobles. Brandon had stumbled upon them unexpectedly, and they'd assaulted him.

Tessa remembered clearly: a bright and flawless September afternoon, the first time Brandon had tried to teach her to drive. They'd both been seventeen, still a year away from what was supposed to be their bloodletting ceremonies to mark them as adults among the Brethren; a year away from the night when

Tessa would be wed to Martin Davenant, a man at least five times her age.

More like sold into slavery to him, she thought as she sat on the motel bed. Memories of that summer were bittersweet for her; sweet because she'd still enjoyed the envelope of naïveté that had always surrounded her at the great house and bitter because those had been the last, fleeting moments of such innocent happiness.

Now down-shift into first again. She remembered Brandon flapping a note in her face, one he'd written on a page from the spiral-bound notebook he carried in a brass case around his neck. He could lip-read and, like all of the Brethren, communicate through telepathic ability—although unlike other Brethren, Brandon's was severely limited, again thanks to his childhood injuries.

Jackson had also taught Brandon sign language, and Brandon, in turn, had taught Tessa, but at the moment, her eyes were on the road in front of her as the engine suddenly died with a shuddering wheeze.

"Damn it," she muttered, slapping the steering wheel and turning to her brother in wide-eyed exasperation. "I did it again."

It's all right, he signed. *You're letting out the clutch too fast, that's all.*

They had driven out to the farm's back acreage, where the Nobles' property abutted the neighboring Giscard horse farm. The "road" in front of Tessa, so to speak, was in actuality an open sea of tall grass and wildflowers, broken occasionally by dense islands of trees. This wasn't one of the Grandfather's pristine rolling fields of lush, tended bluegrass where his prized Thoroughbreds grazed; here was a forgotten corner of land, an abandoned expanse where few among the Brethren ever tread with any frequency, and a place where Brandon had thought Tessa could practice driving undiscovered. Neither of the twins was supposed to know how to drive, but Brandon at least could probably get away with having learned. As a female among the Brethren, Tessa wasn't allowed such luxuries.

Try again, Brandon signed from the passenger seat, with a glance in the side-view mirror, then over his shoulder, his dark eyes somewhat anxious. He'd been doing this off and on for the last several minutes, and Tessa frowned, pivoting in her seat to follow his gaze.

"What is it?" she asked.

He shook his head. *Nothing,* he signed. *Never mind.*

"Do you sense something?" It seemed impossible that anyone might discover them out there in the middle of nowhere, but then again, one never knew. The Brethren employed a staff of more than forty humans called the Kinsfolk. The Brethren weren't allowed to feed on these humans, and the Kinsfolk, in turn, helped keep the farms stocked with migrant workers upon whom the Brethren sated their blood-lust. They also managed the primary, day-to-day responsibilities of the Brethren's combined 1,750-acre properties, so there was always the remote possibility that their duties had taken one or more of the Kinsfolk that far out. "Is someone there, Brandon?"

His telepathy had been damaged during his attack, like his ears and voice, but Tessa had come to notice over the years that he was often more aware of things than she was. She supposed it was because he had less to distract him, no noises or voices to compete for his attention.

He shook his head again, then smiled as he moved his hands in the air. *It's nothing.* He nodded at the steering wheel once in encouragement. *Try again.*

Tessa put the Sentra in gear and turned the key in the ignition. She wondered what Jackson would think if he'd known that Brandon had taken her off the main roads twining through the farm. True, Jackson had said they could borrow the car, but he hadn't said anything about taking it bumping and jostling through fields. *Not to mention letting me grind his transmission all to hell along the way.*

They continued along, bouncing across the rolling hillocks as the grass, blanched from the late-summer sun and nearly as tall as the car's wheel wells, whispered and slapped against the Nissan's doors. She did better this time, making it at least another quarter mile before the car died once more.

Tessa uttered a little cry of disgust, clasping the steering wheel between her hands and giving it a frustrated little shake. "I'm never going to get this!"

Yes, you will, Brandon signed. *It just takes time, that's—* There was more, but she cut her eyes away and missed it. Ahead of them, protruding out of the grass, were what looked like the remnants of walls, crumbling heaps of stone nearly buried beneath an overgrowth of weeds.

Brandon, she thought, forgetting herself in sudden, surprised wonder and opening her mind. *Look at that.*

Brandon followed her gaze and the two of them sat there, silent, for a moment. *What is it?* she thought to him at length, and when he didn't immediately answer, she turned and tapped his shoulder to draw his gaze. "What is it?"

He shook his head. *I don't know,* he signed.

She reached for her seat belt, unbuckling it, and he caught her arm as she opened her door. *What are you doing?* he asked, his eyes wide, his expression inexplicably alarmed.

"I'm going to get out for a minute," she said. "I want to take a closer look."

Tessa, wait . . . he began, but she ignored him, stepping out into the bright, warm sunshine, being immediately enveloped in the thick humidity of early September. The air buzzed and thrummed with the overlapping symphonies of crickets and cicadas. She watched grasshoppers the size of her little finger dart away on the wing as she began to wade through the grass.

Tessa, don't, Brandon thought, opening his car door and standing.

Tessa turned long enough to smile at him. "Olive oil," she said with exaggerated emphasis. It was a long-standing joke between them, one that usually drew at least a smirk from him. Brandon had explained to her once that *olive oil* and *I love you* were pretty much identical to someone who was deaf and could read lips. The way a person's mouth moved to form the sounds were virtually the same. Tessa had seized upon this, and was fond of teasing Brandon good-naturedly with it.

Today it didn't put him any more at ease whatsoever. *We need to get the car back to Jackson. Come on,* he thought. *Besides, I've got a bad feeling about this place.*

What do you mean? She walked again, undeterred despite the obvious apprehension in his words. She felt drawn to the site somehow, a strange and persistent whispering in her mind, pulling her along. *I think these are walls, Brandon. There was a building here or something.*

Which didn't make any sense. The farms the Brethren called home had belonged to them for well over two hundred years, lands chartered in 1790. The only structures that had ever stood there had been built or sanctioned by the Brethren, and Tessa didn't know of any that had ever been constructed—much less torn down—in that spot.

"What the hell is this place?" she murmured to no one in particular as she drew the blade of her hand to her brow, shielding her eyes from the sun's glare. The closer she came, the more of the ruins she could see. Whatever it had once been, it had been enormous; what remained was an expansive circumference that had once been a creek stone foundation crowned with the toppled scraps of brick walls.

I think it was a great house, she thought, turning to Brandon. He hadn't moved; he stood rooted in place beside the car, his dark eyes round and apprehensive.

It's just an old barn, Tessa, he signed. *One that somebody tore down a long time ago. Come on. We need to get back.*

It's not a barn, she signed in reply. He knew it, too; she didn't need to open her mind to sense it. He knew, and it frightened him for some reason.

The grass stood almost to her waist in places. She could part it with her hands as she cleaved a slim path. Yellow flowers like tinted daisies—ashy sunflowers, they were called—wild blue sage and purple waxweed dappled the field around her in bright color, while scarlet pimpernel stood out in vermilion pinpoints among the fallen stones. Near the crumbled foundation, Tessa caught sight of cut stone among the wildflowers and weeds, a long, rectangular tread from what had once been a flight of steps leading presumably to a porch or entrance.

The great houses of the Brethren were sprawling, four-story Victorian mansions that had been constructed during the late 1880s, one of the first directives undertaken by Tessa's grandfather and other Brethren males of his generation when they had been appointed as Elders, the most venerable leaders among the clans. The original houses on the property had been built shortly after the land's acquisition nearly a century earlier; Tessa knew this because paintings depicting them remained on display in the Grandfather's study, along with an old, framed daguerreotype of Augustus Noble as a younger man, standing outside of the house that had once belonged to the Nobles. She had always liked that picture, because the Grandfather was a strikingly handsome man—nearly identical in appearance to Brandon, in fact—and reminded her of her brother in the image.

Was this one of the original houses? she thought, stepping carefully over the ruined stairs and into the circumference of the remaining foundation. *I thought they'd just built the newer ones over the old, but maybe they didn't.*

Not much remained of the building, only the front stairs, the foundation, a few fragments of brick wall and a crumbling chimney left like a listing grave marker to rise from the grass. And yet, to Tessa, it felt as though the air around it tingled, like the broken rocks and fallen bricks were alive somehow, almost electrified.

What is this place? she wondered again as she carefully cut a diagonal path across the foundation. In a far corner, where the weeds grew particularly thick, she saw a hole in the ground, cut into the limestone. Curious, she drew closer, kneeling down and pushing aside the tangled grass and thistles with her hands. The hole was about three feet in circumference, a gaping pit that led downward into darkness. It had been covered with a heavy iron grate that was rusty enough to be antique, and secured in place with a padlock that was shiny enough to be new. *Someone has been out here recently, then,* Tessa realized. *But why? And why would they bother locking up a hole in the ground?*

And then she knew.

The Beneath.

The Brethren farms were reputedly crisscrossed by a network of subterranean tunnels and caverns called the Beneath. All of the great houses were joined by these passageways, and each supposedly had entrances in the cellars. Tessa didn't know what lay in the Beneath. No one among the Brethren did, with the purported exception of the Elders. But rumors ran rampant, especially among the younger Brethren like Tessa, her siblings and cousins, about why the tunnels had been built, and what the Brethren kept secreted away in them.

"It's the Abomination," Tessa's older brother,

Caine, had liked to taunt when they'd been children. "The first one of us. They keep it down there, where it lives on the blood of spiders and rats. It's like an animal itself, gone mad down there in the deep."

Caine also liked to say that if they were bad, the Grandfather would punish them by throwing them into the Beneath, where this horrific creature—the "Abomination"—would eat them, bones and all.

Just as she reached out to touch the padlock, Brandon caught her by the shoulder, startling her.

"Jesus!" she yelped, scrambling to her feet, wide-eyed. She managed a shaky little laugh and gave him a shove. "You scared me, Brandon. Don't sneak up on me like that."

We have to go now, he signed, his motions swift and imperative, his expression stern.

"Look," she said, pointing. "Do you know what that is? I think it leads—"

Tessa. He finger-spelled her name in its entirety for emphasis, rather than simply folding his index finger over his thumb in a letter T and drawing it against his cheek in his pet sign for her. *I mean it. Now.*

He was really spooked. She could see it in his face, his rigid posture. Whatever she could sense about that place, the peculiar, electrical sensation, Brandon could feel it, too, and he clearly didn't like it.

"All right." She nôdded, and he relaxed visibly. Not enough so that he walked back to the car first, however; he waited until she heaved a put-upon sigh and tromped past him before turning and trailing behind her. She kept glancing over her shoulder, her gaze drawn toward the hole in the ground with the padlock and grate. *What happened here?* she wondered, and even though she didn't mean to open her mind and let her twin be privy to her thoughts, it happened anyway.

I don't know, Brandon replied. *But I think it was something bad.*

Tessa had asked her grandmother about the crumbled old ruins later that evening, but Eleanor Noble hadn't known anything, either. "Whatever it was, it's in the past and not for us to know or care about," she'd said.

Tessa hadn't thought much about it in the four years since that day. She might not have ever thought about it again. In fact, had it not been for the side trip Rene had taken that morning as they'd left New Orleans together, a trip that had taken them about an hour southwest of the bustling city and toward the Gulf of Mexico to a place called Bayou Lafourche. Here, along a rutted, winding back road just past a small town called Thibodaux, Rene had stopped, parking his black Audi TT roadster in a swirling cloud of dust and grit in front of a boarded up, one-and-a-half-story house with a broad front porch and dilapidated roof.

The house had obviously been abandoned for some time. The window shutters listed, the porch was littered with piles of dirt and leaves and the white clapboard siding was weather-beaten and worn. The yard was a tangled mess of overgrown grass, weeds and wildflowers—much like that Kentucky back field had been years earlier—and surrounded by the twisted remains of old trees, many of which appeared to have been violently uprooted.

"What happened to the trees?" Tessa had asked quietly, wondering where they were and why in the hell Rene had driven out of their way to reach this place.

"Katrina," Rene murmured, opening the car door and stepping out. He moved slowly, grimacing slightly as his legs unfurled. His right leg was prosthetic from midthigh down; Brandon had explained to Tessa that Rene had once been a police officer and had lost his leg after being shot in the knee. Rene hadn't said anything to Tessa about it, and she hadn't asked him.

As a matter of fact, the two of them hadn't said much

to each other at all during their trip to New Orleans, or their limited stay there, as well. Most anything they *had* exchanged to date had been antagonistic, although before leaving for the Big Easy, they had been at least cordial to each other. That had changed after Brandon and Lina, Rene's former police partner and the woman with whom Brandon was in love, had hit the road for Louisiana, with Rene and Tessa to follow. In addition to not being able to learn how to drive, the Brethren were also prohibited from leaving their sequestered Kentucky estates. Ever. Brandon had broken that fundamental rule; as a result, the Brethren Elders were hunting for him, to kill him in punishment for his defiance. Because she'd fled, too, in order to help her brother, Tessa had sealed her own fate in the eyes of her people as well.

She had mentioned something about one of Martin's cars, a gray BMW sedan, to Rene. She'd taken it when she'd escaped Kentucky, and told Rene she needed to get her suitcases out of the trunk before they left for New Orleans.

Upon which he'd blinked at her as if she had just sprouted a third eyeball. "*Quoi?*" he asked. "What the hell do you mean, your husband's car is here in the city?"

"How else would I get here?" she'd replied, and he'd rolled his eyes skyward and thrown up his hands with an exasperated little snort. "What? Brandon drove, too. He told me he took one of the Grandfather's cars and . . ." Her voice faded as the furrow between his brows deepened. "What?"

"Why didn't the two of you just hang a big fucking sign at the city limits saying 'here we are'?" Rene had exclaimed. "*Mon Dieu,* woman, when you're trying to run away from someone, you don't go stealing cars with goddamn license plates *traceable right back to them!*"

Before they could uncover any more of what Rene

called "goddamn breadcrumbs" she and Brandon
had left for the Brethren to find, Rene had promptly
cut short the three week lead time he'd offered Brandon and Lina. He'd pretty much tossed Tessa unceremoniously into his car—without letting her get her
luggage—and headed south. Things had only gone
downhill from there.

"Where are we?" she had asked him outside of the
ramshackle little house in Louisiana, but he hadn't
replied. He'd left the driver's door standing open, the
little warning chiming alarm beeping inanely as he'd
walked toward the remnants of a picket and wire
fence that surrounded the front yard. The gate hung
at a clumsy angle, loose of most of its moorings, and
Rene eased it open on squealing hinges. Beside the
gate, a rusted, battered mailbox listed hard to star-
board, the hand-painted name *LaCroix* barely legible
on its side.

"Rene?" Tessa unbuckled her seat belt and opened
the car door, following him as he climbed the steps to
the front porch. "Rene, wait!"

He didn't pay any attention to her. Which, she figured, was pretty much par for the course. When he
tried to open the screen door, it fell; he sidestepped
in surprise as it crashed to the rotted plank floor of
the porch with a thin cloud of dust. Tessa hesitated on
the steps. "Rene? What is this place?"

"It's home," he replied without looking back at her
as he walked into the house. "Wait for me in the car,
pischouette."

That was it. Nothing more. He'd dismissed her as
he might have a nuisance child, and she stood there
for a long moment, her blouse clinging to her back
between her shoulder blades with sweat, perspiration
beading along her brow, the bridge of her nose. It was
hot and humid despite the early hour, and the air was
thick and heavy and utterly motionless.

Home? she thought, looking at the shack in disbelief. Rene was a multimillionaire many, many times over, the sole heir of a fortune his family had earned in crude oil, much as hers had in the Thoroughbred horseracing and bourbon distilling industries. *He's kidding, right?*

She could hear cicadas buzzing, crickets chirruping, tree frogs singing and the fading, resonant sounds of Rene's footsteps as he disappeared from her view.

"Rene?" she called, but he didn't answer. Tessa frowned, closing her fingers into fists against her sweat-dampened palms. "The hell with this."

She marched up the stairs, stepped around the collapsed screen door, and followed him into the house. The cracked and dingy hardwood floor was all but hidden beneath a thick layer of dirt and grime broken only by the ghostlike impressions of Rene's footprints. The air inside the house smelled stale and musty; in the muted sunlight that filtered in through gaps between the window boards, she could see glinting fragments of broken glass littering the ground along with heavy shrouds of cobwebs, piles of dried leaves and broken branches, old newspapers and other anonymous garbage.

Her stomach immediately roiled, stirred to uncomfortable nausea as much by the claustrophobic confines of the house as her fledgling pregnancy. She was almost four months along. The ordinarily flat plain of her belly was just beginning to swell, although her morning sickness—which had turned out to be more like *any-time-of-the-day sickness*—and the soreness in her breasts at last seemed to be waning. Being around Rene of late had seemed to rekindle at least the nausea more frequently.

Part of the problem was also that she needed to feed. She'd sated her bloodlust before leaving Kentucky, but that had been almost two weeks earlier. Although normally, that should have sustained her for at least a month, while pregnant, she needed to feed more often, and the bloodlust had been stirring persistently within her. Even now, as she glanced around the empty house, she could feel her gums tingling, a dim ache as they swelled and her canine teeth wanted to drop.

She even imagined she could smell blood, a human from somewhere close at hand. *Which isn't possible,* she thought. *Look at this dump. There's no one here but me and Rene.*

And while Rene may have been half human to her full-blooded Brethren, she sure as hell wasn't going to feed from him. *I'd as soon ram a rusty nail through my eye.*

The sound of Rene's footfalls as he went upstairs, heavy and hollow against the steps, attracted her gaze, and she headed in that direction. *What is he doing?*

She rounded a corner and found the staircase. The corridor beside it led to a bathroom straight ahead, a place where the boards on the window had either been pried away or had blown off during the hurricane. Pale sunlight spilled through and pooled on the floor, seeping out into the hall. The ceiling above had been waterlogged from a leaky roof, and plaster dusted the ground like a fine snowfall, crunching in larger chunks beneath her shoes.

Tessa paused at the foot of the steps, looking up into darkness. She could hear Rene tromping around up there, but couldn't see anything. "Rene? Whose house is this?"

After a long moment, he looked over the railing and down at her, more shadow than distinguishable form. "It's mine, *pischouette*. I told you. This is where I grew up." He ducked out of her view again, walking away from the railing. "Look, just go sit in the car, will you? Before you get something on your little designer pants and then I never hear the end of it."

Her brows narrowed. *Asshole,* she thought. *Fine. If*

that's how he wants it, fine by me. I hope a rat comes up and bites you right in the ass, Rene Morin. You've got it coming, and I'm sure there are at least a couple of them running loose in here somewhere.

She turned to go and heard a soft sound from the bathroom, a scrabbling in the loose plaster that gave her pause. The idea that a rat might actually be close at hand suddenly left her apprehensive, and she glanced hesitantly over her shoulder. *Oh, God, don't let it be a rat,* she thought, as the scratching sound came again. *I hate rats. Please don't let it be a rat. Don't let it—*

A man appeared in the bathroom doorway, a crooked figure nearly silhouetted by the backdrop of sunlight as he shambled into the corridor. Tessa shrank back in startled fright and he paused, squinting blearily at her.

He was older, with gray, wiry hair that framed his face in a wild, disheveled halo and sprouted from his chin and cheeks in a matted, mangy beard. His clothes were filthy and threadbare.

He was human. She could tell by the scent of his blood, discernable even over the stink of his body odor, his need for a bath. And that realization, coupled by her need to feed—which had suddenly, almost instantly swelled to near-desperate proportions—fueled her already stirring bloodlust. Her fangs dropped fully; Tessa felt the distinctive *pop* as her lower jaw snapped reflexively out of socket to accommodate her extended canines. As her pupils widened, spreading in circumference to fill the visible spaces between her eyelids, the shadow-draped interior of the house suddenly became bathed in light from all detectable sources. The bright spill of illumination from the bathroom became like a solar flare, and the jackhammering of the man's heart as he recoiled in clumsy, floundering terror pounded in her ears.

She didn't remember leaping at him, knocking

him backward and to the ground. She didn't remember straddling him or burying her teeth into the side of his neck while he thrashed beneath her and cried out hoarsely. All she could think about was the blood. She tore his throat open with her mouth, plunging her canines into his carotid artery and gulping greedily, hungrily as his frantic heart sent blood coursing rhythmically into her mouth.

She didn't hear Rene shouting her name, hadn't even realized that he'd come racing downstairs at the sounds of the man's shrieks until she felt his hand close sharply, firmly against her elbow. Rene jerked her to her feet, hauling her away from the man. She fought him the entire way, kicking and scratching at him with her nails, screaming and cursing as she struggled to return to her feeding. Rene grasped her by the arms, whipped her around and shook her soundly. "Tessa, goddamn it!"

The sharpness of his voice startled her instantly out of the reverie of the bloodlust, and she fell still, hiccuping for breath and shuddering.

"What's the matter with you?" Rene yelled, giving her another solid shake before turning her loose. He forked his fingers through his disheveled, shoulder-length hair, shoving it out of his face and all the while staring at her as if she'd lost her mind.

"I . . . I couldn't help it . . ." she whimpered. She could still taste blood in her mouth. It was smeared all over her face and neck; a glance down revealed the front of her white linen blouse stained scarlet with it.

Rene walked over to the derelict. The man lay in a crumpled heap against the floor. She could hear him gargling softly for strained breath; she'd punctured his windpipe in her overzealous effort to feed. She'd also swallowed enough blood to leave him hovering on the brink of death. After a few, sodden, struggling breaths, the man fell still and silent. Rene pressed his fingertips against the side of his neck, then glanced at her as he stood again. "He's dead."

Rene could feed without killing, a concept as alien to Tessa as trying to eat a cheeseburger with her feet. The reason her twin, Brandon, had fled the Brethren was because he hadn't wanted to kill; he'd abandoned his bloodletting, the ritual of the first kill, rather than give in to his bloodlust. He'd learned from Rene how to feed without killing, but he'd never fed before then. Tessa had, plenty of times in the last three years. She hadn't meant to kill the old man, hadn't been acting out of any malicious intent. She'd simply been doing what came naturally to her. And Rene clearly didn't approve.

"I'm sorry," she whispered. And then she remembered—to her horror. *Oh, God, Rene's family is half human! What if someone did live here? Oh, my God, what if I just killed someone in his family?* "Who . . . who is he?"

Rene's sharp brows crimped together, draping his brown eyes in heavy, menacing shadows. "How the hell should I know? That's hardly the point." The thin line of his mouth turned down; the hard angle of his jaw was tense and rigid. He closed his hands—smeared now with the old man's blood—into fists and marched past her. *"Viens m'enculer!"*

"I said I'm sorry!" She hurried to follow him, but one of the floorboards in the hallway snapped beneath her, sending her sprawling to the floor. She landed hard on her knees, scraping them raw, and abrading her palms.

"Goddamn it!" she cried. Her foot had fallen into a deep recess beneath the floorboard, and the rough edges of broken wood had cut open her ankle. She winced as she eased her foot loose, then frowned as dim light reflected off something in the hole.

She scooted toward the narrow opening and looked more closely. Reaching inside, she felt something thick and leathery against her fingertips; the spine of a book. She frowned, trying to get a grip on it and pull it free, but the hole didn't grant enough room. Tessa grabbed the next floor plank in her hands and jerked against it, pulling until the old, weather-beaten wood gave way and snapped loose. Again and again, she yanked away floorboards until she'd cleared away a wide enough opening through which to remove the book.

It was huge, thick and cumbersome, and her first thought was that it was some kind of scrapbook. It wasn't until she turned back the heavy cover and flipped carefully through the brittle, yellowing pages that it occurred to her what the book might really be.

"Oh, my God," she whispered, wiping her hands against her pant legs so she didn't get blood all over the parchment.

The book appeared to be written in French, words set to the page by hand in ink, but it was some sort of dialect she'd never seen before. The light was too dim, the handwriting too small for her to make out the text clearly, but as she thumbed ahead, she saw pages outlined with lined diagrams through the last quarter or so of the thick volume. *Family trees,* she thought. *Or at least, one family tree.*

She recognized some of the names transcribed on the diagrams: *Davenant, Trevilian, Morin.*

"Oh, my God," she whispered again, so stunned she forgot about the man she'd just bled to death, or the fury she'd seen in Rene's face. *Oh, God, this is Rene's family tree—his Brethren side of the family. This book is one of the Tomes! Holy shit, it's one of the clan Tomes!*

The Tomes were a series of books maintained by each of the four Brethren clans, the Nobles, the Davenants, the Trevilians and the Giscards. These books not only chronicled the history of the Brethren race, they were used to meticulously track and plan each family's lineage. Marriages were arranged by the Brethren Elders like Tessa's grandfather after careful consultation of the Tomes in order to prevent inbreeding between particular families and to keep the bloodlines clean. Only the Elders were allowed to see the Tomes; the books were kept under tight lock and key and used only behind closed doors, away from any possible prying eyes.

Until now. Tessa stumbled to her feet, hefting the book against her chest. Her ankle smarted as she settled her weight on it, but she gritted her teeth and limped to the front door.

"Rene!" she called as she staggered back outside into the oppressive heat, the blinding sunlight. Rene had returned to the car, popped the trunk and fished out a fresh shirt from an oversized duffel bag. He'd also pulled out a bottle of water.

"Rene, look," she grunted. "Look what I found inside. It's—"

"Clean yourself up." Rene tossed the bottle of water at her, and she yelped, loosening her grip on the book reflexively. It dropped to the ground and the bottle fell beside it, landing heavily in the weeds.

"Be careful!" she exclaimed, snatching the Tome back in hand. "Do you know what this is?"

"No," he replied, striding toward her. He grabbed the book and jerked it away from her, tossing it unceremoniously into the backseat of the car. "And frankly, my dear, I don't give a flying fuck."

Something had fallen out of the book, a postcard or photograph that had fluttered to the ground by the Audi's back tire. Rene leaned over, picking it up. Whatever it was, he stared at it for a long moment, his expression growing momentarily stricken.

"Rene?" she asked. At the sound of her voice, his face hardened again, and he shoved the slip into the back pocket of his jeans.

"I said clean yourself up." His voice sounded strange, suddenly strained somehow, but his brows remained furrowed, his mouth set in a frown. "Take off that goddamn shirt and throw it into the trees over there. You just murdered someone, and I'd just as soon get on the road again before I'm tempted to try it, too."

He said this with a pointed look that left no doubt the person he might feel inclined to murder was *her.* His disgust and aggravation were so apparent, it left her abashed and ashamed. Her shoulders hunched, her eyes burning with the sting of tears. Her bottom lip quivered and she sniffled as she opened the water and splashed it on her face and hands. "You're an asshole."

Rene leaned his hip against the rear bumper of the car, folded his arms across his chest and deliberately turned to present his back to her as she unbuttoned her blouse. She shrugged her way out of the blood-soaked linen, letting it drop to the grass at her feet, then pulled the faded gray T-shirt Rene had given her over her head.

"Get in the car," Rene growled after she'd tossed her blouse into the heavy underbrush as he'd ordered.

Still sniffling, Tessa obeyed, sitting against the pale leather front seat with her shoulders hunched, her fingers knotted in her lap. They sat there in silence for a long moment, him in the driver's seat drumming his fingers against the wheel, and her beside him.

"If you ever do that again, I'll leave your ass behind," Rene told her finally, his voice low and clipped, as if he struggled to sound calm. "You understand me, *pischouette*? You can't just run around killing people. That guy was at least somebody's son, and who knows what else—someone's father, their grandfather." He spared her a glare. "He was something to somebody somewhere and you killed him."

At this, his snide tone and his sharp words, as if she was a naughty child in need of remonstration, something in Tessa snapped. It reminded her too vividly of her life in the Davenant house with Martin.

"I told you I was sorry!" she exclaimed. "What else do you want from me? I couldn't help it. Maybe you and Brandon don't have to bleed someone dry to feed, but I—"

"Who told you to wait so goddamn long between feedings that you had to go and rip that poor son of a bitch's throat open?" he snapped back. "I asked you before we left the city, 'do you need to feed?' I asked you again before we took off out of New Orleans, and both times, you told me no."

"Because you wanted me to feed off hookers! Maybe that's good enough for you, Rene, but I'm sorry. I'm not about to pay some bleach-blond whore to—"

"Oh, no." He barked out a short, mean laugh. "You'll save yourself for some strung out bum stinking of his own goddamn waste, too drunk to even stick up to you in a fight." He spared her a glance, his brow arched. "Or maybe next time, you'll find some migrant worker who doesn't speak a lick of English, just like down on the farm. You take your food there Mexican, no?"

She smacked him, the report of her hand striking his cheek loud and sharp in the heavy morning air. She hit him hard enough to whip his face to the side, and he turned back to her slowly, his brow still arched as he pressed his fingertips against the point of impact.

"You have no right to judge me," she seethed at him, trembling angrily, her voice choked with tears again.

He continued looking at her for a long moment, seeming simultaneously amused by her slap and irritated by it. "Maybe so," he said. "Maybe no."

That had been earlier that day. They'd spent the rest of the afternoon on the road, neither speaking to the other. When they'd stopped for the night at the chain motel with its nondescript suite that smelled faintly of stale cigarette smoke to Tessa's keen nose—despite the No Smoking sign on the door—she'd planned to call Brandon, to beg him to come and get her. But then she'd sat down on the bed and began to study the Tome she'd found—which she'd snatched out of the backseat of the car before Rene could lay a finger on it—and remembered the day years earlier when she and Brandon had discovered the ruins of the old great house.

Rene's name, *Morin,* didn't belong to any of the existing Brethren clans, which had led Tessa and Brandon to believe he was part of a separate sect, or perhaps a family that had splintered from the Brethren. But Tessa had seen another Morin family tree, this one much shorter than the one presented in the Tome, which Rene's human grandmother had put together for him, and through this, she'd clearly seen that the Morins and the Brethren clans had once been affiliated. One of Rene's ancestors had married into the Davenant clan.

What if the Morins had once been part of the Brethren? she wondered.

In addition to the clan names she recognized, there were others still that were unfamiliar to her—some French, like *Durand* and *Lambert* and others with origins not so apparent—*Ellinger, Averay.*

Were all of these clans, too? she thought in amazement. *My God, at some point could there have been so many? What happened to them? What if that great house Brandon and I found had belonged to one of them? What if they never rebuilt it, like they did the others, because they left somehow?*

But why?

The first portion of the book consisted of old, brittle parchment pages that appeared to Tessa's untrained eye to have been carefully removed from another, probably older volume, and bound into the Tome. The pages were intricately adorned with hand-painted borders to resemble climbing vines, tree limbs and other decorations. The text wrapped around large, colorful paintings depicting all sorts of imagery—groups of men gathered together around a large table, as if in conference; farming scenes that appeared to depict different crop harvests; people playing musical instruments or dancing; people traveling by horseback to what looked like castles and closely nestled villages or men in armor on white horses jousting or sword fighting.

Many of the illustrations showed darker images—men and women lying in bed, their bodies covered in boils or sores; others lying naked and strewn on the ground while behind them houses burned and a skeleton rode an emaciated black horse, a scythe slung across its bony shoulder. Several depicted another manner of monster, this one naked, hunchbacked and hairless, with bulging eyes, a mouth ringed with long, sharp teeth, and long, spindly fingers hooked with claws. *Abominacion* was transcribed beneath it, and Tessa didn't need to be a medieval linguist to understand.

"*Abomination,*" she'd whispered, shivering as she thought of the stories her brother Caine had always told about the Abomination living beneath the great house in the depths of the Beneath.

Upon closer examination of the text, it appeared to be written, at least at first, in a strange mix of French and Latin she couldn't decipher. She'd been fighting mounting fatigue, propped up in bed with pillows, skimming through the book when she'd dozed off. The sound of Rene's cell phone, set to speaker mode and turned up loudly as he rang someone's line, had roused her. The phone kept ringing and ringing until finally, irritably, she'd shoved the book aside and stumbled out of bed with every intention of flinging the door wide and screaming at him to hang up already, goddamn it. She stopped, her hand on the doorknob, when she heard a woman's voice—tinged with sleepiness—finally answer.

Who is he calling?

Tessa had opened the door slowly, quietly, cracking it a brief margin and peering into the living room and beyond. She had seen Rene on the couch with a mostly empty bottle of whiskey on the table in front of him. He'd gone out earlier after they'd checked into the room, and now she knew why. He'd been buying booze.

He's drunk. Terrific. Just what I need, she'd thought, tempted yet again to call Brandon and Lina and ask if they had room in their car for her.

"Hello?" the woman on the phone said again.

Rene had pulled the tails of his shirt loose from his jeans and sat with it unbuttoned so it lay open, revealing his chest. Even from her vantage, Tessa could see he was hard-cut with muscles, his stomach chiseled above his waistband.

He wasn't an unattractive man; quite the opposite, in fact—and that was probably the most aggravating thing about him. He'd told her once he was in his fifties, but he looked only in his late twenties or early thirties. Damn near perfect when it came to physique, he had broad shoulders, a slim waist, long legs and strong arms. With caramel-brown eyes, sharp brows, high cheeks and angular features, Rene was handsome in a rugged, if not somewhat disheveled sort of way. He seemed content to let a day or two—or even three—lapse in between shaving, and his idea of styling his dark, sandy blond hair appeared to be simply running his fingers through it and letting the wind take care of the rest—a far cry from the men of the Brethren.

Tessa had never seen her husband, Martin, for example, in anything besides collared shirts and ties, no matter how hot the weather might be. The only exceptions to this seeming rule had been the nights he'd come to her for sex, stealing into the small bedroom at the Davenant great house that Tessa had shared with her cousin Alexandra, who was also one of Martin's wives. Then he'd wear only a silk bathrobe, or at least that's what Tessa had assumed based on the whispering sound of the fabric swishing against his legs as he moved. It was hard to tell anything else because she'd never open her eyes, never even move, not until he had finished and left her as wordlessly as he'd arrived.

Unlike Martin, Rene seemed to have a never-ending barrage of things to say. And he smelled good, too; another distraction Tessa found irritating.

When the woman on the other end of the line hung up, Rene had dropped the phone with one hand and—to Tessa's surprise—raised a pistol to his head with the other. He'd closed his eyes and folded his finger against the trigger like he seriously meant to plug a bullet into his skull, and Tessa had panicked, her heart hammering in a sudden, frightened cadence. He may have been an asshole, and she may have pretty much officially hated him as of that afternoon, but that didn't mean she wanted to watch him shoot himself. She'd bolted from the bedroom.

And the rest, as they say, is history, she thought, sitting on the bed again, her body still feeling tremulous and electrified in the aftermath of his touch. The scruff of his unkempt beard stubble had scraped against her cheek when he'd murmured in her ear and her flesh there still felt sensitive, nearly raw from the friction. She could still recall the sensation of his hand against her skin, his palm sliding along her thigh toward her buttock. She could still smell him, the light, musky, pleasant fragrance of his cologne trapped and lingering in her robe. He'd almost kissed her. And she'd almost let him. Almost.

What the hell is wrong with me?

Chapter Three

The next morning, neither Rene nor Tessa said a word to each other, not even as they knocked elbows changing places in front of the hotel's cramped bathroom to brush their teeth. While Tessa showered and dressed—taking in excess of well over an hour—Rene sat on the couch, leaning his aching head back and keeping the heels of his hands pressed lightly over his eyes. He didn't get a hangover often, a lucky benefit of his Brethren birthright. The Brethren healed quickly, seldom fell ill and aged very slowly, all attributes he'd seemed to inherit, in spite of the fact his mother had been human. But he'd drunk heavily the night before, even heavier than usual for him, and he was paying for it that morning.

I suppose Mrs. Davenant would say I had this coming, he thought, listening as the water shut off—finally—from the bathroom. "Did you prune in there?" he called, and was immediately sorry he had. Even the sound of his own voice ripped through him, making his poor skull throb.

"No." The bathroom door opened and Tessa breezed out, a white towel piled atop her head, another wrapped around her slender torso. He had a momentary but appreciative glance at the coltish length of her legs and the way the terry cloth hugged the contours of her ass beneath, and then she ducked into the bedroom and slammed the door behind her.

Which only rekindled the pain in his head.

"Please don't do that again," he groaned. He'd come to that morning lying on his belly on the couch, the nasty flavors of bile and bourbon thick in his mouth. He discovered that he'd vomited at some point overnight in a nearby plastic garbage can. His pistol lay across the room, his cell phone on the floor by the sofa and the photograph of him and Irene on their wedding day in 1970 on the coffee table in front of him.

Jesus.

He retrieved his phone and flipped it open, thumbing to the last number dialed. He didn't need to see more than the 415 area code to realize what he'd done.

"Viens m'enculer," he muttered. *Fuck me.* In a world with caller ID pretty much standard in every household, the last thing he needed to be doing was getting wasted and calling his ex-wife. At least his cell phone number was unlisted so she wouldn't know it was him.

He had a dim recollection of having called her—only to sit there, as mute as Brandon, unable to summon the balls or voice to talk to her—and of putting the pistol to his head. Whether or not he would have pulled the trigger had Tessa not come tearing across the room, he didn't know.

He also vaguely remembered pinning Tessa down against the couch just long enough to get a massive hard-on from the proximity.

What the hell is wrong with me?

The urge to kill himself had come off and on over the years. He'd served in the Army in the late sixties and had done a tour of duty in Vietnam; the horrors he'd seen there had plagued his mind for a long time afterward—had been part of the reason Irene had ultimately left him, in fact—and still haunted him even now. The previous year, he'd lost his leg, ending what had, to that point, proven to be an enjoyable, burgeoning career as a police officer, and his inclinations toward suicide had been rather persistent ever since. Every time he'd somehow been able to talk himself down from the proverbial ledge, but he supposed there might come a day when even his own voice of reason would fail.

He groaned again as he rose to his feet. He wasn't accustomed to sleeping in his prosthetic leg, and the entire right side of his body felt stiff and sore as a result. For some reason, he felt uncomfortable removing the limb when Tessa was around. It wasn't as though she didn't know about it, because she did, but he still felt self-conscious anyway, like she would look at him differently, think about him differently, if she saw him without it strapped in place.

But why would I give a shit anyway?

He'd seen it before, the looks people would give him—women in particular—a mix of pity, curiosity and disgust. The same kinds of looks people in Thibodaux used to give him: *Look at that poor, filthy little white trash boy.*

Only now, the looks more conveyed: *Half a man. Look at that poor thing—he's only half a man.*

He fished through his duffel bag until he found the battery charger for his computerized artificial knee and frowned when he plugged it in and realized he was due for a recharge.

Stupid, stupid, stupid, he told himself. The battery needed regular charging and optimally that should have been done overnight with the leg removed, if he meant to go several days without fooling with it again. Normally, the knee would vibrate if it was extremely low on power. It wasn't to that point yet, thankfully, and he'd be able to get away with a quick fifteen-

minute charge to get him through the day, maybe
more if he kept it plugged in longer.

*And with as long as it takes Tessa to get ready that
shouldn't be a problem.*

The prosthetic was damn near something out of *Star
Trek* as far as he was concerned. It had cost close to
$50,000 to be custom-built, and in the little more than
a year since he'd had it, he'd endured countless adjust-
ments, refittings and visits to his prosthetist's office.
The knee joint boasted microprocessor-controlled hy-
draulics that allowed Rene to enjoy a relatively natural
gait and to pursue most any physical activity he
wanted. With the press of a button on a small remote
control he kept tucked in the hip pocket of his jeans,
he could even shift the hydraulic mode to compensate
for more vigorous activities like stair climbing or jog-
ging. Not that he had very often, if at all.

That's why God made elevators and sports cars.

Through an interlocking framework, the knee con-
nected to a padded sheath that supported his thigh
and allowed for a seminatural contour beneath his
pant leg, held in place with a silicone sock he wore
over his stump. His foot was thin and flexible, designed for athletes, even though Rene had never put
it to that sort of durability test. He had a foam latex
cover that he could use if he chose to cover the foot
and pylon calf and make them look more like flesh
and bone, but most of the time, he didn't bother. He
felt more self-conscious trying to disguise the leg into
looking lifelike than simply leaving it alone.

Sometimes he still suffered from what his doctors
had termed *phantom sensations,* the peculiar and annoying feeling that his missing leg was somehow still
there—and worse, that it was either cocked at an unnatural and uncomfortable angle, or aching him. His
physical therapist had worked with him on muscle techniques he could use to relieve these bizarre sensations,

and although they didn't prevent them, it did help somewhat. Drugs also didn't hurt; Rene usually kept an assortment of prescription pharmaceuticals on hand in keeping with both the old Boy Scout motto— *be prepared*—and Timothy Leary's sage advice: *turn on, tune in, drop out.*

Although he couldn't just get up each morning and go anymore, as long as he kept the battery in his knee joint charged, Rene was able to do just about everything he had prior to his amputation. He'd trained himself to drive without any special accommodations, such as the installation of a left-side accelerator, and had simply learned how to operate the gas and brakes with his left foot instead. It had felt awkward at first, but now was pretty much second nature to him, something he didn't even lend much thought to.

While his knee charged, Rene went through his daily routine of inspecting his stump and dusting it with powder before returning the silicone sleeve in place. He kept an anxious eye on the closed bedroom door the entire time. He knew he shouldn't give a shit; if Tessa saw the leg, then she saw it, and big fucking deal, but at the same time that stubborn hint of pride remained. He'd had his share of pity and didn't need anymore—especially from Tessa.

He'd often wondered if his accelerated healing ability would have corrected the damage done to his knee when he'd been shot. When he'd been in Vietnam, he'd been wounded in the gut, damn near eviscerating him. He'd fed shortly thereafter—for the first time, in fact—and had been taken by medevac to an Army hospital where he'd healed in a matter of weeks without as much as a hint of scarring. He supposed the knee might have fared as well, but human doctors didn't understand such things as bloodlust or a heightened metabolism. They'd seen a brutally damaged

joint and done the only thing they'd thought viable.
He couldn't blame them for that, and didn't.

Much.

An hour and a half later, they loaded their belongings into the car and walked to a small diner adjacent
to the motel. As Rene stirred powdered creamer into
a steaming cup of desperately needed coffee, he
glanced at Tessa. "I'm going to start calling you Posh."

She looked up from the laminated menu and
frowned. "What?"

"Posh," he said again, tapping his forefinger in the
air to indicate the salmon-colored, sleeveless blouse
she wore over a pair of white capris. He hadn't let her
grab her bags from her husband's car before hitting
the road for New Orleans, and she'd apparently taken
this as an open invitation to spend a small fortune at
the boutiques in the French Quarter. He was willing
to bet she hadn't paid anything less than $150 for the
shirt. "As in Posh Spice. Do you own anything with a
sticker price that wouldn't feed a small family for the
better part of a week?"

Her frown deepened. "If you had let me get my
things, you might have found out."

"I probably would have needed to rent a U-Haul
trailer," Rene remarked, taking a long swig of coffee.

"And you're a fine one to talk anyway," Tessa said.
"Do you have any cars that didn't cost you an arm and
a leg?"

He shook his head. "No. Just a leg."

Her eyes grew round and her hand darted to her
mouth. She looked so comical, so utterly and absolutely mortified, that Rene laughed, choking on his
coffee and nearly spraying it out his nose.

The waitress, a cute young thing with blond hair
and perky breasts named Dee, approached their
table. "Is the coffee all right?" she asked, her pretty
face scrunching up with momentary worry.

"Oh, yes." He smiled up at her winsomely. "In fact, *chère*, I will guarantee you a fifty-dollar tip if you bring me an entire pot of it."

She smiled, appropriately charmed. Dee thought he was *a hottie*, to use her turn of phrase, and if he turned the charm on just a bit thicker, she would let him explore at his leisure all of the curves and contours hidden beneath her creamy pink polyester waitress uniform. That was another benefit of being born with Brethren blood. He could read minds when he felt like it.

Tessa ordered a bowl of plain oatmeal and a glass of orange juice. Rene ordered more coffee and three slices of cherry pie.

"Why?" Tessa asked, looking somewhat repulsed as Dee set the plates down in front of him, like he'd ordered a shit sundae or something.

"Pie's good for breakfast," he said. "Pretty much like a danish or doughnut. And I like cherry the best. Not too sweet. Sort of tart. You should try it sometime."

"No, thank you. And I meant why three pieces?"

"Because," he replied simply, "I like pie."

"You eat like a pig," she muttered as she primly unfolded her paper napkin and smoothed it against her lap.

He shoveled in a wolfish mouthful and smiled. "And you, *pischouette*, eat like a bird."

Dee returned sometime later to collect their empty dishes and refill Rene's coffee. "You're not from around here, are you?" she asked with a smile. He could smell her; the longer she stood beside the table, the faster her heart began to beat, and the more fervently through her slim but curvaceous form it sent her blood. The realization of this made him salivate unconsciously, and his gums ached dimly as they started to swell. Like Tessa, he hadn't fed since before leaving for New Orleans, and even though he didn't need to as frequently as she did, that didn't mean he didn't want to. Or wouldn't.

Besides, feeding would help to ease the throbbing headache that his hangover—and proximity to Tessa—had caused, which was all of the further incentive he needed.

"No, *ma chère*," he told Dee, because she thought it was sexy when he spoke French. He could sense this, too. "I'm from New Orleans."

"Are you really?" Dee's bright smile widened. "I've been there for Mardi Gras a couple of times. At least before the hurricane."

She was too sweet to be the type he ordinarily favored—which generally tended to fall into the "hooker" or "stripper" categories, as Tessa might have disdainfully noted. He didn't care; he liked hookers and strippers. Beautiful, buxom and all business. There were no strings attached, no promises inferred, no miscommunication. Just an exchange of money and services, plain and simple.

Dee wasn't like that, but she was readily available. She'd do in a pinch.

"Excuse me," Tessa said, waggling her now-empty glass in the air. "I'd like some more orange juice, please."

"In a moment, *pischouette*," Rene said, holding Dee's gaze. "I think *ma chère* and I might step away for a bit, if you don't mind."

Tessa blinked. "What?"

"Sure," Dee said, nodding. Her eyes had taken on a dreamy, dazed sort of cast, her smile distant and sleepy. Just as he could read minds, he could also open his mind to others, and through this ability, control them. Or, as he liked to consider it, persuade them to his point of view on things. "Sure, that will be nice."

"What?" Tessa said again as he stood from the table. "What are you doing?"

"Finishing my breakfast." Rene dropped her a wink as Dee turned and began walking toward the restrooms. He followed, ignoring Tessa's sputtered, startled attempts at protest.

Fifteen minutes later, his cell phone rang, vibrating against his hip through his jeans pocket. Rene fished it out and grabbed a paper towel from the wall-mounted dispenser by the sink to wipe at the blood dribbling down his chin. He glanced at the number on the cell phone's caller ID and smiled. "Hey, *chère*, how are you this morning?"

"Hey, Rene," Lina Jones replied. "What are you doing?"

"Me? Just having a bite before we hit the road."

The young waitress, Dee, sat on the sink with her shapely buttocks resting in the basin, her thighs spread wide, her calves dangling, her skirt hiked up to her waist to expose the crotch of her white cotton panties beneath. Her head had lolled back on her neck, and she blinked up at the fluorescent light fixture overhead in a stupefied trance. Because feeding from her throat would have left conspicuous teeth marks, Rene had instead tactfully bitten her high along her inner thigh, nearly to her groin, sinking his canines deep enough into her flesh to puncture her femoral artery. A bit more tricky than hitting the carotid, but Rene had plenty of practice at it.

Not that Dee was aware of what he'd done. Nor would she remember a thing—just a few more perks of his telepathic abilities. He hadn't hurt her, just turned her mind off for a little while, put her in a sleeplike reverie.

"Where are you?" Lina asked. She was probably the

only woman he'd been emotionally close to in at least twenty years—and one of the only women he'd ever known that he hadn't slept with. She'd saved his life in more ways than one, and more times than just once. First, she had shot and killed the son of a bitch who'd blown his right kneecap off. After that, a mental pledge he'd made to somehow even the score with Lina had saved him from suicide; that little, niggling voice of reason in his head would remind him that no matter how lonely he was, how despondent or afraid, no matter how sweet a temptation the muzzle of his Sig Sauer might seem, he owed Lina. She'd never let him down. *And I'll do the same by her.*

"A little café in Boerne," he told her.

He heard the rustling of paper over the line as she checked a map. "How'd you beat us?" she asked with a laugh. "We're stopped overnight in Seguin, not even into San Antonio yet."

"Easy, *chère*," he replied. "Me and Tessa, we don't like each other. We don't need to stop and fuck like rabbits every fifteen minutes like you and Brandon. You get a lot more miles behind you that way."

"Ha, ha," she said dryly, but with just enough hint of affection in her voice that he could tell she was smiling.

He loved Lina. Not like he might have a wife or lover or even a sister—even though in his will, he'd left her everything since he had no real next of kin—but in some strange, deep and intrinsic way nonetheless. He would die for her, something he couldn't say for anyone else in the world.

Except for Irene.

"You still want to meet in Anthony, New Mexico?" she said. "It's going to take me and Brandon a good nine hours to get there. We could all hook up for supper?"

"That would be nice, sure." He was glad that Lina and Brandon had fallen in love. The younger man had brought a light into Lina's eyes the likes of which Rene hadn't seen in ages. And Brandon was a good kid, Rene had to admit, earnest and easygoing, with just enough scrap to stick up for himself if it came down to it. Brandon had broken most of the bones in both of his hands pounding the shit out of his brother, Caine, to prove that. "You call your *mère* yet?"

"Yeah, just a little bit ago." The bright cheer in Lina's voice faltered slightly. Her mother was undergoing chemotherapy following a recent mastectomy and he knew she was worried. "She's got another round this afternoon but seems to be doing okay. As well as can be expected, I guess. She said Jackie's taking good care of her."

He didn't know what she'd told her mother to explain her sudden flight, the complete abandonment of her life, but he suspected that it hadn't been too hard to convince the woman to keep mum about it. Lina's brother, Jackson, who was in Florida with their mother at the moment, had once been Brandon Noble's teacher, and Lina had told Rene that Jackson had long suspected the Nobles of being something far more sinister than what met the eye.

"So we're meeting in Anthony, then?" Lina said, and he didn't need to see her, or read her mind for that matter, to know she forced the smile into her voice. "How about eight o'clock? We'll find hotel rooms and then touch base, see where to meet for supper." In a more relaxed and playful tone, she added, "That should give me and Brandon plenty of fuck time along the way."

Rene laughed. "You're a mess, *chère*," he told her fondly.

He returned to the table and fished his wallet out of his back pocket. "You ready to go, *pischouette?*"

"Where's the waitress?" Tessa asked, frowning. "What did you do to her?"

"Nothing." He pretended to look hurt. "She's right over there."

He nodded to indicate Dee, who had exited the ladies' room shortly after he'd ducked out. Before leaving her, he'd whispered in her ear, quick and quiet words of instruction that had left her with no memory of what had happened—indeed, no memory of him and Tessa whatsoever.

He slipped a fifty spot out of his billfold and dropped it onto the table before dropping Tessa a wink. "Come on. Let's hit the road."

Chapter Four

Tessa fumed as she watched Rene use his hands to help maneuver his prosthetic leg into the Audi. "Good news," he said. "I talked to Lina on the phone inside. We're meeting her and your brother tonight for supper in Arizona."

"Good," she said coolly, clicking her seat belt in place. "Because I'll be riding with them to California after that."

"What?" he asked with a sideways glance.

He thought he was so clever, that the stunt he'd pulled in the restaurant with the waitress was oh-so-charming, and meanwhile, he'd never even bothered to notice that she was infuriated with him, murderously so, in fact.

Asshole, she thought, fuming.

"Look, you've been a big help to Brandon, and I really appreciate it," she said, struggling to keep her composure, her tone of voice steady and unaffected. "And I know you're friends with Lina, but this just isn't going to work anymore."

He cocked his eyebrow, an annoying, condescending expression. "What the hell are you talking about? You make it sound like you want to break a date to the prom or something. We aren't supposed to be in love here, *pischouette*."

"No, we're supposed to be riding in a car together. And we can't even do that without fighting all of the time. You make fun of the way I look, the way I dress— I'm tired of you acting like I'm an idiot or a child or you're better than me somehow."

At this, he uttered a sharp bark of laughter. "*I* act like I'm better than *you*? There's a crock of shit. You know what your problem is, *pischouette*? You've never had someone tell you no before. You've gotten used to having everything just the way you want it, exactly when and how you want it at that little pony farm of yours, and you can't stand it out here in the real world, where that kind of shit doesn't fly. You're a spoiled rotten little brat."

"And you're a hypocrite!" she snapped. "After all of the things you said yesterday, all that crap about how that man in Louisiana was something to somebody somewhere and then you have the nerve to turn around and do the exact same thing to that waitress."

He jabbed his forefinger at her, his brows narrowed. "Now wait just a goddamn minute, *pischouette*. I didn't do the 'exact same thing to that waitress.' I didn't kill her. Hell, I didn't even hurt her. She doesn't remember—"

"Don't curse at me." Tessa slapped his hand out of her face. "And *you* wait a goddamn minute. I don't have the right to kill someone, but you have the right to brainwash them? Strip away their memories? Make them pretty much your personal walking-talking feed sack?"

"That's not what I—" he began, but she cut him off hotly.

"I'm tired of you talking to me and treating me as if everything I do, think and say is wrong! I don't know if losing your leg has made you such an asshole or if you were like this before, but I don't care. I'm not like you, and you sure as hell aren't like me! You don't know anything about me, or . . . or my life and I . . . I just . . . !"

Her voice dissolved into tears. Thanks to her pregnancy and all of the hormonal turmoil that came along with it, she seemed to weep at the drop of a hat, as if her body had forgotten any other physiological response to stress but this. She uttered a frustrated little cry and clapped her hands over her face. "Goddamn it!"

He didn't say anything; merely sat there like a big dumb rock while she hiccuped and sobbed in the passenger seat of his car. After a long moment, she felt his hand drape lightly against the back of her head, and she swatted him away. "Don't."

"Tessa," he said. "I'm sorry."

He tried to touch her again, this time on her shoulder, and she flapped her arm furiously to shoo him. "I said *don't*, Rene. I don't want your apology." She tried to glower at him through a hazy curtain of tears. "Just . . . just leave me alone. By tonight, you'll be rid of me, all right? You can go back to your boozing and playing with your gun and prank calling your hookers, or whatever else constitutes your stupid, sorry, messed up life."

His face clouded with momentary hurt, and she almost felt sorry for what she'd said. But then his brows narrowed and his mouth turned down in that cold, dismissive way he had and he snorted.

"Fine by me." He jerked the key in the ignition and the engine roared to life. "Just fucking fine."

The Audi lurched as he dropped it into gear, and the rear tires squealed against the parking lot asphalt.

As they drove through the open Texas countryside with bright sunlight spilling through the windows, Tessa leaned her head back, closed her eyes and dozed. She hadn't slept much the night before, between trying to decipher the mysteries of the Tome she'd found and Rene's little stunt on the sofa. Napping was not only needed, but also a welcome reprieve from the heavy, brooding silence in the car. She and Rene hadn't said a word to each other in hours.

He can keel over dead for all I'm concerned, she told herself. *I should have done myself a favor and let him shoot himself last night.*

But she didn't feel that way. Not really. She was too hard on him and she knew it, but sometimes . . .

Like whenever he opens his mouth.

. . . she felt powerless to stop herself. He could be sarcastic and acerbic, true, but he could then turn around and offer clumsy attempts at gentleness, like trying to comfort her when she'd burst into tears. Secretly, Tessa found that sort of charming and endearing. Nice, even. Not that she'd ever admit this aloud.

God, I'd never hear the end of it, she thought as her mind faded and the warm sunshine lulled her to sleep.

She dreamed of her grandmother. Not surprising, Eleanor Noble had been on Tessa's mind a lot since she'd left Kentucky. To Tessa's knowledge, Eleanor had been the only woman among the Brethren who had ever traveled beyond the confines of the farm compounds. Tessa had always envied her adventures.

And now here I am, off on one of my own.

Tessa had enjoyed dressing up in Eleanor's clothes, even into her teen years, up until the time of Eleanor's death. In her dream, she imagined herself in her grandmother's bedroom, standing in front of a full-length mirror and admiring a white sundress she wore. Eleanor sat behind her in a winged-back chair, watching and smiling.

"It looks beautiful, darling," Eleanor said, her voice deep and rich, nearly silken. "It fits you perfectly."

"Do you think, Grandmother?" Tessa asked, beaming. She'd been staring down at the dress, and glanced up to meet Eleanor's gaze through the mirror. To her shock and horror, she caught sight of a man's reflection behind her own—her husband.

"Martin!" she gasped, drawing back from the mirror.

Martin Davenant was handsome in a haughty, pristine sort of way; the polar opposite of Rene Morin, with his unruly hair and beard scruff. Martin wore his dark hair combed back from his wide, high brow, and his sharp, square jaw seemed perpetually settled at a stern angle. His mouth was small, his lips full but set in an unyielding frown. His eyes were small and wide-spaced, his gaze so piercing she'd been able to feel— even from across a crowded room—whenever he'd pin her with it. As he did right now.

She whirled in surprise, and uttered a breathless gulp as Martin's hand clamped against her throat, seizing her just beneath the chin. He slammed her backward, crashing against the mirror, and she felt the glass crunch, splintering at the impact.

"Tell me where you are," he seethed, leaning close enough for spittle to spray from his lips against her own. She could smell him—the awful, familiar combination of spicy cologne, laundry starch and cigarette smoke. He was a chain smoker; sometimes the stink of cigarettes in his hair or on his skin had been enough to gag her when he'd come to have sex. Tessa pawed helplessly at his hand, choked and mewling. "You miserable bitch—*tell me where you are!*"

Tessa snapped abruptly from sleep, her breath hitched to scream. She realized she was still with Rene, still in the car, and that they'd come to a stop.

"Where . . . where are we?" she croaked, sitting up, tucking wayward strands of hair behind her ears.

"Rest area," Rene replied, unfastening his seat belt.

He opened the door and swung his legs around slowly. "I need to take a piss."

"How charming," Tessa murmured as he slammed the car door shut behind him. Even though the back of her blouse was sticking to her spine with perspiration from where the intense Texas heat had permeated the car's interior, she shivered, the downy hairs along her forearms rising. Her heart was still racing with residual fear from the nightmare about Martin. If she closed her eyes, she could still feel his hand shoved against her windpipe, smell him, hear his voice hissing.

Tell me where you are.

When she'd first fled Kentucky, he'd tried to call her, over and over again leaving messages on her cell phone. They'd been benevolent enough at first, his voice soothing and calm, nearly purring . . .

I'm not angry with you, Tessa. I just want you to come back.

. . . but with each passing day, his tone had grown colder, his words more malicious . . .

You're trying my patience, Tessa. It's time to come home. Right fucking now.

. . . until at last, any hint of his customary, cool composure had dissolved, and she'd understood what Brandon had always meant when he'd told her the Brethren were monsters.

You answer this goddamn phone! You think this is funny? You think this is a fucking game? Tell me where you are or so help me God, I'll make you sorry! Do you hear me, you stupid bitch? Tell me where you are!

She hadn't told anyone about the voice mails, and had laughed off Martin's phone calls so Brandon wouldn't worry. She'd never told him the truth about her marriage, the nightmarish four years during which she'd lived under the Davenants' roof. During that time, Martin's attention toward her had careened between nonexistent and sadistically violent at the drop of a dime.

She opened the car door and stepped out, pausing long enough to glance around anxiously. They were alone at the rest stop, the parking lot empty, and the highway was vacant of any traffic coming or going, eerily silent in the hot afternoon.

He can't hurt me anymore, she told herself for at least the millionth time since leaving Kentucky. *He can't find me here. Me or my baby.*

The ladies' room was on the far side of the building, next to a freestanding kiosk that housed an assortment of snack and soda machines. Tessa stood, hands on hips, and perused the selections, eyeing a Snickers bar with melancholy, sentimental interest. That had been one of her grandmother's favorite candies.

With her long, chocolate-colored hair, bee-stung lips and catlike eyes, Eleanor had been a stunning woman. Tessa had inherited Eleanor's beauty, her long, slim frame and fiery spirit; the same light that had always flashed in Eleanor's sharp eyes still sparkled in her granddaughter's. Eleanor had been Augustus Noble's first and favorite wife, the only woman Tessa imagined that he had ever found the heart enough to love. No one knew the cause of Eleanor's death. All that Tessa had been told was that the Grandfather had found her lying cold and lifeless on her bedroom floor.

Tessa felt a funny little fluttering from somewhere deep in her belly and blinked, startled out of her distant thoughts. Smiling, she pressed her hands lightly against the waistband of her capris; she was far enough along in her pregnancy that she'd begun to feel the baby stirring now and again. She opened her mind just enough to enjoy a momentary sense of the growing life within her.

This was why Martin was so determined to get

her back, not any real affection or sense of possession.
My baby.

Tessa had been Martin's sixth wife and yet, despite
this, he had only twelve children who had survived
beyond infancy. She'd often heard him arguing about
this, most often with his father. As big a son of a bitch as
Martin was, he was eclipsed by Allistair Davenant, from
whom he'd apparently inherited his brutal disposition.

"Can you do nothing right?" Tessa had heard Allistair shouting at Martin one night from the foyer. "Do
you want to live like this—pushing papers and licking
goddamn boot heels for the next goddamn century?"
His voice had echoed with resounding, sharp emphasis throughout the entire house, loud enough to wake
both Tessa and her cousin Alexandra from sound
sleeps. When they'd crept from their room to peek
over the balustrade, they'd watched in wide-eyed disbelief as Allistair had thrust his hand between Martin's
legs, grabbing him by the crotch with enough force
to double Martin over, *whoofing* for sudden breath.

"You have balls, at least," Allistair had growled as
Martin had crumpled to the floor, retching. He'd
wiped his hand on his slacks as if his hand was soiled.
"Use them for once. Give me some goddamn heirs."

Childbearing had become a real issue among the
Brethren over the last few generations. Pregnancies
among Brethren women were on a sharp and alarm-
ing decline, while the mortality rate for babies and
Brethren children under the age of three was on the
increase. No one seemed to know why, but it was
enough of a growing concern to make someone like
Tessa—with proven fertility and still youthful enough
to have many more children in her lifetime—a precious commodity.

She fished a couple of dollars out of her purse and
fed them into the snack machine. After she'd grabbed
a Snickers, she shelled out another two bucks for a

plastic bottle of Diet Coke. As she walked toward the restroom door, snack in hand, she heard the distinctive sound of a car engine and glanced over her shoulder, her heart momentarily pounding beneath her breast.

It's not him. She tittered slightly in audible relief to see an old, gray sedan pulling into the parking lot. *Not Martin, not in a piece of shit like that.*

She closed her eyes and sighed as she ducked into the restroom. *He can't hurt me anymore,* she reminded herself again. *He can't find me here. Me or my baby.*

Chapter Five

Rene squinted as he walked out of the rest stop men's room. It was goddamn bright outside and he wished he hadn't left his sunglasses in the center console of his car. He forked his fingers through his hair, pushing it back from his brow, then shoved his hand into his hip pocket, fishing for change as he limped toward some snack machines. He hadn't seen an exit off the interstate in more than two hours, and from what he could tell by checking out the map mounted on a bulletin board in front of the building, there was nothing ahead of them for at least another fifty miles.

Looks like it's Cheetos for lunch, he thought, frowning as he studied the snack machine. He glanced down at his palm and began to poke through the assorted loose change he'd dug up. *Have to grab something for* la pischouette, *too,* he figured. She was awake now and with the baby, she needed to eat.

No matter how much Tessa infuriated him, how much she grated on his last fucking nerve like fingernails scraping across the surface of a chalkboard, something in him always softened when he thought about her pregnancy. Probably because he hadn't been able to enjoy much of Irene's. She'd left him, though he could hardly blame her. He'd suffered what was now known as post-traumatic stress disorder when he'd returned from Vietnam; between his hellish tour of duty, the catastrophic wound he'd suffered and the subsequent, horrifying realization of what he was—a vampire—he'd been a wreck by the time he returned stateside.

Hell, I'm still a wreck.

Irene had been about as far along as Tessa when she'd left him. She'd lost the baby shortly thereafter, a miscarriage he hadn't learned about until later. He'd been heartbroken, and remained so even now. Not much had given him hope back then, or a reason to live, but the promise of his child had. That had slipped through his fingers, as had any happiness he might have known with Irene. Seldom a day went by that he didn't wish he could take it back somehow, that he could have made things right for all of them.

A wire coil inside the machine rotated slowly, dropping a foil bag of Cheetos, and Rene leaned over to retrieve it. He didn't see anything in the machine that resembled the sticks and twigs healthy crap that Tessa seemed to favor, so he hoped that dehydrated cheese powder would constitute nutritious enough to satisfy her. And a snack might make for a sort of peace offering on his part, a way to smooth things over from earlier that morning.

He'd made her cry and even though she'd provoked him—par for the course—he still felt like shit about it. He'd been too hard on her—yet again par for the course—and he knew it, but sometimes . . .

Like whenever she opens her mouth.

. . . he felt powerless to stop himself. She was a smart girl, high-strung but also wide-eyed and innocently oblivious to a lot of the world's more unsavory aspects, thanks to the privileged, sheltered life she'd known in Kentucky. He'd known too many people—himself included—who had been beaten down by reality's harshness, made jaded and cynical because of it, and he secretly found that naïveté sort of charming and endearing about Tessa. Nice, even. Not that he'd ever admit this aloud.

God, I'd never hear the end of it, he thought.

"Hey, you got a light?"

Rene looked up to find a young man in his early twenties standing between him and the restroom building. The kid had long, dirty-blond hair caught back beneath a red bandana tied over the cap of his skull. He wore an old AC/DC T-shirt, grease-spotted, ratty blue jeans and a pair of faded black Chuck Taylor sneakers.

Rene had been a police officer long enough to recognize the nervous, darting light in the kid's eyes. *Strung out on something,* he thought, wishing all of a sudden that he hadn't left his Sig Sauer in the glove compartment of the car. "Sorry, pal. I don't smoke."

The kid nodded, cutting his eyes to the snack machines. Rene decided to hedge his bets and get the fuck away from him. Just as he turned, presenting his back to the younger man, he heard the distinctive *snict!* of a gun hammer being drawn back.

Shit.

"I guess I'll just take your wallet then, *pal,*" said the kid, with pointed, sarcastic emphasis. "And your car keys, too. Hand them over."

Rene pivoted, stepping in a slow semicircle toward the kid and found himself facing the business end of what appeared to be a .45-caliber Smith and Wesson revolver.

Shit.

"Your wallet," the kid said again, giving the gun a little demonstrative waggle in emphasis. "And your car keys, too. Come on."

Rene could see beads of perspiration beading along

his brow line below the edge of his bandana. He could smell the kid, a mix of sweat and adrenaline, and could sense the mounting, anxious rhythm of his heartbeat.

Christ, he's wired. What's he on?

"Take it easy," Rene said, keeping his gaze steady on the kid as he reached slowly for his pocket. Unbeknownst to the young man, he opened his mind.

Tessa, where are you?

"You sure you want to do this?" he asked aloud, because he had no fucking intention of handing over his car keys if she was still sitting in the front seat. The gun would be a problem he'd then have to deal with somehow, but he figured he'd cross that bridge if and when he came to it.

The kid glanced beyond Rene's shoulder at the sleek Audi sports car, then back to Rene, his brow arched slightly. "Oh, yeah. I'm sure."

Tessa? Rene thought again.

I'm using the bathroom! she snapped back, sounding irritable. *Jesus, I'll be right out!*

No, that's okay. Rene slipped his hand into the hip pocket of his jeans and hooked the ring to his car keys with his fingertip. *Just stay there for a few minutes. Take your time.*

Don't tell me what to do, she groused in his mind. *I'm sick and tired of you doing that—bossing me around.*

Goddamn it, I'm not bossing you around, he thought, bristling as he held up his hand, the key ring around his middle finger. The key dangled against his palm for the kid to see. *I'm just asking you to stay put for a bit.*

"And your wallet," the kid said, jabbing again with the gun. "Give me your wallet, too."

Don't you curse at me, Tessa said. *I'm tired of you doing that, too, goddamn it. Asking means you phrase something as a question. It means you say 'would you mind to do this, please, Tessa?' Not just 'do this' or 'do that.' That's* telling, *Rene. You were* telling *me what to do. Again.*

The kid's eyes cut about uncertainly, wide-eyed with startled fright as a semi roared by on the interstate. "Hurry the fuck up, man. Give me your goddamn wallet."

"Take it easy," Rene said again, moving his free hand for his back pocket. "I'm getting it for you."

He didn't give a shit about the car or his wallet. What mattered was Tessa; getting the kid, his pistol and his hyped-up, itchy trigger finger the hell out of there before she came out of the ladies' room, even though she *was* picking the absolute worst time to pull one of her Miss High-and-Fucking-Mighty routines on him, and if she had been standing in front of him, he might have been momentarily tempted to shoot her himself. He pulled out his wallet and held it up with the keys. "Take them. They're yours."

"Damn right," the kid said, stepping forward and reaching for the wallet.

Right about that time, the door to the restroom swung open wide and Tessa marched out, her brows narrowed, her face twisted in a scowl. *And furthermore, you asshole—*

She skittered to an uncertain halt when she saw Rene, then shrank back, her eyes flying wide when the kid whirled to her in surprise, pointing the muzzle of the pistol directly at her face.

"Don't move!" he screamed, and she dropped the bottle of Diet Coke she'd been carrying. She'd opened it in the bathroom, and it spilled in a sudden, frothy puddle around her feet.

"Rene!" she hiccuped, looking to him in bright, desperate fright.

"You don't move, either!" the kid screamed, whipping the gun back to momentarily aim at Rene. "Both of you just stand the fuck still!"

"Take it easy, kid," Rene said, keeping his voice calm and quiet, locking eyes with the boy. "We don't want any trouble. There's more than five thousand dollars in my wallet. It's yours. Take it—the car, too."

The kid cut a glance at Tessa, letting his eyes crawl along her body, his gaze lingering at her bosom. Rene didn't need to read his mind to know what he was thinking. "Maybe I just found something else I want, too," he said, the tip of his tongue darting out to swipe across his lips. He shoved the gun toward Tessa and she flinched, hunching her shoulders and crying out softly. "Move, bitch. You're coming with me."

Rene saw the world suddenly become cast in brilliant, nearly blinding glare as his pupils opened fully, filling his corneas. He felt the sudden rush of blood to his gums and his canine teeth extended, the bloodlust coming over him almost instantaneously. "No," he said, reaching out, clapping his right hand against the kid's arm. "She's not."

The kid swung the pistol back around. Rene clapped his left hand over the front of the muzzle, meaning to shove it aside, but when the younger man saw his face, his eyes and teeth, he uttered a breathless shriek: "What the fuck—!" and pulled the trigger.

The sound of the gunshot was like thunder trapped in the narrow confines between the snack machines and the bathrooms. Tessa's scream overlapped the booming report, and pain ripped through Rene's hand, spearing up his arm and slamming into him like a head-on collision with a locomotive.

He doubled over, gasping on the smoke, blinking at the shocking agony. When he looked up, his eyes smarting with tears, he saw the kid dancing clumsily back, the gun dangling limply in his hand, his mouth agape.

"Oh!" he whimpered. "Oh . . . oh, shit . . . !"

"Why . . . why did you . . . have to go and do that?" Rene seethed from between clenched teeth as he staggered upright. He cradled his wounded hand against his belly and felt blood coursing down his arm, spattering heavily on the sidewalk between his feet. "You . . . you stupid son of a bitch . . . now I'm going to have to kill you."

The kid had a half second to flounder backward, his eyes wide as he raised the pistol again, and then he shrieked as Rene leapt at him, knocking him off his feet and sending the gun flying from his fingers.

Rene heard Tessa crying out his name, her voice choked with tears, as he stumbled back against the snack machines. His face and the front of his shirt were now soaked with blood and not all of it his own. The kid lay sprawled against the grass, his throat ripped open, his eyes wide open and unblinking, his mouth wide and frozen in a scream.

"Rene!" Tessa cried, her hands fluttering against him. He blinked at her and was absurdly touched to see she was crying, her cheeks streaked with a steady torrent of tears. "Rene, oh . . . oh, God . . . he shot you!"

"Je suis bien," he murmured. "I'm all right, *pischouette.*"

A glance down at his hand told the truth, however. The .45-caliber round had punched clear through, in his palm-side and out the other, leaving behind a shredded mess of bloody, exposed meat.

"Oh, my God!" Tessa gasped in horror. "Oh . . . oh, my God, Rene! Your hand . . . !"

It wasn't as bad as his knee had been, or his gut, for that matter, back in Vietnam, but his hand sure hurt like all hell. He couldn't catch his breath for the pain, and remained doubled at the waist, leaning heavily against the Coke machine.

"It's all right," he managed, because she was frightened and panicked, clutching at him, her eyes wide and frantic. "Tessa, listen to me. I've been shot before. This . . . this is no big deal. *Ce n'est rien.* I'm all right."

He hooked the front of his shirt with his uninjured hand and gave a mighty yank, jerking buttons loose and splitting it open. He shrugged his way out of the sleeves, then gritted his teeth and wrapped it around his hand. "Help me move him," he said with a nod toward the kid. "Grab a foot, *pischouette*. We need to hide him before somebody comes."

They each grabbed one of the kid's ankles and together, hauled him unceremoniously back to his car, a gray, beat up Toyota Corolla. "Check his pockets," Rene told Tessa, out of breath with pain and exertion. "See if you can find his car keys."

She did, and he popped the trunk. "We'll put him in here," he said.

"What about the blood?" Tessa looked uncertainly behind them, at the smeared, gory trail they'd left behind them in the grass and on the sidewalk.

Rene shook his head. "Nothing we can do about it," he said. "But at least this will buy us some time. Come on. Help me with him."

When they were finished, Rene limped back to the snack machines, retrieving his fallen key ring and wallet. "Check my trunk, would you, *pischouette*?" he asked, tossing her the key. "Get me a shirt out of my bag, *sie tu plais*. And I think I have a first-aid kit in there somewhere. Would you bring it here? Oh—and there's an unopened fifth of Bloodhorse. I'll need that, too."

Tessa nodded, scurrying toward the Audi. Rene picked up the kid's revolver, shoving it into the waist-band of his jeans at the small of his back. He limped into the men's room and stood at the sink, unwrapping his hand and then dousing it under a steady stream of cold water.

Goddamn, that hurts. It wasn't the worst he'd ever felt, but it was a far goddamn cry from the best. He closed his eyes, clenching his teeth and steeling himself against the pain. Grabbing a paper towel from a nearby dispenser, he set about cleaning the blood off himself, mopping at his face and chest. When he walked back outside, he found Tessa waiting for him with shirt, Bloodhorse and first-aid kit all cradled between her arms.

"What are you doing?" she asked, watching as he poured bourbon on his wound and sucked in a sharp, hissing breath.

"I don't know where that bullet's been," he replied, managing a wink and a crooked smile. "And alcohol kills anything."

Following his instructions, she helped him wrap his hand, pressing thick pads on either point of penetration and then binding them in place with gauze. "He was trying to rob us," she whispered when they had finished. She looked up at him, her large, dark eyes swimming with new tears.

"Yes, *pischouette.*" He nodded, easing his way into the clean shirt she'd brought to him.

"He hurt you." Now her bottom lip quivered and her tears spilled, leaving glistening trails against her pale skin. "He . . . he was going to hurt me . . . and my baby."

Rene reached for her with his good hand, brushing the cuff of his knuckles against her cheek. "No one's going to hurt you or that baby. Not while I'm here." Her narrow frame began to shudder, and he drew her against his shoulder. "It's all right," he breathed, closing his eyes. "Hush, now, *pischouette.* It's all right."

Chapter Six

"She wasn't a hooker," Rene murmured from the passenger seat.

"What?" Tessa sat rigidly behind the wheel of the Audi, clutching it so tightly her knuckles had blanched. She hated to drive because she'd never had the opportunity to learn how to do it well. She'd made the long trip from Kentucky to follow Brandon, but she'd been motivated by desperate fear for his safety, and it had felt like she'd held her breath the entire time. Whenever a semi truck had gone barreling past her on the interstates, she'd nearly hyperventilated. Other cars and trucks had flown past her, some blaring on their horns because she'd grow nervous and wouldn't drive fast enough.

When Rene had first told her she would need to get them to New Mexico, she'd nearly choked. "No, let's just wait," she'd said. "Let me call Lina and Brandon. They're somewhere on the highway behind us. They can meet us here and Brandon can—"

"Brandon's hands are broken," Rene had reminded her. "He can't drive, remember? And we can't stay here. Someone could come along in the meantime, before them. *Nous devons aller.*" We have to go.

He'd told her to get into the trunk once more before leaving, this time to look for a bottle of prescription pills. When she'd been unable to find one in his bag, he'd run his fingers through his hair in frustration. "I must have given them all to Brandon," he'd muttered.

"All what?" she'd asked.

"My pills," he'd replied. "Pain pills, *pischouette*. I take them sometimes for my leg."

Which hadn't made any sense to her, because his leg had been amputated more than a year ago. *How could it still hurt him?*

"That's what I get for trying to go clean cold turkey," Rene had remarked more to himself than her, sounding rueful. He wouldn't admit it, but he was in a tremendous amount of pain. His hand had stopped bleeding, and he held it cradled against his lap in the car as he sat, slumped in the seat, his eyes heavily lidded.

He was fighting unconsciousness, nodding his head as his mind would fade in and out. His pallor was ashen, his breathing shallow, and when he was awake, he seemed dazed and confused. Like right now.

"You told me earlier I could go back to my boozing and playing with myself and prank-calling hookers," he said. "Or something like that. She wasn't a hooker . . . the woman I called last night. *Elle était mon épouse* . . . she was my wife."

Tessa blinked at him in surprise.

"You were right," he said. "I don't know anything about you or your life. And you don't know about mine, either." He smiled, his eyelids fluttering closed as he leaned his head back. "Maybe it's time we learned, no? I married Irene in May of 1970. She left me that December, the day after Christmas, in fact."

"I'm sorry," Tessa said. She glanced down at the speedometer and realized she was going 85 miles an hour. With a startled gasp, she jerked her foot back from the accelerator. The Audi had a powerful engine and a very easy gas pedal, Rene had warned her—as she kept inadvertently discovering.

"Not your fault," he replied, still smiling. "It was mine. All mine." He opened one eye and glanced at her. "Bet you find that hard to believe, *est-ce vrai?*"

He kept lapsing between French and English as he spoke, and Tessa kept racking her brain, trying to recall her French tutelage from years earlier at the great house. For example, he'd just said, *is this true?*

Her grandmother, Eleanor, had been fluent in French; their ancestors from many long generations ago had come from France during the Middle Ages. The night before, as she'd been studying the Tome— and the unfamiliar French-Latin combination part of it had been written in—Tessa had wondered if it had been transcribed in the dialect of these medieval predecessors.

Rene also kept cracking jokes, trying to make Tessa smile, like right now, as if he felt badly or responsible for her growing concern over him, and wanted to make her feel better.

"*Ici,*" he said, wincing as he leaned forward and popped open the glove compartment. *Here.* He took something out, a faded, creased photograph. "Take a look."

She didn't really want to take her eyes off the road, but there was no other traffic in either direction, nothing for miles, so she risked a glance. He held it out and curious, she took the photo from his hand. Forgetting herself for a moment in surprised wonder, she stared at the picture of a very young Rene, no older than she and Brandon, and the smiling, pretty blond beside him.

"That's our wedding day," Rene said. "My *mamère* must have kept it for me. It fell out of that book of yours, that Tome, yesterday in Thibodaux."

The young woman in the photograph looked so

happy. Her cheeks were flushed with joy, her eyes sparkling, her mouth spread in a wide, beaming grin, as if all of her hopes, dreams and desires had come true in that one moment and had been captured on film. *She's in love,* Tessa realized. *That's what it looks like. That's what it must feel like.*

"*Joli drôle,* no?" Rene asked. *Funny, isn't it?* "Not at all like your fancy wedding, I'm sure." He settled back in the seat. "Irene lives in San Francisco now. She's re-married, at least the last I'd heard, and got herself a nice, shiny life." He closed his eyes and murmured, "Better than she would've ever had with me."

"You . . . you should rest," Tessa said, handing the picture back to him. She didn't want to look at it any-more, the joy in Irene's face. It made her feel too lonely inside, envious somehow. "I'll find a place where we can stop, a town or something, and we'll call Lina, tell her what's happened."

He shook his head as he put the picture back in the glove box. "Why, *pischouette*? There's nothing she can do except worry."

"But you killed that man."

He nodded. "First time in damn near forty years." His eyes had closed again, and his voice had grown quiet, somewhat slurred.

You killed him for me, Tessa thought. Not because of the car or his wallet—because Rene had offered those freely to the man. Rene hadn't tried to resist or fight back until the man had turned the gun toward Tessa.

"We'll see Lina tonight," Rene said. "We can tell her then. I've fed twice today . . . made a glutton of myself. Once that kicks in, I'll be fine." He didn't open his eyes but the corner of his mouth hooked slightly, wryly. "That or whatever the hell that kid was high on. Either way, there's hope for me yet."

Tessa glanced at him as he drifted off into uncon-sciousness. She didn't know much about Rene, but she knew that killing humans was something he took neither lightly nor arbitrarily. He'd taught himself how to feed without doing it. And yet he'd killed to protect her. He'd nearly torn the man's head from his neck with his bare hands.

You might be right, Rene, she thought. *There may be hope for you yet.*

She wished that she'd been able to face her own wedding day with the same uninhibited joy she'd seen in the photograph of Rene's young bride, Irene. Instead, Tessa had been filled with trepidation and anxiety, not to mention a fair share of sorrow.

She remembered her first day at the Davenant house, stepping through the front doors and into the main foyer to be greeted by Monica Davenant, Martin's first and eldest wife.

"I can smell your cunt." Monica had been statuesque, tall and whip-thin, with pale skin and auburn hair, her features delicate and pristine, her beauty nearly frigid. Her eyes had been icy, piercing and lucent, filled with nothing but disdain for the young woman who'd stood before her. "Or is that Eleanor's? Augustus's whores are so alike—you all share the same stink. However does he tell you apart enough to know which to fuck?"

Tessa had been shocked by the woman's vulgar language and frightened, as well, but struggled not to show it. She'd been warned about Monica—all of the Davenants, in fact.

"They'll hate you because you're a Noble," her mother, Vanessa, had told her once.

"They'll hate you because you're Augustus's granddaughter," Eleanor had warned. She'd tried to smile, but her eyes had glistened with tears as she'd stroked her hand against Tessa's dark hair. "Allistair Davenant is jealous of your grandfather because of his dominance. It's a hatred that's been brewing for more than two hundred years and spilled over to his entire clan. You stay close to Alexandra. She's your cousin. She'll look out for you, protect you if she can."

Protect me from what? Tessa had wondered and worried, but she'd soon learned.

"Before you do anything in this house—the *Davenant* house," Monica had told her that gray, gloomy morning as she'd pinned Tessa with her gaze in the Davenant great house foyer. "You'll go and take a bath, wash that nasty Noble stench off your skin before I gag."

Her eyes had cut to the necklace around Tessa's neck. It had belonged to Eleanor, a simple gold chain with a solitary but enormous stone pendant—a rare ten-carat green sapphire that Augustus Noble had custom-ordered from Sri Lanka for his favorite wife.

"This is the first gift your grandfather ever gave to me," Eleanor had told Tessa, upon presenting the necklace to Tessa on her sixteenth birthday. Tessa had sputtered in flabbergasted protest, but Eleanor hadn't listened. When her mother had warned Tessa not to bring it with her to the Davenants, Tessa likewise hadn't paid heed. Eleanor hadn't been dead a week at this point. Tessa had still been very much in mourning, the gift even more precious to her because of it.

Monica Davenant's eyes had danced with a wicked sort of glee as she'd reached out to touch the pendant. "This is lovely," she murmured, her voice low, nearly a purr.

"It . . . it belonged to my grandmother," Tessa said, uncertain of what to say but struggling to be polite.

Monica locked gazes with her. "Yes. I know."

Tessa gasped in startled disbelief as Monica closed her hand quickly about the sapphire and with one swift, sudden jerk, snapped the chain and yanked it from about her neck. She reacted instinctively, not as the new wife—the least among six in Martin's part of the Davenant family hierarchy—but as she would have had she been standing beneath her own family's roof. Her hand shot out, her fingers closing fiercely around Monica's slender wrist. "That's mine," she'd said, her brows furrowed. "Give it back."

Monica had blinked at her, her lucent blue eyes flying wide in surprise. "You little bitch," she seethed, wrenching her arm loose and stumbling back a step. Tessa caught a blur of motion out of the corner of her gaze, and then Monica slapped her in the face—the first time Tessa had ever been struck in her entire life. It stunned more than it stung, but then Monica grabbed her roughly by the hair and shoved, sending her sprawling to the floor and making her bark her knees painfully against the granite tiles.

"Nothing in this house is *yours* anymore," Monica snapped, snatching a handful of Tessa's hair again and twisting hard enough to make Tessa cry out. "Whatever you walked through that door with—kiss it good-bye, you spoiled little bitch. It's *mine* now, and so are you. You belong to *me*."

Later that evening, she'd overheard Monica complaining to Martin: "Don't you remember how that stupid cunt would parade around with this dangling from her neck like it was some kind of goddamn prize?"

Tessa had been going upstairs to the small room she would be sharing with Alexandra, when she heard voices from the third-floor landing, filtering out from behind a nearby closed door. The word *cunt*, again delivered with nearly tangible venom, drew her short.

"I remember," Monica said. Tessa crept to the door and knelt to peek through the keyhole. She could see Martin sitting in a winged-back armchair with Monica behind him—one of the first times Tessa had seen him since he'd come to take her from the great house. Monica leaned over his shoulder, holding something in her hand, something that flashed and

glimmered in the glow from the nearby lamp—
Eleanor's green sapphire pendant.

"She wanted all of us to see it," Monica hissed. "All
of us to know—Augustus Noble spends money that
rightfully belongs to *all* of us however he damn well
chooses. It's bad enough he used to take her with him
all over the goddamn free world, but then he lavished
that slut with stuff like this—look at it, Martin!"

Martin seemed bored as he swatted the necklace
out of his face, apparently more interested in the half-
empty tumbler of bourbon in his hand. "I see it," he
growled, tilting his head back. Tessa heard ice cubes
clink softly together as he drained the glass.

"Well, it's mine now," Monica declared, and Tessa
had felt her face flush angrily as she watched the woman
draw the chain about her neck, fastening the clasp.

Like hell it is, you bitch, she'd thought, and in that
moment, she'd resolved that somehow, someday she
would get the pendant back. It was a promise she'd ultimately been unable to keep; even though Monica
had worn the sapphire nearly every day without fail,
Tessa had no chance to grab it from her before she'd
fled Kentucky. The idea that the necklace—a symbol
not only of her grandparents' love, but of Eleanor's
love for Tessa, as well—remained in Monica's possession killed her.

"Augustus sits at the head of the Brethren Elders,
puts his sons in all of the choice positions with the
farms and distillery, and what does he leave for the rest
of you?" Monica had said to Martin that night four
years earlier. "Grunt work and mid-level management.
Why doesn't he put you out with the Kinsfolk or the laborers shoveling shit in the barns? It's not fair."

"I know it's not," Martin replied, standing. He
crossed the room to refill his glass. "But there's nothing I can do about it, Monica. You want to change
things? Give me *sons*."

"One male heir is all that's made them the leading clan," she said. "That's why Augustus didn't just clap his hand over that little bastard Brandon's mouth all of those years ago and see him smothered when he realized he wouldn't bleed to death. It's why he didn't kill him for defying the bloodletting. He'll keep him alive if only to force him to it. And now Vanessa's given birth to another misbegotten whelp that might make it to adulthood. Two sons—two lucky births, that's all."

Tessa had been frozen with shock, because she'd known that Monica meant her brother Daniel, who had been born only two months earlier.

He'd been the third of Sebastian and Vanessa's sons; in addition to Brandon and Daniel, who was now four, there had been the eldest, Caine. But Caine was dead now; he'd come after Brandon and Lina had killed him. The Elders, including Augustus, were hunting for Brandon with the intent to murder him, which was why they were cutting such a desperate path across the country—to escape the Elders somehow.

But maybe we don't have to. Not now. Not anymore.

The leading Brethren clan—the family that held dominance over all others—had always been determined by the house with the most adult male heirs at any one time, those who had gone through the bloodletting and fed for the first time. For generations that distinction had belonged to the Nobles. But because of the mounting fertility problems and infant mortality, over time it had become a slim margin of victory over the other clans, and the Davenants in particular.

"It's only one son who keeps the Nobles dominant," Monica had complained that night years earlier. "Until Brandon and Daniel Noble complete the bloodletting—*if* they complete the bloodletting— that's the only thing keeping Augustus in power. Take out one . . ." She'd reached over Martin's shoulder, pinching a half-melted ice cube from his drink and tossing it into the fire. ". . . and he'd have to share with the Davenants. Take out another . . ." Again, she flicked an ice cube into the flames. ". . . and your father, Allistair, becomes the lead Elder with the dominant clan—and *you* next in line when he's gone."

"What do you want me to do?" Martin had griped, moving his glass out of her reach and cradling it somewhat protectively against his belly. "Walk up to their front door and shoot Caine Noble in the goddamn head? You said so yourself—they've got two more of the little bastards right in line behind him." He'd slurped the rest of his drink down. "I'd be doing my father the goddamn favor, not me."

Now Caine was dead. That left the Nobles and Davenants equal in the number of male heirs. Monica had been right; this would mean the two clans would share dominance equally.

But only once word reaches the Elders. They didn't know that Caine was dead. At least, she didn't think they knew. *Because if he did, the Grandfather would change his mind,* she thought. *He'd rescind his order to have Brandon killed.*

Eleanor had told Tessa that Allistair Davenant hated Augustus Noble and the feeling had been more than apparently mutual. They would share control of the Brethren as readily as they might have cut off their own balls, and Brandon would be the key to avoiding that scenario.

The Grandfather needs Brandon now, needs him to complete the bloodletting if the Nobles are to be the dominant house.

Caine had slipped away from Kentucky on his own; the Elders might not yet have realized his absence. There was a very strong possibility that they were completely unaware of what had happened.

She glanced at Rene, then lifted her foot off the gas pedal. As the Audi slowed, she pulled over onto the shoulder of the road. The car jostled in the loose gravel, and Rene stirred, groaning and sitting up somewhat.

"What . . . what is it?" he murmured, blinking dazedly.

"Nothing," she said, opening her car door. "I . . . I just . . . I need to stop. I feel sick to my stomach. The baby, I think."

"Oh." He nodded once, his eyelids drooping closed.

Tessa walked around to the back of the car and fished her cell phone out of her pocket. She squatted against the rear bumper so that Rene couldn't see what she was doing clearly if he looked through the side-view mirror. Not that she needed to worry; he'd been out again before she'd even closed the door.

She felt badly for him, and knew she needed to get him to New Mexico so they could meet up with Brandon and get some of Rene's pain medication. She needed to stay on the road, but at the moment, she just couldn't. "I'm sorry, Rene," she whispered as she flipped back the cover to her phone. She thumbed through her address book until she found the number she needed, then hit *send*.

"Tessa?" Her father, Sebastian, answered his cell phone on the second ring, his voice tinged with static, nearly shrill with alarm. "Tessa? Is that you?"

He'd recognized her number undoubtedly, and the concern in his tone brought immediate tears to her eyes. "Hi, Dad," she said. "Yes, it's me."

"Where are you? Is Brandon with you? My God, we've been worried sick, Tessa, and Martin is—"

"Dad, listen to me," Tessa cut in. "I can't talk long, but you need to know. You need to let the Grandfather know. Caine is dead."

Stunned silence from the other end of the line. "Emily's dead, too," Tessa said, because her younger sister had been with Caine; they had both attacked Brandon and Lina had shot her, as well.

"What?" Sebastian asked, sounding breathless and strained, like she'd just kicked him in the balls. "How? I . . . I don't . . ."

"They followed me to look for Brandon and they . . .

they were killed." Her voice quavered as her tears spilled. "I'm sorry, Dad." She clapped her hand over her mouth as a little sob escaped her. "I love you."

She hung up on him before he could say anything more, and squatted on the side of the road for a long moment, struggling to compose herself. She hadn't been particularly close to either Caine or Emily, but they'd been her siblings nonetheless, and she hadn't yet allowed herself to mourn for them. She closed her eyes, knowing she'd just broken her father's heart.

But hopefully I just saved Brandon's life.

Although it had been an arrangement dictated by the Elders just after she had been born, she'd been wed to Martin Davenant shortly after her eighteenth birthday, two weeks after her bloodletting. It was supposed to have been Brandon's first kill, as well as her own, but her brother had defied the customs of the Brethren and refused. He'd fled from the bloodletting ceremony and holed up in his tutor, Jackson's guest house on the farm, waiting there until the following morning before returning home to face the Grandfather's wrath.

But it was a wrath that had never come. Terrified of what Augustus would do to Brandon, Tessa had pleaded with her grandmother, Eleanor, and her father, Sebastian, to intercede on Brandon's behalf. As with Eleanor, Augustus had seldom refused their son, and Tessa had desperately hoped that this united front might persuade him to spare Brandon punishment.

And it had worked. Brandon's teacher had been fired, an act that had broken her brother's heart, but that had been the extent of any retribution against Brandon. A week later, Eleanor had died. A week after that, Tessa had been shipped off to the Davenant great house to assume her life as Martin's wife. In retrospect, she wondered if this had been further punishment for her brother; with neither Tessa nor Eleanor remaining in the house, and Sebastian often consumed by his responsibilities to the daily operation of the horse farm, Brandon had been left virtually on his own, his most stalwart champions gone. But while Tessa knew some of the Brethren—including members of their own family—looked down at Brandon and treated him derisively because of his handicaps, she'd never thought that anything truly bad would happen to him. Certainly not from their own grandfather.

But something had happened to Augustus Noble upon Eleanor's death, and whatever soft spot she'd held in his heart had hardened to match the rest. More than just cool and distant, as was his customary demeanor, he'd become vindictive and cruel. Three years later, Tessa had realized to her horror just how much so he could be.

He'd crushed Brandon's hands, shattering the bones and leaving her brother crippled. Tessa had rushed to the great house as soon as she'd learned, and remembered finding Augustus standing before the fireplace in the first floor study upon her arrival.

"How could you?" she'd cried, marching up to him, her eyes flooded with tears, her hands balled into fists. "You . . . you *monster!* How could you do this to Brandon?"

The Grandfather had struck her so hard she'd stumbled sideways and crumpled to her hands and knees, momentary stars dancing in her line of sight. She'd blinked at the floor in silent, absolute shock.

"Watch your mouth, girl," he'd said, his face icily stoic. "Or you'll be laid out along with him."

Only then had she realized he wasn't alone; on the far side of the room, at least five Brethren men stood in a tight and stern-faced ring—Elders from other clans. She recognized one of them in particular, a man with sharp, cold eyes the same shade of steel gray

as his hair and a doughy face that tugged the corners
of his mouth into a perpetual frown—Allistair Davenant, Martin's father.

"I see it only takes a minute, eh, Augustus?" he remarked, sparing a cool, brittle glance at the Grandfather. "Not two footsteps through your door and your
granddaughter forgets her place."

"She's not my granddaughter anymore, Allistair."
Augustus had turned his eyes to the fire, his words—
his cold dismissal—hurting Tessa more than any physical blow ever could. "She's yours."

Rene woke again as she got back into the car. "You
all right, *pischouette*?" he asked, squinting blearily and
wincing as he inadvertently moved his hand.

"Yes." Tessa nodded, muffling a sniffle against the
back of her hand. She'd already rubbed at her eyes
before opening the door, and hoped he couldn't tell
she'd been crying. "I . . . I'm fine. How are you doing?"

He looked bad, pale and haggard, but managed a
smile. "Still here." He tried to wiggle the fingers of his
wounded hand, but sucked in a hurting breath at the
effort.

"Try to rest, Rene," she said and without thinking
about it, she reached out and brushed his hair back
lightly from his brow. Her fingertips trailed briefly
against the side of his face, and he closed his eyes, as
if drawing comfort from her touch.

"Sounds good," he murmured, then faded
once more.

Chapter Seven

Rene had met Irene in the fall of 1967, his senior year in high school. He remembered sitting beneath the cool eaves of a magnolia tree on the grounds of Thibodaux High School. It was the first day of classes, his lunch break, but he hadn't touched much of the bologna and cheese sandwich his grandmother had packed. Instead, he sat pinching bits of bread loose between his fingertips and flicking them out onto the lawn, where a small finch waited.

He'd lured the bird to him by opening his mind. Although at this point, he was unaware of what exactly he was, and the bloodlust hadn't yet come upon him, he knew he was different. It hadn't taken a fucking rocket scientist. If you could make animals, and birds in particular, do whatever you wanted them to just by thinking about it, you definitely weren't your average, everyday, run-of-the-mill teen in Thibodaux, Louisiana.

He'd been able to summon birds for a long time, since his early childhood. He had always felt like an outsider in the small community he called home and had never had many friends growing up, so the birds had been companions to him. They didn't judge; they didn't care if he was poor, his clothes secondhand, or that his grandmother worked in the local grocery store while his grandfather drew disability. They would come to him, their thoughts innocent and simple; he could close his eyes and have them fly about him in a fluttering swarm, their wings brushing against him, tickling his flesh and tugging at his hair. He could see through their eyes, hear through their ears and lose himself in their world of sensory perceptions.

The finch hopped closer, its small, dark eyes glittering like polished buttons as it drew within a few inches of Rene's foot. He sat with his knees drawn toward his chest, his elbows resting atop, and when he dropped another crumb, the bird darted for it, snatching it up in its beak. Holding its gaze with his own, Rene reached out, a piece of bread balanced on his fingertips. As his hand lowered to the grass, the bird crept closer, its head turning this way and that, wary and curious, until it stood only millimeters away.

"Oh, my God!"

The voice was soft, nearly breathless with wonder, but enough to startle both the bird and Rene, snapping the mental bond he'd forged between them. The finch flew away with a sudden rustling of feathers, darting back for the shelter of overhead magnolia limbs.

Rene turned and saw a girl standing behind him, having just ducked her head to walk beneath the tree. He froze, paralyzed, unable to speak, breathe or think clearly.

Mon Dieu, *she's beautiful.*

She blinked at him, blue eyes wide and filled with wonder. "Did you see that?" she gasped. "That bird almost jumped right into your hand!"

He knew who she was, of course. There wasn't anyone in Thibodaux who didn't recognize Irene Hunt. Her father was president of the Thibodaux branch of Whitney National Bank. While Rene's family was probably the poorest in Lafourche parish, the Hunts were undoubtedly the wealthiest.

Rene stared at her until she giggled, drawing her hand to her face. "Of course you saw it," she said. "It's *your* hand."

She wore a sleeveless dress in a colorful print of scarlet, black and white horizontal bands with a short hem cut to mid thigh. Her blond hair fell in a heavy sheaf to just below her shoulders, fastened back in a ponytail at the nape of her neck. She wore little discernable makeup, and her face was round, her features gentle and sweet. She smelled good to him, even at a distance, like lavender soap and baby powder.

Mon Dieu, he thought again. *She's beautiful.*

"Hi," she said with a small, clumsy wave, as if his silence disconcerted her and made her feel shy. "My name's Irene." When he still said nothing—because his throat felt like it had closed, nearly strangling him—her bright expression faltered further. "I . . . I'm sorry. I didn't mean . . ." She turned around. "I'll leave you alone."

"No," he said, the word bursting out of his mouth as he forced himself to speak. "No, wait. Don't go."

She turned, smiling hesitantly again, and that was probably the moment he'd fallen in love with her, utterly, hopelessly, helplessly.

"I'm Rene LaCroix," he said, because it would be years yet before he met Arnaud Morin, his father, and assumed his last name.

Irene was new at school that year. Her father had sent her to private schools in Shreveport prior to that, and Rene later learned that it had only been through her near-constant pleading that John Hunt had eventually consented to let his daughter attend public school in the parish.

"You hassling this young lady, LaCroix?" a loud voice asked, and Gordon Maddox, one year Rene's senior and a good twenty pounds heavier, strode into view, shoving aside tree boughs with his big, meaty fists. His family was wealthy, too; his father was the third-generation owner of the town's leading drug store. Gordon was your garden variety privileged pretty-boy asshole type—quarterback on the football team, president of the student council, homecoming king. All that happy horse shit. He'd bullied Rene since grade school for no reason other than the fact Rene was poor, and Rene had long since lost count of how many times Gordon had punched, pounded, pummeled or otherwise plowed the shit out of him over the years.

"I wouldn't stand too close to this Cajun trash," Gordon had warned Irene as he'd draped his arm around her shoulders. "You might get shit on your pretty dress."

"Funny . . ." she'd replied, and she'd made a point to deliberately duck away from him. "I was just thinking the same thing about you."

She was fifteen; Rene was seventeen. Because her family would never have approved of their relationship, they spent that academic year meeting in secret, late-night rendezvous. After his graduation, he'd enlisted in the Army, hoping to make enough money to build a life for himself with Irene. Before he'd shipped off to basic training, and from there, to Vietnam, he'd given her an engagement ring, a thin gold band with a chip for a diamond solitaire; the best he could afford. She'd tearfully accepted his proposal, and that more than anything had seen him through his tour of duty at Dong Tam in the Delta.

But he'd returned from Vietnam a changed man in more ways than one, and while Irene had tried her best to make things work between them, Rene knew that it had been impossible. The wound to his gut had left no visible scars, but the damage from his stint in

Vietnam had run cruelly and deeply. He'd retreated from her and his family; he'd rejected and repelled anything in his life that might have made him happy. He'd started drinking heavily, the first of many times in his life when he'd turned to the bottom of a liquor bottle for comfort.

The added discovery that what had happened to him in Vietnam—the rush of the bloodlust—wasn't a one-time deal, but something recurrent and beyond his capacity to control was especially devastating. When Irene had come upon him in his grandmother's pigpen early one Sunday morning, the fresh carcass of a spring suckling between his hands, his face smeared brightly with blood, it had been the last straw.

"Just go!" he'd screamed at her—hateful, hurtful words he wished he could take back. He'd followed her back into Odette's house, letting the screen door slap shut behind him. She'd told him she was leaving; she'd crossed the kitchen for the corridor and the staircase beyond to pack her bags. "Go back to your daddy! Let him buy you a fresh new life! I don't need you here! I don't want you here! Do you hear me? *I don't need you!*"

He'd kept screaming because she'd kept walking, and she hadn't stopped until she'd gone out the front door. She'd cried the entire way, her shoulders twitching and shuddering with hiccuping sobs. When Odette had come home from her shift at the Piggly Wiggly and found out what had happened, she'd slapped Rene across the face.

"*Tu êtes un couillon!*" she'd cried. *You're a fool!* "*Quel est le problème avec tu, laissant cette fille marcher hors d'ici?*" *What's the matter with you, letting that girl walk out of here?* She'd shaken her head, her eyes filled with tears. "You push everyone away—anyone who tries to love you. *Tu êtes un couillon!*"

Odette had never forgiven him for driving Irene

away, not even after Arnaud Morin had shot and killed himself, leaving his fortune to Rene and rescuing them all from a life of abject poverty. She'd been diagnosed with stomach cancer a year after his inheritance, a particularly aggressive and ultimately lethal variety. Even though he'd kept a constant vigil at her bedside and made sure she received the best medical care money could afford, he knew that Odette had still died angry with him, her heart broken because of what he'd done.

There had been something so innocent and vulnerable about Irene; she'd lived a spoiled and sheltered life but hadn't been jaded because of it. Come to think of it, there were a lot of things about Tessa that reminded him of Irene.

Maybe that's why I've been thinking so much about Irene lately, Rene thought, his head resting back against the passenger seat of the Audi, his eyes closed. *And why I've been so hard on Tessa.*

Tessa had surprised him—something few people did anymore, and never women. He'd worried that what had happened at the rest stop would cause her to have some kind of irreparable break down, but it hadn't. Her initial tears had waned, and she'd helped him with a relentless and stony sort of determination as they'd hidden the body together. She'd helped him dress his wounded hand and taken over driving duties without complaint. There was something tough beneath that pretty, pampered exterior, just as there had been in the end with Irene. Rene had to admit that it had shocked the hell out of him and he had to admire Tessa for it.

He opened his eyes and glanced at her. The hot Texas sun streamed through the windshield of the car, spilling directly upon them, and even with the air-conditioning at full blast, beads of perspiration had formed along the contours of her face, dampening her bangs. She'd tucked her hair back behind her ears and sat somewhat scooted forward, her hands draped against the top of the steering wheel as she kept her gaze pinned on the road ahead.

Mon Dieu, *she's beautiful.*

"It wasn't fancy," she said, seemingly out of nowhere, and he jumped, startled.

"What?"

She looked at him briefly. "My wedding. It wasn't fancy." Her gaze returned to the highway. "We don't do anything to celebrate marriage."

She adjusted her grip on the steering wheel, craning her neck slightly from side to side to resettle her spine. "The Elders arrange all of our marriages. They use the Tomes, like the one I found in Louisiana . . ." She pointed over her shoulder, toward the backseat, where the voluminous book had been stowed. ". . . to determine who marries whom. The Tomes keep each clan's records all the way back to the beginning. That way, the bloodlines stay clean and they can make sure there's no inbreeding among the clans."

"The beginning of what?" Rene asked, and she shrugged.

"Everything, I guess. As far as the Brethren are concerned, anyway; back to the thirteen hundreds, I think. Around the Middle Ages."

"Is that what you read in that book?" Rene asked.

Tessa shook her head. "I can't read it. At least not so far. It's written in French, but it's not like any French I recognize—an old dialect, I think, maybe medieval. Maybe you can take a look at it later, see if it makes sense to you."

"Yeah. Because I'm that fucking old," Rene remarked, and immediately felt bad. Here, they had been having the introductory strings of an actual, honest-to-Christ conversation—the first he and Tessa had enjoyed thus far in their travels—and he had to go and blow it with a smart-ass comment.

To his surprise, Tessa laughed. "No, because your French is better than mine," she said, seeming completely unbothered by his remark. "Didn't you tell me you grew up speaking it?"

"My grandmother seldom spoke anything else when she was home," Rene admitted. His mother's side of the family had come from long-standing Acadian lines, and Odette LaCroix had been fiercely proud of this distinctive heritage.

"Anyway, you said something earlier about my fancy wedding, and it wasn't. I was Martin's sixth wife."

"His *sixth* wife?" Rene asked. *Jesus, and I couldn't keep one happy long enough to make a go of things.*

She nodded. "He was older than me. Much older. Brethren men can have multiple wives as long as they've passed their bloodletting and are members in good standing of the Council."

"The Council? You mean the ones who are after you and Brandon?"

Tessa glanced at him and smiled. "No. Those are the Elders. They're different. The Council is made up of all married adult males who have undergone the bloodletting. They propose rules and regulations, vote on things that affect all of the Brethren. The Elders are the head males from each of the clans, the strongest ones, our leaders. Whatever passes at the Council has to be agreed upon by the Elders before it becomes mandate. And my grandfather has final say on everything, because he's in charge over the Elders."

The bloodletting. The Council. The Elders. Clans and mandates. *Jesus Christ, it sounds like they operate their own goddamn third-world country.* "So how did your *grand-père* wind up in charge? Is he the oldest or something?"

Tessa shook her head. "He has the most male heirs. You know, sons and grandsons."

"He with the most *bibettes* wins, no?" Rene remarked, arching his brow, and Tessa laughed.

"I don't know what that means, but I'm pretty sure the answer's yes."

He tried to re-situate himself more comfortably in his seat, and accidentally jostled his hand. To that point, the pain had grown if not tolerable, then at least not overwhelming anymore, but at the movement, fresh pain speared up through his arm and into his chest and he grimaced.

"Are you all right?" Tessa asked, draping her hand against his arm. It was the second such time she'd touched him like that; she'd caressed his face earlier, if only for a moment, and he had to admit, there had been something welcome in the gesture. Now, as before, she let her hand linger against him, and again, as before, he found he didn't mind at all.

"Yeah," he said, managing a smile. "It's feeling much better, in fact."

"Really?"

"Yes, really," he lied, because he didn't want her to worry. "How about you? How's your belly?" When she looked puzzled at this, he said, "You stopped earlier. Said you felt sick."

"Oh," she said. "That. I . . . I'm all right. Much better now."

He had the distinct impression she was lying, though not necessarily about feeling better. Rather, he thought maybe she'd lied to him about stopping in the first place, that something else and not nausea had caused her to pull the car off the road.

What are you hiding, pischouette?

He could open his mind to her and try to find out, but Tessa had telepathic abilities of her own and she could keep him out of her head if she wanted. There would be nothing surreptitious on his part about it, as there would have been had she been human; she'd know what he was trying to do and she'd undoubtedly get pissed.

And he couldn't blame her for not trusting him enough to tell the truth. He hadn't exactly proven himself trustworthy with his behavior. She'd been right earlier when she'd said he treated her like an idiot or a child. *Not the sort of thing that endears you to someone else,* he thought.

"So your husband had six wives, no?" he asked. She had started fidgeting in the seat, alternately relaxing and tightening her grasp on the steering wheel, and he respected her nonverbal cues to change the subject. "He must have kept busy."

"With his work, yes. Martin works in the accounts payable department for the distillery. I didn't see him much." She continued fingering the steering wheel anxiously, keeping her eyes fixed on the road. "He's a very hard worker."

It felt like she was feeding him some sort of rhetoric, something she'd regurgitated so many times, it came out sounding nearly robotic. And like absolute bullshit. *So what's the truth?* Rene wondered, raising his brow. "How long have you been married?"

She slipped her hands from the steering wheel one at a time and swatted them against her pant legs, as if her palms were suddenly clammy. "Four years."

"Oh." Rene nodded. "And here you are, coming along with his *bébé.* I bet he misses you. It must have been a hard choice, leaving him behind to come after Brandon."

"I don't think that's any of your business," she said, the sharp edge to her voice startling him. After a moment of uneasy silence, the tension in her body visibly drained, loosening through her shoulders. "I'm sorry. I shouldn't have said that. I . . ."

"No, you're right," he told her, shaking his head. "It's not my business."

Again, there was silence between them. Clearly he'd touched on a nerve, but wasn't sure what else he could say or do to make amends. He'd just been getting to a point where things seemed cordial and even friendly with her, like they'd been before leaving for New Orleans. *Leave it to me to fuck it all up.*

"Things with me and Martin weren't like you and your wife," Tessa said finally. "The way you were in that picture—happy, in love." She glanced at him. "Marriages among the Brethren don't have anything to do with love. I wouldn't even see Martin most of the time. And when I would, it was because he wanted sex or . . ."

Her voice faded. *Or what?* he wondered, because he could see in her face that it was something that caused her pain and anxiety.

"Never mind." She shook her head and forced a smile. "Choosing between staying in Kentucky with him or leaving to follow Brandon was a no-brainer. Especially now." Her hand draped lightly, briefly against her belly, and her smile softened, growing less strained.

"Speaking of which," he said as they passed a sign for restaurants in an upcoming town called Junction, "you need to eat. There's a pair of twenties tucked up there in the sun visor. Let's swing through a drive-thru off the next exit and grab a couple of burgers."

"Are you sure?" She looked uncertain, and again, he found himself touched by her concern for him.

"Yes, *pischouette.*" His hand was still hurting like all hell, but he did his best to smile and put her at ease. She needed food. The baby needed food. His hand— and the pain pills he'd given Brandon—could wait. "Trust me."

Chapter Eight

Martin used to beat Tessa, but the admittance of this would have been too painful. She'd never told anyone, especially not Brandon. Her twin might have been a gentle soul, but he was also a black belt in aikido. He would have done more than just kick Martin's ass if he'd known. *Brandon would have killed him.*

More than wanting to keep Martin from harm, Tessa didn't mention the abuse because she was ashamed of it, of what her family would think of her. Even now, hundreds of miles away from Martin—free from him at last—she couldn't bear to say the words aloud, because she still felt self-conscious, like Rene would look at her differently, think about her differently if he knew the truth.

It had started almost immediately, within days of her arrival at the Davenant house. Women among the Brethren tended to all of the daily household duties, from cooking to cleaning, childcare to laundry, and everything else in between. At the Nobles' great house, Tessa had helped her mother teaching the elementary-aged children, offering instruction in reading and writing, as well as offering ballet classes. Tessa had received extensive private training for years in classical dance, gifts from both her father and grandmother Eleanor. She'd assumed this experience would be well put to use under the Davenants' roof, but had been surprised and disappointed when Monica had assigned her to work in the laundry instead.

"Working with children is a privilege reserved for older women and established wives," Monica had told her with an air of icy disdain. "Not for lesser wives little more than children themselves."

Tessa had known next to nothing about laundry, though she'd struggled to learn. Two days after becoming Martin's bride, she'd been awoken in the wee hours of the morning by the sharp report of her bedroom door flying open, slamming into the wall. She'd sat up in bed, frightened and bewildered, as had her cousin Alexandra from the adjacent bed. A silhouetted figure had plowed across the room, stomping noisily, and Tessa had a bleary, startled moment to realize it was Martin.

She'd thought at first, and to her dismay, that he'd come to her for sex again. He'd already come once and she'd stayed still as a board beneath him while he'd gone about his business, grunting in her ear and crushing against her. They hadn't exchanged a word, and Martin had come and gone from the room hardly making a sound.

That night, however, his hand had clamped so hard against her arm, seizing her above the crook of her elbow, that his fingers had left bruises. "What is this?" he'd demanded, shoving something in her face. He'd flapped it furiously, a white cotton shirt. "Tell me what this is supposed to be!"

He'd dragged her out of bed and down the corridor, forcing her in staggering tow. Because Martin expected his wives to be ready to accommodate his desires on any given night, none were allowed to sleep in nightgowns. Tessa had been naked, frightened, fighting against tears as Martin had marched her downstairs to the basement laundry room.

Here, he snapped on the lights, and a flood of brilliant, dazzling fluorescents had spilled down against the rows of stark white washing machines and industrial-sized dryers.

"Do you expect me to wear this?" Martin had shouted, again shoving the shirt in her face. "I want starch in my shirts, enough to hold some shape, and creases in the middle of the sleeves, not off to one goddamn side!" He'd struck her, sending her crashing to the floor. Tessa had sprawled against the linoleum tiles and blinked dazedly at the sudden spray of lights dancing in front of her eyes.

Martin had beaten her that night, stripping his belt from the waistband of his slacks and swinging it, driving the strap over and over against her shoulders, buttocks and spine. He'd grabbed her by the hair and hauled her, stumbling and weeping, to her feet. "Wash it," he'd ordered, pushing the shirt into her hands. "Then dry it. Then iron it again. Correctly."

For four years, the abuse she'd suffered at Martin's hands had been routine. At least twice each week, he'd fly into a rage and lay into her. Sometimes he'd settle for simply slapping her with his hand a time or two, but most of the time, he opted to use his belt. And Tessa hadn't been the only recipient; her cousin Alexandra was also beaten, as were all of Martin's wives . . . except for Monica. Martin had never raised his hand to his first bride, which had only made Tessa hate Monica all the more.

I'm sorry I can't tell you the truth, Rene, she thought. Growing up, she'd always been resilient and feisty, the strong one between her and Brandon, who'd been unafraid to stand up to anyone—even the Grandfather— in her brother's defense.

"You remind me so much of myself sometimes, I'd swear I was looking in a mirror," Eleanor used to tell Tessa fondly.

Eleanor would have never allowed anyone to beat her, much less her own husband. And until that first night, when Martin had taken his belt and whipped her, Tessa would have expected nothing less from herself. She'd hoped that incident had been a fluke, something that would never happen again, but it hadn't, and her humiliation and despair had only grown with each new and terrible occasion.

Tessa didn't want Rene to know. Since the incident at the rest stop, that antagonistic tension between them had been gone, and she liked the way things were now, friendly and comfortable. She didn't want to ruin it, the way she knew she would if she said anything. He'd look at her differently, down on her again. *The way Martin used to.*

They arrived in Anthony, New Mexico, shortly after six o'clock that evening, still well ahead of Lina and Brandon. They stopped at a Super 8 Motel so they could get a room in the meantime.

"My wallet's in my back pocket," Rene said, leaning forward in his seat and craning his uninjured arm behind him. "Hang on . . ."

"Do you want me to get it?" she asked, and he raised his brow, smirking wryly.

"You trying to cop a feel of my ass, *pischouette*?"

She laughed as he handed her the wallet. "Don't flatter yourself."

She paid in cash. When the clerk had asked if she wanted a double or king-sized room, she was at a loss. "What's the difference?"

"How many beds do you need?" the clerk replied.

Rene had gotten them a suite the night before, with one bed but a separate living room. "I'm not much on sleeping," he'd told her. "This way, I can stay up and watch TV and you can close the door and get some shut-eye."

So Tessa asked for one bed, and was somewhat dismayed when she unlocked the door to their room and got exactly what she'd requested. And not a single thing more.

Rene, at least, enjoyed a good laugh over it. "*Ça ne fait rien,*" he told her. *Never mind.* "I'll sleep on the recliner, *pischouette.* You take the bed."

She'd protested. After all, he was hurt, and that should have taken precedence over any misguided sense of chivalry he might have been feeling.

"I'll make a deal with you, how about that?" Rene said with a glance at his watch. "We've got at least two hours before Lina and Brandon get here. How about I stretch out on the bed and nap in the meantime?"

She agreed, parking herself in the cornflower blue recliner so that he couldn't renege on his end of the deal. He chuckled but hadn't argued with her, and lay down on the bed while she turned on the TV.

She channel-surfed for a while, thumbing through a seemingly endless array of infomercials, evening news broadcasts, televised court shows and cartoons before turning off the television in bored exasperation. Rene had fallen asleep, but it didn't seem to be restful, she realized. He moaned quietly, squirming slightly atop the comforter, and Tessa stood to check on him.

"Rene?" she asked softly. Clearly he was still in pain, despite his reassurances to the contrary and his attempts to act like everything was fine. His face was slightly flushed, peppered lightly with perspiration, his brows lifted slightly, his expression twisted with distress. He murmured something breathlessly but she couldn't make out the words.

"It's all right," Tessa said, brushing his hair back from his face. She lay down facing him, curled up on the mattress. It was something she and Brandon used to do as children. She'd been afraid of the dark and would steal into his bedroom at night, crawling into bed with him. They'd lie facing each other, and she'd fall asleep, safe in her twin's company, comforted by his presence.

She felt somewhat foolish but didn't know what else to do for Rene; he was in pain, and there was nothing she could offer besides comfort that would take that away from him. He was hurting, and it was all her fault; he'd been shot because he'd tried to protect her.

"It's all right," she said again, whispering as she reached between them, finding his uninjured hand. She let her fingers slide between his, and his restless murmuring quieted as he fell still, relaxing.

It was nice, being close to him—more than she would have expected. *I could get used to this,* she thought. The warmth of his body seeped through his clothes, enveloping her and she closed her eyes as it lulled her to sleep.

Chapter Nine

Rene felt his cell phone ring, thrumming from inside his hip pocket, rousing him begrudgingly from sleep. He tried to ignore it, but the vibrations continued, pulsating against his groin, aggravating him.

"Goddamn it," he muttered, opening his eyes blearily. He blinked in puzzled surprise, the cell phone forgotten, as he found himself lying face-to-face with Tessa in bed.

What the hell . . . ?

For a moment, his sleep-addled mind couldn't quite process what he was seeing. It took him a moment to realize where he was, and it wasn't until he tried to move his left hand—sending immediate, sharp pain shooting up his arm—that he remembered everything that had happened in the last twelve hours.

Well, almost everything, he thought, momentarily paralyzed by his proximity to Tessa. She rested on her side, her face close enough to feel the soft press of her breath against his face with each exhalation. Her eyes were closed, her dark lashes curled against the high arches of her cheeks. Her hand was draped against his uninjured one, her fingers between his. He could feel the warmth of her body filling the narrow margin of space between them; he could smell her, a light, floral fragrance, the hint of her perfume.

He hadn't slept with a woman since Irene. He'd taken plenty of lovers, of course, more than he could count or keep track of, but he'd either left after fucking them, or, in the case of the prostitutes he used for feeding, they would leave him. He hadn't shared his bed for anything but sex with anyone in almost forty years.

I'd forgotten this, he thought, gazing with fascination at Tessa's hand, their intertwined fingers and running the pad of his thumb lightly against her knuckles. *How good it feels.*

He drew his hand slowly away, watching a slight crease form between her brows. She murmured in her sleep, something incoherent, and then her expression softened, relaxing once more.

She was a beautiful woman. He'd thought that all along, from the first moment he'd laid eyes on her. Although she'd originally struck him as being stubborn as a mule, he was beginning to realize that this was just a front she presented, some kind of emotional shield. Judging by everything he'd learned about the Brethren, both from her and her brother Brandon, Rene didn't blame her for putting defenses like that in place.

They sound like a bunch of sadistic control freaks, no better than a pack of dogs, he thought. *Was your husband like that, too,* pischouette?

Things with me and Martin weren't like you and your wife, she'd told him. *The way you were in that picture—happy, in love . . . I wouldn't even see Martin most of the time. And when I would, it was because he wanted sex or . . .*

Or what? he wondered again, and he drew his hand up between them, brushing the back of his fingers lightly against her cheek. *What did he do to you,* pischouette?

At his touch, Tessa woke with a start, her large, dark

eyes flying open wide, her breath cutting short in a gasp. "Oh!"

"*Il est bien,*" he said quietly, with a smile. *It's all right.* "Good morning, sunshine."

She blinked at him in groggy bewilderment, then sat up, tucking her hair behind her ears. "What . . . what time is it?"

He glanced at his watch. "Almost eight thirty." He rolled slightly, fishing his cell phone from his pocket to glance at his caller ID "Looks like Lina and your *frère* just arrived in town."

"Oh." Tessa nodded, scooting quickly toward the edge of the bed and standing. She seemed visibly uncomfortable at having been caught lying so near to him, and drew her arms about herself. "That's good."

"You're almost rid of me, then," he said, and she looked at him, puzzled. "You want to hitch a ride with them the rest of the way to Tahoe, no?"

"Oh." Her eyes swept the room. "I . . . I don't think that's such a good idea right now." She glanced at him. "Do you? I mean, with your hand the way it is. You can't drive."

"*C'est vrai,*" he said as he sat up. *That's true.* He'd fed well enough that day between the young waitress in Boerne and the kid at the rest stop that his accelerated healing ability had kicked into overdrive. The heavy nap he'd just taken had helped, too. The wound to his hand still hurt like all hell, but he could sense an improvement. He moved his fingers experimentally; earlier, such effort would not only have left him breathless with pain, but would have been difficult if not impossible, given the damage to bones, muscles and tendons.

"I guess you're right," he said, adding with a wry hook of his brow. "You sure that's the only reason you've changed your mind, *pischouette*?"

She blinked. "What?"

It had been nice, waking up next to her; the sort of tender moment his life had been decidedly lacking, and he had been missing. He reached out and hooked his fingertips against hers, giving a playful tug. "You sure you just don't want to stick close to me?"

She smiled, her mouth unfurling hesitantly at first, then widening as she relaxed, her posture softening, her cheeks blooming with shy, sudden color.

Mon Dieu, you are beautiful, Tessa, he thought.

"Admit it, *pischouette.* I'm growing on you, no?"

"Oh, yeah. Just like a fungus." She laughed out loud, making no effort whatsoever to pull away from his grasp.

A half hour later, Rene and Tessa's twin brother, Brandon, stood together on the landing outside of the motel room, gazing out at lights from the nearby interstate. Brandon and Lina had checked into a room on the first floor, and brought pizza to share for supper. The two men rested their elbows against the wrought iron railing and nursed a bottle of Coke apiece while Tessa and Lina stayed in the room, chatting together.

"Pizza just isn't the same without beer," Rene remarked, making Brandon laugh. He tipped the bottle back and swallowed a mouthful of soda. "Or at least a shot of whiskey to give this shit some flavor."

Good old Lina. She was constantly riding his ass about how much he drank or how many pain pills he'd been popping. Never mind that after the miserable hangover he'd endured earlier that day, he didn't plan on touching as much as a drop of liquor any time soon. He had asked Brandon for his Percodan back, but hadn't taken any of the pills—and didn't plan to, either. Not because he wasn't in any pain, but because he'd decided he was sick of it—drinking or drugging himself to oblivion.

Weird shit happens when I do, he thought, remembering the press of the pistol against his temple, the sound of Irene's voice, sleepy from the other end of the phone line, and the silken smoothness of Tessa's thigh against his hand as he'd reached up beneath her gown. *Too much weird shit.*

So what really happened to your hand? Brandon asked in Rene's mind.

Although Rene didn't understand American Sign Language, Brandon had originally communicated with him either through the psi-speech he was using at the moment or handwritten notes. His broken hands prohibited this, however, and Rene reluctantly left his mind pretty much wide open to the younger man so they could converse, even though doing so made him uneasy. Not because he disliked Brandon, but because Brandon was an extremely powerful telepath, the likes of which Rene had never seen. He suspected Brandon was the likes of which none of the Brethren had ever seen before, either, and that was part of the reason they were so determined to hunt him down.

Rene thought maybe some among the Brethren, like Brandon's grandfather or the Elders, might have been blocking Brandon's powers in Kentucky. Now that the kid was away from them, free of their influence, his abilities seemed to be growing on a daily basis. Upon their initial introduction, Brandon had damn near rattled Rene's skull, plowing past any mental defenses he might have had to keep his thoughts guarded. It wasn't something the younger man had done on purpose, but Rene wasn't keen on the idea of tempting fate—or Brandon's fledgling ability to control himself.

I told you, petit, Rene thought in reply. *We had a flat tire earlier today. I cut myself on the jack trying to change it.*

Brandon looked at him, his brow cocked at a dubious angle as Rene regurgitated this paper-thin line of bullshit. He hadn't told Brandon or Lina the truth because he hadn't seen the point. There was nothing that could be done about it now, and both of them had enough weighing on their minds without adding to it. Rene had sworn Tessa to secrecy, too, and had considered it somewhat of a testimony to the tentative and affable peace that had been forged between them that she'd agreed to it, albeit reluctantly.

"I don't like keeping secrets from Brandon," she'd said, but there'd been a look in her eyes, a slight edge to her voice that had clearly imparted that she had before, and would this time, too.

So what else haven't you told your brother? Rene had wondered. *What other little secrets are you keeping, Tessa?*

Brandon knew Rene was lying, and Rene knew that he did. They both also knew that if Brandon had felt so inclined, he could have just skimmed the contents of Rene's brain and learned the truth for himself.

And there wouldn't be a damn thing I could do to stop him.

"I'm all right, *petit,*" he told Brandon, holding up his bandaged hand and wiggling his fingers—an act that was growing more easy and less painful by the hour. "Really. How about you?"

Brandon glanced at his own hands. *It's amazing,* he said. This was the first day he'd apparently foregone swaddling them in bandages. It had been almost two weeks since he'd broken his hands, but already the bones had knitted back together, however fragilely.

It took months for my hands to heal in Kentucky, but they're almost as good as new now. They still ache sometimes, and I can't grip things very tightly . . . He mimed pinching his fingers together but stopped just shy of the tips fully touching. *I can't hold a pencil yet, but it's getting close.* He glanced up at Rene. *Amazing.*

"That's what happens when you feed, *petit*," Rene told him with a wink. Even though he could witness such seemingly miraculous healing in his own body, it still amazed him, too. "It accelerates everything—your metabolism, healing, all of that."

Like Rene, Brandon was enjoying the effects of having fed twice in rapid succession. That kind of gluttony had heightened his healing ability just as it had Rene's. Brandon had fed for the first time in his life from Lina. The second time, after he'd shattered his hands, he'd fed from Rene. It had been a desperate gamble to help him, one that had paid off; with only his father being Brethren, Rene had hoped there was enough human in his blood to benefit Brandon.

Rene took another swig of Coke. *So tell me about this book your sister found,* he said. *This Tome thing of hers. What's so special about it, anyway? She said you use it to play matchmaker, set up marriages and whatnot?*

Not me. Brandon shook his head. *The Elders. No one else is supposed to see the Tomes. They keep them under lock and key at all times. Each clan has its own. As for what's in them, I don't really know. I only got a quick look at the one Tessa found. She said you were going to help her translate it?*

Yeah. Rene nodded. *Or try to anyway. It's written in French, at least parts of it. Some of it's really old. Who knows what the hell language it is.*

What I saw looked like your family tree, Brandon said. *Which makes sense. That's what the Elders use to arrange marriages.*

"My family," Rene murmured, then he turned so Brandon could read his lips. "So this makes it official, then? My family has one of these Tomes, so they must have been part of the Brethren at some point."

Sure looks that way, Brandon said. *What I'm wondering is if they were, how did they get the Tome out of Kentucky?*

The books are kept at the dominant clan's house. Each family doesn't keep their own. Like right now, all of the Tomes are locked in my grandfather's library.

Rene arched a curious brow. "You think my clan must have been dominant at some point, *petit*? That's how they had access to the book?"

I don't know, Brandon replied.

And if that's true, then what happened? Rene wondered, closing his mind momentarily, his brows furrowed thoughtfully. This was a point that had been niggling at him, the way a mosquito bite will itch—just barely at first, enough so that you'll reach for it to scratch, and from there, inexorably worsening until it's absolutely maddening and you'll claw your flesh open and raw. *What happened to my family? Did they leave the Brethren willingly? Were they kicked out somehow? Either way—why?*

Whatever the circumstances, obviously the Brethren had gone to some effort to make sure the Morins were forgotten. But when and why this had happened remained a mystery. Rene's father, Arnaud, hadn't offered him any clues. In fact, he had led Rene to believe they were the last of their kind anywhere in the world.

Did he not realize then? Did he not know? Whatever happened, was it before my father's lifetime? Or did he know, and just lied to me about it?

As if he'd been reading Rene's mind—despite the fact Rene had deliberately closed it—Brandon said, *Makes you wonder how your human grandmother wound up with it, huh?*

"My father must have given it to her years ago," Rene replied. "When he came to find me. That was . . . 1971, I think."

The year after Irene left me.

"He came to our home in Bayou Lafourche," he said to Brandon. "Maybe he knew I was there all along, maybe it took him that long to find me. I don't know. Either way, I came home from this factory job I'd taken down in Houma, and there was this fancy car I'd never seen before parked in front of the house. I walked inside to find my *mamère* sitting in the living room, serving tea and store-bought gingersnap cookies on her best set of bone china to some slick-dressed *salaud* I'd never seen before, either. She introduces him as Arnaud Morin. 'This here is your *papa*,' she says to me, even though the guy on the couch doesn't look much older than I did at the time."

Rene took another long swallow of Coke, emptying the bottle, and wished his head didn't ache at even the idea of adding a dollop of Bloodhorse Reserve. *Could probably use at least two-fingers' worth right about now.*

"In retrospect, I think he must have done something to her mind, the way I do now when I go to feed," he said, and he flapped his bandaged hand at his temple. "I sort of turn them off in a way. Make them do what I want, so they don't make a fuss."

Brandon nodded. *The Brethren do that, too, except during bloodletting ceremonies. The rest of the time, it's really low-key. They keep the humans subdued with their minds.*

"I don't know if he gave the book to her to hide, then made her forget about it somehow, but she never told me about it at any rate." He glanced at Brandon. "When I read about him blowing his brains out two days later, I showed the newspaper to *Mamère* and she didn't even bat an eye. It was like she didn't even know who he was, like he hadn't just spent half a goddamn day parked on her sofa not forty-eight hours earlier."

Strangely, though, his grandmother at some point had written out a family tree of her own, one that had traced Arnaud's side as well as her own, at least back to Rene's great-grandfather. The dates had all been recorded correctly, which seemed to suggest that Odette had known about Arnaud's heritage, what he

was—and what Rene was. At least at some point, she
had. Whether or not Arnaud Morin had walked out
of the house that sunny afternoon outside of Thibodaux, Louisiana, and left those memories intact, Rene
would never know.

"Maybe he never meant for me to find that Tome,"
he said. "Who the hell knows. Either way, he didn't do
me any favors. All of my goddamn life to that point,
I'd felt like I was different than everybody else . . . not
quite in step with the rest of the world. Finding out
the truth from him didn't make much of a difference." He glanced at Brandon. "I guess you know how
that goes, no, *petit*?"

I used to, Brandon said. *But I don't anymore. Not since
finding you and Lina.*

Rene smiled, thinking of how good it had felt to
wake up in bed with Tessa curled up beside him; right
somehow. He had Brandon to thank for that, for the
day only weeks earlier in which Rene had sensed the
younger man outside of the dilapidated high-rise he
called home. It had been the first time since Arnaud
that Rene had experienced the peculiar, tickling sensation inside his mind that had alerted him to the
presence of another just like him. Rene could still call
the birds, just as he had when he'd been young, and
he'd summoned them to him, sending them in sweeping paths around the building, seeing through their
eyes as Brandon had walked away from the front entrance, his shoulders hunched against a steady rain.
Brandon had been robbed and shot in a nearby alley,
and would have been murdered if Rene hadn't witnessed the crime in time to save him; if he hadn't sent
the birds swooping down at the gunmen, attacking
them, driving them away. He'd brought Brandon
inside and tried to nurse him back to health, a part of
him so elated, he could hardly breathe. *Like me*, he'd

thought, in dumbstruck wonder. *Like me.* Saint merde, *this boy is just like me.*

He could have been Rene's brother, for all he'd known; a cousin or nephew, anything. It hadn't mattered. He was like Rene and that was all that had counted. *I'm not the only one after all.*

Rene reached out and tousled Brandon's hair with a fond smile. "You know what, *petit?*" he asked. "I don't feel so alone anymore, either."

Chapter Ten

Tessa stifled a yawn against the back of her hand as she sat cross-legged on the king-sized bed. Rene glanced at her, sitting next to her, his legs dangling over the side of the mattress. "Past your bedtime, *pischouette*?" he asked with a wry smirk.

"I'm fine," she said, and to prove it, she settled herself more comfortably, tucking her hair behind her ears and leaning forward to peer down at the opened Tome before them.

"Well, it's past mine, then, how about that?" he said with a laugh, grimacing as he stood, unfurling his legs slowly and stretching his back. *"Mon Dieu,* I think my ass has gone numb."

Lina and Brandon had left several hours earlier and they'd been awake ever since, poring through the voluminous old book page by brittle, yellowed page. Rene had hauled in a notebook computer with wireless Internet capability from the car, and between the two of them, they'd been able to tentatively identify the dialect in which portions of the book were written. Unfortunately, neither had been able to translate it.

Langues d'oïl, Rene had called it. "Old French, influenced by Latin and some Celtic way of speaking called

Gaulish." He'd glanced up from the laptop. "Wikipedia says it was spoken from around one thousand to thirteen hundred. Also says there was no one specific language, that it varied from region to region."

In addition to being an archaic dialect, the transcriptions were also written in a tiny script, old ink set to brittle parchment, and nearly illegible. He'd been able to read some of the words, but not enough to make much sense of the entire text. Together, they'd settled for trying to make sense of the pictures, the wealth of ornate but enigmatic illustrations adorning the pages.

"Abominacion," Rene read, his voice low and thoughtful as he stared down at the peculiar painting of the armored knight and the bald, snaggle-toothed creature. *"Abomination.* What the hell do you suppose this is?" He glanced at her and arched his brow wryly. "Distant relation, perhaps? A mother-in-law no one much cared for?"

"Ha, ha." Tessa slapped his shoulder. "Must be a relative of yours."

"Oh, come on, *pischouette.* She's not so bad. Sure, someone's whacked her a time or two with the ugly stick, but maybe she has a sparkling personality, no?"

Tessa hit him again, laughing. "Why do you think it's a *she* anyway?"

He tapped his fingertip against the page, pointing out something she'd failed to notice before. "Because *she* has tits, *pischouette.* Saggy, *oui,* and nothing I'd find appealing, but still . . . either a *femme* or a really, really, really old man."

Tessa laughed again, giving him a playful shove. "You're terrible."

She told him about her brother Caine, the stories he fed them as children about the Abomination.

"Lovely," Rene murmured. "After everything you and Brandon have told me about your *frère,* why am I not surprised Caine would try to scare the *merde* out of you with tales of some creature in your basement?"

"Not the basement. The Beneath. It's supposedly this network of tunnels that run all beneath the Brethren farms, under the houses and fields, everywhere."

"The Beneath," he repeated and she nodded. "And the Abomination lives down there, just waiting to eat you if you fuck up." She laughed, but nodded again. "You got a weird goddamn family, *pischouette*."

Further into the book, they found old photographs and yellowing daguerreotypes tucked or pasted among the pages—one of a woman, her dark hair caught back in a bun, her clothing antiquated and modest. Another was of two children, a boy and a girl posed together, stern-faced and stoic. In another, a handsome but solemn young man gazed at the camera, while in another, this same man stood outside of an old brick house, eerily reminiscent in design and façade to the old great house in which Tessa's grandfather had once been photographed. *Michel Morin* had been written on the back, underscored with *July 12, 1815*.

"That's your grandfather, Rene," Tessa said softly. Rene didn't say anything; he gazed down at the photograph for a long time, wordless, his expression unreadable.

"We had a picture like this in the study at home," she said. "That's one of the original great houses. They tore them all down in the late eighteen hundreds and built the ones we live in now."

"You think this was my family's great house?" Rene asked.

"I don't know," Tessa said. "That's sure what it looks like to me."

They flipped ahead to the pages that traced the Morin family tree. Though interesting, what they'd perused thus far hadn't offered them any clues as to what might have happened to the Morin clan, or why they were no longer part of the Brethren.

"I have an attorney by that name—Gregory Lambert," Rene had remarked, pointing out the notations that had so intrigued her: *Lambert, Durand, Ellinger, Averay.* When she'd looked momentarily excited, he'd shaken his head and laughed. "Trust me, *pischouette.* He's a lawyer not a bloodsucker . . . although the two are often mistaken."

After studying the names again, he'd frowned. "Some of these others look sort of familiar, too, now that I think about it."

He hadn't been able to place any of them as easily as he had Lambert, however, and Tessa had been moderately disappointed. She'd been fascinated by the prospect of so many other potential Brethren families out there in the world. Because if Rene's family had survived, even if only to him, then surely if there had been others, they could have, as well.

"It's probably nothing," he'd said. "I would have known if I'd ever run across another Brethren. I would have sensed that, no? I mean, like I did Brandon that first time in the city."

The only notation they'd found of even moderate interest had been scrawled in the margin on the last page of the extensive family tree. *October 12, 1815,* followed by *le feu* in French, words scrawled so heavily against the paper, the quill point had nearly torn through the page.

"Fire," Rene had said, although Tessa hadn't needed translation. She spoke enough French to understand it on her own. "You know of any fires on that date?"

She shook her head again. "No, but that's my birthday, mine and Brandon's. October twelfth." She felt a peculiar little shiver go through her. "That's a weird coincidence."

Was it a barn fire? she wondered. It wouldn't have

been unheard of. The Brethren had been involved with horses since colonial times. From the little bit she'd learned of the Brethren's origins, she knew they'd originally left France to live in Virginia just prior to the French revolution. Here, they had been forced to live among humans, at least for a time—a fate Tessa imagined they would have found detestable.

They'd been acquainted with a man named William Whitley who had gone on to explore and establish a settlement in Kentucky. The area had been unpopulated at the time, still very much considered the frontier. It had been Whitley who had inspired the Brethren to move west into what would one day become the bluegrass state. The promise of wilderness solitude, a place where they could build their own isolated developments and live free from the prying eyes of humans—much as they must have in France for centuries—had been too appealing to resist.

William Whitley had also had a penchant for horse breeding and racing, something else the Brethren had been introduced to through him. Whitley had instituted counterclockwise horse racing in America, in fact; a deliberate opposite of the British way of doing things. Among the Brethren, it was said that Andrew Giscard, Elder of the clan, had proposed the idea to Whitley over drinks one night while still in Virginia. Giscard had once built a turf racetrack on the Brethren lands in Kentucky, much as Whitley had on his own. So the Brethren would have owned valuable horses, even in 1815. A barn fire, which could have theoretically killed the animals inside, would have been a catastrophic enough event to note in the Tome.

Rene's grandfather, Michel Morin, was the last name noted in the book, born in 1707. Before that was the listing for his great-grandfather, Remy, and his marriage to Marguerite Davenant that Tessa had seen before in the family tree Rene's human grandmother had made.

"Why isn't my father included?" Rene asked. "He's here." He pointed to his grandmother's tree, which Tessa unfolded and spread out beside the Tome on the bedspread. "See? Arnaud Morin, born July 12, 1818."

She didn't know the answer to that, and the book didn't provide any other clues.

"I say we hit the hay," Rene told her. "It's after two in the morning already, and we've got a long drive ahead of us today. Hopefully one that's less eventful than yesterday's."

He said this last with a little wink that made her smile. Things had changed between them since the attack at the rest stop, a subtle but distinctive shift in the dynamic of their relationship. There was a sweetness about Rene that had caught her by surprise. She'd expected him to make some wisecrack about finding her beside him when he'd woken up earlier, but he hadn't. Instead, it hadn't seemed to bother him at all.

"So you want to call it, heads or tails, to see who gets the bed tonight?" he asked, making a show of reaching into his pocket and digging for a coin.

She laughed, hefting one heavy half of the Tome and plopping it closed. "That's okay. You take it. You're the one with the bullet hole in him."

"That?" He laughed, glancing at his hand almost dismissively. "That's nothing, *pischouette*. I've had worse bug bites."

He definitely seemed to be feeling better. Tessa wondered if it was because he'd taken any of the Percodans he'd given to Brandon. Even though they hadn't told Lina and Brandon the truth about what had happened to Rene's hand, when she'd been alone with Tessa, Lina had still expressed concern.

"He wasn't drinking when it happened, was he?" she'd asked, because they'd said that Rene had hurt himself changing a flat tire. "Sometimes he has a problem with that . . . and his pills, too. Ever since his leg. He's not drinking while you guys are out on the road, is he?"

"No," Tessa had replied, shaking her head and managing a laugh. "No, of course not, Lina. I . . . why, I haven't seen him touch a drop since we left for New Orleans."

She still wasn't quite sure why she'd lied, why she hadn't told Lina about the night before, when Rene had gotten drunk and tried to shoot himself, except she'd felt some sudden and fierce need to protect him, even if only from Lina's disapproval. *Because he protected me,* she thought. *Everything is different now. That guy with the gun changed everything.*

"I'm perfectly fine to sleep on the recliner," she told Rene as she grunted, hoisting the Tome. "You just—"

"You take the bed," Rene said, reaching out and drawing the cumbersome book out of her arms. "I'll take the book. I need to sit up tonight anyway, so don't worry about it."

"What do you mean?" she asked as he carried the Tome to the bedside desk. He'd said something the night before about being an insomniac. "You can sit up in the bed and watch TV. It's not going to—"

"It's all right." He shook his head, then cut his eyes toward the bathroom, looking suddenly uncomfortable. "I just . . . there are some things I need to do with my hand . . . and my leg and all . . ." His voice faltered clumsily and he cleared his throat. "Anyway, it's easier if I just do them sitting up."

"Oh." She glanced at his right leg. He hadn't said anything about the prosthetic during their travels together, and she'd never seen him do a lot with it, much less remove it. *Is he embarrassed?* she wondered.

Why? I know he has it. He and Brandon both told me. "I can help you."

"That's all right . . ." he began.

"With your hand, at least," she insisted, crossing the room to his bag. She poked through it until she found the first-aid kit they'd tucked inside, and a brown paper bag full of medicinal supplies they'd grabbed from a convenience store near the motel. He was already trying to sputter out some kind of protest, but she shook her head. "I can help you," she said again. "Go stand over there by the sink. We'll change your bandages."

He sighed, his shoulders hunching in resignation, but stood still and unflinching as she slowly unrolled the white gauze bandage from around his palm. Although he'd regained a small amount of mobility in the maimed appendage, any healing was from the inside out. Underneath the stark glare of the vanity's overhead fluorescent lights, the wounds looked as gruesome as ever.

The edges of torn flesh were jagged and ashen, the exposed meat bright red and spongy. It looked painful as hell, and as she dabbed at his palm gently with cotton balls soaked in hydrogen peroxide, she glanced into his eyes. "I'm sorry."

"It doesn't sting," he said. "It's just cold."

Earlier in the day, there had been enough damage from the bullet that Tessa had been able to see clear through Rene's hand at a point in the center. That part of the wound, at least, had closed, for which she was grateful, because that had been disturbing. Rene, in fact, had held his hand up to his face, pretending to peek through the hole in a morbid attempt to amuse her.

He'd been doing that all day, as if her concern for him bothered him more than his hand. *Which is kind of sweet,* she thought, glancing up at him again.

"You know, you surprise me, *pischouette*," he said.

"How's that?"

"This," he said with a nod at his hand. "Everything that happened today. I really thought you'd fall apart on me. But you did real good."

She laughed, pressing squares of gauze against either side of his wound. "Thank you, I think."

He helped her hold the pads in place as she wound a fresh ribbon of bandage around them. "Come on, *pischouette*. You know what I mean. Your clothes . . . your makeup . . . it takes you three goddamn hours in the bathroom every morning."

Only earlier that day, this might have pissed her off, but now, Tessa just laughed along with Rene.

"You aren't exactly what I'd call 'low maintenance,' *chère*," he told her.

Her smile faltered as she reached for a roll of white first-aid tape. "My grandmother taught me to appreciate nice things," she said, peeling back a strip. "She was very beautiful and very elegant, and I always wanted to be like her."

She pressed the tape in place against his hand, then tore off another. "She was the only woman in the Brethren who ever got to leave the compound. My Grandfather would take her with him whenever he'd travel. She visited all over the world. He loved her very much." She looked up at Rene as she finished bandaging his hand. "I know you probably think the Grandfather is a monster, and he is in a lot of ways. But he wasn't always like that."

It had always occurred to her that one of the reasons the Grandfather had always been so hard on Brandon, and yet at the same time had allowed her brother to enjoy a private tutor and to forgo his bloodletting for as long as he had—luxuries other Brethren never would have been allowed—was because of Eleanor's intercession.

"I think after my grandmother died, Brandon reminded him too much of her in too many ways," she said, her mind turning back to the afternoon in which she'd confronted Augustus about breaking Brandon's hands. That had been the last straw for the Grandfather, she suspected; Brandon's determination not only to escape the Brethren, but to go to college, as well. It would have been something that Eleanor might have tried; a moment of Eleanor in Brandon's otherwise ordinarily quiet and reserved nature that must have just seemed too reminiscent in the Grandfather's eyes.

"I think a part of him died along with her," she said softly, her eyes distant, her voice nearly a whisper. She cradled Rene's swaddled hand gently between hers and felt dim tears well in her eyes. She blinked against them, snapping out of the reverie of her distant, melancholy thoughts, and managed a small laugh. "Anyway, that's where I get it—all of that with my hair, makeup, clothes and whatnot. My grandmother taught me."

And for four years, I couldn't have any of it.

Martin had stripped her of all the fine clothes Eleanor had bought for her. In the Davenant house, Tessa had worn plain clothes, often hand-me-downs from other women in the clan. She hadn't been allowed to put on makeup. On the occasions she was allowed to leave and visit her family, she remembered pinching her cheeks like Scarlett O'Hara in *Gone With the Wind* just to lend them some semblance of healthy color.

When she'd left Kentucky, she'd taken several thousand dollars with her, money that Martin kept tucked inside a large manila envelope. He stowed the envelope away with a leather-bound ledger in a hollowed-out book in the library and over the years, Tessa had seen him put cash in and take it out of this secret cache, even though he'd been unaware of her.

She'd taken both the money and the ledger and gone to a department store in Lexington. Here, she'd bought a pair of suitcases and filled them to overflowing capacity with all of the designer clothes and shoes she could afford.

My way of saying a great big fuck you to Martin, she thought.

At that moment, she sensed the warm, fluttering presence of the baby in her mind as it stirred within her womb and pressed her hand to her belly reflexively.

"Êtes-tu bien?" Rene asked, his brows raised in concern. *Are you all right?*

"Yes." She smiled. "It's just the baby. It moves sometimes. I can sense it. Do you want to feel?"

He blinked, taking a small, hedging step back, as if surprised, and Tessa laughed. "Come on. You grabbed hold of the barrel of a loaded gun today. I think touching my stomach will be a piece of cake."

She caught him by his uninjured hand and pulled her shirt up, exposing the slightly rounded swell of her belly. "Here." She pressed his hand against her and was immediately, acutely aware of the warmth of his palm against her skin. In that moment, her mind snapped back to the night before, when he'd pressed her down against the couch, laying atop her, and his hand had slid with electrifying friction along the length of her thigh, caressing the outermost curve of her buttock.

Tessa blinked up at Rene and found him looking back at her, directly in the eyes. He didn't say anything, but she could feel the hesitation and tension in his arm.

"Is it kicking?" he asked after a moment, giving his head a small shake and averting his gaze to his hand.

"No." Tessa giggled quietly. "It's too little to feel anything like that yet. You have to open your mind."

His brow arched slightly. "Oh. *Je suis désolé.*" *Sorry.*

She watched his expression change as for the first time he allowed himself to be aware of the tiny, delicate life growing inside of her. Any hint of uncertainty drained from his face as his eyes widened, his brows lifting with wonder. He stared at his hand, at her belly beneath, the corners of his mouth unfolding in a soft, marveling smile.

"*Saint merde,*" he said. *Holy shit.*

"Do you feel it?" she asked, even though she could see the answer plainly in his face.

His smile widened as he nodded. "That's amazing, *pischouette,*" he said, his voice small and quiet. "That . . . that's damn likely the most amazing thing I've ever felt in my life."

"I can't sense it all of the time," Tessa said. "Not yet anyway. It's still too early. But sometimes I do, like right now. It doesn't have thoughts yet, not like you or I do. There's just that—all warm inside, light somehow."

"Like sunshine," he said, and when she nodded, he glanced at her, raising his brow. "So if all we can do is sense it in our minds, why are you holding my hand against your belly?"

She could have told him that it was because the baby must have been able to feel it whenever someone pressed against her stomach, that this awareness was enough to stimulate the little growing bundle of neurons that served as its primitive brain stem. She could have told him that this was what they were sensing together, the baby's reaction to his touch, the pressure of his hand against the shelter of her womb. She could have told him this, but instead, she said something else, something equally as true. "Maybe I like it there."

She'd never met a man like Rene before, someone who could make her laugh out loud or want to wring his neck all in the course of one conversation; one who could charm her, move her, infuriate, amuse, challenge and fascinate her. All that afternoon, she'd been reminded of how her grandmother Eleanor had been with the Grandfather, how they had behaved together, interacted with each other, how much emotion they had been able to convey without saying a single word. She'd been reminded because she'd seen it happening with her and Rene, and she'd come to realize that it had been growing between them all along.

Grandmother Eleanor would have loved Rene, she thought. *And oh, dear God, I think I do, too.*

His brow arched a bit more and he stepped toward her, collapsing the space between them to no more than mere inches. He moved his hand from her stomach, trailing the cuff of his knuckles up between her breasts, caressing the side of her neck, making her shiver. "Is that so?" he murmured, his fingers uncurling against her face, his palm cradling her cheek.

He leaned toward her, and Tessa felt her heart— which had started pounding beneath her sternum in a frantic, fluttering rhythm—quicken all the more. Her breath hitched once, twice, then fell still, caught in the back of her throat. The pad of his thumb brushed lightly against her lips, making her hiccup softly, a shudder going through her entire body. He smiled and cocked his head, leaning closer, until the front of his shirt touched her breasts.

His lips lightly brushed hers as he used his hand to guide her face, tilting her chin up. Then his mouth settled against her, a gentle, lingering kiss that made her heart hammer, and sent chills trembling all the way through her. The tip of his tongue slipped between her lips, dancing against her own, and he uttered a low, hungry sound, like a cross between a growl and a groan as he pulled her near, kissing her deeply. He pressed her so tightly against him, she could feel the heat from his chest through the fabric of his shirt, and the hardening strain of his growing arousal against her through his jeans.

When he pulled back, just enough to draw his lips away from hers, leaving their foreheads nearly touching, the tips of their noses together, Tessa gasped quietly, trembling.

"Merde," Rene breathed with a quiet, shaky laugh. *Shit.* After a moment, he stepped back, leaving an abrupt chill in the air and against her body. "I . . . I shouldn't have done that. I'm sorry, Tessa. I don't . . . I don't know what got into my head."

"It's all right," Tessa whispered. She didn't seem to be able to summon any more voice than this.

He shook his head. "No, it's not." He forked his fingers through his hair and turned, walking away. "You're married, *pischouette.* I mean, your husband may have had six wives, but I'm sure he still cares about you and wouldn't—"

"He doesn't care," Tessa said. "Trust me."

"Sure, he does," Rene replied. "He must. You're carrying his baby, for Christ's sake. He's probably—"

"He used to hit me," Tessa said, and Rene's voice cut off in mid-sentence. He turned, visibly startled, and she looked down at the blue carpet beneath her feet. She wanted to clap her hands over her mouth and take it back somehow. Worse, now that she'd admitted it, she found herself saying even more, the words spilling out of her mouth in a rapid-fire tumble. "Martin was a horrible man. He hated my grandfather and punished me because of it. He'd punch me, slap me, knock me to the ground. He'd take off his belt and whip me with it, leave me black and blue . . . sometimes so much I couldn't even walk."

She glanced up at him, her eyes clouded with tears. "I hate him," she whispered, her voice tremulous. "I never told anyone about it, not the Grandfather, not my father . . . not even Brandon . . . especially not Brandon . . . because I . . . I just couldn't . . ."

The words faded and her tears spilled. She pressed her hand against her mouth and turned toward the wall. Rene didn't say anything at first. He simply went to her, draping his hand against her shoulder and turned her around.

"Come here," he said, drawing her into an embrace.

"He doesn't even care that I'm gone," Tessa wept, huddled against his chest. "That bastard, he . . . all he wants is the baby. He wants the baby back . . . he wants to take my baby!"

"No one is going to take your baby." Rene tucked his fingertips under her chin, making her look up at him. "Listen to me. I won't let anyone hurt you or that baby. Not now. Not ever. I swear to you, *pischouette*."

He leaned forward, his lips pressing against hers again, first in promise and then with growing passion. He pushed her back against the nearest wall and pinned her there, holding her face with his uninjured hand, kissing her the entire time.

"Tu es sûr avec moi," he told her. *You are safe with me.* He let his lips trail lightly across her cheek, tracing the contours of her ear.

Tessa touched him, feeling the roughness of his face, the unkempt beard stubble, and the contrast of his hair, soft and thick, nearly silken through her fingers. His heart thrummed against her, its rhythm mirroring her own and she sensed the blood racing through his veins, coursing through his body, making her gums ache with sudden, mounting need.

Not to mention other parts of her.

She reached between them, cupping her hand against the hard swell of his arousal, straining against the fly of his jeans. He groaned softly as she moved, gripping him firmly, then caught her wrist to stay her. "Don't," he said in a hoarse, ragged voice.

She blinked at him, drawing back, somewhat wounded and confused, but he slipped his fingers through her hair, cupping the back of her head in his palm and kissed her again. He turned, guiding her until the backs of her legs met the mattress. When she sat, he moved with her, laying her back against the bed and stretching out beside her. He began to explore her with his good hand, caressing her breasts, toying with her nipples until they grew firm through the thin fabric of her blouse. The sensation of it left her breath hitching, and she hooked her fingers into the curve of his shoulder, digging her nails into his sleeve.

"Tell me to stop, *pischouette*," Rene whispered, looking down at her.

She met his gaze, trembling. She wasn't naive when it came to sex. Martin had spent four years forcing himself on her to get her pregnant. She'd never felt anything on those occasions but repulsion, but at Rene's touch, his kiss, she found herself suddenly on that same brink of tenuous self-control as when the bloodlust would come upon her.

"Tell me to stop," he said again, and she shook her head.

"No." She caught his face between her hands and pulled him down, kissing him again. He touched her through her pants, sliding his hand between her thighs and rubbing against her, sending sudden pleasure shuddering through her. No one had ever touched her like that before; sure as hell not Martin. She found herself moving with Rene, and when he paused, unbuttoning her fly and slipping beneath her waistband, she moaned softly.

She felt his fingertips steal through the tangle of dark curls hidden just beneath the edge of her panties, then move lower still. She raised her hips slightly from the bed and he caressed her, delving between her folds, stroking against a wonderful, almost electrified point deep at her core.

"*Tu es étonnant, femme,*" he whispered as she clutched at him, gasping for breath. *You are amazing, woman.* When he slid his fingers inside of her one at a time, slow and deliberate, she moaned again. He kissed her, his mouth pressing hungrily against hers as she moved with a nearly desperate urgency, grinding against his hand, drawing him deep inside, filling her. Faster and faster he moved, plunging his fingers in and out. She could feel something massive and wonderful building with his pace, some mounting pleasure that crashed down on her all at once, making her cry out, writhing against the bed.

When it was finished, leaving her breathless and trembling, she huddled against him, her eyes closed as he stroked her hair. "You all right?" he asked, and she laughed, nodding.

"Yes," she said, resting her chin nearly against his sternum to look up at him. "Very much all right."

He smiled, lifting his head enough to kiss her forehead through her bangs. "Good," he said.

Tessa wondered why he hadn't made love to her. He could have. She would have let him. Impossible as it seemed, given she'd never felt anything but a rigid disgust when it came to sex with her husband, when Rene had been touching her, kissing her, she'd wanted him, a foreign but fascinating—and damn near maddening—sensation.

She felt certain that Rene had wanted to, as well; that much had been obvious from the fervency in his kisses, not to mention the fact that he'd been so aroused, she'd thought for sure he'd burst through the front of his jeans. He'd been as desperate for her, as much on the tenuous brink of self-control as she'd been.

Then what stopped you? She rested her cheek against his chest and listened to the heavy, racing measure of his heart as it slowed back to its normal rhythm. *Why didn't you make love to me, Rene?*

Chapter Eleven

Stupid, Rene thought. *Stupid, stupid, stupid.*

He'd damn near waited too long before plugging in the lithium ion battery in his knee joint to recharge. It was designed to warn him of this sort of little oversight by vibrating. He'd felt the thrumming at about the same moment as he'd kissed Tessa for the first time, and had ignored it as a result.

Would've been real romantic, too, he thought with a scowl. *If the damn thing hadn't frozen up and left me stuck there, unable to move without dragging it around with me— a goddamn 15-pound titanium anchor.*

He sat in the motel room recliner with a blanket draped across his lap and his prosthetic leg propped against the chair arm beside him, the knee fully bent while the battery recharged through a nearby wall outlet. Tessa was sound asleep in the bed; he'd lain with her for a while until she'd drifted off in his arms, that damn knee joint vibrating all the while in friendly reminder. He kept stealing anxious glances at every soft sound, each time she'd shift or murmur in her sleep.

I don't want her to see me, he thought. *Not like this.*

He didn't mind particularly if men saw him without

his prosthetic; in fact, Tessa's brother, Brandon, had once, and Rene hadn't been bothered at all. But women were different. He didn't like for them to see him without the leg in place, and few ever had. He hadn't made love to a woman face-to-face since Irene; when he had sex with the prostitutes he'd hire to feed on, he'd always done so from behind. It made things easier that way . . . in more ways than one.

While waiting until the last minute to tend to his leg had been foolish enough, that wasn't exactly why he was remonstrating with himself at the moment.

Stupid, he thought again. *What the hell was I thinking, messing around with her? And what the hell was she thinking, letting me?*

He watched Tessa sleep, admiring the soft play of lamplight against the contours of her face, alight against her glossy hair, remembering how it had felt to touch her, taste her. He hadn't meant to, but hadn't been able to stop himself from kissing her. And then when she'd told him about her husband, the way Martin used to abuse her, his heart had nearly broken. Here was the secret she'd been so careful to hide all along, the truth she'd been unable to share with anyone, not even her own brother. She'd confided it to him, and he'd been moved by her trust. He'd lost his mind for the moment, just like he had at the rest stop earlier. Only this time, he hadn't acted impulsively to protect her from some drugged-out kid with a gun. He'd wanted to protect her from herself, from memories that obviously haunted and terrorized her. He'd wanted to show her that not every man in the world would hurt her.

There's irony, no? a mean little part of his mind said. *Because Christ knows you've never hurt anyone, right, Rene? Especially a woman.*

Goddamn it, I need to get up, he thought, tearing his eyes away from Tessa and shoving the heel of his hand against his brow. He hated walls. That was why his home in the city was utterly devoid of them; nothing but a broad, open loft with drapes to mark boundaries. Right now, the claustrophobic confines of the motel room were damn near suffocating to him. *I need to walk right out through that goddamn door, get in my car and get as far away from here as I can.*

But he couldn't. Not now, because of his leg. *My goddamn leg,* he thought, and in that moment, he was tempted to hoist it up and throw it across the room, ruining a fifty-thousand dollar investment. He blinked against sudden, frustrated tears and hated the goddamn prosthetic more than anything else in the entire world. Worse than that, he wanted a drink. Vodka, bourbon, beer, something—anything to take away that horrible edge, to make him stop feeling.

Because that's what got me into this fucking mess, he thought. *Feeling. Letting myself get caught up in the moment.*

He looked at Tessa again, the outline of her body beneath the crisp, pale sheets, all long legs and gentle curves. She was breathtaking, her figure flawlessly proportioned, slender and strong, graceful and lean.

And here I am, half a man, he thought. *I couldn't even make love to her because I had to charge up my goddamn leg.*

She would have let him, too, and that had been the most humiliating part. He hadn't needed to read her mind to know this; it was obvious from the urgency in her kiss, the way she'd moved her body against him, undulating to match the rhythm of his hand. When she'd climaxed, she'd jerked against him, uttering a soft cry, and he'd damn near shot off in his pants like an adolescent schoolboy. And all the while, his goddamn knee had been buzzing: *Hey, Casanova! I'm about to die here! You'd better fucking charge me!*

When it was over, Tessa had curled up against him and fallen asleep. His erection had withered along with his ego, and he'd lain there, feeling frustrated and humiliated, hating his goddamn leg.

And what would you have done if your knee had been fully charged? he asked himself sharply. *You can't just drop your Levi's anymore,* mon ami, *not so she wouldn't notice. She'd see your leg. She'd see* you, *asshole, and talk about a fucking mood killer! You aren't some goddamn romance novel hero, Rene Morin. Half a man, that's what you are. That's what she'd see. Half a man.*

He glanced across the room at her, his brows furrowed deeply as he struggled defiantly against his tears, his lips pressed together in a stern, crooked line. "Stupid," he whispered.

Before he'd left her in bed, he'd felt the baby again. He'd touched her stomach through her clothes and that dim but wondrous sensation—which he could only liken to a broad beam of sunshine spilling into an otherwise darkened room—had flooded his mind, an awareness of some basic, inherent consciousness that had been sweet and innocent, like the thoughts of the birds he could call and command, but amplified ten-thousand fold. Just as it had before, this sensation had momentarily made him lose his breath, and he'd lain in the bed, dumbstruck.

Do you wish it could be yours? that spiteful part of his brain whispered. *Do you, Rene? Stupid, stupid, stupid—you couldn't be a father to the one you had the right to call your own. You drove Irene away. You broke her heart, made her lose the baby.*

"No," Rene whispered, closing his eyes, his brows narrowing even more. "No, I didn't."

It was a mistake, what you did with Tessa. A big fucking mistake, and if you don't stop things now, it's only going to get worse. You're going to end up disappointing her, hurting her—just like you did with Irene. Do you really think you could ever make someone like Tessa happy? You couldn't with Irene. Do you really think someone like Tessa would ever love you?

Half a man—that's all you'll ever be. Damaged goods, Rene. You're as fucked up in the head as you are everywhere else.

"No, I'm not," Rene seethed.

No? his brain quipped back. *Then why the hell are you sitting here arguing with yourself?*

He opened his eyes. "Goddamn it."

His cell phone sat beside him on a small table. He reached for it, flipped back the cover, then cradled it in his hand for a long, uncertain moment, staring at the small, glowing display screen, his thumb hovering above the keypad. *You won't do it. Not sober anyway. You don't have the balls.*

At this, Rene defiantly punched the redial button and drew the phone to his ear. *Fuck you,* he said to that little inner voice as he sat in rigid silence, his jaw locked at so stern an angle, his back teeth hit together, nearly grinding. He listened to the phone ring once, then again, then a third time.

Maybe she's not home. Maybe she's out on a date with her husband.

Several years ago, he'd hired a private investigator to track down Irene. He'd learned that she had remarried several years after leaving him, some college-educated accountant type Rene was sure her father had approved of. They'd moved to California in the early 1980s, when her husband had taken a job with some multibillion-dollar tech firm in Silicon Valley. He was now the chief financial officer of the company, or some such bullshit, and they lived in a posh Victorian mansion in the exclusive Pacific Heights area of San Francisco. They'd had two children, both of whom were grown. She lived the proverbial life of Riley.

She probably never even thinks of me at all.

"Hello?" Irene's voice was sleepy; he'd roused her from bed again.

Rene closed his eyes and remembered the day forty years ago when he'd first set eyes on her, the way she'd smiled, the sweet fragrance that had surrounded her, the way sunlight dappling down through magnolia limbs had fallen against her face and shined in her hair.

"Hello?" she said again, this time the tone of her voice lending itself to a frown.

She'd never known about Rene's money. By the time Arnaud Morin had found him, Irene was long gone, moving on with her life. She didn't know that in one fell swoop, he'd acquired a hundred times the fortune her husband had spent years to earn; that he could have bought the sprawling house she called home a thousand times over and still have spent little more than pocket change to him.

She'd only known him dirt damn poor, and it had never mattered to her. She'd been one of the few people he'd ever known in his entire life who had loved him simply as he was, with no expectations, no demands. Lina was one of the others.

And now Tessa, he thought, closing his eyes and pinching the bridge of his nose. *Tessa is falling in love with me like that, and oh, sweet Christ, I don't know what to do, because I'm falling in love with her, too.*

"Is somebody there?" Irene asked.

"No, *chère,*" Rene said softly, lowering the phone from his ear as he hung up. "Nobody at all."

He slept for a couple of hours, waking some time just before dawn. Tessa was still sleeping, and his leg had charged, so he pulled it on long enough to get up off the recliner and duck into the bathroom. He needed a shower. Taking one involved removing his leg again, and he wanted to get a quick one in before Tessa roused just to avoid the risk of her seeing him. He needed to shave, too, but figured that would wait; the buzz of his electric razor as he stood over the vanity sink would have disturbed Tessa.

Once safely behind the closed bathroom door, Rene sat down against the side of the tub and removed his clothes and leg, propping the prosthetic within his reach in the corner near the toilet. He turned the hot water tap open wide, watching it splash down against the tub drain, sending steam curling up in thick tendrils that quickly filled the small room.

He had a folding shower chair in the trunk of the car, but didn't want to risk waking Tessa by going outside to get it. At home, as a general rule, he simply stood in the shower; he had a large, walk-in stall instead of a tub and could balance himself by leaning against the wall. The floor of his shower was some kind of special, nonskid surface, while the basin of the motel's porcelain tub was glossy and potentially slippery. That, combined with the fact he'd need to avoid getting his hand wet, if possible, meant he was going to have to be really careful. If he fell, he'd have a hell of a time getting up on his own, because the bathroom wasn't handicapped equipped; there were no bars or rails for him to grab hold of for leverage. As he turned the showerhead on, Rene frowned, again toying with the idea of going to get the bath chair.

"Fuck it," he muttered, swinging himself around on the edge of the tub. Resting most of his weight on his leg, he shoved his good hand against the shower wall and stood. Once upright, he leaned his shoulder against the wall and closed his eyes, feeling the spray of hot water stinging his chest, peppering his face. *Heaven*, he thought.

Within moments, the cotton gauze wrapped around his left hand was soaked. He'd had to force his fingers into reluctant movement in order to unwrap the little bar of motel soap, something he'd not thought to do before getting into the shower. The wound had healed considerably since the day before, but was still incredibly sore, and trying to manage something that had required at least some modicum of dexterity had left his hand throbbing and aching.

He wound up using the soap to wash his hair, because he'd also forgotten to grab one of the miniature bottles of shampoo from the corner of the tub. Since bending over to get it was pretty much out of the question, he was stuck with what he had on hand. Literally.

And when the little bar of soap slipped out from between his fingers, clattering to the floor of the tub and skittering about like a runaway hockey puck, Rene stared down at it with a frown. "Goddamn it."

He had the urge to reach out with his right foot and poke it with his toes as it came to a rest against the chrome-plated tub drain. Which was odd considering he had no right foot anymore, no toes with which to poke anything.

He glanced at the far corner of the tub, where the edge of the white nylon shower curtain was plastered against the wall with moisture. There was another bar of soap there, and the little bottle of shampoo, as well. *If I just lean over a little bit, I can reach it.*

Ordinarily, he might not have bothered. He wasn't particular or picky about his appearance, but yesterday had been hot, and he'd also torn open the kid's throat at the rest stop. Even though he'd washed in the bathroom there, he'd still felt kind of grimy and unclean ever since, if only in the Lady Macbeth guilt-ridden sort of way. *And messing around with Tessa last night sure as hell didn't help any.* Out, out, damn spot— *and all of that.*

He shifted his weight slightly, blinking against water droplets beading in his eyelashes as he reached out, his fingers splayed for the soap. *You're not going to make it.* Now the mean little niggling voice in his head had turned into an annoying little nagging one. *You're going to slip and fall and wind up stuck in this goddamn tub like a turtle turned up on its back.*

"I am not," Rene muttered, leaning over, arm outstretched. All at once, he lost his balance, and he had a wide-eyed, startled moment to realize that nagging voice had been right after all before he crashed down into the tub, dragging the shower curtain with him. It ripped loose of the thin metal loops holding it onto the curtain rod and came spilling down atop him like a sopping, cream-colored shroud. He landed hard, catching the brunt of the blow with his right side and sending a bright spear of pain shooting up from his stump. He tried to catch himself reflexively—and put too much weight down on his injured hand, causing him more pain. His chin smacked the lip of the tub so hard, his back teeth clamped down against his tongue, drawing blood.

"Goddamn it!" he cried, swatting the curtain off his face. The shower was still going full blast; now the water pelted down on the top of his head, and he sputtered, choking for breath, spitting out a bitter mouthful of blood.

"Goddamn it!" he gasped, struggling to push the soaked shower curtain away from him. *Oh,* viens m'enculer, *that hurt like a son of a bitch!*

"Rene?" He heard a light but urgent rapping against the bathroom door. "Are you all right?"

Terrific. So Tessa was awake now. His humiliation was complete.

"I'm fine." He grimaced as he shoved his good hand against the side of the tub and tried to sit up.

"I heard a big crash . . ." she said, sounding uncertain.

"Yeah, *pischouette.* That was me." He couldn't stand up. Not on his own, he realized to his dismay. He might have been able to somehow struggle upright if he'd been able to use both of his hands, but with his left one injured, there'd be no way.

Viens m'enculer. Fuck me.

Rene saw the doorknob start to turn and his eyes

widened in alarm. "It's all right," he called out, but it
wasn't all right of course. He was stuck in the tub for all
practical purposes, and if he didn't want to spend the
rest of his life there, he'd need Tessa's help. "Just . . . just
give me a minute, *pischouette.*"

If she'd walked in on him jerking off, he wouldn't
have been as mortified. He shoved his dripping hair
back out of his face and struggled not to laugh. If he
didn't laugh, he'd probably burst into tears. *Just bring
me my pistol, Tessa, and slide it through the goddamn door.
Let me kill myself, for Christ's sake.*

"Are you hurt, Rene?" Tessa asked, turning the
doorknob again. "I'm coming in. What happened?"

"Tessa, don't—" he began, but it was too late; she
was already through the door. He grabbed a wadded
handful of shower curtain and jerked it over his
midriff, struggling to hide both his crotch and stump
from view.

"Oh, my God!" she exclaimed as she rushed over to
the tub, wide-eyed and reaching for him. "What happened?"

"What the hell does it look like?" he growled, embarrassed. "I fell down."

"Are you hurt?" she asked, but he shook his head.
Just my pride, he thought as her hands fluttered
about him. "No," he said.

Her hands fell still and she blinked at him. "You're
bleeding . . ."

He shook his head and spat blood. "It's nothing,"ter
he said. "I bit my tongue, that's all. I'm going to need
your help here. I . . . I can't get up on my own."

"Oh." Tessa stared for a moment longer, then
shook her head as if snapping out of a reverie. "Okay."

She turned off the water and leaned over, hooking
her arm around him. He tried to hold the shower curtain in place and grunted, his brows furrowed with
effort as together, they hauled him up enough to sit

against the side of the tub. When they were finished, she squatted beside him and reached out, brushing her fingertips against his chin, dabbing at the rivulet of blood leaking from the corner of his mouth.

"It's nothing," he said again, ducking away.

He hadn't been able to look her in the eyes since she'd walked in the bathroom. He risked a peek now and found her looking at him, or rather, at the open air where his right leg had once been. The shower curtain had wadded beneath his ass and around his waist as he'd sat down; now, the folds had pulled back enough to reveal the end of his stump.

"Just . . . just go in the other room, please." He jerked at the shower curtain, struggling to cover his stump. It was caught beneath him though, and wouldn't budge.

"Okay." She nodded, noticing that he'd noticed her attention. Bright color blazed in her cheeks and she cut her gaze to the floor as she backed out of the room. "You sure you're all right?"

"I'm fine." *I'm about to start bawling like a girl who's been stood up on the night of the homecoming dance, but otherwise perfectly goddamn swell.*

The door closed behind her, and Rene breathed for what felt like the first time. He huffed out a long, anguished breath and forked his fingers through his hair. Tessa had seen him. She'd seen his leg, the ruined remnants of it, anyway. She'd seen him like no one else had in a long, long time—utterly helpless.

Half a man, he thought, blinking against the dim heat of shamed tears. *Nothing more than a cripple.*

"Goddamn it," he whispered.

Chapter Twelve

It was the blood that had done it.

Tessa hadn't meant to stare, but the sight of that solitary, slender trickle of blood leaking from the corner of Rene's mouth, trailing along the contour of his chin had struck her with every bit as much force as a physical blow.

Rene was half human, and when he bled that percentage of his humanity—the part of him that made him so inherently different from her—was acutely apparent. The day before, when Rene had been shot, she'd been too frightened, her body too seized with adrenaline, for his blood to have affected her. But that morning, she noticed it. She'd smelled the heady, distinctive fragrance of it as soon as she'd burst through the bathroom door. And then she'd seen it on his face, bright red in contrast to his pale skin, and it had shocked the bloodlust to life within her.

She'd only fed two days earlier, but everything about her body had become difficult and unpredictable with her pregnancy—especially her bloodlust. It would come upon her out of nowhere, like at that moment, and no matter how recently she'd last sated it, it would feel like she hadn't fed in months.

She'd felt her gums suddenly tingle, the roots of her canine teeth throbbing as they reflexively started to lower. She'd stared at the blood on his face like a woman mesmerized, until at last, a voice of reason had snapped in her mind, shaking her out of her reverie.

What the hell is the matter with you? It's Rene, for God's sake! Stop gawking at him like he's food!

Tessa didn't say anything as Rene limped out of the bathroom. He didn't say anything, either; simply fished a small traveling case out of his bag, then went to the sink to brush his teeth and shave.

"Are you sure you're all right?" she asked finally in a small voice. She watched him through his reflection in the mirror as she sat on the bed, her hands in her lap, her fingers twining anxiously together. As he'd finished in the bathroom behind closed doors, she'd stood over the sink and splashed cold water on her face, trying to rid herself of the damnable bloodlust. She wanted to talk to him about what had happened, but she wasn't sure how to broach the subject.

He saw me.

He'd glanced up just as she'd torn her eyes away from his face. He'd undoubtedly realized what was going on; her teeth were partially descended, her face flushed with rising bloodlust. He wasn't a moron. *Oh, God, what he must think,* she thought, and she wanted to plead with him, explain somehow. *I didn't mean it, Rene! I couldn't help myself.*

"I'm fine." He walked back to his bag and tossed the electric razor inside. "Why don't you get ready? We're meeting Brandon and Lina for breakfast."

God, after yesterday . . . and last night . . . what he did to me, what he did for me and this is how I repay him?

She wanted desperately to tell him she was sorry, but didn't know where to begin. "Rene . . ." She stood, crossing the room toward him. He had his back to

her, and stiffened visibly when she brushed her fingertips lightly, hesitantly, against his shoulder. She
wanted to touch him, hold him, kiss him. *I'm sorry,
Rene. I didn't mean it. Please, can't we just pretend like it
never happened?*

I would never hurt you, she wanted to tell him, but
she pressed her lips together and said nothing.

"We need to get going," he said, deliberately sidestepping away from her proffered caress. He didn't
turn around as he spoke, lifting the overnight bag in
hand. "Go on and get ready, *pischouette*. You'll make us
late."

At breakfast, Lina chattered cheerfully at them over
an unfolded road map that she'd spread out across
the table while they waited to place their order. Tessa
only pretended to pay attention and kept cutting
glances at Rene, who sat across from her. He seemed
equally distracted, stirring the same packet of
creamer into his coffee for at least five full minutes
without taking as much as a sip. He'd occasionally
nod or grunt in agreement with something Lina said,
or put on a strained looking smile in mute response.
He didn't look at Tessa, not even a passing glance.

". . . so I figure we can stop outside of Tucson for
lunch," Lina said. "That's about four and a half hours
from here and there are a couple of places we could
try—a town called Cortaro here . . ." She pointed on
the map, leaning forward and frowning a moment
before planting her fingertip. "Or here, Rillito. What
do you think, Rene?"

Rene set his spoon aside and pushed his chair back.
"I think I need to take a piss."

Lina frowned quizzically as he walked away. "What's
with him?"

Tessa shrugged.

You two are getting along, aren't you? Brandon asked. He'd been practicing picking up his fork and spoon, folding his newly healed fingers carefully around the slim metal handles, but frowned now, leaning toward his sister.

"We're fine," Tessa replied, smiling. It came naturally to her, without seeming outwardly forced or insincere. She'd had four years to perfect it; four years of hiding from Brandon the truth about her nightmarish marriage. "I . . . I guess he's tired, that's all. We stayed up pretty late last night, looking through the Tome together."

"Did you find out anything new?" Lina asked.

Tessa shook her head. "Not much." *Unless you count Rene introducing me to the finer points of an orgasm,* she added to herself. "Something about a fire in 1815, but no details. And a picture of Rene's grandfather like the one that's in the study at home, Brandon—the one of the Grandfather in front of the old great house. It was dated 1815, too, July, I think. Oh, and someone had written down another date for that year, too—the twelfth of October."

Brandon raised his brows in surprise at the mention of their birthdate and she nodded. "I know. Coincidence, huh? Beside that, they'd written the French word for *fire*. But I don't know what that means."

Fire, Brandon repeated, his dark eyes suddenly growing troubled, though he offered nothing more.

"There were lots of pictures, too, drawings and paintings," Tessa said. "One of them was of this weird-looking creature. I'll have to show it to you later—someone had written *abomination* underneath it."

Abomination? Brandon said. *Like that bunch of bullshit Caine made up to frighten us when we were kids?*

"You ready to order?" the waitress asked, appearing beside the table with a fresh coffeepot in one hand, her ticket tablet in the other.

Because she looked expectantly at Tessa first, Tessa said, "Sure, I guess. I'd like oatmeal, please. Just plain, with butter on the side and a glass of orange juice." She nodded to indicate Rene's empty chair. "He'll have three slices of cherry pie."

Pie? Brandon looked puzzled, and Lina laughed.

"He still does the pie thing, huh? Jesus," she said, then looked up at the waitress. "Give me the pancake platter, please, with a side of sausage links."

While Lina ordered for Brandon, Tessa caught sight of Rene emerging from the restroom. He walked back toward the table, but when his eyes momentarily met hers, he looked away.

I'm sorry, Tessa thought unhappily. *Please stop being angry with me, Rene.*

"You and your pie," Lina remarked as he sat down again. When he just looked at her, clearly at a loss, she laughed again. "Tessa ordered for you. Three slices of cherry pie. You've always been a pie junkie. I remember you used to make special detours in the squad car just so you could hit this one bakery on East Twenty-second street and get—"

"I think today I'll have eggs," Rene interjected, holding up his hand to flag the waitress back to the table. When she returned, he said, "Eggs, *ma chère.* Hard-scrambled, with hash browns, buttered toast and bacon."

"No pie?" the waitress said, and he shook his head.

"No thanks." He spared Tessa a momentary, withering glance. "I'm not really in the mood."

By the end of the meal, Tessa had barely touched her oatmeal, letting it grow cold, hardened to near-mortar consistency in the bottom of her bowl. She moved robotically, sullen and quiet, as the four of them left the restaurant together and exchanged good-byes in the parking lot.

"We'll see you in Rillito," Lina said, giving Tessa a hug and a smile. If she noticed anything tense or strained in Tessa's demeanor, she didn't mention it, but Brandon did.

What is going on? he thought as Lina and Rene conferred over the map one last time. Brandon hooked his hand against the crook of her elbow and led her aside, looking her in the eyes, his brows furrowed slightly in concern.

Nothing, she replied.

Tessa . . . he began, but she shrugged away from him.

It's nothing, Brandon. I told you—I'm just tired.

He wasn't buying it, not one bit. He'd known her too long and too well, and she could tell just by looking at him that he knew she was feeding him a line of shit. His feelings were hurt; she could tell that by looking, too, and felt badly. During the four years of her marriage, he hadn't understood why she'd kept herself so distant, both emotionally and physically from everyone in the Noble family, but most of all from him.

When the Grandfather had broken Brandon's hands, Martin had begrudgingly agreed to let Tessa return to the great house to help tend to her twin, a concession he'd offered because Tessa's father, Sebastian, had come and practically pleaded it from him. She'd often imagined that Martin had enjoyed that moment of her father's anguish and had reveled in not only the opportunity to watch Sebastian beg a favor of him, but to be in a position of power enough over the Noble house to grant it. During her brief return, however, Brandon hadn't wanted much to do with her. Unable to write or sign, he'd refused to use psi-speech much, no matter how much she'd tried to initiate conversation with him. He'd told her once, in a quick exchange, that the Grandfather had forbidden him to use his telepathy and he was in trouble enough without inviting more on himself. But she'd known the truth—he had been angry with her for her absence and hurt by it.

I stayed away to protect you, Brandon. She wished so desperately that she could make him understand. *And myself. I didn't want you to think badly of me, or worry about me, and I knew if you realized what Martin was doing . . . the way he treated me . . . that you'd try to protect me somehow.*

They were only just now reconnecting, rediscovering the closeness that had always bound them to each other, and she could tell from his expression he felt wounded that she wouldn't confide in him.

It's not because I don't want to. I'm ashamed, Brandon. I'm ashamed of what I did and it's bad enough Rene won't talk to me now. I don't want you to be angry with me, too.

She made herself smile for him; forced herself to hold it until his expression softened, the worry in his eyes fading.

You'd tell me, wouldn't you? he asked and he reached out, brushing the cuff of his newly mended fingers against her cheek. *If there was something wrong? Whatever it is, Tessa, I'd be here for you. I love you.*

She hugged him, holding him fiercely for a moment and closing her eyes as tears flooded her eyes again. *I know, Brandon. I love you, too.*

She sat rigidly in the passenger seat of the Audi, her shoulders hunched, and flinched as Rene lowered himself into the driver's side, slamming the door hard enough to rock the little sports car.

"Are you sure you're okay to drive?" she asked in a small, hesitant voice. "With your hand, I mean?"

"I'm fine." He fired up the engine and dropped the car in gear. She didn't miss the way he gripped the steering wheel lightly, gingerly with his injured hand, or the wince that momentarily twisted his brows.

The tension in the car was thick enough to stifle. Rene drove out of the restaurant parking lot and across the street, pulling up to a gas station and killing the engine. "I need to fill up," he said, reaching for the door handle and wincing again as he forced his fingers to grasp it.

"Rene." Tessa caught him by the sleeve. All she'd said was his name, but already, she could feel tears welling up, threatening to choke her.

He glanced at her, his brows narrowed slightly, draping his eyes in stern, disapproving shadows. It might have been her imagination, but at the sight of tears glistening in her eyes, some of that severity in his face seemed to abruptly falter.

"I want to talk to you about this morning," she said, forcing her voice out. "About what happened. I . . . I didn't mean . . ."

"Don't worry about it." He drew his arm away.

"But you're upset," she protested. "I just want to explain. Please, Rene."

He looked at her for a moment, his face unreadable. "What's to explain, *pischouette*?" he asked at length. "It's happened before. Plenty of times. I'm used to people staring at my leg."

Tessa blinked in surprise. "What?"

"And while I don't normally keel over in the bathtub like that, it doesn't mean I'm not used to people gawking," he continued, his voice growing sharper, his brows narrowing again. "I mean, after all, it does come with the territory and all—good ol' Rene, half a man, the poor cripple gimping around on his Tin Man leg, no?"

What? Tessa thought, so caught off guard, for a moment, she couldn't speak. "What are you talking about?" she managed finally.

"The Tin Man—you know, from *The Wizard of Oz*," Rene told her dryly, leaning over to rap his knuckles demonstratively against the titanium shaft of his prosthetic calf. "What? Is that too far before your time, *pischouette*? You don't have TNT on your cable channels out there in Kentucky?"

He hadn't realized after all. *He has no idea,* she thought.

"I don't care about your leg, Rene," she said with a frown, feeling her own anger stoking slightly at the confrontational edge to his voice. When he uttered a mean little bark of laughter, her frown deepened. "I don't give a shit about that, Rene."

"*Ah, vraiment?*" he asked, arching his brow. *Oh, really?* "Then what *were* you gawking at this morning, *pischouette*? Cause if it wasn't my stump, your eyes were sure bugging halfway out of your skull over something."

He has no idea, she thought again, and in that moment, she clammed up, pressing her lips together, too ashamed to admit the truth: *I was looking at your blood, Rene. I wanted to feed from you.*

When she said nothing, his brow raised all the more. "*Voilà,*" he said and he pivoted, opening the car door and swinging his leg around.

She watched him get out of the car and slam the door behind him, sending another shudder through the Audi's sleek frame. A tear slipped from the corner of her eye and rolled down her cheek; she rubbed at it with her fingertips. *How could things have gone from so wonderful last night—like something out of a dream—to this, like something out of a nightmare?*

She got out of the car and stood beside it for a long, uncertain moment, watching as he pumped gas and deliberately kept his eyes turned away from her. The longer he ignored her, the more incensed and hurt she became. *Why would he think his leg matters to me?*

Didn't last night prove anything? Didn't it mean anything to him?

And then it hit her with all of the shocking force of a slap in the face.

It didn't. It didn't mean anything at all to him.

Rene cut her a glance over the Audi's roof. "Get in the car, *pischouette.*"

No different than anything he's ever done with his hookers, she thought. *That's how he sees last night. That's how he sees* me—*no different than one of his hookers.*

Another tear fell and again, she swatted it away. "You know something, Rene?" she said, trembling with sudden outrage, pain and shame. "You really are the Tin Man, but it doesn't have a goddamn thing to do with your leg. Neither one of you has a heart."

She turned and marched toward the convenience store entrance. Her tears spilled out along the way, despite her struggle to contain them. She rubbed her cheeks furiously with her hands as she stepped inside the shockingly cold, air-conditioned store.

"You okay, honey?" the woman behind the counter asked, even though Tessa knew it was pretty damn apparent that, for the moment at least, she was anything *but* okay.

"Yes." She sniffled, dragging her finger beneath her nose and struggling to compose herself. "I'm fine, thank you." She grabbed a Snickers from a nearby candy rack and pushed it toward the register. She hadn't swallowed two bites of her oatmeal, and her stomach was grumbling. If ever she'd needed a chocolate fix, it was now. "Just this please."

The cashier rang up the candy bar and waited while Tessa dug through her purse for spare change. "Where are your restrooms?" Tessa asked, dolling out quarters and nickels.

"Outside and around the corner to your left," the

woman replied, reaching beneath the counter. "Here. You'll need the key."

The bathroom was a tiny, dingy room on the far end of the building, away from the gas pumps. Lit by a solitary fluorescent fixture that buzzed and flickered overhead, it sported cracked, gray linoleum floors, a beat-up toilet with hard-water stains, a sink with a perpetual, steady drip and a wall-mounted machine that offered latex prophylaxes in a wide variety of neon colors and tropical fruit flavors. Tessa didn't want to touch anything, but plucked a slip of toilet paper from a roll on the back of the commode and stood in the middle of the room to dab at her eyes.

Damn you, Rene Morin, she thought, blowing her nose. *You absolute asshole.*

Of course Brandon and Lina had already hit the road. Of course Rene would wait until they were gone to pull something so downright mean-spirited and nasty, leaving her with no other recourse than to spend yet another miserable day trapped in the car with him for unpleasant company.

I can't believe I let him touch me, she thought. *I can't believe I thought he cared. I can't believe I thought I cared!*

The worst part was, she *did* care about him, even now. She'd let him touch her because she had wanted him to; she'd wanted him. She still did.

I love him, she thought. *Goddamn him.*

After a few moments, Tessa tossed the wadded up paper into an overflowing trash can and left the bathroom. She paused, squinting against the bright contrast of the sun's glare, after having stood in the relatively dim restroom for so long. She also wiped her hands against the thighs of her cargo pants before pulling the Snickers out of her purse, because it hadn't been dim enough to hide how filthy everything had been.

As she walked toward the front of the building

and the gas pumps again, she felt a peculiar, tickling sensation inside of her mind that immediately sent the downy hairs along the nape of her neck rising. It was the same sort of feeling that would come upon her whenever Brandon or Rene drew near—or any other of the Brethren, for that matter. They could sense one another, even at great distances sometimes; the way that she and Brandon could sense the Elders coming after them. This was nothing like sensing the Elders—which felt in Tessa's mind like a heavy, looming shadow threatening to engulf her, swallow her whole. Instead, it felt like someone close by, maybe even standing behind her, and she realized.

Rene. He just stepped out of the men's room.

She turned around, unsure whether or not she meant to chew him a new ass or simply grab hold of him and kiss him, and noticed for the first time, out of her peripheral vision, the streamlined silhouette of a maroon Jaguar sedan parked immediately outside of the restrooms, just beyond a brick wall meant to shelter the doors from view.

That's funny, she thought. *That looks like—*

And then she realized who had stepped out of the men's room behind her, who now stood less than a foot away, his eyes sharp and filled with menace, the corner of his full mouth hooked in an icy smile. The Snickers fell from her hand and she gasped.

Hello, Tessa, Martin Davenant said inside her mind. *I've missed you, darling.*

Chapter Thirteen

"Martin . . . !"

That was all Tessa had time to breathlessly gulp before Martin's hand clamped against her throat, snapping her windpipe shut. Practically hoisting her off her feet, he forced her backward in skittering, clumsy tow, opening the door to the women's restroom again and pushing her inside. He shoved her against the far wall hard enough to rattle her brain momentarily. Her purse slipped from her shoulder and fell to the floor, spilling coins, loose peppermints, her cell phone and lipstick across the battered linoleum.

"You bitch," Martin seethed, his face flushed with rage, his brows knitted deeply. "You goddamn stupid, sneaky bitch!"

"Please . . . !" she croaked, pawing desperately at his hand, struggling for air. "Martin . . . please . . . !"

"Did you think I wouldn't find you? You stupid fucking bitch, did you really think you could get away from me?"

He raised his hand to slap her and she mewled weakly, holding out her own to try and stay him. "Wait . . . !" she gasped. "Martin, please . . . ! The baby . . . !"

He hesitated, and the palm against her throat pulled away, leaving her knees to buckle. She collapsed to the bathroom floor, clutching her neck, gagging for breath. "Please . . . please don't hurt my baby . . ." she wheezed.

Pain ripped through her scalp as Martin closed his fist in her hair, wrenching her head back and forcing her to look up at him. "It's not *your* goddamn baby— it's *mine*," he snapped, and now he did slap her, striking her hard enough to whip her head sideways, bouncing against the dingy cinderblock wall. "It's my baby, you stupid fucking bitch, and you'd better fucking believe me—once it's born, you'll never see it again. You'll never see the goddamn light of day again for this, you lousy fucking whore."

He jerked her by the hair again and she cried out. "I know you took my money," he seethed, leaning over to speak against her ear, his breath hot, his spittle spraying her face. "I want it back. My ledger, too. Where is it?"

She'd taken both from his secret cache in the library when she'd fled Kentucky. A ledger had been tucked inside the manila envelope along with the thick bundle of cash, and it wasn't until some time later that she'd curiously peeked inside, discovering what appeared to be thick stacks of invoices and bank records for a company called Broughman and Associates, of which she'd never heard. As she thumbed through them, puzzled, she realized the Brethren's distillery, Bloodhorse, had paid in excess of three million dollars to the company over the last ten years.

How did Martin get all of this? she'd wondered. Martin worked in the accounts payable department for Bloodhorse Distillery, but beyond that scope, his interaction with humans was strictly prohibited. *So why would he have all of these financial records for this company?*

"I said where is my goddamn ledger?" Martin

demanded, smacking her in the face again, this time hard enough to bloody her nose.

"My purse," she cried, tears spilling down her cheeks. "I . . . I put it in my purse . . . please don't . . . !"

"Shut up." He shoved her away from him, knocking her head into the wall again, leaving her crumpled on the floor. He turned and stooped again, snatching her fallen purse in hand, then turned it upside down, spilling the rest of its contents. When the manila envelope plopped to the floor, he grabbed it, tossing the purse aside. She watched him through a bleary haze of frightened tears as he opened the envelope and pulled out the ledger, the money that remained.

"You spent some of it." He glared at her, his eyes so filled with murderous rage, she cowered. "It's coming out of your hide, Tessa. So help me Christ, it is."

"Please don't hurt me," she pleaded, trembling. "Please, Martin . . . the baby . . . !"

"The baby?" He snorted, closing the distance between them in one broad stride. Again, his fingers closed in her hair and again, she cried out as he jerked her, stumbling, to her feet. "The only reason you're still drawing breath at the moment is because of that baby. Do you understand? The *only* goddamn reason."

She nodded, pressing her lips together to stifle a terrified whimper. She could have called mentally to Rene for help, but kept her mind shut tightly. Obviously Martin had followed her, but she didn't know if he knew about Rene—and even if he did, she was willing to bet that he didn't realize Rene was like them, of Brethren descent. She hadn't, either, the first time she'd met him; she'd been able to sense him, as she'd sensed Martin outside, but she'd dismissed it as having only been aware of Brandon. *Martin probably thinks he's just sensing me. He doesn't know yet who Rene is—what he is. If he did, he'd kill him.*

Please stay where you are, Rene, just stay outside, she

thought. *Please, God, don't go trying to prove you're not really an asshole and come knocking on this door to apologize.*

"What are you going to do?" she whispered to Martin as he let go of her hair.

He arched his brow. "Do? I'm going to drag your sorry ass back to Kentucky, that's what I'm going to do. I'm going to tie you to the goddamn bedposts until that baby's born and after that, I'm going to wear out your sorry goddamn hide."

Oh, God! Tessa's mind raced as she struggled to think of some way out of this, some desperate hope of escape. She couldn't let Martin return her to Kentucky; she couldn't leave Brandon alone to face the Elders. *And I can't leave Rene.*

"Wait," she said. "Martin, please . . . listen to me."

His hand clapped roughly against her throat once again, and he pushed her back against the wall. "And why would I want to do that, Tessa? You stole my car, my money, my baby, for Christ's sake. What makes you think I want to listen to anything that might come out of your lying, thieving goddamn mouth?"

"I did it for you!" she gasped. "Please, Martin . . . I was trying to find Brandon for you!"

"Oh, give me a fucking break," Martin said with a laugh. "You were trying to find your pansy-ass, deaf-and-dumb brother so you could protect him somehow. You wanted to escape right along with him!"

"No!" She shook her head, clutching at his hand, trying to pry his fingers away from her windpipe. In that moment, with tiny pinpoints of light dancing in her line of sight as she strained for air, she decided to take a desperate chance. "I . . . I followed Caine and Emily to find him. Caine wanted to bring him back, impress the Grandfather, but I was going to bring him back for you! Caine told me he and Emily were going to leave the farm, so I followed them. I was going to bring Brandon back, let you deliver him to the Elders."

Martin didn't say anything, but he removed his hand, leaving her to choke and wheeze again.

"I just . . . I wanted to please you," she said. "I wanted you to think of me . . . like you think of Monica. I wanted you to be pleased with me like that." She looked up at him, shuddering. "I know where he is—where Brandon is going. Please, I was following him and I can take you there. He won't run from me. He trusts me. Think of how pleased the Elders would be—the whole Brethren council. I can show you where he is. I can take you there, Martin."

"And what precisely is supposed to prevent Caine and Emily from finding him first?" Martin asked.

"Because they're dead," she said, and watched Martin visibly react. He stepped back slightly, his eyes widening in undisguised surprise. "They're dead, Martin, both of them."

Just as her father and grandfather would understand the implications of Caine's death, so, too, would Martin. Especially since his family, the Davenants, stood to gain the most from the loss.

"Caine is dead?" he asked softly, his voice filled with something nearly like wonder; a child on Christmas morning who's come downstairs to discover Santa's boot prints in the cinders by the hearth.

Tessa nodded, gulping for breath. "He was shot in the head. He died. Emily, too." Here it was, her final card, what she hoped would be her ace in the hole. "But not before she called the Grandfather and told him about Caine."

Martin's face darkened, his brows narrowing again, and she knew her hasty plan had worked. He knew— as she did—that Augustus Noble wouldn't hold to his word to kill Brandon now. In light of Caine's death, the Nobles were equal to the Davenants now in male heirs; by Brethren law, the two clans would have to share supremacy until Brandon or Daniel underwent the bloodletting. Then the Nobles would rule again. And considering Daniel was only four years old— more than a decade away from his first kill—that left Brandon as the most reasonable ace in the hole. But only if he lived.

"So you were going to lead me to your brother— your twin," Martin said slowly, locking eyes with her. "You'd let me kill Brandon. You'd screw your family— your own brother—to help mine."

"I'm a Davenant, Martin. My loyalty lies with you— my husband." He rolled his eyes, opened his mouth to shoot back some derisive remark and she reached for him. "My grandfather said so—right to my face. Your father was there, too. Ask him about it. He told Allistair I'm his granddaughter now."

"So if something was to happen to your youngest brother . . . ?" Martin asked, his gaze unflinching. "If Daniel was to die . . . some tragic accident like your poor bitch of a grandmother . . . and the Davenant domi- nance secured . . . Your loyalty would still lie with me?"

Oh, God, she thought, suppressing an inward shud- der. *What is he saying?* Not only a thinly veiled threat against Daniel, but Martin's words seemed to imply some sort of culpability in Eleanor's death, as well, and for a moment, she couldn't breathe, much less speak. She stared up into Martin's dark eyes, smeared with reflected glow from the fluorescent tubes over- head, and trembled. *You son of a bitch, what did you do to my grandmother?*

He was waiting for an answer, and it took every ounce of deception that Tessa had practiced and honed over her four years of marriage to deliver one to him. "Yes, Martin," she said.

Martin dragged her out to the Jaguar, holding her tightly by the crook of her arm and leaving her purse behind, all of its contents scattered across the bathroom floor. He thumbed off the alarm, opened the car door and shoved her unceremoniously inside. As he walked briskly around to the driver's side, Tessa scanned the lot. She saw the low-slung Audi still parked at the gas pump; Rene was just finishing filling the gas tank. She watched as he returned the nozzle to the pump, her lips pressed together in a thin, anxious line, her breath bated, her heart pounding. *Don't turn around, Rene,* she thought. *Don't look this way. Please don't see us.*

Martin got in the car; the report of the car door slamming startled a quiet yelp from her. "I don't believe you, Tessa," he said, as Rene punched a button on the gas pump's automatic credit card payment pad and stepped back, waiting for a receipt to print. "Not for one goddamn minute, not about wanting to help me or my family."

He started the Jaguar, pumping the gas pedal so the engine gunned. As he put it in gear, he shot her a dark glance from beneath furrowed brows. "But I *do* believe you know where your brother is. And you *are* going to take me there. You do that, and you and I can negotiate the matter of your punishment for leaving."

She nodded as they drove past the Audi toward the parking-lot entrance. "I'm not lying to you, Martin," she said in a hush. Rene glanced over his shoulder as the car passed, his brow raised slightly, his expression puzzled, as if someone had just tapped him on the shoulder unexpectedly.

"Really?" Martin pulled out of the parking lot, heading toward the interstate entrance ramp. "Then who the fuck was that guy?"

Oh, shit. From the feel of things, her heart had collapsed into the middle of her gut. Had she really been so stupid as to think Martin would have missed the fact she wasn't traveling alone? "Wh-what guy?"

His hand shot out, his fingers closing painfully

against the shelf of her chin. "What do you think—
I'm fucking blind? The guy with the goddamn Audi—
the guy you pulled into the station with."

He'd seen enough, tailed her long enough to know
about Rene, then, but he still clearly had no idea what
Rene really was. Like Tessa had at first, Martin simply
thought he was human. "Nobody!" she whimpered
and when his hand crushed all the more against her
jaw, she cried out hoarsely. "He . . . he's nobody,
Martin, really! A private investigator I hired, that's all."

"A private investigator?" He gave her head a rough
shake.

"Yes!" she cried. "Like on TV, Martin, to help me
find Brandon!"

"Did you fuck him?" Another painful shake. "Because if so help me Christ, if you've disgraced me and
my family by fucking some goddamn human carcass,
I'll—"

"No! No, I swear, Martin! He's just been helping me
track Brandon!"

All the while, she thought, *Oh, God, please don't let
him know we spent the night together at the motel last night.*

He glared at her. "If you fucked him, Tessa, I'll kill
you both. I'll turn this goddamn car around and
bleed that son of a bitch dry right in front of you.
Then I'll turn your sorry ass over to the Elders and let
them deal with it from there."

"I didn't!" she pleaded, mewling around his
clamped fingers. "Please, I swear! I just hired him to
help me find Brandon!"

Martin let go of her face, pushing her away. "And
used my money for it."

"How else do you think I could find him?" She cowered in her seat, struggling not to weep. "Why do you
have all of that money, anyway?"

"That's none of your goddamn business," he
warned, shoving his forefinger in her face. "And so

help me Christ, if you ever mention it to anyone, you'll never walk without a limp again."

Tessa nodded, mute and frightened, as they pulled onto the interstate heading west at her direction. She turned her gaze out the passenger-side window as the landscape suddenly grew blurred, whizzing by in her view. A small bird kept pace with the Jaguar for a brief moment, flying along the shoulder of the road with its little wings beating furiously as if it meant to race, and then Martin floored the accelerator, leaving it behind.

Help me, she thought, closing her eyes as her tears spilled. *Oh, God, Rene, please help me.*

Chapter Fourteen

Brilliant, shit for brains, Rene thought for the millionth time as he finished pumping gas. *Real goddamn charming. Another Romance Novel Hero moment.*

Tessa had stormed off for the convenience store, and it hadn't taken a fucking genius to see the tears in her eyes, the wounded bewilderment. He'd just made a big deal out of nothing and broken her heart.

His grandmother's words reverberated in his mind, as apropos now as they had been nearly forty years earlier: "You push everyone away—anyone who tries to love you. *Tu êtes un couillon!*" You're a fool.

He returned the nozzle to the pump and pressed a button to print his receipt and stop the machine's incessant beeping. Life, he realized, was full of friendly little reminders. A chime on a gas pump so you didn't walk off without your receipt. A vibrating battery in your prosthetic leg to let you know it was time for a recharge. A memory imbedded so deeply in your brain, it replayed itself at every eerily similar moment.

"Quel est le problème avec tu, laissant cette fille marcher hors d'ici?" Odette cried inside his mind, and she may as well have been speaking about Tessa. *What's the matter with you, letting that girl walk out of here?*

He folded the receipt, tucking it in the back pocket

of his jeans and felt a strange, nearly electrical tingling run through him, like the hint of a cold draft seeping through a crack beneath a door. He'd felt it several times since pulling into the gas station, but never as strongly as he did at that exact moment. Someone was behind him, close enough to raise the hairs along his forearms. Someone like him.

Tessa.

He turned, his shoulders hunched. "Look, *pischou-ette,* I'm sorry. I was a real ass and I . . ." His voice faded as he realized in surprise that no one was there. A maroon Jaguar was turning out of the parking lot just as a white Chevy Blazer turned in. It was a busy morning, with people walking in and out of the store, cars parked or idling along the rows of gas pumps. He scanned all of the passing faces but didn't see Tessa.

That's funny, he thought. *I could have sworn she was there.*

He waited by the car for a few moments, until the morning heat began to get to him and his shirt began to stick to his back between his shoulder blades with a light film of sweat. A glance at his watch told him they'd been at the gas station for a good fifteen minutes at least.

Tessa, we need to get on the road, he thought and when she didn't answer, he began to get irritable with her again, despite himself. She was making him sweat— literally—by taking her damn sweet time. She had to know her words had hurt him, cut him to the quick in fact, and she was leaving him out there to suffer a bit more, to twist the knife in a bit deeper.

He gave her another minute—which to him, felt like thirty years—and then frowned, walking into the store. *Two can play this game of yours,* pischouette, he thought, browsing along the snack food aisle and grab-bing three Hostess cherry pies. He tucked a bag of bar-becue pork rinds atop these, then went to the cooler section and grabbed a bottle of sweetened iced tea.

"How'd you hurt your hand?" the cashier asked, making idle conversation as she rang up the food.

"Got shot yesterday," Rene replied, drawing a dubious, if not withering glance. "Say, *chère*, where are your bathrooms?"

"Outside and around the corner to your left," the woman replied, reaching beneath the counter. "Here. You'll need the key."

Rene cradled the brown paper sack with the food and drinks in the crook of his injured left arm and walked out the front door, back into the oppressive heat. He followed the sidewalk to his left and around the building, meaning to knock on the door to the ladies' room and try to convince Tessa to come out. *And if that doesn't work, I'll just kick the goddamn door down and drag her out.*

He stopped in surprise to see the key to the women's restroom lying on the ground just outside the closed door. Beside it was an unopened Snickers candy bar, Tessa's favorite. She'd told him this only last night, back before he'd gone and fucked everything up.

"My grandmother would always bring these back for me and my brothers and sister when she'd go on trips away from the farm," she'd told him as she'd unwrapped one and taken a wolfish bite. He'd grabbed it for her from the motel vending machine, and had found it cute, if not sort of sexy, the way a string of caramel had drooped down over the curve of her bottom lip to drape momentarily against her chin. "One for each of us, and we'd all sit on the floor of her bedroom and eat them together."

Rene leaned over, hooking the restroom key ring with his finger, picking it up off the sidewalk. He rapped his knuckles lightly against the door before trying the knob. "Tessa? You in there, *pischouette*?"

When she didn't answer, he frowned and set the bag on the ground. He knocked again, louder this time. "Tessa, it's Rene. Open the door or I'm coming in."

Still nothing. His frown deepened and he used the key to unlock the door. He felt his heart shudder to a sudden, dismayed halt when he found the bathroom empty, Tessa's purse upturned on the floor, her belongings scattered across the chipped gray linoleum.

Viens m'enculer. Fuck me.

He turned, letting the door slam behind him as he rushed around the front of the building again. He looked around frantically for any sign of her, opening his mind, straining to sense her. *Tessa!* he called out. *Tessa, where are you?*

He couldn't think straight. He couldn't breathe. His heart hammered in his chest, and a thousand horrifying images flew through his mind—the strung-out kid from yesterday . . .

He survived somehow. He wasn't dead and he followed us here, grabbed her!

. . . the Brethren Elders . . .

Did they block our telepathy somehow and keep hidden from us? Did they take her?

. . . any number of potential circumstances, each more horrendous than the last.

Christ, she's been abducted . . . beaten . . . robbed . . . raped . . .

Oh, viens m'enculer, *the baby!*

Tessa! he shouted mentally, darting in and around parked cars at the gas pumps. *Tessa, open your mind! Tell me where you are! Tessa!*

There was no sign of her. No one he spoke with, no one he stopped had seen her. The cashier remembered her, but hadn't seen her since she'd left with the bathroom key.

"Do you want me to call the police, honey?" she'd asked, because Rene's alarm must have been apparent in his face. "There's a state police post just up the—"

"No." He'd shaken his head, cutting her short. "No, thanks."

As he said this, he had held the cashier's gaze,

opening his mind and reaching out to hers. He hadn't said another word aloud, but hadn't needed to. In that moment, one reflexive, split second, he'd eradicated the woman's memories not only of him and his inquiry, but of Tessa, as well. The last thing he needed was for her to call the police and report a missing person, despite his insistence not to. *The police do not need to be involved in this.*

He returned to the ladies' room and collected Tessa's things, her cell phone and lipstick and whatnot off the floor. He didn't know what else to do. He felt exactly as he'd felt when he'd been shot in Vietnam, when the initial pain had worn off, and he'd been left with a handful of his own entrails, his gut blown open. Then, as now, he'd reacted mechanically, his brain utterly on bewildered autopilot.

Christ, what have I done? he thought, distraught. *Why did I have to take so fucking long in the store? What if that's when it happened? What if she screamed for help and I missed it? She wouldn't have even fucking been in here if I hadn't been such a jackass, if I hadn't picked a fight with her.*

Tessa! He opened his mind again, straining to sense her. *Tessa, please, tell me where you are!*

And then it occurred to him.

The birds.

There were trees around the convenience store and telephone wires lining the street. He was literally surrounded by birds.

Rene left the bathroom and stood out in the sunshine, closing his eyes, tilting back his head and opening his mind. He called to the birds as he had since he'd been a boy, sensing the fluttering, darting impressions of their thoughts within his mind. There were dozens and he summoned them, sending them out, flying in all directions. He could see through their eyes, rapid-fire, overlapping images in his mind of the sprawling New Mexico landscape around him, miles covered in literally the blink of an eye. The birds swooped and darted along the interstate, and one car in particular drew his attention—a maroon Jaguar.

I've seen that car before, not ten minutes ago, he thought. *It was here at the gas station. It drove right past me.*

When he saw through the bird's eyes that the car had a Kentucky-issued license plate, his brows furrowed, his hands closing into reflexive fists. *Son of a bitch, they took her,* he thought. *The Elders—those bastards. They found us.*

He sent the bird in more closely; the Jaguar was accelerating but through the bird, he caught a quick, heartbreaking glimpse of Tessa in the passenger seat, her eyes tearful, a thin crust of blood beneath her nose. There was only one other person in the car that he could see; a man who didn't look much older than Rene, and sure as hell not like anything he'd ever consider an Elder.

But he's Brethren, he thought, as the car sped away and the bird was only able to follow now from above. *He's got to be—those tags are from Kentucky. If he's not one of the Elders, then who the hell is he?*

Even as he thought this, he realized.

"Martin was a horrible man," Tessa had told him. *"He hated my grandfather and punished me because of it. He'd punch me, slap me, knock me to the ground. He'd take off his belt and whip me with it, leave me black and blue . . . sometimes so much I couldn't even walk."*

"Oh, Christ," Rene whispered, aghast. He hurried for his car, clutching Tessa's purse in his injured hand and digging his keys out of his pocket with the other. *Oh, Jesus,* he thought. *He followed her somehow, found her, took her. That son of a bitch is her husband.*

He drove like the proverbial bat out of hell, throwing the little Audi into gear and leaving rubber from his tires seared against the pavement. It hurt like a son of a bitch to close his injured hand around the steering wheel, but as he floored the accelerator and headed for the interstate, he gritted his teeth and bore it.

Martin Davenant had found Tessa, and it didn't take a wealth of imagination to figure out what he had in store for his runaway bride.

He'd punch me, slap me, knock me to the ground. Tessa's words kept reverberating in his skull, brutal knife points scraping at his heart. *He'd take off his belt and whip me with it, leave me black and blue . . . sometimes so much I couldn't even walk.*

He'd never tried to drive before while maintaining a mental link with birds. It took all of five seconds to realize there was no way in hell he could make it work. The main problem was that birds weren't like human beings. Their thoughts were simple, their memories limited and most of their brain capacity was reserved for instinct. They didn't have distinctive personalities to distinguish them from one another, and the only way Rene could tell one bird's point of view from another was if he held an exclusive and unbroken mental connection with them. Which, as he discovered, was impossible when one was trying to drive.

He realized this at about the same time the Audi drifted across the center lines of the two-lane highway leading to the interstate ramp, and headlong into the path of an oncoming tractor trailer. He wasn't watching where he was going because his mind was fixed on the flurry of images he was receiving from the bird still tailing Martin's maroon Jaguar. When the eighteen-wheeler blasted its horn at him, Rene jerked, severing the mental connection with the bird in his startled fright.

"Viens m'enculer!" he cried, wrenching against the steering wheel, cutting the Audi back into its rightful lane. The semi flew by, close enough for the wind off its trailer to rock the little sports car violently, and Rene was pretty sure he wasn't only imagining the hand thrusting

out from the window of the cab—the one balled in a fist with its middle finger strategically pointing skyward.

"Christ," Rene whispered, his voice breathless and shaky. In fact, his whole damn body was shaking and it took him a long second before he realized he'd lost the bird. And therefore he'd lost Tessa, as well.

"Goddamn it."

He hadn't seen the Jaguar get on the interstate, so he had no idea which way it had been traveling. But he had a pretty fucking good idea. *This interstate only goes two ways,* he thought. *East and west. And that pony farm of Davenant's sure as shit isn't west of here.*

And with that, he turned the wheel, sending the Audi whipping down the entrance ramp for the east-bound lanes, racing back across the New Mexico countryside in the direction from which he'd come the day before.

Interstate 10 might have only gone two ways, but a hour and a half later, as he stood beside his car, parked on the shoulder, Rene wondered if maybe he hadn't picked the wrong goddamn one.

"Viens m'enculer," he said, then uttered a hoarse little cry and smashed his fist against the roof of the Audi.

His left fist. The one with the gunshot wound.

"Owwww, goddamn it!" Rene howled, clutching his hand against his belly and staggering backward as pain lanced through the entire left side of his body. When it had subsided down to a dull, throbbing ache and he could breathe again, he stumbled back toward the car and leaned heavily against it.

"Son of a bitch," he whispered. For at least the millionth time, he opened his mind and strained to sense any hint of Tessa's presence whatsoever. He didn't expect to feel her and was no longer dismayed or disappointed when he couldn't. *Where are you,* pischouette?

Give me a sign, a thought, a big "fuck-you-Rene"—anything. Come on, Tessa. Help me here.

He'd fought traffic as the interstate had cut through the heart of El Paso, and was now somewhere south of the city, just past exit 42. *Did they stop in El Paso for some reason?* he wondered because he'd seen no sign of the maroon Jaguar. *They can't still be ahead of me somehow. I've been driving damn near ninety miles an hour all this time!*

"Where are you, Tessa?" he asked as traffic rushing by on the interstate sent a smart, hot breeze flapping into his face. *Jesus Christ, am I going the wrong way? Could they be going west instead? But why? Martin Davenant wouldn't know where Brandon is, where he's going, and Tessa sure as hell wouldn't tell him.*

"It's east," he told himself, shoving his hair back from his brow. "It's east, goddamn it, they have to be going east. I just haven't caught up to them yet, that's all."

Since he was still for the moment and didn't have to worry about plowing headlong into oncoming traffic, Rene closed his eyes and opened his mind again, this time reaching out to the birds. He'd never tested himself, never pushed the limits of his abilities, and figured now would be as good a time as any. *What the hell,* he thought, widening the scope of his telepathic range for miles in all directions like a big, broad, mental umbrella.

The effect was immediate and staggering; he didn't know how many birds he'd inadvertently stumbled upon, but from the looks and feel of things inside his skull it was thousands of them, if not ten thousand, all crashing into his brain at once.

"God . . . !" he gasped, buckling at the waist, nearly crumpling against the side of his car. He shoved the heel of his hand against his forehead, his brows furrowed, his teeth gritted as he struggled to make sense of the maelstrom of thoughts he was picking up from the birds. He saw what they saw, felt what they felt, heard what they heard, and it overwhelmed him in a dizzying internal cacophony. It was so disorienting, nearly painful, he moved to break the connection, to close his mind.

And then he saw it—a low-slung maroon sedan. His mind had come across a hawk floating on a thermal draft over the interstate; through its small but sharp eyes, he could see the telltale, shield-shaped red and blue sign with the unmistakable numerals, *10,* emblazoned across the center. As the hawk swooped over the maroon car, Rene caught it with his mind, simultaneously breaking his mental bond with all of the other birds and focusing solely on this one. The hawk circled the highway in a broad circumference, following the sedan until it drove past a landmark by which Rene could orient himself—a ramp for exit 49.

Son of a bitch, they're less than ten miles ahead of me!

Rene jerked himself out of the hawk's brain and hurried around to the driver's side of the Audi. He didn't bother with a seat belt, and only barely bothered to swing his prosthetic leg around and out of the way of his left foot—this only out of necessity, because he needed the space to reach the accelerator. When he'd bought the car, he'd been told it was electronically limited to topping out at 130 miles-per-hour. *Guess it's time to find out for myself,* he thought grimly, as he put it in gear and roared back onto the highway.

He didn't hit 130, but came awfully damn close. He might have reached it, had he not seen the maroon sedan parked in the emergency lane just before the ramp for exit 55, its emergency flashers marking a pulsating, staccato beat. As he approached, he watched a man get out of the driver's seat and jog around toward the passenger's side, where upon he opened the back door and leaned inside, all but disappearing from Rene's view.

Rene stepped on the brakes, slowing the Audi and pulled it to a sliding, skidding halt in the gravel-strewn lane behind the sedan. Along the way, as he'd been driving, he'd wrestled with the steering wheel using his injured left hand—gritting his teeth against pain the whole time, as he'd forced himself to curl his fingers about the wheel—and fished his Sig Sauer P228 out of the glove box with the other. He held the pistol—loaded, cocked and potentially lethal—in his lap and didn't even bother turning off the Audi's still-growling engine after throwing it in park.

He got out of the car and walked toward the sedan, his stride wide, his pace brisk, his brows narrowed with murderous intensity. Davenant hadn't even noticed him yet, still too fucking busy with whatever he was doing in the backseat. When Rene drew closer and heard the hoarse but distinctive sounds of someone screaming, shrill and nearly sobbing, he moved even faster, raising the gun to level it at head-height.

"Get your fucking hands off her," he seethed, ignoring the pain that ripped through his arm as he clapped his left hand against Davenant's shoulder. He jerked the other man backward and spun him around, slamming him against the car door frame. He shoved the business end of the nine-millimeter into Davenant's face, flattening his nose beneath the steel muzzle.

And then realized.

He'd never seen Martin Davenant in his life, but was willing to bet the man wasn't traveling with a wailing infant in the backseat. A second glance now revealed what he'd been too seized with emotion to realize before—the car he'd been following wasn't a Jaguar at all, but a Hyundai, the sleek silhouette of the sedan similar, but not identical, to Davenant's.

Viens m'enculer, he thought, watching in dismayed horror as a pale pink pacifier dropped from the man's hand and bounced to the gravel and dirt below.

"Oh, Christ . . . !" the man whimpered, his eyes

enormous and nearly crossed as he gawked at the pistol against his nose.

There was a woman in the front passenger seat, a woman who shrieked loudly now, her voice momentarily drowning out the peals of the unhappy baby. She all but scrambled over the center console inside the car, fighting against the restraint of her seat belt's shoulder harness, trying desperately to throw herself protectively over the child.

Viens m'enculer.

Which turned out to be *children*—in addition to the baby, a little boy no more than three years old sat belted into a booster seat on the driver's side, round-eyed and frightened as he blinked at Rene.

"Please don't!" the woman screamed, trying to wrap her arms simultaneously around both the little boy and the bucket of the baby's car seat. "Oh, God, please don't hurt my babies!"

Viens m'enculer, Rene thought. *Fuck me.*

"Please," the man said, his voice shaking, his hands raised. "Please . . . take whatever you want. Anything you want, mister. Just please . . . please don't hurt my family. Please."

"I'm sorry," Rene whispered, lowering the gun. In that instant, he opened his mind, reaching out to both the man and his wife, calming them as abruptly and effectively as an intravenous sedative. The woman stopped screaming; she moved, sliding away from the children and back into her seat, her expression softened and nearly dull, her gaze distracted and dazed.

The man's hands dropped limply to his sides and he stood there, blinking over Rene's left shoulder like a marionette at the ready, waiting for someone to come along and pick it up by the strings. In that moment, Rene obliterated from their minds any memory of him whatsoever.

I'm sorry, he thought.

"Mommy?" the little boy inside the car whimpered. "Daddy?"

Rene leaned over to look into the car, and the boy shrank in his car seat, all wide and frightened eyes. The baby—a girl to judge by the fuzzy pink, ruffle-trimmed jammies—continued to howl, drumming her small hands and feet in indignant outrage.

The man's name was Vincent Thomas. The woman was his wife, Yvonne. These were their children— Nathan James, who was two and a half, and Olivia Marie, who was three months old.

Rene knew these things because he could see them plainly in Vincent's and Yvonne's minds, just as he could see they'd been on their way to Vincent's mother's home in Alamo Alto.

Christ have mercy, I'm sorry.

"Hush now, *petit*," he said softly, reaching into the car and brushing his fingertips lightly against the baby's face. At this caress, the baby instantly hushed, blinking up at him with wide, glistening, curious eyes. Her skin was impossibly soft, nearly velveteen, flushed and warm to his touch. He could smell her; a sweet infusion of baby lotion, lavender soap and underlying these, the hot rush of her blood. He could feel her in his mind, the same sensation of sunshine and warmth that he'd felt when he'd touched Tessa's belly, only stronger this time, more developed and cognizant.

"Her name is Olivia," said the boy, Nathan. Rene was aware of his thoughts, as he was the baby's, but made no move yet to control or manipulate either of them. Surprisingly, there seemed no need; Nathan's momentary fright had likewise waned as Rene had touched the baby and now, seeming somehow satisfied that Rene posed no threat, the boy smiled at him shyly. "She dropped her binky."

"Here." Rene reached down, picking the fallen pacifier from the ground. "Why don't you hold onto it for her then, *petit*?"

The painful realization that he'd missed out on this, that he might have built a life with Irene and raised their baby together, that they might have taken midmorning drives to Grandma's house, left him nearly breathless with remorse and heartache.

"Is my daddy sleeping?" Nathan asked.

"*Oui, petit.* Daddy's sleeping." Rene smiled and nodded once. "But he'll be awake again when I'm gone. Don't you worry."

He would have given anything—traded all of his money, every last fucking dime from his considerable fortune—to have someone say that to him, that magic, precious, powerful word: *Daddy.* He might have had a second chance for that; he'd thrown it all away with Irene, but he might have had it again with Tessa and her unborn child. *If I hadn't fucked things up. And oh, Christ, now she's gone and I'm never going to get her back. I've lost it all again and it's my fault.*

He drew back from the car, seized with a sudden, powerful loneliness. "You forget about me now, *petit,*" he said, opening his mind again. "You and your wee *souer,* no?"

He saw the little boy nod, his gaze growing dreamy, just as his mother's had. Only the baby, Olivia, continued blinking at Rene as he turned to walk away, her eyes bright and fascinated, her little mouth forming an endless series of *oooo*s and *aahhh*s.

Chapter Fifteen

Brandon had always been more perceptive than Tessa, more aware of what he called the *chi* of things in many ways. Like the afternoon when they'd discovered the crumbled remnants of what she now believed to have been the Morin clan's original great house; the electricity in the air Tessa had sensed about the rubble—and been eerily fascinated by— had affected Brandon on some deeper, more visceral level. The place had disturbed him.

The *chi* of things. That's what he had always called it, some kind of foreign term associated with the martial art of aikido, which Brandon had studied through Lina's older brother, Jackson.

"Aikido" means "the way of harmony with ki," he'd told her once, when they had been sixteen, only a couple of months after they'd found the old ruins out in a field. He'd accompanied her to the third floor of the great house, to the ballet studio, and while she'd practiced at the barre, he'd stood nearby, practicing aikido moves in a choreographed fashion he called *kata*. He had taught her some aikido maneuvers over the years, wrist locks and other techniques that seemed simple enough in the demonstration, but proved to be devastatingly effective in the implementation.

When they had finished, they'd sat together on the floor, their backs pressed against one floor-to-ceiling mirror panel while facing another of identical proportions on the opposite side of the room.

Ki—as in the middle part of aikido—*is a derivative of the Chinese word,* chi, he'd signed, finger-spelling the unfamiliar terms, his hands moving swiftly, deftly in the air.

What does it mean? she'd signed in reply, to which he'd offered a shrug.

Some people say it's in everything and everyone, he signed. *Everywhere—all around. It's a sort of energy that flows through you and surrounds you.*

She'd given him a dubious look, the corner of her mouth hooked in wry amusement. "Use the Force, Luke," she'd deadpanned, and he'd laughed silently.

Exactly, he signed, giving her a playful shove.

She had shoved him back, then leaned her temple against his shoulder, resting. *Grandmother Eleanor and the Grandfather come home today,* she thought, opening her mind so he could hear her. It had been November; Augustus and Eleanor had traveled to Lexington for a nearly three-week long annual breeding stock Thoroughbred auction. As she spoke, Tessa toyed, in fond habit, with the green sapphire pendant around her neck, her sixteenth birthday gift from Eleanor. *I hope she brings us back Snickers bars.*

It had been a while since Eleanor had indulged in what had once been a standard wrap-up to her adventures. As her grandchildren had grown older, animosity between Brandon and their older brother, Caine, had magnified, and the two young men seldom made or found the opportunity to be in the same room together anymore. It was an arrangement Eleanor seemed to respect, and her habit of bringing candy for them and telling them about the world beyond the farm had fallen by the wayside as a result.

I miss that. Tessa sighed wistfully, gazing across the room in a distracted fashion at her reflection to find Brandon watching her through the mirror as she tugged the sapphire lightly to and fro along its chain. She had thought he would echo her sentiment; had expected it, actually, and was surprised when he said nothing in reply. She tilted her head, glancing up at him, quizzical. *Don't you, Brandon?*

He shrugged. *I guess.*

She poked him lightly in the ribs with her elbow. *Oh, come on. Sure you do. Caine wasn't always such an asshole to you—especially not when we'd all sit around with Grandmother and listen to her stories. We all looked forward to it.*

Again, she expected agreement from him, some manner of concession, but again, none came. He didn't say anything and Tessa sat back from his shoulder, puzzled. She touched his arm to draw his gaze. "Didn't we?"

He shrugged again. *I guess.* He flipped his hand dismissively, as if to say, *Whatever.*

Tessa pulled against the crook of his elbow again so he could watch her lips move as she spoke. "Maybe we could just go together," she suggested. "You and me."

She couldn't blame Brandon for wanting to steer clear of Caine. What had always been pretty much prankish bullying in childhood had swelled to out-and-out abuse as they'd grown older. Sometimes Brandon stood up to Caine, but most times, he simply endured his brother's contemptuous remarks and physical blows, despite the fact that he could have probably kicked Caine's ass. Tessa had never really understood it until she'd moved to the Davenant house a year later, and fell victim to abuse of her own. Sometimes it was simply better to weather a storm without complaint if there was no hope of ever escaping it.

"We won't tell Caine," Tessa had offered. "It'll

just be the three of us—you, me and Grandmother Eleanor." With a smile, she leaned forward, poking him again in the ribs. "And all of the Snickers bars just for us."

He shrugged away from her, his smile more polite than anything. *No, thanks,* he signed. *But you go ahead.*

Again, he cut his eyes momentarily to her necklace, the green sapphire pendant, and Tessa had blinked in surprise. Their birthday had only been a month ago, the twelfth of October. Was Brandon angry that Eleanor had given such an obviously extravagant gift to her?

"Sweet sixteen is more special for girls," Eleanor had told her with a wink and a doting smile.

Just before Eleanor had surprised and delighted Tessa with the gift, she'd caught sight of her grandmother and twin brother together in the great house foyer. Neither had seen Tessa at the top of the stairwell at first; Eleanor had been cradling Brandon's face between her hands in fond fashion, smiling and speaking quietly, words Tessa didn't glean. She suspected she'd been forewarning Brandon about the necklace, offering some explanation as to why she was giving it to Tessa, because all at once, Brandon had frowned, his brows narrowing, and shook his head, jerking himself rather forcefully away from Eleanor.

Was he jealous?

"Grandmother Eleanor loves you, Brandon," she said. "She loves us both. Don't you know that?"

I know plenty about Grandmother Eleanor, he replied with a quick glance at the necklace again, his brows narrowing, his expression clouding.

"What?" she'd asked. "What's that supposed to mean?"

But he didn't answer her at first, keeping his mind enigmatically closed. She didn't know how he could do this; he could communicate with her through his mind, but somehow keep his thoughts otherwise utterly blocked from her. At the time, she'd simply dismissed it as an idiosyncrasy in his mental abilities, something that was the result of the grievous head injuries he'd suffered as a child.

"What's that supposed to mean?" she asked again, frowning now.

His expression softened, his mouth unfolding in a slight, crooked smile. *Olive oil,* he mouthed, a turnabout of her favorite, long-standing joke; the words, when spoken aloud, looked identical to *I love you* to one who was deaf and read lips. He meant to diffuse the sudden, peculiar tension with this. *Nothing,* he said, his mind open enough to speak—but the rest like some broad and impenetrable wall, the thick and impregnable battlements of some medieval castle. *It's nothing, Tessa. Never mind.*

Rene had told her he thought Brandon was stronger than even the Elders, that this was part of the reason why they were so determined to find him, but whether that was true or not, Brandon had always been more telepathically sensitive than Tessa—even though he refused to believe this. That morning over breakfast, he'd kept cutting his eyes toward the restaurant window, his gaze drawn to the interstate, his expression inexplicably puzzled. He hadn't said anything about it, and Tessa had been too preoccupied with the brewing tension between her and Rene to ask him, but now she wondered.

Did you sense Martin following us? Did you know somehow, Brandon?

As she sat in the passenger seat of Martin's car, watching the landscape whip past beyond the window, she wished with all of her heart for even one brief minute of Brandon's ability, the way he could keep different parts of his mind opened or closed, like water-tight compartments in a ship. *Help me, Rene,* she wanted to cry out in her mind without Martin noticing. *Please, Rene—I'm need you!*

Not that she might have needed Brandon's power. Martin had been on his cell phone nearly from the moment they'd hit the interstate, too distracted to do more than glance occasionally in her direction, much less notice whether or not she used her telepathy.

". . . I don't know," he said for at least the thousandth time, his brows furrowed, his expression exasperated. It hadn't taken a genius to figure out to whom he was speaking. "Goddamn it, Monica, we're heading west on I-10, and beyond that, I don't fucking know! I didn't expect to grab her at a goddamn gas station bathroom, so I didn't plot out a fucking itinerary."

Tessa dabbed at her nose with her fingertips, sniffling experimentally. The blood had dried, sticky and crusted against her skin, and she tried to rub it away.

"No, you stay there," Martin groused. "Just stay put, goddamn it. You have a credit card for the Broughman account if something comes up. Use it."

She decided to risk it, at least in part, and opened her mind. She didn't say anything; she just tried to sense Rene, see if she could feel him somehow. Surely by now he'd figured out she was gone. Even if he thought she'd holed up in the bathroom to piss him off, he'd have gone to look for her. Hopefully he'd found her purse spilled all over the ladies' room floor and realized something had happened. Hopefully he was looking for her somehow, some way—no matter how angry they'd been with each other.

Because last night meant something to him, she thought, closing her eyes against a stinging swell of tears. *I know it did. I was stupid to think otherwise, to get mad at him over nothing.*

She tried to sense him, but she couldn't, not even when she braved opening her mind further, straining to feel even a trace of Rene's presence anywhere close by.

Where is he? she thought, bewildered and frightened all over again. *Why isn't he coming for me?*

She jerked, gasping in start as Martin reached out, shoving his hand roughly beneath her shirt. He balanced his cell phone between his left shoulder and ear while driving with his left hand and he pushed the flat of his right palm against her stomach. For one wild, panicked moment, she thought he meant to keep right on reaching up, to grope her breasts and she shoved him away.

"Yes, I can still sense the baby," Martin said into the phone, frowning. "Hold on."

He slapped her hard before she could raise her hand to try and ward him off, sending fresh blood trickling from her nose.

"I can sense it," he said again, returning his attention to the phone. "Yeah, she had the ledger, too. How the hell do I know if all the records are there? I haven't had a chance to check yet."

He prattled on, telling Monica about the deal to follow Brandon. Tessa could hear bits and pieces of the woman's end of the conversation whenever her voice would raise, growing sharp or imperative, like now. She couldn't make out the words exactly, but that tone told her plenty—Monica didn't think it was a good idea.

"Look, do you want this or not?" Martin snapped finally, nearly shouting into the phone. "Jesus Christ, do you want to keep the status quo for goddamn chump change or do you want to be the first wife of the dominant house? Isn't that what you're always fucking harping on me about?"

The status quo. Tessa thought about the mysterious ledger she'd taken from him, the invoices, statements and three million dollars in payments to a company called Broughman and Associates. And hadn't he just said something a few minutes ago to Monica about that? *"You have a credit card for the Broughman account if something comes up. Use it,"* he'd told her.

Why would Martin have a credit card in that company's name? she wondered. *Is he working for them or something?*

It didn't make sense. Martin worked as a mid-level accounting manager for Bloodhorse Distillery, but like any other Brethren, his contact with the human world beyond this scope was strictly prohibited. And even though all of the Brethren had contributed to their considerable wealth over the centuries, control of it rested solely in the hands of the dominant clan and its Elder. While that changed as male heirs were born or died, at the moment, it meant that the Brethren's fortune belonged, for all practical purposes, to Tessa's grandfather.

Martin was paid a stipend for his work for the distillery, at least on paper, but he had no need for money outside of this. The Elders, with Augustus Noble's approval, provided him with everything he needed—clothes, food, shelter, cars, even the disgusting cigarettes he smoked so manically.

"I don't trust the stupid bitch, either," Martin said. Aside from the blow he'd just delivered to her, he seemed to have forgotten Tessa was even in the car with him. He ranted and raved furiously on the phone, and she watched in undisguised alarm as the speedometer on the Jaguar edged over the ninety-miles-per-hour line. "Not for one minute. But what choice do we have? Do you want that son of a bitch Augustus Noble to find Brandon first?"

Martin balanced the phone against his left shoulder again and fished around in his sport coat pocket, pulling out a rumpled pack of Marlboro Reds. He shook one loose, popping it butt-first through the opened end, and slipped it between his teeth. She held tightly to the door handle as he then dug about for a lighter, and the car—now pushing the century mark speed-wise—meandered recklessly back and forth between lanes.

"Because if he does, Monica, you can kiss all of our goddamn dreams of dominance good-bye," he said into the phone, lisping around the cigarette butt as he fumbled, lighting it with a gold-plated Zippo. A sudden, stinking cloud of smoke filled the car, and when Tessa coughed slightly, he frowned and cracked his window. "You do realize that, right? He'll guard that goddamn kid himself now—lock him in his room and shove the key up his own ass for safekeeping."

Tessa moved her hand hesitantly away from her nose. Her fingertips were smeared with blood; bright red droplets had fallen and stained the lap of her pants. The arch of her cheek was still stinging, and she had no doubt that there would be a bruise there. It would be gone as quickly as it came; her accelerated healing would see to that, but in the meantime, it ached just the same.

Rene . . . oh, God, please help me, she thought.

"The Elders aren't going to give a shit if I'm not back by then," Martin said to Monica. "I'll call Father when we stop for the night and he'll handle things from there." He paused as Monica jabbered at him, a sharp flurry of garbled sounds muffled to Tessa's ear. "Yes, I said stop for the night! What, do you think I'm going to drive straight on through clear the hell to Lake Tahoe?"

The Elders know he's left the farm, Tessa thought in surprise. Brandon had left Kentucky without permission, as had she when she'd followed him. Their brother and sister, Caine and Emily, had tailed Tessa to hunt Brandon down, but they, too, had been acting without the Elders' knowledge. *Or at least, Allistair Davenant knows. What's going on?*

Martin uttered a bark of humorless laughter and spared Tessa a withering glance. "Don't worry about that," he said into the phone. "I have no intention of touching the little bitch."

"Martin . . . please . . . !" Tessa gasped, frightened as Martin dragged her by the arm, marching her smartly across the parking lot toward a motel. She'd been sleeping and was now bewildered and disoriented; Martin had driven the entire day through and well past dusk. For more than ten hours now, they'd been on the road, the only occasions to stop coming when she needed to relieve herself—in which case, he'd pull off to the side of the road, force her out of the car and then stand within an arm's length of her while she squatted.

"Yeah. Like I'm going to let you duck into a bathroom all by yourself," he'd scoffed when she'd dared to protest. This had been followed by a sharp, painful cuff to the back of her head, and she hadn't objected anymore.

She was hungry, thirsty, stiff and sore, and she stumbled, falling to her hands and knees when he shoved her unceremoniously across the threshold and into a small motel room.

"Get up." Martin followed behind her, close as a shadow, and she flinched as he slammed the door behind him. He locked the door, then jerked her to her feet. He spun her around to face him, then shoved her backward, sending her sprawling against the bedspread.

"Take off your clothes," he told her, shrugging out of his coat and tossing it against the back of a nearby chair. She watched as he loosened his tie, then the buttons at the cuffs of his shirtsleeves. There was no mistaking what he meant or wanted; if she needed any further clue, the grotesque swell of his erection suddenly bulging from the front of his slacks made it clear.

Oh, God, she thought, scooting back on the bed and shaking her head. *Not that, not now. God, please—not ever again. Not with him.*

"You . . . you told Monica you weren't going to touch me," she said, because now she understood—Monica had been jealous, angered by the fact that Martin had mentioned stopping for the night with Tessa. The only person who'd ever seemed to wield any control or power over Martin outside of his father had been Monica, and Tessa hoped desperately that mentioning her name would be enough to curb his sudden, unwanted interest.

"I lied," he said. "Now take off your goddamn clothes."

The idea of Martin touching her, of his hands falling anyplace against her body where Rene's had caressed with such welcome passion made her feel sick. "No," she said, her voice warbling.

He'd unbuttoned his shirt but paused now, his brow arched as he glared at her, looking momentarily surprised—if not somewhat irritated—by her refusal.

"I said . . ." He stepped toward her, catching hold of the front of her blouse in his fist. She uttered a quiet, frightened cry as he jerked violently against the thin fabric, sending buttons bouncing off the mattress to the floor and ripping seams open wide. ". . . take off your goddamn clothes."

She had never dared to fight back against him even though Brandon had taught her some simple aikido moves, because she'd been trapped in the marriage, trapped in Martin's house. But she wasn't anymore—she had escaped Kentucky and him, and in that moment, as she blinked at the torn front of her shirt, she felt outrage boiling in her, four years' worth overriding her reflexive fear. She felt her grandmother's spirit well up inside, whatever fire she'd inherited from

Eleanor that she'd long believed dormant or dead stoking suddenly, fiercely.

She caught Martin's hand between her own as he released her shirt. Just as she had with Rene only two nights earlier, she jerked against Martin's arm, suddenly craning his wrist at an unnatural, painful angle. The shocking, unexpected pain of such a simple gesture had left Rene all but paralyzed in her grasp, and the effect was nothing less with her husband. Martin's eyes flew wide in surprise, then wider still at the unexpected pain, and he cried out hoarsely as she wrenched his wrist all the more, forcing him to crash against the floor, dropping to his knees.

"Goddamn it!" he gasped, his face flush brightly, his mouth hanging open. "You . . . you fucking bitch! Let me go!"

"Fuck you, Martin," Tessa seethed, jerking his arm again, taking admittedly sadistic pleasure in seeing pain flash in his eyes. She planted her foot against his chest, the wedge heel of her sandal squarely against his sternum and punted him away.

On her feet in an instant, Tessa scrambled off the bed and bolted for the door. Martin had dropped his keys onto a small table by the air-conditioning unit, and she snatched them as she darted past. Already, a plan had flooded her mind—yank open the door, run across the parking lot, get into the Jaguar and drive like hell. Rene was out there somewhere; she hadn't been able to sense him all day, but she knew he had to be. She clung to this desperate, frantic hope with everything she had. He was out there and he was looking for her.

Rene! she screamed in her mind, grabbing the handle to the motel room door. *Rene, help me!*

She felt a strong, heavy hand suddenly clamp down brutally against her shoulder. Martin whirled her around, shoving her back against the door and she rammed her knee up, catching him squarely in the crotch. His eyes bulged as he uttered a breathless grunt and crashed to his knees.

"Bitch!" he gasped as she darted past him, his hands fumbling against her legs. His fingers closed around her ankle and Tessa yelped, floundering and falling face-first to the floor. "You . . . goddamn bitch . . . !"

She rolled onto her back, scrambling like a crab, driving her heels over and over at his face. "Get away from me!" she screamed, kicking wildly, and in her mind, she cried again: *Rene! Rene, help me! Oh, God, please!*

She stumbled to her feet, trying to dance over Martin's sprawled body and reach the front door. He pawed at her, his hands slapping clumsily for purchase, and she kicked some more, driving him away. She wrenched the door open, but in her blind panic, didn't realize or remember that he'd fastened the chain. The door snapped open no more than four inches before being caught by this short tether, and for a frantic moment, overcome with terror, Tessa couldn't do anything except blink at it, jerking desperately, vainly against the chain.

At last she came to her senses enough to close the door and rip the chain away, leaving it to swing against the alabaster door frame. She moved to open the door, but Martin's hand shot out over her shoulder, smashing it closed once more. His other hand closed in her hair, jerking her back, and she cried out as he tossed her the length of the room. His eyes had rolled over black like a shark's, and his fangs had extended in his fury; he threw Tessa with the preternatural strength of one filled with the bloodlust, and she crashed brutally into the far wall before crumpling to the floor, knocking over the bedside lamp and telephone as she went.

He was on her, leaping across the breadth of the motel room like he was an extra on wires in one of those Chinese fighting movies. She barely had time to get her hands beneath her, to struggle and raise her head before his feet slammed into her immediate view, landing with enough force to shiver the floorboards beneath the carpet.

"Don't!" she gasped, holding out a pleading hand, because he wasn't thinking rationally now; he was in a blind rage, consumed with the bloodlust. He wouldn't feed from her—to do so from another Brethren was considered an abomination—but he meant to hurt her—badly. "Oh, God . . . the baby . . . !"

"Fuck the baby." He grabbed her hair and jerked her to her feet, sending pain searing through her scalp. She cried out again, then her voice cut off sharply as he caught her by the throat, shoving her back against the wall. She felt the drywall crunch beneath her, splintering at the forceful impact, and then Martin raised her aloft, hoisting her off the ground, leaving her feet to pedal and drum helplessly in the air while she gagged for breath.

"You fucking bitch," he seethed, his voice lisping and distorted. His fangs had dropped fully, and his jaw had snapped out of place to accommodate the gruesome lengths. "You could be carrying a goddamn litter of sons in your gut and it wouldn't save you."

Tessa slapped vainly at his hands, her mouth open wide as she gulped for any hint of air. She couldn't force any past the massive, crushing force of his palm against her windpipe and began to see tiny lights flickering in front of her eyes, the room beyond fading into heavy, dusky shadows.

Oh, God, she thought. *Rene . . . oh, God, help me . . . my baby . . . !*

"You're a goddamn lying, stealing Noble whore," Martin said, spraying her face with spittle, leaning close enough so that she could see herself reflected against the glistening, black planes of his corneas, her face twisted as she strangled. "Just like your slut grandmother. So I guess that makes it only fitting that you fucking die like Eleanor."

She didn't even have time to consider this; the shadows closed in on her, a dark and heavy shroud, and her eyes rolled back into her skull. When she heard a sharp report, the sound of the motel room door flying wide open and smashing into the wall; when Martin's hand fell away from her neck and she collapsed to the floor in a shuddering, gagging heap, she thought she was only dreaming. When she heard a screeching, squawking, fluttering din and realized the tiny confines of the room were suddenly filled with a swarm of birds—dozens, if not hundreds of them—she knew. *Oh, God, I'm dead . . . dreaming all of this . . . my God, Martin killed me . . . and the baby . . .*

She heard Martin shrieking, his heavy footfalls as he staggered about, his hands thrown up toward his face as the birds attacked. Shielding her head feebly with her hand, still panting and choked, she looked up blearily and watched him flounder around the room, swinging his fists, trying to ward them off. They tangled their talons in his hair, tore into his face with their beaks, snapping at his eyes, leaving bloody streaks and pockmarks in their wake. There were too many and he couldn't fend them off; he danced in broad, clumsy circles, his voice ripping up shrill octaves as he screamed.

Then, impossibly, she felt a tingling sensation in her mind, like a light caress along the back of her neck, a soft voice whispering near her ear and her eyes flew wide in realization.

"Martin Davenant, I presume?" Rene said, materializing into view like a ghost from behind the swirling cloud of birds. Martin whirled, as startled by his approach as Tessa. She caught a quick wink of light flashing off something metal—a pistol in Rene's hand—and then he smashed the butt of the gun into the side of Martin's head, knocking him out cold and sending him sprawling to the carpet. "Yeah. That's what I fucking thought."

Tessa blinked at Rene, dazed and disbelieving as the birds settled down, either flying out the open door or landing against his shoulders. His hair was swept about his face in disarray and he needed a shave even worse than usual. His shirttails were untucked, his shirt rumpled and wrinkled, and to judge by the scarlet stain on the bandages, his wounded hand had bled again at some point. Like Martin, his fangs were extended, his eyes glossy, featureless and black. He looked a sad, sorry, pissed-off and disheveled mess, like some disgruntled cat that had fallen in the toilet during a flush.

"God, I love you . . ." she murmured, then fainted.

Chapter Sixteen

"Where the hell have you been?"

Rene winced, drawing the cell phone back from his ear slightly as the sharp, angry voice cut loudly through his skull. "Lina, *chère*," he said with a forced smile and even more forced nonchalant cheer in his voice. "Hey, how are you? I was just—"

"Don't give me that 'Lina, *chère*' crap, Rene. You were supposed to meet us in Rillito. I've been trying to call you all goddamn day."

Damn. She sounded really pissed off.

He'd taken a room for the night at a small but charming mom-and-pop motel in Banning, California. By day, the view from just outside the room would probably be spectacular—the slopes of Mount San Gorgonio and Mount San Jacinto were visible in the distance. By night, there wasn't much to see at all but a large, pale moon suspended overhead, draping the valley in dim illumination.

He sat on the side of a full-sized bed—the largest the motel had to offer—and glanced down at Tessa, who lay beside him. She was curled up on her side with her hands near her face like a small child. He reached down and brushed the cuff of his knuckles gently against her cheek, where a large, dark bruise had developed, marring her pale, porcelain skin. She had similar bruises around her neck, a violent splay of purple and black where Martin Davenant had tried to throttle her and more contusions around her right eye. She hadn't roused from consciousness long enough to tell him what had happened, but he didn't really need her to.

Christ Almighty, pischouette, he thought, momentarily choked.

He'd tried his best to clean her up once he'd carried her from the car into the room. Using a cool, wet rag, he'd bathed her face gently, dabbing at the blood smeared and crusted. Her shirt had been torn nearly to shreds, and he'd eased her carefully into one of his, slipping the old T-shirt over her head and drawing each of her long, slender arms through the sleeves.

There had been nothing arousing in this act of redressing her. She had seemed frail to him, and he'd handled her gingerly, with all of the deliberate and delicate care he might have a fragile, priceless piece of glass. She'd whimpered in her sleep as he'd moved her, even though he'd tried his best to disturb or hurt her as little as possible and he'd spoken softly to her all the while, murmuring nonsensical things to her in French; comforting words and phrases his grandmother had offered him in his youth whenever he had been hurt, sick or scared.

"Rene?" Lina snapped hotly in his ear. "Are you there?"

"Yeah," he said, and he had to tear his eyes away from Tessa and clear the sudden, hoarse strain from his voice. "I'm here, *chère.* I'm sorry. My cell phone hasn't been able to get any service all day. This is the first time I've been able to get it to work."

"What about Rillito? We waited for damn near two hours for you guys. We've been worried sick."

"Why?" Again, he feigned a bright tone. "We're fine. Tessa forgot to stop, that's all. She was driving and I was sleeping, so we stopped when I woke up and grabbed some tamales at this little roadside Tex-Mex stand. I tried to call and tell you, but like I said, my phone's been out."

Lina sputtered for a minute. Clearly she still wanted to be angry with him, but he wasn't giving her much of a reason. "Besides, *la pischouette* and I have made a nice day of things," he said, glancing at the bedside table and grabbing a handful of glossy, trifold brochures someone had left out promoting local attractions. "You know, doing the whole tourist thing. We stopped to see the dinosaurs in Cabazon."

"The dinosaurs?"

"Uh, yeah," Rene said, balancing the phone between his shoulder and ear and thumbing open the pamphlet. "Two big concrete dinosaurs. You can see them from the highway. You guys missed them? There's some kind of brontosaurus or something, one of those big ass things from *Jurassic Park*. I don't know." He skimmed through the literature. "There's a creationist museum inside its belly."

Lina was quiet for a moment. "A creationist museum."

"Yeah. You know, that whole Garden of Eden–ible thing. Man and dinosaurs hanging out together. Don't eat the apples. That kind of shit." He threw the brochures on the floor, grimacing. *Christ, shut up, Rene.*

Another long silence. Lina could smell bullshit a mile away and apparently that keen nose of hers worked over the telephone, too. "I'll see you tomorrow in Tahoe," she said, her voice flat.

"What? Come on, *chère.* Don't—" he began, but she hung up abruptly on him, leaving him sputtering into dead air.

Terrific. He flipped the phone closed. *I can look forward to hearing more about that, I bet.*

Tessa moaned softly from the bed. *"Il est bien,"* he murmured, turning and stroking his hand against her face again. *It's all right.* She jerked at his touch this time, her eyes flying wide, her breath tangling in a sharp, frightened breath.

"My baby!" she gasped, her hands darting reflexively for her belly.

"It's all right, *pischouette,*" he said again. "You're safe now."

She still looked wild-eyed and panicked for a moment, as if it took her sleep-dazed mind a few seconds to fully take in where she was, and who she was with. At last, realization dawned on her, and her eyes flooded with tears. "Rene!" she whimpered, pushing herself to a sitting position. She reached for him, hands outstretched and he drew her into his arms, holding her fiercely. "Oh, God!" She shuddered against him. "You came for me! You . . . you came . . . !"

"I'll always come for you, *pischouette,*" he whispered, and as she drew back from him, sniffling and struggling visibly against tears, he cradled her face between his hands. "Always," he promised. "No matter what you do or how much you piss me off, I will come for you."

She tried to laugh, but wound up crying instead, and he hugged her again, closing his eyes and drawing her near. He held her while she wept, her narrow frame racked with tears, and when at last, she'd quieted, he rose to his feet to get her a cup of water. As he brought it back to the bed, he saw her press her hands against her stomach again, her expression twisted with worry.

"The baby is fine," he said, and she glanced anxiously up at him. "I felt for it while you were sleeping. I could sense it inside of you, bright like before."

She must have simultaneously sensed the growing

child, too, as he spoke, because her face softened, and she closed her eyes, heaving a long sigh. "He slammed me into the wall," she whispered. "Threw me across the room. I was so afraid. I thought he would kill my baby." She looked at him, the fear and anxiety suddenly flashing in her eyes once more. "What happened to Martin?"

"He's in the trunk of his car," Rene replied, and when she blinked at him, startled, he added, "Don't worry. I put a bullet hole in it so he could breathe." He reached into his pocket and pulled out a car key hooked to a remote entry pad. "I couldn't just leave that Jag sitting around for the Elders to track down and find, so I figured I'd upgrade our ride. They're not going to think twice if they come across my Audi."

"He . . . he's here?" Tessa's posture grew stiff, her eyes wide like a deer pinned by oncoming high beams. "He's outside in the parking lot?"

"It's all right."

She shook her head. "You don't understand. When the bloodlust comes on him, he's really strong. He . . ."

Rene smiled crookedly, and her voice faltered, fading. "Trust me, *pischouette*," he told her. "Your husband isn't going to be bothering anyone again for awhile yet to come. Least of all you and that baby."

He'd dug out the bottle of Percodan that Brandon had given back to him and crushed a handful of the pills into a fine powder he'd then dissolved in a glass of tap water. The blow to the head from where he'd pistol-whipped Martin hadn't kept the other man out long, but by the time Martin had started stirring again, Rene had already used the electrical cord from a lamp in the other motel room to hog-tie his hands and feet.

"Good morning, sunshine," Rene had muttered, wrenching Martin's head back by the hair and forcing him to drink the cup of drugged water. Martin had sputtered and tried to cough it up, but Rene had clapped a hand over his mouth and forced him to choke down nearly every damn drop. Even with Martin's accelerated Brethren metabolism, Rene figured he had put enough narcotics in to dope a baby elephant. And he had plenty more where that came from. Martin Davenant wasn't going to enjoy the business end of conscious awareness for quite a while.

"What are we going to do with him?" Tessa asked. Obviously the idea that her abusive husband was alive and well and still within close proximity left her uneasy, despite his reassurances.

Rene shrugged. "For starters, I thought we might let Brandon have a few minutes alone with him. I thought your *frere* might appreciate first dibs on the son of a bitch who knocked his sister around like—"

"No!" Tessa grabbed hold of his arm, stricken. "No, Rene, no, you can't tell Brandon!" She looked frantic, nearly desperate, her fingers hooked deeply into the meat of his elbow. "Please, Rene. Please don't."

As he watched, she rose slowly to her feet, her brows twisted, her breath caught between her teeth with pain. When he tried to help her, slipping his arm around the narrow margin of her waist, she shook her head, limping away from him. She went to the bathroom and turned on the lights, flooding the tiny room with stark illumination. He could see her as she leaned over the sink, staring aghast at her reflection in the overhanging mirror.

"Oh . . ." she whispered, round-eyed and trembling, as her hands fluttered toward her face, her fingertips lighting hesitantly against the bruises on her cheeks and throat. "Oh, my God."

She pressed her hand to her mouth and closed her eyes as tears spilled, and Rene went to her, drawing her into his arms again. "*Pischouette,*" he whispered, because it killed him to see her like this, to know how much pain she had to be in and to imagine how horribly she must have suffered.

It had taken all that he had not to kill Martin Davenant. There had been a long, uncertain moment in the other motel room in which he'd stood over Davenant's fallen form, the barrel of the pistol pressed against the other man's temple. Tessa had fainted, and he'd knocked Martin out; there was no one and nothing to stop him from flexing his finger against the Sig Sauer's light trigger and sending a nine-millimeter round through the son of a bitch's corpus callosum and into the floorboards beneath him.

He'd told her that he'd kept Martin alive so that Brandon could have the first crack at him, but that was only partially true. He imagined that the younger man would indeed have appreciated some quality time alone, just Martin Davenant and Brandon's decidedly impressive aikido skills. But there had been another reason.

As he'd stood there, staring down the barrel of the Sig Sauer at Davenant's face in chiseled profile, that little voice inside of his head spoke up.

You might need him alive.

Yeah? he thought in reply. *What the fuck for?*

Leverage, the voice whispered and Rene had glanced across the room at Tessa, who lay on the floor, unconscious. *She's got a monkey on her back,* mon ami. *Ten of them, in fact—the Elders. They're coming for her and Brandon and maybe this guy's the ticket for getting rid of them once and for all.*

His finger had eased against the trigger, his aim wavering. *How?*

I don't know yet, the little voice said. *But we'll see. Besides, if you wait to kill him, your hand will be healed and you won't need Brandon to beat the shit out of him. You can do it yourself.*

That's a very good point, mon ami, he'd conceded, and he'd thumbed the safety back on.

"I . . . I don't want Brandon to see me like this," Tessa said, her voice muffled against the front of his shirt. "Please, Rene. I don't want him to know . . . not about this . . . about any of it . . . the way Martin is." She looked up at him, tearful and battered. "Please."

"All right," he said, cupping her face between his hands and using the pad of his thumb to lightly stroke away her tears. She could have asked anything of him— cut off his remaining leg with a pair of hedge clippers, rip out his own heart, kill someone, kill himself—and he would have in that moment. *Anything for you, Tessa,* he thought. *Anything.*

Chapter Seventeen

"You need to feed," Rene said, but even though she knew he was right, Tessa still shook her head in protest. The last damn thing she wanted was to rip the throat out of some derelict or prostitute while in the throes of the bloodlust.

"No," she said with a wince. Shaking her head hurt. *Everything* hurt. She felt like she'd bruised, strained, sprained or otherwise injured every visible part of her body. *And some invisible ones, too,* she thought ruefully.

"Tessa, listen to me," Rene said. She was mortified that he'd seen her beaten up and battered but there was nothing she could do about it now, no point in trying to cover her face or hide it from him somehow. He'd seen it—the ugly, shameful truth of her relationship with Martin. He knew all about it; hell, it was laid bare and in stark, apparent detail all over her face.

"I know you don't want Brandon to know about Martin hitting you," Rene said. "But we're going to be damn pressed to keep it from him when we're supposed to be meeting him and Lina tomorrow afternoon in Lake Tahoe."

She could see herself in the bathroom mirror over his shoulder, the ruined mess that was her face. Just looking at her reflection was enough to make fresh tears well in her eyes, and she jerked her gaze away.

She remembered being fifteen years old, standing in one of the bathrooms at the great house, using the corner of a damp washcloth to blot at a busted lip Brandon had gained during one of his seemingly never-ending altercations with their brother Caine.

"Why don't you just stand up to him, Brandon?" she'd asked. She'd felt sorry for him, but exasperated, too. "Jackson taught you all of that aikido. Why don't you use it?"

It would be years yet until she married Martin and endured her own litany of abuse, learning firsthand that sometimes things were much more easily said than done. Brandon had eventually stood up to Caine, indeed, only weeks earlier. While he wouldn't say much about it, Lina had told Tessa plenty. Brandon had beaten Caine's face to a mashed and bloody pulp. All those years of shame and intimidation had exploded out of him with brutal force.

I wish I could have fought back against Martin like that, she thought. *I wish I'd been as brave as you, Brandon.*

"You need to feed, *pischouette,*" Rene said again, hooking his fingertips beneath her chin and directing her gaze to his face. "I can buy us another day, tell Lina and Brandon we can't meet them until the day after tomorrow, but after that, the whole sightseeing line isn't going to fly anymore. Lina's not real patient when it comes to bullshit, and she smelled mine a mile away. She just hasn't called me on it yet. If you feed, it will help you heal, make the bruises fade so maybe they won't notice."

Tessa pulled away from him and sat down against the foot of the bed. She didn't want to kill anybody because no matter what he said now, Rene would be angry with her for it. He didn't understand. She wasn't like him; she couldn't control her bloodlust. "I can't, Rene. There's no one I can feed from, and I can't just go out and . . ."

"Yes, there is," he said quietly and she looked up at him, puzzled. "Me, *pischouette.*"

Her eyes flew wide. "What?"

"I'm half human."

"But . . . but . . ." She was so stunned by his offer, for a moment, she could do nothing but sputter. "But you're half Brethren, too." She shook her head. "I can't do that, Rene. It . . . it's an abomination. It's not allowed. It's—"

"A bunch of bullshit from your family," Rene interjected. "Yeah. I know. Look, Brandon fed from me before we left the city, and there wasn't any kind of plague of locusts afterward or—"

"No!" Tessa shot to her feet, her eyes round and alarmed. On the night of her bloodletting four years ago, she had all but blacked out, her mind clouded and consumed by the bloodlust—just as it had been at Rene's old house in Thibodaux. She didn't remember anything except the smell of blood, the bittersweet taste of it, the heat of it as it flooded her mouth.

The next morning, she had slipped out of the great house early, wrapping a long overcoat atop her nightgown and plodding across the cool, dew-draped grass in her bare feet. She'd walked through the fields, ducking around the white-painted slats of fences until she found herself deep in the property, far away from any road or prying eyes. Here, the farm workers lived in rows and rows of small, neat, tended little cottages, bunkhouses that slept ten to twelve farmhands apiece.

The hunting grounds, she had thought, because this was where the bloodlettings were held, where the Brethren converged in a blood-crazed wave during the indoctrination ceremonies. Ordinarily the Brethren fed in discreet fashion, but during bloodlettings, they killed with brutal abandon, tearing open throats, thighs, groins—sometimes three and four Brethren at a time ripping into a single body, gorging themselves wherever and however they could.

Tessa had stood at the crest of a pasture hillock and watched the Kinsfolk humans as they hauled the bodies of those slain toward waiting pickup trucks. The corpses would be burned, then buried elsewhere on the farm. There were hundreds of them, mostly illegal immigrants from Mexico who would never be missed or sought; during bloodlettings, every man, woman and child not of the Kinsfolk were hunted down and slaughtered, and they lay strewn in all directions, ashen corpses with their bodies torn open, their mouths hanging ajar in terrified, eternal shrieks.

"They are cattle," Eleanor had told her with a gentle smile, when Tessa had gone to her, troubled by what she'd seen. Neither could have known that the older woman had less than a week to live past that moment. "Fresh meat for the celebration of slaughter."

Tessa thought of coming to, snapping out of some bloodlust-induced reverie to find Rene lying sprawled on the motel room floor, the flesh of his neck torn back in a gruesome flap to expose meat and tendons, blood vessels and bone, his face frozen in an unflinching mask of terror.

Fresh meat for the celebration of slaughter.

It made her stomach knot at the idea; more than this, it made some visceral place within her heart ache.

"No, Rene, I am not feeding from you," she said. "I'm not like you. I can't do the things you and Brandon can do. I . . . I just can't!"

He looked bewildered. "Of course you can. I'm not special, *pischouette*. Neither is Brandon. Not like that, anyway."

Oh, God, yes you are, Rene, she thought desperately, thinking back to that morning in Louisiana, of the old man struggling and screaming beneath her, the gurgling as he'd sucked in his last, feeble breaths. *You're half human and Brandon had never fed before. Maybe that's what made it easy for him, what keeps it easy for you. But I've fed before—killed lots of times—and I don't know how to stop myself. That's all I know how to do.*

"Tessa . . ." Rene stepped toward her, his hand outstretched. "Listen to me."

"No. You're not going to talk me into this," she said, as he caressed the side of her face, his fingers slipping into her hair. "Stop it, Rene." She tried to swat him away, but he touched her again anyway, his palm warm and comforting as it pressed against her cheek. Eleanor's words kept echoing in her mind, overlapping with the sodden sounds of the dying old man in Thibodaux.

Fresh meat for the celebration of slaughter.

"Stop it, I said!" she exclaimed, giving him a push.

"Tessa, you need to feed if you want to heal fast. There's no other way to do it but this."

"Then I'll just have to tell Brandon the truth," she replied. Rene was looking at her like she was crazy, a mixture of confusion and hurt on his face, and she wanted to explain somehow, make him understand. *I love you, Rene,* she thought, her mind closed so he couldn't overhear. *I don't know what I'd do if I hurt you or . . . or worse . . . ! I could never forgive myself. Never.*

He'd already done so much for her, risked everything, including his life to protect her. *Now it's my turn,* she thought. *I have to protect you this time, Rene— from me.*

An hour later, they sat together on the bed, and she watched uneasily as Rene went through the contents of Martin's suitcase, which he'd apparently pulled out of the Jaguar's trunk when he'd deposited Martin inside. She pressed a cold pack against her cheek, ice cubes wrapped in a little plastic waist-paper bag, then tucked inside one of the motel hand towels.

"What we need is a nice, raw porterhouse," Rene had remarked as he'd presented it to her. When she'd looked at him, puzzled, he'd told her that raw meat helped ease bruising and swelling, particularly black eyes. "And you, *pischouette*, are sporting one hell of a shiner."

"That's absolutely disgusting. Where do you come up with these things?"

"The school of hard knocks—literally," he'd said with a shrug. "I used to get the shit beat out of me all the time as a kid."

"By who?" she'd asked and he'd shrugged again.

"Lots of different people. Mostly this one asshole, Gordon Maddox."

"But why?" she'd asked. "Didn't you fight back?"

"I guess because I was poor. My *mamère* worked at the local Piggly Wiggly and that was all we had to live on besides the good graces of Uncle Sam, on account of the fact my grandpa hurt his back working a shrimp boat, gimped himself to where he couldn't do much of anything except sit around and get drunk. And yeah, I fought back. But it doesn't do you much good when the guy gunning for your ass is twice your size."

It was one of the first times Rene had told her much about himself, outside of the occasions when he'd talked about his wife, Irene, and he'd said this last with a long, pointed look in her direction, as if he knew she was still berating herself for not fighting more against Martin.

"No," she'd murmured, shaking her head, touched not only that he would confide in her, but try to empathize, too. "It doesn't."

"So what is Broughman and Associates?" Rene asked. He'd been sifting through the invoices and records Martin had tucked inside the mysterious ledger, a thoughtful pinch cleaving his brows.

Tessa shook her head. "I don't know. But I think it must be something important." She told him about how furious Martin had been with her for taking the ledger, how frantic he'd been to get it back, and about how his first wife, Monica, had apparently shared these sentiments based on the phone call she'd overheard. "He asked her something about keeping the status quo for chump change—that's how he put it— or becoming the dominant family. But I don't know what he meant. He has a credit card for them, too. I heard him mention that to Monica on the phone. He told her to use it if she needed."

Rene's pensive frown deepened as he scanned the papers again. "You said he's an accountant or something for your grandfather?"

"At the Bloodhorse Distillery, yes," she said. "For all of the Brethren, not just the Grandfather."

"But your grandpa holds the Brethren purse strings, no?" Rene asked, and she nodded. "My guess, then, would be your husband's been skimming off the top of the family till, so to speak. You know, stealing."

"What?" Tessa blinked in surprise. "How could he do that? Those payments are to a company, that Broughman and Associates, not Martin."

Rene dropped her a wink. "He can do that, *pischouette*, because Martin *is* Broughman and Associates."

She must have looked like a fish, her mouth dropped open and gaping, her eyes suddenly flying wide, because he took one look at her and laughed. "It's easy, really. All done on a computer." He waggled his fingers demonstratively, as if at a keyboard. "He figured since he handles some of the bills, why not pay himself through one, too? So he sets up a bank account in the name of this pretend company, gets a couple of credit cards in its name—one for him, one for Monica—then mocks up invoices he processes himself and deposits the money electronically to the account every time. Nobody notices. Nobody knows. Bloodhorse Distillery probably gets bills left and right for all sorts of shit. Who's going to pay attention to one extra?"

"He could get away with that?"

"Sure," Rene said. "As long as no one goes snooping around too much, finds the financial records or double-checks his books. It happens all the time."

Tessa couldn't believe Martin had the balls to steal from the Brethren. *From the Grandfather, no less. My God, he'd be killed if the Grandfather found out about it. What the hell would make him take that kind of risk?*

But she knew.

Augustus sits at the head of the Brethren Elders, puts his sons in all of the choice positions with the farms and distillery, and what does he leave for the rest of you? she'd overheard Monica complain to Martin. *Grunt work and mid-level management. Why doesn't he put you out with the Kinsfolk or the laborers shoveling shit in the barns? It's not fair.*

For as much as she had hated Eleanor for her fine clothes and exquisite jewels, all of the elaborate gifts the Grandfather bestowed upon her, Monica had also coveted them. She was a spiteful bitch whose jealousy toward Eleanor had spilled over to Tessa, as well. Tessa could still remember the momentary bite of chain links against the back of her neck as Monica had snatched the green sapphire necklace from about her throat.

"I had an accountant try the same thing with me a couple of years ago," Rene said. "Only I'm not nearly as fucking stupid as he thought. I like my money." He tapped his brow with his fingertip. "I keep an eye on my money."

"What did you do when you found out?" Tessa asked.

"I ate his liver with some fava beans and a nice chianti," Rene replied solemnly, then laughed. "What the hell do you think I did, *pischouette*? I had the *salaud* arrested. He's serving four years in prison now for embezzlement and fraud."

He folded the records neatly together and tucked them back into the ledger. "What are you going to do with them?" she asked, and he laughed again.

"I don't know, but I'm going to hang on to them, that's for damn sure. I bet we can find ourselves a good use for them."

He glanced over and caught her touching her stomach again. She'd been doing this almost nonstop, either pressing, stroking or rubbing her hand against the slight slope of her belly. She had also kept her mind open, a mental eye of sorts on the baby, with the irrational but unshakable fear that somehow, it wouldn't be all right; that if she broke her mental connection with it, even for a fleeting moment, something might happen, some residual damage from where Martin had hurt her, and the baby would be lost.

I don't know what I'd do if that happened. She'd suffered a maelstrom of emotions since learning that she was pregnant months earlier, a mixture of exuberance and trepidation; joy because of the promise of motherhood, and by that same promise, reservation and fear. But while she'd doubted her own abilities to be a good mother, and she'd been tormented by the idea of raising the baby under Martin and Monica's roof, one thing had always been unquestioned in her mind and heart—she loved the baby. She dreamed of the baby, holding it in her arms, nestled against her breast. She imagined its warmth and softness, the sound of its voice, the fragrance of its skin.

In her mind, she'd imagine the child—a daughter sometimes, a son in others—walking with her on the farm in Kentucky, following the rutted roads that bisected the Grandfather's land. "Do you know how much I love you?" she'd ask.

It was a game Eleanor used to play with her and Brandon, usually right before she would leave on one of her adventures beyond the farm with the Grandfather. While he'd wait, stern-faced and stoically impatient in the foyer, surrounded by luggage, Eleanor would scoop the twins up and kiss them, making them squeal with giggles. "Do you know how much I love you?" she'd say to them, and Brandon, like the son in Tessa's dreams would answer: "To the moon and back again!"

Tessa, like her imaginary daughter would always cry, "More than all of the fishes in the sea!"

She'd daydream about these things, fond games with her child, but had never imagined a father because Martin wasn't one, not like Tessa's had been to her, someone nurturing, protective and caring. Martin had taken after his father, Allistair. She'd lived in the Davenant house; she'd seen Allistair with his children—the incident in which he'd grabbed Martin by the balls in the foyer being par for the course—and Martin had spared his own offspring no similar disdain.

"Tessa?"

She looked up, Rene's voice drawing her from her thoughts. His brows were lifted with concern, and he reached for her, draping his hand lightly against her wrist. "The *bébé*," he said. "It's all right still, no?"

She managed a feeble smile. "It's fine. I just . . . I want to keep checking, that's all. Just to be sure."

Martin had never given a shit about her or, apparently, their baby. And while half the time, Rene seemed exasperated, pissed off or otherwise put out with her, he had still cared enough to take a gunshot to the hand to protect her, not to mention track her somehow across the breadth of New Mexico and come to her rescue. Rene cared about her, as well as the baby, even though he had no right to, and she sure as hell hadn't given him much of a reason to.

I wish you were my baby's father, Rene, she thought.

His expression softened, the worry fading. "You do what you need to, *pischouette,*" he told her with a smile. "Whatever makes you feel safe."

He leaned across the bed and kissed her, pressing his lips gently against the corner of her mouth. It was a tender gesture, nothing sexual or passionate; just a gentle empathy that might have once surprised her coming from him. But no longer.

She closed her eyes as he pulled away, letting the scruff of his beard stubble rub coarsely against her cheek, drawing the light fragrance of him—warm, pleasant and familiar—fill her nose. *You make me feel safe,* she thought. *You're what I need, Rene.*

Chapter Eighteen

Rene waited until Tessa was asleep before going out to the car. He popped the trunk and stood there, looking down at Martin, still hog-tied and gagged. The other man had roused at the rush of fresh air coming into the trunk, the dim orange glow from the light on the underside of the door. He moved feebly, uttering a low, muffled groan around the wadded up washcloth Rene had shoved between his teeth and fettered in place with a torn strip of bedsheet.

"Bon jour," Rene said, closing his hand roughly in Martin's hair. He jerked the man's head up and pulled down the gag.

"You . . . son of a bitch . . ." Martin gasped hoarsely, squinting up at him. His face was a mess of oozing pockmarks and scab-lined scratches from where the birds had attacked and there was dried bird shit and feather down visible in his hair.

"Yeah. Fuck you, too," Rene said. "Tell me, when you slap your wife around, does it make you feel like a man?"

He shoved a plastic bottle to Martin's lips, spilling tainted water into his mouth again. "I mean, do you get off on it, hitting someone half your size? Does it make your dick hard to beat up on a woman, you sick, twisted fuck?"

After Martin's initial gag reflex left some of the drink splashed and slopped, Rene managed to force the rest down his throat. "I really want to know, Davenant." He wrenched Martin's head back farther, forcing a strangled cry from him. "What does it feel like to hit a woman?"

He opened his hand, letting Martin's head drop back to the floor of the trunk. He promptly folded his fingers in toward his palm and sent his knuckles careening brutally into Martin's cheek. He punched the shit out of Martin, hard enough to rattle a tooth loose from the feel of things, the moist, sickening crunch he heard at impact.

"Oh," he said, stepping back, shaking his hand out, his knuckles stinging. "That's how."

Martin choked and sputtered around the washcloth as Rene crammed it unceremoniously back between his teeth, cinching the scrap of sheet tightly against the back of Martin's head. He slammed the trunk closed on Martin's garbled protest, then went around to the backseat and pulled out his folding shower chair.

Birds had relatively short digestive tracts and no sphincters, which meant they pretty much shit anywhere and everywhere without really meaning to. And when you had more than two dozen of them flapping around in close confines, like Martin's motel room, sooner or later, you were going to get dumped on, telepathic control over them or not. Rene had changed his shirt since finding Tessa, but he still felt decidedly grimy. He wasn't a vain man by any stretch of the imagination, but bird shit was bird shit no matter how you looked at it. And since he didn't feel like taking another accidental, graceless swan dive in the tub, it was time to swallow his pride and get out the chair.

Keeping a wary eye on Tessa, he brought it back into the motel room and carried it into the bathroom. He unfolded it, extending and locking the aluminum legs into proper place, along with the molded plastic backrest. The seat was wide and contoured, roomy enough to accommodate his ass while leaving plenty of elbow room to either side. It was comfortable enough, but Rene hated it; hated the way sitting in it made him feel old and crippled and goddamn useless.

But bird shit was bird shit, and so into the shower he went, leaving his prosthetic leg propped against the toilet, his clothes in a heap on the floor. He closed his eyes and reached blindly for the soap as hot water, nearly scalding, hit his head in a stinging spray.

Both his hands hurt now. *But* saint merde, he thought with a wicked little upturn of his mouth as he recalled the sound of his fist hitting the side of Martin's head. *It was worth it.*

Every time he thought about that son of a bitch laying his hands on Tessa, it infuriated and pained him. After she'd fallen asleep, Rene had sat awake for a long time beside her in the bed, stroking his hand lightly against her dark hair, feeling something deep within him ache as he gazed at her bruised, battered face.

It's my fault, he'd thought, anguished. *Goddamn it, if I hadn't been such an asshole to her . . . if I hadn't let her walk away from me at the gas station . . . if I'd gone to look for her sooner instead of taking my goddamn sweet time in the store . . . if I hadn't gone the wrong goddamn way on the interstate . . .*

None of this would have happened if it hadn't been for me.

"*Je suis désolé,* Tessa," he'd whispered to her. *I'm sorry.*

More than just her injuries, her fear for her baby had broken Rene's heart. He'd watched her touch her stomach time and again over the course of the evening, her face fraught with worry, her dark eyes anxious and afraid. Again and again, his mind had turned to Irene, the miscarriage she'd suffered. He had probably been the cause of it, the strain he'd put on their relationship, the stress that had finally destroyed it. He hadn't been there to comfort or reassure her. He'd let her down—just like he'd let Tessa down. And it had damn near cost Tessa her child, too. *Never again,* he swore in his mind. *Never again—by Christ and all that's holy, Tessa, I'll never let you down again.*

He scrubbed his face, opening his eyes and watching water stream down, spattering against the floor of the tub. He sat hunched forward, relaxed and relatively comfortable, his elbows resting on his left knee and the stump of his right leg. His hair clung to his cheeks and forehead in drenched strands; water dripped from the sharp tip of his nose, his lips. Soap bubbles swirled, gathering in a frothy foam against the chrome drain plate while steam curled up, bathing him in misty tendrils.

More than just a bully, a sick, sadistic freak, Martin Davenant was a fool. The man had everything Rene had ever longed for—a bright, beautiful wife like Tessa, the amazing glow of life that was their baby growing inside of her. *A family.* Rene had been so lonely for so long, he would have given anything in the world for what Martin had thrown away with such seeming, callous ease.

I wish you were mine, Tessa, he thought. *You and the* bébé.

The shower curtain drew back, letting in a gust of sudden, cool breeze and he jerked in wide-eyed surprise; he hadn't even heard the bathroom door open. When he saw Tessa standing there, holding the white fabric curtain aside with her hand, he jerked again, choked for breath, momentarily dumbstruck.

She was nude, her petite frame lean and strong, her small but shapely breasts crowned with rose-colored nipples, her flesh creamy and smooth, like a porcelain doll's. She had a ballerina's legs—slender and muscular—and elegant, graceful arms. The delta of her lovely thighs lay marked by a thatch of dark, silky curls; just above these, the outward swell of her womb was slightly pronounced and visible.

"Tessa . . ." he whispered, a sort of stunned, breathless croak. He stared at her for a long, confused, mesmerized moment. And then it occurred to him that just as sure as she was naked, he was, too, his maimed body—the disfiguring absence of his right leg—laid bare and exposed for her to see, stark against the white backdrop of the shower walls and tub.

"Tessa . . ." he said, tearing his eyes away from her beautiful form, looking down in dismay at his own. *Oh, God, oh, Jesus, oh, fuck me, Christ,* his mind rattled, and where the fuck was that niggling little voice of reason when he needed it the most? He reached for his thigh, covering the stump with his hands, his face blazing with bright, humiliated color. "Tessa . . . I . . . I didn't . . . I . . . what are you doing?"

He saw her step into the tub out of his peripheral vision, but couldn't look up at her. He heard the soft rattle of the shower rings as she drew the curtain closed, then she stood in front of him under the heavy stream of hot water. He could see her feet. Her toenails were painted, he noticed with a detached, stricken sort of fascination. A sort of pearlesque shade of pink. Nearly the same color as her nipples, he realized, with a slight glance up.

"What . . . what are you doing?" He found his voice, ripping his eyes away again and oh, Christ, if the ground were to have opened up and swallowed him right the fuck whole, he wouldn't have complained, not one goddamn bit.

"It's all right," Tessa said, her voice gentle and quiet. He felt her touch his face, tilting his gaze up toward her. When he tried to protest again, stammering and choked, she leaned down to kiss him sweetly, silencing him. "It's all right, Rene," she said, cradling his face in her hands, meeting his eyes.

Tessa kissed him once more, pressing her mouth against his, the tip of her tongue slipping between his lips, and Rene groaned softly, his body instantly responding.

He pulled her near, tangling his hands in her wet hair and kissing her deeply. Water streamed down her face, spilling against his own. He touched her, running his hands hungrily along her sleek, soaked curves as she straddled him in the shower chair, placing her lean thighs on either side of his hips. He cupped her breasts in his hands, kneading the bullet points of her nipples between his fingertips as his lips trailed from her mouth to her chin, the angle of her jaw, and from there, along the graceful, downhill slope of her throat.

She leaned back and gasped, clutching at his hair as he slipped her left nipple into his mouth. Using his tongue, he traced circles lightly against the sensitive flesh; with every sweeping pass, her fingers closed more fiercely in his hair. God, he had wanted to taste her for so long; her skin was sweet against his tongue, flushed with blood and desire, hot and wet from the shower's downpour.

His left hand still wasn't worth much of a damn, but with his right, he reached between them, slipping his fingers against her apex and then between the wondrous, warm folds. Tessa began to move against him, undulating against his hand as he touched her at her core, the place that obviously pleased and pleasured her. She moaned lightly, catching his face with her hands, pulling his mouth from her breast and up to her own. She kissed him again and he slid his forefingers inside her, up her hot, slick sheath. She was tight, but another moan and a sudden increase in the pace of her hips let him know she was eager for him.

He whispered her name against her mouth, pulsing his fingers in and out of her, touching someplace deep inside of her and palpating, making her breath hitch against his tongue, her fingernails dig into the

muscles of his shoulders. He was fully aroused; hot,
hard and throbbing with aching, urgent need. The tip
of him brushed with repeated, excruciating friction
between her buttocks every time she writhed against
him, and at last he had to pull his fingers away and
hold her still, catching her hips between his hands.

"Stop," he whispered breathlessly, hoarsely. When
she tried to move again, grinding against his lap, kissing him and whimpering, he laughed softly and again,
forced her to stillness. "Stop, *pischouette. Sie tu plais.*"

She blinked at him, her large, dark eyes round and
confused, somewhat wounded. "What is it?" she whispered, afraid she'd done something wrong. God, it
had been so long since he had last been even this
close to making love to a woman face-to-face, let alone
see it through—close enough that he could read her
every thought and emotion, even without his telepathy, all through the subtle nuances in her face. It had
been so long since he'd last known a woman well
enough to read her so well and goddamn, but he'd
forgotten how good it could feel.

"Nothing," he told her, smiling and kissing her.
"You're just . . . *saint merde,* woman, you're going to
make me shoot off like a clumsy goddamn kid on his
first time." He grasped her hips again and maneuvered
her atop him until the head of his arousal pressed
against her, sliding up between her folds and resting
lightly—agonizingly—against her threshold.

He looked up into her eyes and held her here, pro-
longing the moment, savoring the hungry, veiled look
in her eyes, the way her body trembled against him in
eager anticipation, water streaming down her every
curve and contour in steady, intertwining rivulets.

"Rene . . ." she whispered, and then he plunged
into her, pulling her down against him and entering
her fully in one deep motion. She gasped sharply, and
he caught it against his mouth with a kiss. He kept
one hand against her hip and pressed the other

against the back of her head, drawing her near. As they kissed, he guided her to move again, setting a slow pace at first but letting her build it steadily, each stroke deeper and more powerful than the last. Again, he touched that visceral place inside of her, that deep recess of pleasure, and knew by the way she moved, her hips grinding more quickly, with ever increasing urgency; by the way her breathing grew sharp, hitching, that she was on the brink of climax.

"*C'est lui, Tessa,*" he breathed, lapsing into French without even being aware of it. *That's it.* "*Venez pour moi.*" *Come for me.*

When she came, he could see it—something he had not enjoyed since Irene. He watched her eyelids flutter closed, her brows lift, her mouth slightly ajar almost in a delicate "O." She tightened around and against him, writhing, digging her nails into his skin, her voice escaping her in a breathless cry. It was too much for him to take; he arched his back from the chair, clamping his hands against her hips and spearing into her one last time, crying out hoarsely in release.

When they were finished, he drew his arms about her, holding her against him, tucking his head against her shoulder and gasping as water pelted the back of his skull.

She turned her face down toward him; he felt her lips brush against his ear through his sopping wet hair, and looked up at her. "You all right?" she asked with a smile, her cheeks flushed brightly.

I'm in love, he thought as he kissed her lips. He touched her face, tracing her lips with his fingertips, her nose, lighting against the bruises. *Goddamn, you're beautiful, pischouette.*

"I've never been better," he told her, making her smile widen all the more.

Chapter Nineteen

That night, Tessa slept peacefully, likely the first sound and restful sleep she'd enjoyed since fleeing Kentucky. When she woke the next morning, it was dawn, the first hints of rosy sunshine seeping through the window curtains and Rene was spooned against her from behind, his arm around her waist. She had slept well, but not long; after the shower, they'd tumbled into bed together for another round of lovemaking, a pattern that had repeated itself frequently—and fervently—throughout the night.

She lay there for a long moment, a soft smile playing against the corners of her lips as she enjoyed the simple closeness of him, the warmth of his body. His bandaged hand rested lightly at her stomach, as if even in sleep, he felt protective of both her and the baby. She slipped her fingers through his, still smiling, and drew his hand to her mouth, kissing the back of his knuckles lightly.

He groaned softly as he roused, moving behind her, and when she felt the first hints of arousal, the hard, dim heat of him poking her lightly, it stirred sudden, almost immediate want within her, the way even a glimpse of blood, a momentary whiff of it in the air would stoke her bloodlust.

"Good morning," she said, wriggling her buttocks against his groin and making him groan again.

"Good morning," he murmured groggily, delivering a light kiss to her shoulder but when she rolled over, crawling atop him, straddling him beneath the sheets, he grew tense, his expression apprehensive. "Tessa . . ."

He kept doing this; never in a million years would she have guessed that Rene would remain insecure about the matter of his leg. Every time they made love, Tessa would think that it would be enough; he'd realize it didn't bother her. But then the next time would roll around, so to speak, and he'd grow shy and anxious all over again—so uncharacteristically so, it charmed her.

"Shut up," she told him, grasping him by the wrists and halfheartedly pinning his arms to the mattress. She leaned over, brushing the tip of her nose against his until he smiled. "Now kiss me."

He arched his brow slightly. "Yes, ma'am," he said, obliging her request. As the kiss lingered and deepened, she could feel him growing, the hot, hardened length of him pushing up between them. He didn't need an invitation; she didn't offer him one. She raised her hips slightly, then lowered them again, letting him sink into her, sliding in, deep, slow and full.

"*Mon Dieu* . . ." Rene breathed, closing his eyes. It was all she let escape his mouth; she fell into a swift, grinding rhythm against him and he could do nothing but gasp and cup his hands against her breasts for the ride. By the time she was finished some twenty minutes later, he lay beneath her, gasping and trembling, the muscles in his chest, stacked in his abdomen all sharply defined with a gloss of exhausted perspiration.

"You're going to wear me out, *pischouette*." He looked up at her and smiled, his hands still covering her breasts, his fingertips lightly, almost idly toying with her nipples.

"Tough shit," she replied, giving a playful wiggle against his groin.

"Ah, vraiment?" His brow arched again in amusement. *Oh, really?* "Is that so?" His fingers slipped from her breasts to hook beneath her arms, and she shrieked, writhing in a sudden, convulsive jerk as he tickled her.

"Rene, stop!" she squealed, pitching sideways, landing on the mattress. He leaned after her, catching her again between the ribs, and she laughed, kicking and struggling. "Rene, stop! That tickles!"

"Est-ce que c'est ainsi?" he asked, laughing and ducking as she slapped at him. *Is that so?* "Tough shit."

They tussled together for a few moments and at last fell still, lying side by side and face-to-face in bed, laughing. As his laughter subsided to a soft smile, he brushed her hair back from her cheek.

"How does it look?" she asked. She felt better, the soreness in her body from her fight with Martin all but vanished, but hadn't gotten up to look in the mirror yet that morning. She'd have to face her brother soon; Brandon would see the bruises on her face and at last learn the shameful truth about Martin's abuse, and she wasn't looking forward to it.

"Beautiful," Rene replied, his fingertips lingering against her face.

Her cheeks burned with bashful heat. "I meant the bruises," she said, slapping his hand lightly away. She rolled over and slipped out of the bed, not missing the way he self-consciously drew the blankets across his waist, keeping his leg from view.

She walked into the bathroom and looked at herself in the mirror. Her healing had helped fade the bruises, but they still remained, unmistakable. She had makeup in her bag, another luxury she hadn't been afforded as Martin's wife, and wondered if some powder and foundation, if applied heavily enough, would camouflage the damage.

"You could feed from me, take care of all that this morning," Rene remarked from the bed.

She turned and glanced past the doorway at him. "No."

"There's still time. We're not hooking up with Lina and Brandon again until later on this afternoon," he said.

"No," she said again. "I just can't, Rene. Please stop asking me."

He sighed, sounding frustrated, nearly exasperated, and she closed the bathroom door, cutting him off before he could even begin to argue.

After dressing, she watched as he sat against the edge of the bed, shook baby powder into his hands, then rubbed them briskly against the end of his right thigh. He slipped the stump down into a pale, silicone sheath at the top of his prosthetic, a sleek set of gray and blue metal tubes affixed between the mechanized knee joint and the frame of his foot. She'd never seen anything like it before, and found herself staring, curious and fascinated.

Rene noticed her attention and seemed embarrassed but resigned. "It's something else, no?"

"It's neat." She reached out to touch the cool titanium shaft of his calf. "Does it hurt to wear it?"

"Not usually." He shrugged. "As long as this top part fits right, it's okay." He patted his hand against the silicone sleeve. "I had to go and have it resized several times after the surgery. As the swelling went down, the fit would change. It took it a while, and I'll probably need to have it adjusted a time or two more."

He leaned over, tossing the little bottle of Johnson's

baby powder into his bag. She watched as he hooked his jeans with his left foot and pulled them toward him, slipping them on as he sat. "How did it happen?" she asked in a quiet voice. "Your leg, I mean."

Brandon had told her about the incident in general terms, but it was the first time Rene had seemed willing enough to even remotely open up to her. "Well . . . let's see . . ." he said, and she worried all at once that she'd pressed too hard too soon; he wasn't ready to confide in her and would be angry with her for prying.

"That's okay," she said quickly, kicking herself mentally in the ass. *Why do you have to go and try to push things, spoil it all, just when it's going so good again?* "Never mind, Rene. I shouldn't have—"

"It's all right, *pischouette*. I don't mind," he said, surprising her. He dropped her a wink and a smile. "I mean, we've seen each other naked. Not much point in keeping secrets anymore, no?

"Lina and I were partners, you know, both of us on the police force. So one night, we get this call down in the projects, this ratty twelve-story tenement complex, a 10-103—domestic disturbance."

His smile grew somewhat forlorn. "I still remember all of the call codes. I'll never use a goddamn one of them again, but they're filed away up here." He tapped his brow with his fingertip. "I never had much thought about what I wanted to do with my life, but I sure liked being a cop. I was good at it."

Another sad smile, this one directed to her. "That's the way it goes, no? So anyway, Lina and I show up for this 10-103, knock on the door all official like, and while one guy answers the door, the other tries to duck and run out the window. Since most folks aren't inclined to run from the cops unless they have something to hide, I took off after him while Lina cuffed his buddy. We found out later it was a drug deal, the guy out the window was a mule with a half kilo of cocaine crammed up his ass—about fifty grand worth. So no wonder he didn't want to get caught."

His eyes took on a distant cast. "It was cold out," he said, his voice low, nearly a murmur. "I remember that. And it had been raining. You could feel the moisture in the air, see it in the way your breath would mist around your face. The steps were slick. I was trying to hold on to the rail with one hand and unholster my gun with the other. I saw him below me. He stopped for a minute, and I remember I had this crazy thought that hey, this son of a bitch is going to listen to me after all, he's going to stop the chase. Then he holds out his hand at me . . ." Rene pointed his index finger at Tessa's nose. "And the next thing I see is a big flash of light."

He stood, tugging his jeans up, hiding the prosthetic from her view again. "I must have blacked out. I don't remember it hurting when he shot me. He missed me the first time, but caught my knee with the second round. I remember falling down the stairs, praying to God that I didn't spill ass over elbows over the side of that goddamn fire escape. And Lina crying—I remember that, because it scared me more than anything. I knew I was fucked up pretty bad if it made Angelina Jones bawl."

He blinked as if coming out of a reverie. "Sometimes my leg hurts. Or at least I think it does. It's like the nerve endings don't know there's nothing there . . . they forget or something. *Phantom sensations,* that's what my doctor calls them. I'll wake up in the middle of the night thinking I've got some hell of a leg cramp. Either that, or like my foot's turned all cockeyed." He glanced at her. "Crazy, I know."

A cell phone rang, loud but slightly muffled, startling them both. Rene laughed, reaching reflexively for his pocket. "I bet that's Lina," he said as he pulled out his phone. "Wish me luck as I feed her another line of . . ." His voice faded, his expression puzzled. "It's not me."

Tessa quickly crossed the room, grabbing her purse off the back of a chair. "I don't know who might be calling me," she said, with a bright moment of panic seizing her. She'd called her father only two days earlier and had hung up on him abruptly after delivering the news of Caine's death—news she hoped had reached the Elders by now. As she fumbled around inside the small bag, she hoped like hell it wasn't Sebastian. *Because then I'd have to explain to Rene why my dad would be calling,* she thought. *And I bet he'll be pissed as hell to find out.*

She frowned when she pulled out her phone only to find it dark and silent. "It's not me, either," she said, bewildered, even as a cell phone rang again from somewhere in the room.

"Ici," Rene said as he grabbed a dark coat from atop the air-conditioning unit. *Here.* "This is Martin's coat. I grabbed it when we left the other motel. I didn't want to leave anything behind the Elders could track us by."

He reached into the interior pockets as the phone continued to bleat, pulling out Martin's cigarettes and lighter, tossing them aside with a disgusted little snort. Finally, he pulled out a slim, silver phone. By then, Tessa had moved to stand beside him, and peered around his arm to see. Martin had obviously set the phone to both ring and vibrate; it thrummed, nearly jumping, like something alive against Rene's outstretched palm. She didn't recognize the number on the caller ID display, but she sure as hell recognized the name, which had been preprogrammed into the phone.

"It's Monica," she said, just as the phone at last fell silent. At Rene's curious glance, she added, "Martin's first wife. She's a real bitch."

"Ah." Rene raised his brow.

"She stole something from me once, a necklace my grandmother Eleanor gave to me," Tessa said, bristling even now to think of Monica yanking the green sapphire from around her neck. *It's mine now,* she'd hissed.

"Well, maybe we should call her back," Rene remarked, tucking Martin's cell phone into the hip pocket of his jeans. "Offer her a little trade. Speaking of which . . . I bet our little pal in the trunk is ready for another doping."

"I'll come with you," Tessa said, and he blinked at her in surprise.

"No, *pischouette.* You stay here. Let me deal with that *salaud.*"

"No," Tessa replied. Brandon had faced his demons when he'd stood up to their brother Caine. Rene had stood up to his by letting her see him without his prosthetic in place, by confiding in her. Everyone around her had made some measure of peace with their pasts. *Now it's my turn,* she told herself firmly. She might not have been able to confront Monica or take back Eleanor's necklace, but there was one score at the moment she could settle. *I need to stand up to Martin.*

"I take it you were close to your grandmother, *pischouette?*" Rene asked as they walked outside together.

Tessa nodded. "I guess you could say I idolized Eleanor when I was growing up. She and Brandon . . . they were my best friends."

"*Drôle,*" Rene remarked. *Funny.* "I don't remember Brandon ever mentioning her."

Tessa thought of their sixteenth birthday, how she'd seen Brandon jerk away from Eleanor in the foyer, a mixture of anger, bewilderment and hurt on his face.

"He wasn't as close to her as I was, at least not after we turned sixteen," she said. "Grandmother Eleanor gave me a very extravagant gift—that necklace I told you Monica stole from me. It had a green sapphire pendant, ten carats." When Rene raised his brows and whistled, she nodded. "It was beautiful. My grandfather had given it to her—his first gift, in fact, after they were married. It was very special to me, but I think Brandon must have been jealous, his feelings hurt. After all, it was his birthday, too. But Eleanor told me sweet sixteen is more special for girls." She watched Rene pull the keys to Martin's car out of his pocket and thumb off the car alarm. "I always wished they would have reconciled before she died, but I guess they didn't."

"How did she die?" Rene asked.

"I don't know exactly . . ." Tessa murmured as he opened the trunk.

You're a goddamn lying, stealing Noble whore, Martin had said as he'd tried to strangle her. *Just like your slut grandmother. So I guess that makes it only fitting that you fucking die like Eleanor.*

". . . but I'm about to try and find out."

Martin looked like hell.

The places on his face where bird beaks and talons had torn or pecked him open were beginning to heal, but still, it was hard to look like anything less than warmed-over shit when you were hog-tied and gagged in the trunk of your own mid-sized luxury sedan.

He squinted blearily against the abrupt glare of morning sunshine as the trunk swung open. When he caught sight of Tessa, his brows furrowed and he bared his teeth around the wadded up washcloth in his mouth, wriggling and mumbling at her, an inarticulate mess of sounds.

"Good morning, sunshine," Rene said to him. He held up a plastic water bottle, in which he'd dissolved a handful of crushed up Percodan tablets. "Breakfast is served."

The cleft between Martin's brows cleaved more deeply and he muttered and growled around the gag, angry and defiant.

"Now, now," Rene said, setting the bottle down and grabbing Martin roughly by the hair, forcing his head up. "That's no way to talk, what with a lady present." He jerked down the gag and moved to cram the mouth of the bottle between his lips. "Down the hatch."

"Wait," Tessa said, catching him by the arm. He and Martin both blinked at her in mutual surprise.

She stared at her husband, feeling tremulous and frightened, as if he could somehow still hurt her. She stared at him as she would have a rattlesnake curled by her feet; despite the ropes and her proximity to Rene, she still could feel that threatening potential energy surrounding Martin, coming off him in thick, stinking, nearly tangible waves.

"You said something yesterday," she said, her voice choked and quiet. "You told me I was going to die like Eleanor. I want to know what you meant."

He held her gaze, his eyes cold and filled with contempt. "Go fuck yourself," he croaked, spittle spattering against his cracked, blood-crusted lips.

Rene jerked his head, tearing hair loose from his scalp, and Martin uttered a hoarse cry. "You want to join the Hair Club for Men, asshole? Keep up that charming attitude."

"Tell me what you meant," Tessa said, clearing her throat and narrowing her brows. In that moment, as he'd cursed at her, the illusion of intimidation had fallen away and she'd seen him for what he truly was—not the monster who had beaten and terrorized her for the last four years, but something pathetic, battered and helpless, so consumed with greed and jealousy, she doubted he had room in his heart or mind for anything else. "You tried to kill me. You tried to kill my baby. You son of a bitch—did you kill my grandmother, too?"

When he said nothing, turning his eyes away as if bored with her, she felt the same rage that had filled her the day before—that fire that had been Eleanor's— ignite again. Tessa grabbed him by the collar of his shirt and shook him furiously. "You tell me!" she cried. "You son of a bitch, you tell me *right now!* What happened to my grandmother?"

He locked gazes with her again, the hatred in his eyes spearing into her. "Why don't you ask your grandfather?" he hissed and, startled, Tessa let go of his shirt and drew back. Martin chuckled at her surprise and bewilderment. "Go on. Call him on the phone, you stupid cunt. Ask him about it. He should know how Eleanor died—he's the one who killed her."

"Liar!" Tessa punched him hard enough to knock him loose from Rene's grasp and send him crashing back to the floor of the trunk. But she wasn't finished. She launched herself after him, all but scrambling into the back of the Jaguar as she began to pummel him, scratching, slapping and pounding his head and face over and over. "Liar! *You're a goddamn liar!*"

"Tessa!" Rene caught her by the waist and hauled her backward.

"You're a liar!" she cried at Martin, squirming against Rene. "My grandfather would *never* have hurt Eleanor! He loved her!"

"Yeah?" Martin spat out a mouthful of fresh blood; her knuckles had sheared open his bottom lip. "My father was there. He saw the whole thing, told me all about it. Augustus Noble crushed her goddamn throat with his bare hands, until her eyes bulged out of her goddamn skull and she pissed her fucking panties—how's that for love?"

"Liar!" Tessa yelled again, but she couldn't get to him to punch him anymore, not with Rene holding on to her. He hoisted her aloft, leaving her feet to pedal in the open air, and carried her forcibly back from the car.

"That's enough, *pischouette*," he said against her ear. He dropped her unceremoniously against the curb and gave her a warning look from beneath crimped brows. "Let me finish with him."

"But I need to—" she began, objecting.

"You need to sit tight and be quiet before you wake up the entire place and have cops crawling all over my ass, wondering why I've got your husband cinched up in the trunk," Rene said in a low voice. "Now stand still and stop it, goddamn it."

He returned to the car and leaned over the trunk. Martin uttered a choked, gurgling cry that cut off quickly. When Rene finished forcing him to drink the contents of the bottle, he stood again, looked about warily, then slammed the trunk down.

For a moment, she thought he'd be angry with her, but as he approached, his expression softened and he touched her face with a gentle hand. "You better now?"

She nodded, looking away, sullen and upset. "He's lying."

He canted his head to catch her gaze. "He's trying to push your buttons, *pischouette*," he said, leaning forward to kiss her. "And you let him. Come on. Let's get on the road."

"My grandfather didn't kill Eleanor." Tessa turned, following him back to the motel room. Here, she began to collect her things, shoving them with angry emphasis into a bag as she continued to speak. "He adored her, would have done anything to make her happy. They were everything I grew up thinking love was supposed to be."

He loved her like I love you, Rene, she thought, closing her mind and mouth. *He couldn't have hurt Eleanor any more than I could you.*

Rene made a strange little coughing sound and she paused, glancing over at him. "What?"

"Nothing, *pischouette,*" he said, shaking his head and shouldering his traveling bag. "It's just . . ."

His voice faded and he shrugged, making her frown. "What, Rene?"

He met her gaze, his brow raised slightly. "To hear you and Brandon talk about your grandfather, it doesn't seem to me like you're describing the same person at all. I'm not saying anything one way or the other, but this great man you keep mentioning, the one who loved your *mamère* so much . . . he's the same son of a bitch who broke Brandon's hands, punished him for wanting to go to school."

She blinked at him. "I'm not saying the Grandfather was a great man. I'm not saying that at all. I didn't live in the great house after Eleanor died. I don't know what things were like for Brandon then. I—"

"Sounds to me like things were bad off for Brandon for a long time before your grandmother died," Rene remarked.

"What the hell are you saying, Rene?" she asked, her voice growing sharp.

He shrugged again. "*Rien,*" he said. *Nothing.* "Just making an observation, that's all."

He walked out the door, leaving her to stand in the middle of the room, blinking after him.

He's right.

She had long struggled to reconcile within her mind the Augustus Noble who had so doted on Eleanor—the loving and adoring husband Eleanor had always described, who had smiled easily, laughed often and shown nothing but warmth to his wife—and the domineering patriarch who had so cruelly ostracized and abused her twin brother, offering Brandon nothing but icy contempt and condemnation.

She'd tried to tell herself that he hadn't been cruel before Eleanor died, that the bitter malice in his heart had come about in the aftermath of that loss. But that was a lie.

Because he was always cruel. Brandon was always afraid of him.

She slipped the strap of her bag over her shoulder and pressed her lips together in a thin, troubled line. *I've never wanted to believe that. I still don't want to. Because if that's true . . . if the Grandfather really is that kind of monster . . .*

"It means Martin's right," she whispered. "He murdered my grandmother."

Chapter Twenty

Lake Tahoe was twenty-two miles long and twelve miles across, encompassing a surface area of more than 190 square miles and bridging the outermost edges of California's eastern snowcapped Sierra Nevada mountains and the high desert plains of western Nevada.

And what a surface it is, Rene thought, looking down the steep slope of mountainside toward the plane of dusk-draped cerulean below. The sun was sinking beneath the Sierra Nevada peaks behind him but even without the full benefit of daylight, the view was extraordinary, damn-near breathtaking.

They'd followed Interstate 10 to the outskirts of Los Angeles, then turned north to take highway 395 to Carson City, Nevada. From there, he'd taken highway 50 and hugged the southern shoreline of Lake Tahoe's impressive and expansive circumference until hitting state route 89 west toward Emerald Bay. He'd have to double back along 89 in another hour or so to meet Lina and Brandon at a local restaurant for dinner.

"What is this place?" Tessa asked. Her voice was small, her eyes enormous as she took in the sweeping vista of dense pine forests, rocky peaks and that stunning view below. It was at least ten degrees cooler in the mountains than at lower elevations as a general rule of thumb; after sunset, you could notch that down another ten degrees at least. He'd stopped in the town of Stateline and bought a coat for her; it was always either ski season at Lake Tahoe, or damn near it, so finding something stylish enough to suit her and warm enough to be practical hadn't been a problem. The lightweight pink parka had cost him almost three hundred dollars, but it was quilted and down-filled, and she seemed grateful for it now as she tugged the collar flaps up toward her face and stuffed her hands into her pockets. The wind flapped dark strands of hair across her cheeks as she followed his gaze down to the water.

"It belonged to my father," Rene said, turning away from the edge of the slope and walking around the front of a Jeep Wrangler Unlimited. He'd stowed the Jaguar sedan at a hotel in South Lake Tahoe when he'd checked in, and rented the Jeep to better navigate the rough-hewn terrain. "And now it's mine. Come on, *pischouette*. I'll give you the grand tour."

They were north of Emerald Bay, looking down upon the expansive inlet, on twenty-five acres of relatively untouched wilderness accessible only by four-wheel drive. Rene didn't know why or how the property had come to be among his father's assets; the deed had been included among the documents left to him upon Arnaud's suicide, but the origin remained a mystery.

A loud, rustling crash from somewhere in the woods startled Tessa and she jumped, wide-eyed. "What was that?"

"Probably just a pinecone falling out of a tree." There were black bears in the forests surrounding the lake, enough to warrant them being considered an official nuisance by most area residents, but Rene decided now was probably neither the best time nor place to point this out to Tessa.

"A pinecone?"

He leaned down, hefting one from the thick carpeting of dried pine needles on the ground. Not your run-of-the-mill, residential variety of conifer seed cluster, it was as big as a softball at the circumference of its base, thick and heavy with sap. He tossed it to her and she caught it with both hands, her eyes widening again at the surprising heft.

"Pinecone," he said again, chuckling at her. "Watch your head when you're under the trees."

Although the land itself was extremely valuable, it was relatively vacant. Surrounded on either side by state park acreage, the area was virtually undeveloped, and the only building on Arnaud's property had been what Rene had surmised to be some kind of fire lookout about 900 square feet in circumference, with windows on all sides to award a panoramic view. The windows were hidden beneath hinged shutters that could be propped up and open, but were closed and padlocked in place otherwise. There was no plumbing, phone service or electricity, although there was room in a crawl space beneath the house to install a generator if Rene had ever wanted. Which had been his plan, once upon a time.

"The road up here from the highway is pretty much impassable in the winter, but I used to come every year in the summer," he remarked, fishing a set of keys from the pocket of his own down-filled ski jacket. "I don't know what it is, but I've always felt something . . . like I'm supposed to be here, like I'm home." He glanced over his shoulder at Tessa and smiled. "Once upon a time, I was going to retire from the police force and move here. Of course, then I got shot. Kind of messed up the whole idea."

"Are we going to stay?" Tessa asked, a bit apprehensively as he led her up a rickety flight of wooden steps to the plank porch that wrapped around the entire breadth of the house.

"*We're* not, no." He couldn't remember which key was which. It had been at least three years since he'd been out here. The last vestiges of daylight were rapidly dwindling, too, and he handed her a large Maglite he'd been carrying beneath his arm. "Here, *pischouette*. Do me a favor, no? Shine that light over here so I can sort through these keys."

She did and after several clumsy attempts, he found the right one for the front door. It opened on rusty, creaking hinges into a solitary room; the air inside smelled musty and stale. It was sparsely furnished: a twin-sized cot in one corner with a bare, lumpy mattress; a small, propane-powered one-burner stove on a wooden table in another corner, along with a dust-covered box containing pots, pans and other household items. No sink or toilet.

He glanced at Tessa again, offering a feeble smile. "Be it ever so humble," he remarked, sidestepping across the threshold so she could follow him inside.

"You were going to live here?" Tessa panned the flashlight around, sweeping its wide yellow beam across the wooden floor, the stark white walls. The only fixture was a single vertical beam, a post in the center of the room spanning from floor to ceiling. "But there's nothing here. No rooms."

"I don't need them," Rene said, walking slowly toward the center of the room, listening to the soft crunch of dust and grit beneath his shoe soles. "Or walls, either. Never have liked them much."

"Why?" Tessa asked.

With a laugh, he shrugged. "I don't know. I'm claustrophobic. Can't stand to feel shut in for too long."

"I didn't know that," Tessa said, looking surprised.

"It started when I came home from my tour of duty in Vietnam," he said. "We used to go humping around in the middle of the night through some of the densest goddamn jungle you can imagine. You could never relax because as soon as you did, someone would take a potshot at you. I remember always feeling smothered, like everything was closing in on me and I was suffocating. I guess that just stayed with me."

Dark places were particularly bothersome for him, maybe because light—particularly from windows—helped lend the illusion of space. He always kept the lights on at his loft in the city; a restored Victorian gaslight burned perpetually in the center of his living space. If he had no light to see by, he'd become disoriented, panic-stricken, suffering nearly full-fledged anxiety attacks. Sometimes in his mind, he'd even have flashbacks to his time in Vietnam, delusions that were realistically intense, even down to the remembered fragrance of mud and rain, the stink of his own ripe, pungent fear. In fact, being in that dark room, with only the flashlight's glow to orient him, was making him feel a bit edgy. *Should have thought to open the windows first,* he thought.

Not that he intended to stay long enough for it to matter.

"Good thing our sort don't really have to camp out in coffins, no?" he said with a wink. "I'd be in real trouble."

She smiled, and he watched as she traced little concentric circles on the top of the mattress with the flashlight beam. "You want to break that in or something?" he asked.

She swung the light directly into his face, blinding him. "No," she said, laughing.

He laughed, too, groping against the glare, shoving the light aside. "No?" He caught her by the wrists and pulled her against him, making her dance momentarily on her tiptoes. The simple prospect of making love to her—even in the dark in these close quarters—was enough to get his heart pounding, and the fly of his jeans to suddenly feel tight and strained. "You sure about that, *pischouette*?"

She could feel his arousal against her; he could tell by the mischievous reflection of light in her dark eyes. When he reached between them, sliding his hands deliberately, firmly against her breasts, reaching for the zipper of her coat, she giggled, pushing his hand away. "Don't even think about it. It's freezing in here."

He hooked his brow, smiling wryly. "Don't worry about that," he said. "I'll keep you warm."

She laughed against his mouth as he kissed her, walking her back toward the bed. "There's no way that mattress is going to hold both of us," she told him, muffled against his lips.

He glanced over her shoulder, then steered her to the right, crossing the room. "Fair enough."

Tessa laughed again as he knocked the stove and box of pans off the tabletop, sending them clattering to the floor. He lifted her up, hooking his hands beneath her ass and hoisting her atop the table. As he laid her back, her face was draped in yellow glow and heavy shadows from the fallen flashlight and he unbuttoned the front of her slacks.

"Raise your hips," he told her, and she did, letting him slide the pants and her underlying panties down her legs, bunching them around her ankles. Goose bumps immediately raised along her skin at the chilled air, and he leaned over, kissing her lightly on her belly, huffing a warm, soft breath against her groin. God, he was tempted to taste her there; he let the blade of his tongue flick lightly, quickly against her, delving ever so slightly between her folds, and she jerked in surprise. He wanted to spread her legs wide and explore her with his mouth, but he knew there wasn't time. The idea of it left him throbbing with painful, urgent need; that aside, he'd promised to meet Lina and Brandon at a specific time, and he was in deep enough shit by Lina's estimation without adding to it further. He'd have to settle for the proverbial quickie.

He unzipped his jeans and lifted her legs, propping them against his shoulders, hooking her pants around his neck and raising her buttocks slightly off the table. He turned his head, kissing the creamy, silken flesh along the side of her knee, stroking his hand against her skin. *My God, I love this woman,* he thought, gazing down, admiring her in the dim light.

Her breath was already hitching with anticipation; her eyelids fluttered closed, her fingernails hooked into the tabletop. She was wet and ready for him; he could feel it as he prodded lightly against her. He could smell her eagerness, the light fragrance of her arousal and he couldn't contain himself, even if he'd wanted to. He groaned her name, his voice husky with need, and buried himself inside of her.

The height of the table was perfect for his long legs, the angle it provided even more so, keeping Tessa tight around him. They didn't have time for anything slow or sweet; he took her hard, fast and fierce, making her moan aloud. She arched her back and he ripped open the zipper on her coat, shoving her shirt and bra up toward her neck to expose her breasts, the cold-hardened points of her nipples as they bounced with each thrust. He folded himself atop her, drawing one rose-colored nub lightly between his teeth and the tip of his tongue. She closed her fingers in his hair, holding him there, urging him on.

"Rene . . . oh, God . . ." she whimpered, and when she came, her legs tightened against his neck, her entire body tensing, her voice cutting short in a sharp, fluttering gasp.

Christ, I will never get tired of making love to this woman, he thought, shuddering with his own release. He gripped her buttocks with his hands and grinded against her, closing his eyes and uttering a hoarse cry.

He winced to pull away from her, to feel the biting chill of the air against parts of his body that had been enveloped by her warmth only moments earlier. "*Saint merde,*" he whispered shakily.

"You say that a lot," she said as she sat up to kiss him. "What does it mean?"

"Holy shit," he replied by way of translation, making her laugh. "It's a compliment. I promise."

After redressing, they walked back outside onto the porch together. "So why did we come here?" Tessa asked, hooking her arm through his and sidling beside him. She looked up, smiling winsomely at him. "Besides so you could have your way with me on the table."

"Have my way?" He laughed. "Woman, you haven't let me have my way on a damn thing since I met you!"

She laughed, too, and when she leaned against his shoulder, he kissed the crown of her dark hair. "I figure this is as good a place as any to keep Martin out of trouble," he told her, and she immediately grew tense and wary.

"What do you mean?"

"You'll see," he replied.

They went back to the Jeep and he opened the rear hatch. Martin was unconscious, still bound and gagged, but he stirred, groaning lightly as Rene hauled him out by the arm. He'd adjusted the bonds so that Martin's hands were tied behind his back, his ankles unfettered, and forced the other man to walk now in stumbling, dazed tow for the house.

Martin grumbled around the gag, bleary and disoriented, and grunted in pain when Rene shoved him through the front door, knocking him to his knees.

"Can we freeze to death?" Rene asked Tessa, dragging Martin over to the vertical post in the center of the room. He squatted, loosening the electrical cord around Martin's wrist long enough to cross his arms behind him around the beam, then lash them together again.

"What?" She stood hesitantly nearby, angling the flashlight so he could see what he was doing by its swath of illumination.

"Our kind, you know, Brethren. Can we freeze to death?"

"I don't know. Sure, I guess."

Rene nodded, giving an experimental tug on the cord to make sure it was secure. He rose to his feet, giving Martin a rough pat on the shoulder. "Well, don't worry, *mon ami*. Unless there's a late-season snowfall, you probably won't have to worry about that."

Martin glared up at him, shrugging against his bonds and snarling around the washcloth between his teeth. "*Mmmfllffrrr!*"

The cell phone in Rene's pocket, the one belonging to Martin, suddenly vibrated against his hip, startling him. Monica Davenant had been calling her husband all goddamn day. He'd finally become so sick of the constant ringing, he'd pulled out the phone and figured out how to switch off the ringer. "Looks like your old lady is calling you," he remarked, fishing the phone out of his pocket. He held it out, waggling it at Martin. "Your first one, anyway. Anything you'd like me to tell her?"

"Rene, don't—" Tessa began, but it was too late. He answered the line.

"*Bon jour.*"

He heard a clipped intake of surprised breath, a pregnant pause, and then a woman said, "Martin?"

"I'm sorry, *chère*," Rene said. "Monica, is it? But your husband is sort of . . . tied up at the moment. No wait, hold on. He'd like to speak with you."

"*Mmmrrrgggllrrrrpphhh!*" Martin yowled around the

gag as Rene again held the phone out toward him. Or something to that effect anyway.

"Did you catch all of that, *chère*?" Rene asked with a chuckle, drawing the phone to his ear again. "The reception out here is for shit most times."

"Who the hell is this?" the woman asked, her voice icy and brittle, like the edge of a razor blade scraping against a tin roof. "What have you done to Martin?"

"Nothing he didn't have coming," Rene replied wanly. "*Au revoir, madame.* The pleasure's been all mine, I'm sure."

He hung up the phone and tucked it back in his pocket. "She sends her love," he said, dropping Martin a wink as he walked toward the door. "We'll check back with you in a couple of days. I'd leave you some food, but it attracts bears."

"*Grrrlllmmffrrr!*" Martin yelled in garbled protest.

Rene slipped his arm around Tessa's shoulders and turned her around, steering her in step with him. He didn't doubt for a moment that Martin could smell the lingering scent of their lovemaking in the air and that made the entire arrangement all the more satisfying. "Come on, *pischouette*," he said as they left. "I'm starving."

Less than thirty minutes later, Rene parked the Jeep in the parking lot outside of the Burger Lounge in South Lake Tahoe. It was the perfect place to meet Lina and Brandon, because even though they had never been to Tahoe before, there was no way to miss the distinctive sign, shaped like an enormous beer mug overlooking the road.

"You sure you want to do this?" he asked, as she checked her reflection in the sun-visor mirror for at least the thousandth time since leaving Emerald Bay. She kept dabbing and redabbing powder and makeup on her face, trying to disguise the purple discoloration left in the wake of Martin's attack. He might have told her there was no use; Brandon was deaf, not blind, but knew she realized this, just as she recognized her own futile efforts.

Tessa closed the mirror, her eyes anxious and fearful as she glanced around the parking lot. Lina and Brandon were already there; the silver Mercedes 280 they had borrowed from Rene was parked almost directly across from them.

"I can call Lina," he offered. "Tell them something came up, we can't meet them until tomorrow."

She shook her head, closing her little powder compact and tucking it back into her purse. "No," she said. "No, that's all right, Rene. I . . . I should do this. It's probably about time anyway."

He took her hand because she was trembling, and drew her knuckles to his mouth, kissing her lightly. She glanced at him and smiled. "Thank you, Rene," she said. "For everything. You've done so much for me . . . and for Brandon, too, and I . . . I'm really grateful."

He leaned across the SUV's center console and kissed her on the lips. "It's been my pleasure, *pischouette*. Now stop talking like we're about to die. Lina's not *that* pissed, I promise."

At least, he hoped Lina wasn't pissed enough to kill him. As they walked into the small, crowded dining room and caught sight of Lina and Brandon at a four-top table, he could tell that she was still pretty damn close.

"I'm sorry I didn't call," he said as they approached, not even bothering with a greeting or other bullshit. She wasn't about to believe it anyway, so he figured he'd best save his breath. "My phone's been acting up. I told you. Maybe it's busted."

He'd also hoped that Tessa's cosmetics might buy them at least a few minutes, but that didn't work, either. Before they'd even reached the table, Brandon was on his feet, his dark eyes round with alarm.

Jesus Christ, Tessa! What happened? he asked, his voice nearly frantic in Rene and Tessa's minds. He rushed toward Tessa, visibly upset, and tried to cradle her cheeks between his palms.

I'm all right, Brandon, she said, ducking away from him. *It's nothing. I—*

Nothing? That's bullshit. His eyes cut toward Rene, his brows narrowing slightly. *Who did this to her? What the hell happened?*

"Let me guess," Lina said, rising to her feet. She no longer looked pissed; she looked as worried as Brandon. "Tessa got busted along with your phone." She cut a glance down at his bandaged hand—another crock of shit she wasn't buying—and then back at Rene. "Or maybe you had to change a flat tire and the jack slipped again?"

"*Touche, chère,*" Rene said, then clapped his hand against Brandon's shoulder. "Let's sit down. Everybody relax. We'll order some food and tell you all about it. I promise."

He let Tessa do the talking, at least through her mind, while they occupied their mouths eating. As nervous as she'd been to tell her brother the truth, once she'd started, it was like a dam had broken, and the words had flowed like an unleashed torrent.

So Martin's here? Brandon asked. He and Lina both looked decidedly anxious about this revelation, neither particularly pleased with the news. *In Lake Tahoe? Why did you bring him with you?*

Because the last thing you need is to have Martin running loose in the world to tell the Elders where you are, Rene replied, drawing the younger man's gaze. Their food had arrived—half-pound burgers all around—and he thought this as he munched a bite of a three-cheese behemoth the menu touted as a "Happy Cow." That a group of vampires sat around sharing an oversized basket of garlic-laden French fries was an amusing paradox not lost on Rene. Had the circumstances been different, a little less tense all around, he might have shared the observation and a laugh over it with Tessa and Brandon.

"You guys are all telepaths," Lina said. "Martin Davenant doesn't need to run loose in the world to tell the Elders. He can just think it—and is probably up at this cottage of yours in the middle of fucking nowhere doing exactly that." She slapped her napkin down and glared. "What the hell were you thinking, Rene?"

It's okay, Lina, Brandon thought before Rene could swallow and reply. *That's not how it works. We have to be near someone in order to communicate with them.*

"So if the *salaud* is out in the middle of fucking nowhere—your words, *chère*," Rene said to Lina. "That's the best place for him at the moment. Trust me. He's not going anywhere."

Rene thinks we can use him to get the Grandfather off our trail for good, Tessa said. She'd ordered a "Sticks and Twigs" veggie burger with avocado, but hadn't eaten much of it. Now she unconsciously draped her hand against Rene's, sliding her fingers between his against the tabletop; a tender gesture that Brandon didn't miss, to judge by the momentary surprise in his face . . .

Oh, shit, Rene thought again.

. . . or Lina, either, to judge by the fact the daggers in her eyes had returned . . . only this time, they were fucking broadswords à la the movie *Braveheart.*

Oh, shit.

Martin's been stealing money from the Grandfather through Bloodhorse Distillery, Tessa said, making Brandon blink at her in new surprise. She nodded. *We have the papers to prove it—a bunch of invoices and bank statements*

for a company called Broughman and Associates. Rene thinks
Martin made it all up—the company, the invoices, credit
cards, everything—all so he could take money from the
Brethren and not get caught.

"How did you get a hold of these papers?" Lina
asked.

"I took them accidentally when I left Kentucky,"
Tessa replied.

How are they supposed to help us call off the Elders? Brandon asked.

"Because Martin chased me halfway across the
country to get them back," Tessa said. "He and
Monica don't want anyone to know about them, that's
for sure. So we convince him to help us, to get the
Elders to go home in exchange."

Brandon raised a dubious brow. *He's not going to do*
that. Why would he?

"Because we're not going to give him a choice,
petit," Rene said.

"He'll either help us or I'm dropping all of his
papers in the mail to Dad," Tessa added. "Dad can get
a hold of the Grandfather and tell him all about it."

"Which will leave Martin Davenant up shit creek
with no paddle," Rene said. He tried to smile, but
didn't miss the fact the sentiment wasn't shared
by Lina as again, Tessa reached for him, holding
his hand.

"Are you sure you know what you're doing?" Lina
asked him an hour later back at the motel. She and
Brandon had checked into a room down from Rene
and Tessa. Each room had its own small patio, big
enough—barely—to accommodate two adults standing shoulder to shoulder, but offered a nice view of
the mountains and lake. She and Rene stood in their
coats watching their breath frost in the air, hazy and

iridescent in the moonlight while they took swigs
from bottles of beer.

"Sure I am." Rene shrugged. "I know you think I'm
this strung-out loser ever since I lost my leg, *chère,* but
I promise you, I can have a beer now and then and not
get wasted. Besides . . ." He awarded her a wink and a
smile. "I can't get addicted. My healing won't let me."

"You can still overindulge," Lina said pointedly.
"Which you do. A lot. And that's not what I meant."

Tessa and Brandon were behind closed doors in
Rene's room having a little one-on-one follow up to
the conversation broached over supper. He was worried about her, half tempted to use his telepathy to try
and overhear their conversation. Facing Brandon
alone, confiding in him all of the details she'd only
hinted at during dinner would be difficult.

"Look, you don't have to worry about Martin Davenant," he said to Lina. "I'm sure about that, too. I've
got him trussed up like a goddamn Christmas goose,
and even if he somehow gets loose, he's got nothing
but forests all around him for a good twenty miles.
He's got no coat, no flashlight, nothing, and it's the
middle of the night with a frost advisory issued. I told
you—he's not going anywhere."

Lina raised her brow. "That's not what I meant,
either." After a long moment of dark scrutiny, which
he tried his damndest to ignore, she said, "Are you
sleeping with Tessa?"

"What?" He tried to feign surprise. "No, *chère,* why
would you—?"

"Because if you are, you'd better knock it off," Lina
warned. "Jesus Christ, what the hell's the matter with
you? She's not one of your little hired guns, Rene.
She's a nice girl and—"

"What are you saying?" he asked, bristling. "I'm not
good enough for her?"

"Don't be an ass, Rene. That's not what I meant,"

Lina replied coolly. "All I meant was that Tessa doesn't need a fuck-buddy right now. She needs someone who's going to look out for her and the baby."

Even Lina—the woman who knew him better than anyone in the world—thought he didn't deserve Tessa and that wounded him to the core. It was just like Thibodaux, Louisiana, all over again; just like Gordon Maddox, his childhood nemesis who had bullied him for being poor. *It's never enough, is it, chère?* he thought about saying, but pressed his lips together, forcing himself to remain mute. *No matter what, I'll still just be white trash, no? Here's a news flash—I've been shot in the hand and burned 10 hours worth of rubber off my goddamn tires looking out for Tessa and the baby. If that doesn't make me fucking good enough, I don't know what will.*

"You sure you know what you're doing?" she asked.

"Are you?" He glanced at her. "I'm not the only one sleeping with one of the Noble twins. And you've got a lot more to lose than I do, *chère.*"

"It's not the same thing."

He took a swallow of beer. "How do you know?"

"Because I love Brandon. Are you going to tell me you love Tessa?"

"I am, yes, and I do," he said, meeting her gaze. When she rolled her eyes, it stung all the more. "*Quoi?* You think you have a monopoly on feelings, Lina? You're the only one who can fall in love these days?"

"No," she said. "That's not what I meant at all. It's just . . . I've known you a long time, Rene, and I've never seen you fall in love with anybody. You're just . . . you . . ." Her voice faded and she averted her eyes.

"What?" He frowned. "I'm what, Lina? Don't be shy. Whatever it is, just come out and fucking say it."

Lina's eyes flashed angrily. "You're still in love with your wife," she said, startling him. "Yeah. You've told me about Irene. You don't remember? You've given me earfuls over the phone during several of your

'I-can't-get-addicted' drinking binges. You told me
about her and the baby. And I'm worried that you're
trying to get that back with Tessa, all of the stuff you
lost with Irene."

He blinked, as shaken as if she'd physically struck
him. "Thanks, Lina." Shoving the beer bottle at her,
he turned, walking back through the door into the
motel room. "Thanks a hell of a lot."

"Rene, wait." She hurried after him, but when she
hooked her hand against his coat sleeve to stay him,
he flapped her away. "Come on, Rene. I didn't—"

He slammed the door behind him, leaving her
alone in the room.

Chapter Twenty-one

Is the baby all right? Brandon asked Tessa, his brows lifted, his eyes round with worry. She sat against the edge of the bed while he knelt before her, draping his hands against hers at her knees and looking up into her face.

Yes. She nodded, brushing his knuckles lightly with her thumbs, struggling to smile at him in reassurance. *I can still sense it and everything feels okay. I think I would know somehow . . . sense something different . . . if the baby was hurt.*

He reached for her neck, tugging lightly against the high collar of her turtleneck sweater. Rene had bought it to help hide the bruises—dark violet splotches against the pale skin of her throat that formed ghost-like impressions of Martin's hands. She tried to shrug away from her brother, but he eased the collar back enough to catch a glimpse.

Jesus, Tessa. Brandon leaned forward, drawing her into his arms. She tucked her head against his shoulder and closed her eyes against the sting of tears. *I'm so sorry,* he whispered helplessly in her mind. *All of this time . . . all of these years. I wish you had told me.* When he sat back, his eyes were hurt and confused. *Why didn't you?*

"There was nothing you could do," she said, cutting her gaze to her lap, knotting her hands together.

Nothing? Brandon hooked his fingertips under her chin, forcing her to look up at him. His brows had narrowed, his mouth turned down in a frown. *I would have killed that son of a bitch if I'd—*

"And that's exactly why I didn't say anything," Tessa cut in. "You would have gone after Martin and then the Grandfather would have gone after you. It's not like you didn't have enough trouble living in the great house and I . . ." Her voice faltered. "I didn't want you to know. I didn't want anyone to know. There was no undoing it. I was stuck there." She brushed his hair back from his brow and smiling sadly. "Kind of like with you and Caine."

His eyes traveled along her face, from one bruised and battered place to another. "It's all right," she told him. "We're safe now—all of us. You, me and the baby. They can't hurt us anymore, Brandon."

I don't know what I would have done if something had happened to you, Brandon said. *If Rene hadn't been with you . . . if he hadn't found you and Martin . . .* He stood, forking his fingers through his dark hair, his expression strained. *I don't know what I would have done,* he said again.

He walked away, standing before the closed drapes, his arms folded across his chest, his back to her. His posture was rigid with stress and, as always, it amazed Tessa how Brandon could communicate so much so well—all without saying a word. He was blaming himself, probably delivering a mental reaming and she rose to her feet.

Brandon . . . she began gently.

None of this would have happened if I'd just stayed in Kentucky, he said without looking at her. *If I'd just gone through the goddamn bloodletting like you asked me to, like everyone fucking wanted. If I hadn't run away, Lina's life would still be normal, not like this—fucked up and on the run . . . Caine and Emily wouldn't have followed me . . . you wouldn't have, either.* He turned, pained. *Martin wouldn't have done this to you.*

"He would have hurt me anyway," Tessa said. "He never needed a reason, Brandon, just like Caine never needed any to bully you. He's a monster, just like Caine was. Just like you always said. And I never would have been brave enough to leave him if it hadn't been for you."

I never would have met Rene if it hadn't been for you, she thought, closing her mind momentarily so Brandon wouldn't overhear.

I should go, Brandon said. *It's getting late and we've been on the road all day. You need to sleep. The baby—*

"Wait." Tessa caught his arm. "There's something else, something Martin told me."

Brandon raised a curious brow. *What?*

"He said the Grandfather murdered Grandmother Eleanor," she said and when his eyes widened in surprise, she nodded. "When he was choking me, he said that's how Eleanor died, and then later . . . once Rene had him tied up, I asked about it and he told me. He said his father had witnessed the entire thing. Do you think it's true, Brandon? Do you think the Grandfather could really do that? You know how much he loved Eleanor."

Brandon's brows narrowed slightly. *I don't think the Grandfather has ever loved anyone in his entire life. I don't think the son of a bitch is capable.* He shook his head. *It wouldn't surprise me at all if he killed her. Frankly, I don't give a shit either way.*

Tessa bristled at this. "What the hell does that mean?"

Nothing, he replied. *It means I'm tired and I need to go to bed before I say something I'll be sorry about later.* He moved to lean forward, kiss her cheek good night, but she startled him by giving him a shove.

"No, don't do that. Don't just make some smart-ass quip and then walk away or play it off, like you did that day in the dance studio years ago." When he clearly didn't remember this, to judge by the bewildered look on his face, her frown deepened. "You've had a problem with Grandmother Eleanor since we were sixteen years old, ever since she gave me that green sapphire pendant for my birthday. I know you were angry about that, jealous even, but—"

What? Brandon interrupted, his eyes widening again. *I wasn't jealous. Or angry, either.*

"I saw you in the foyer," Tessa said. "When Grandmother Eleanor must have told you she was going to give it to me. I was standing on the staircase and saw the whole thing—the way you reacted, how you pulled away from her."

Brandon moved to walk around her. *You don't know what you're talking about.*

"I know you think she slighted you by giving it to me," Tessa said, stepping directly into his path, blocking his way to the door. "I know you've acted angry with her ever since. But she loved us both, Brandon."

Tessa. He locked gazes with her. *You don't know what you're talking about. So just leave it alone.*

He brushed past her, but she grabbed him by the sleeve, wheeling him forcibly about to face her. "I will not!" she exclaimed. "I think it's high time we talked about this, Brandon—that you deal with it. It's not fair for you to be angry with Grandmother Eleanor."

You want me to deal with it? He frowned, jerking his arm away from her grasp. *You don't think I'm being fair? You don't know what the hell you're talking about, Tessa. You don't know anything—only some half-assed conjecture about what you think you saw that day on the staircase. And you're wrong. You're dead fucking wrong.*

"Then tell me what I saw." He kept trying to get by her; she kept preventing him. "Tell me, Brandon! I want to know. If you're not mad at Eleanor for giving me the necklace—if you're not jealous—then what have you been pissed about all these years? What did she say to you? Tell me!"

Get out of my way, Tessa, he told her with a frown.

"Not until you tell me," she shot back.

I mean it—move, he said, and when he sidestepped, she cut him off.

"Tell me, Brandon. I want to know," she said. "Tell me!"

It should have been you! Brandon snapped. *Are you fucking happy now, Tessa? Grandmother Eleanor told me what happened to me—getting attacked, losing my hearing, getting my throat slit—it all should have happened to you!*

And in her mind, he showed her, opening up his memories, letting them replay inside of her head like her own. Through Brandon's eyes, she saw Eleanor on their sixteenth birthday, their grandmother cradling his face between her hands and leaning forward to press her full, cool lips against the corner of his mouth.

"Beautiful Brandon," she murmured, smiling as she stroked her hand against his cheek, her fingertips trailing down to trace along the scar at his throat. Brandon hadn't been able to hear her voice, but he'd read her lips; her words whispered through his mind, soft and intimate. "Such a pity, what happened to you. Such a waste."

She met his gaze, wearing a sweet but melancholy smile. "I wish it had been Tessa instead," she remarked. "A Brethren man should be strong—speak his mind and stand his ground, especially a Noble. Women don't need to hear or speak to make babies, no matter their clan. And, in the end, isn't that really all Tessa can ever hope to accomplish?"

At this, Brandon had recoiled, startled and dismayed, and that was what Tessa had seen from the stairs.

When Brandon snapped his mind closed to Tessa,

it was like a heavy steel door slamming abruptly shut in her face. She stumbled back, wide-eyed and dumbstruck.

Women don't need to hear or speak to make babies, no matter their clan.

Eleanor's words echoed in her mind, stabbing into her stunned heart again and again like the point of some cruel and relentless knife.

. . . in the end, isn't that really all Tessa can ever hope to accomplish?

Her hands darted to her belly, to the baby growing inside of her womb. "Oh, God," she whispered. *Oh, God, is that all she thought of me?*

She remembered Eleanor giving the necklace to her, how she'd smiled at Tessa's surprise, and entertained none of Tessa's sputtered protests. "Sweet sixteen is more special for girls," she'd said.

But she didn't think I was special, she thought, her eyes welling with tears. *Not then, not ever . . . oh, God, not at all.*

Tessa . . . Brandon reached for her, round-eyed and remorseful. *Oh, Jesus, I'm sorry. I didn't mean for you to . . . I didn't mean . . .*

He tried to touch her, but she shrugged him away. "Get out."

I didn't want you to know that, he pleaded. *I didn't mean for you to see, Tessa. I was angry and I'm tired and I . . . it just slipped . . .*

She pointed one shaking hand toward the door. "Get out, Brandon. Just . . . just go away. Leave me alone."

Tessa . . . He tried to touch her again but she recoiled.

"Get out!" she cried. "Get out, Brandon! You get the hell out of my room!"

Tessa, please . . .

Again, he reached for her and this time she shoved him back. "Get out!" she cried again. "Just go away!"

Chapter Twenty-two

Rene ran damn near headlong into Brandon on the walkway outside of their respective motel rooms. Both men had been walking swiftly, their heads down, their minds clearly distracted, and when they bumped into each other, knocking shoulders and each stumbling sideways, they both blinked in mutual surprise.

"Oh, hey, *petit*," Rene said. "Sorry about that. I wasn't watching where I was going."

That's okay, Brandon said. *I wasn't, either. You all right?*

"I'm fine." Rene glanced over his shoulder, back in the direction of Brandon and Lina's room. "Can't say the same thing for your other half, though, *petit*." When Brandon looked at him, clearly puzzled, he elaborated. "Lina and I just had a bit of a spat."

Oh. Brandon nodded. *Fair enough. Tessa and I just had one, too. What was yours about?*

Rene shrugged, stuffing his hands into his pockets. "Nothing really," he said. "It's just that Lina doesn't seem to think I'm good enough for Tessa, that's all."

What? Brandon cut his eyes toward his door and then back to Rene. *You're kidding. She said that?*

"Not in so many words, no," Rene said. "But

she didn't have to. I understood her meaning perfectly well."

Brandon glanced again, this time over his shoulder to Tessa's room. *Are you sleeping with my sister?*

The dreaded question. Rene braced himself, straightening his spine and settling his jaw at a stern angle. He met Brandon's gaze, fully expecting yet another confrontation, another rousing round of the same old "good enough to hire, not good enough to marry" bullshit he'd heard time and again his entire life. "I am, *oui*."

Brandon looked up at him, his expression uncharacteristically unreadable. *Do you love her?*

"Yes, *petit*. I do. You can hit me if you want. I probably have it due. But that's the God's honest truth of it, Brandon."

After a moment, Brandon shook his head and laughed soundlessly. *I'm not going to hit you, Rene,* he said. *Jesus, I could hug you. I don't know why Lina would tell you that you're not good enough for Tessa, but she's wrong. You're more than good enough for her—you're good to her. She needs someone like you. She's needed that for a long time.*

This caught Rene completely off guard and he stood there for a long, awkward moment, unsure of what to say.

Martin would have killed her if it hadn't been for you, Brandon said. Then, with a pointed look that let Rene know he still wasn't buying the whole "the jack slipped while changing a flat tire" story, either, he added, *I don't know the truth about your hand, but I suspect something else happened—something that put you and Tessa both in danger—and you took care of it. You took care of her.*

He glanced again toward Tessa's door. *She probably hates me right now . . .* he said, his brows lifting, his eyes growing sorrowful.

What? Rene interjected mentally, because Brandon's gaze was averted; he wouldn't have been able to read his lips or realize he was speaking. *No,* petit. *Don't be silly. Why would you say that?*

She's pretty pissed, Brandon said. *I told her something . . . something about our grandmother that I shouldn't have . . . something I didn't mean to.*

"That one *mamère* she thinks hung the moon?" Rene asked and Brandon nodded. "What about her?"

Nothing. Brandon shook his head. *Never mind. You'll probably find out from Tessa soon enough. Anyway, she's pissed at me, and I deserve it. I hurt her.* He forked his fingers through his hair, shoving it back from his face. *I didn't mean to. I was angry, too, and it just came out.*

He looked up at Rene. *I keep fucking things up, so thank you for taking care of her. She needs that right now. She needs you.*

Rene had been ready for Brandon to rip into him. The last thing he'd expected was this—Brandon's earnest candor, his approval. He found himself choked up, as ridiculously on the verge of tears as he'd been with Lina moments earlier, only this time because he was touched, not hurt.

You really think that highly of me petit? he asked.

Of course I do. Brandon looked surprised by the question. *You're my friend, Rene.*

Rene hooked his hand against the back of the younger man's head and drew him into a brief, one-armed embrace. *Thanks,* petit, he thought, closing his eyes. *I needed that.*

When Rene walked into the motel room, he found Tessa curled up on the bed, her back to the doorway, her narrow shoulders trembling visibly. He could hear her sniffling mightily against tears. She didn't look back or otherwise acknowledge his entrance, but when he lay down beside her and draped his hand across her waist, she caught his hand, sliding her fingers between his own.

"I ran into Brandon outside," he said. "He told me you two had some kind of argument . . . ?"

"I don't want to talk about it," she said simply, still without looking at him.

"C'est juste," he said. *That's fair.* He felt her stiffen against him despite this, anticipating some sort of lecture, perhaps a well-intended but ineffectual attempt to empathize with her. "Say, have I ever told you about Baldy Bertie?"

She sniffled again and canted her head slightly to glance over her shoulder. "What?"

"Baldy Bertie. Have I ever told you about her?"

Tessa offered a feeble, somewhat tearful laugh. "No."

"Ah." Rene snuggled closer, drawing her against him. "Baldy Bertie was the nickname for Miss Florence Bertram, the head librarian at the Thibodaux Public Library when I was a boy. All of the kids called her that because she had this bald patch on her head right about here . . ." He touched the cap of Tessa's head with his hand.

"Stop trying to make me feel better," Tessa said, shaking her head to dislodge him. "She did not."

"Hand to God, *pischouette,* I'm telling the truth. She looked like a goddamn Benedictine monk or something. This was back in the days before Rogaine or hair plugs, anything like that. She'd try to comb the rest of her hair over and hide it, but it never did any good."

He smiled somewhat sadly. "Back then, my *mamere* worked at a local grocery store, and when she'd go to town for work in the summers, she'd bring me along with her, drop me off at the library to keep me out of trouble. I'd stay there until midday, then walk or hitchhike home for lunch and chores.

"I didn't have many friends growing up," he remarked, his mind turning momentarily to his childhood nemesis, Gordon Maddox, and the gang of boys who would often join in his bullying. "So I never minded spending so much time at the library. Aside from all of the books, they always had other things there for me to get into, like these self-illuminating little stereo viewers that looked sort of like cameras, only you used them to look at pictures, not take them. They showed you things in 3D, the way they'd look in real life, if you were right there in the middle of them, and the library used to have all kinds of slides with pictures of big cities, foreign countries, national landmarks, that sort.

"*Mamère* couldn't afford to take me anyplace like that—going to New Orleans or maybe Shreveport was as big a deal as things got in my house growing up. But I could look at those pictures and pretend anyway. When you don't have a lot of friends as a kid, a good imagination is a damn close substitute sometimes."

He could feel Tessa relaxing against him, the unhappy tension that had made her body tight in his embrace fading as he spoke. "So there was this boy named Gordon Maddox who used to always make fun of me, pick on me and fight because my clothes were all hand-me-downs, my family was poor and worse than that, we were Cajun, which was just about a half step up from being black back in those days in the bigoted deep south. Gordon Maddox was rich and golden, everybody's all American, and even though he beat the shit out of me more times than I can count off the top of my head, a part of me still wanted him to like me.

"So one day when we were both in the library at the same time and he couldn't get me in trouble by punching on me, he decides he'll get me another way. He and his friends dare me to jerk my pants down in the library foyer, where the ceiling is high and the floor is polished granite, and say 'Baldy Bertie! Baldy Bertie!' And me, like a stupid *salaud*, agrees to do it."

"You didn't!" Tessa said with a laugh.

He chuckled against her hair. "I did. She was sitting behind the main counter, right past the foyer, where the big glass doors were propped open because of the heat. I dropped my britches right in front of her and yelled at the top of my lungs, my bare ass flapping in the breeze all the while. 'Baldy Bertie! Baldy Bertie!'"

Tessa laughed again, the strain of tears almost fully gone now. "God, Rene."

"*Je sais,*" Rene said. *I know.* "Trust me, *pischouette.* I know. To this day, I don't know what the hell I was thinking, or why I didn't think *Mamère* would find out. She'd grown up in Thibodaux. She and Bertie had gone to school together. And it wasn't like no one in that library knew me by sight, or how to get a hold of my grandmother.

"So I spent the rest of that afternoon just sort of fucking around, and by the time I get home, it's nearly supper and *Mamère's* back from work. She's standing in the living room when I get home, and little do I know but she's got her whippin' belt off its hook in the kitchen and behind her back.

"'So tell me, Rene,' she says to me in that deep voice of hers with a French accent thick like *roux.* 'How was your day? Did you have fun at the library?'

"'Oh, *oui,*' I said, and I have no idea the licking I am in for, the hide blistering that is waiting for me. To which she replies, 'I just bet you did,' and then she pulled out that belt and laid into me like my ass was a sinner and it was the second coming. The next day, she took off her lunch at the grocery to march me down to the library and have me apologize in person. I don't recall ever calling her Baldy Bertie again . . . not until just now."

He meant for her to get a giggle out of the story, as he did now in retrospect, but as soon as he finished, he realized. *Jesus Christ, her husband likes to beat the shit*

*out of her, and here I am with an anecdote whose punch line
has me whipped upside the ass with a belt.*

"I'm sorry, *pischouette*," he said with a grimace.
"I shouldn't have told you that. I don't know what
I was . . ."

His voice faded as she rolled over to face him.
"That's all right, Rene. I know what you were trying to
do. Your heart was in the right place . . . and it *was*
kind of funny." She reached up, stroking her hand
against the side of his face gently. "I'm sorry your
grandmother hit you."

"She didn't mean it out of spite," he told her, feeling
goofily obligated to try and explain, to assure Tessa that
Odette LaCroix hadn't been some belt-wielding abusive monster like Martin. "That's the way things were
back then, *pischouette*. There weren't things like time-
outs or getting grounded. And *Mamère* had enough
on her mind without me making things harder. My
granddaddy was a drunk and he didn't do much but
draw disability, so that left it up to *Mamère* to take care
of things—the house, the laundry, the yard, me."

"What about your mother?" Tessa asked.

"I never knew her, outside of her name—Cécile
Marie LaCroix—and her face. She died when I was a
baby, a car accident, but *Mamere* kept pictures of her
all over the house, like it was a goddamn shrine. She
used to tell me I looked like her, that I was headstrong
and stubborn just like she'd been."

"Everyone used to say that about me, too," Tessa said,
growing sorrowful again. "That I looked just like Grandmother Eleanor . . . acted like her, everything." Her eyes
clouded with tears and her bottom lip trembled. "Everything I thought about her has been a lie, Rene," she
whispered, tears creeping from the shelter of her lower
eyelashes, rolling slowly down her cheeks. "Everything
I felt about her . . . anything she ever told me . . . all of
it lies."

He wrapped his arm around her, drawing her near. "I'm sorry, *pischouette,*" he said softly, kissing her ear through her hair. "I'm sorry."

She fell asleep in his arms and Rene dozed lightly, her hair soft and fragrant against his face. He had restless dreams of being back in Thibodaux, the LaCroix house again, just as he'd been only days earlier.

The dream was vivid, utterly convincing in its realism. Everything from the stale odor of stagnant dust in the air to the light crunch of plaster chips and grit beneath his shoe soles was just as it had been in person. He dreamed of walking down the front corridor toward the rear of the house, his eyes cutting easily through the heavy shadows of night that had settled through the shack's darkened interior.

My pupils have dilated, he thought, even though he felt none of the other heightened awareness that typically came with the bloodlust. His pupils had spread wide; to anyone observing, it would have looked as if they'd swallowed every margin of space across his corneas, leaving his eyes smooth, featureless planes of black. In reality, this allowed for even the faintest hint of discernable light to be detected; to Rene, the world looked like it might have through night-vision goggles.

Where derelicts had pried loose the boards covering the bathroom windows, he saw a smear of moonlight against the gloom, enough to cast an eerie glow across the sprawled, fallen body of the man Tessa had killed. By now, the insects of the Louisiana bayou had found the bum's corpse, as had rats; from the corner of his gaze, he saw several large ones scamper and scurry away, frightened by his encroaching footsteps.

He smelled the pungent, cloyingly sweet stink of decay and could see that the body was beginning to bloat slightly, baking in the stuffy, hot confines of the vacant house. He stood for a long moment, gazing down at the man, then turned and knelt beside the hole in the floor in which Tessa had discovered the Morin clan Tome.

The book had been in the secret alcove beneath the floor long enough to leave a faint, musty scent lingering in the narrow opening. *Funny,* Rene thought, as he reached down into the hole. *I never noticed that smell before.* Now it seemed somehow familiar to him—more than this, like something he'd been specifically searching for, a fragrance that had drawn him to that house, that place.

He felt something in the dusty, cobweb-lined opening and picked it up, pulling out an old photograph like one of the daguerreotypes they'd seen inside the Tome. Rene recognized the stern-faced man in the portrait; he'd been the principle subject in other photos.

Michel Morin.

The name whispered through Rene's mind in a voice that was surprisingly unfamiliar to him. The feelings associated with those words were equally as surprising—a sudden, unexpected mixture of fondness and sorrow, as if seeing Michel's image had brought his heart both pleasure and pain all at the same time. The only problem was, he couldn't account for either emotion. *Because I don't know who in the hell Michel Morin was outside of a face in a photograph, a name in a book.*

Yet in his mind, as if through memory, as plain as any of his own, he saw a young boy on a bright spring morning, standing beneath a grove of trees so that daylight dappled through the new vernal foliage and against his face in splayed shadows.

Michel.

He saw the glint of sunshine off metal; a short-handled knife in the boy, Michel's hand, and felt the sharp sting as the blade drew against his palm.

Strangely, looking down at his hands in the dim light of the house in Thibodaux, he could see a scar—a thin line bisecting his right palm at a crooked diagonal. *Because I was too young to heal,* he thought inexplicably, because the scar was part of the dream, nothing he'd ever seen before. *Not all of the way, at least. When Michel cut me, it left a scar.*

"Now we're like brothers," he remembered Michel saying as he cut open his own hand and pressed his palm against Rene's, clasping fiercely. "Nothing will ever come between us. Not ever."

In the dream, Rene walked slowly toward the light of the bathroom in Thibodaux. He glanced down to find himself in a charcoal-gray sport coat and dress slacks, a button-down shirt and silk tie—clothes he'd never seen before, much less had packed to take with him. He tucked the picture of Michel Morin into the inside breast pocket of his jacket and watched light glint momentarily off a gold cuff link affixed to the juncture of his sleeve; a gold cube with the initials *A. S. N.* engraved atop.

Inside the bathroom, Rene approached the old porcelain sink, which listed against the crumbling wall, a battered medicine cabinet above it. With the moon's glow all around him, he looked into the cracked surface of the mirror. To his shock, it wasn't his own face reflected at him in the glass; rather it was someone older, a man who appeared to be in his late forties or early fifties, with a heavy sheaf of white hair that spilled down from the crown of his head, past his shoulders in a thick fall. His face was handsome, his features angular and somewhat familiar to Rene; his brows narrowed as he frowned into the mirror.

He sort of looks like Brandon, Rene thought, realizing who it was, what he was dreaming about. *The Elders!* Saint merde, *that's Brandon's grandfather!*

And in his mind, a flurry of sudden images struck:

Michel Morin in boyhood, smiling as they had clutched their bloody hands together. *Now we're like brothers . . . Nothing will ever come between us. Not ever.*

A woman who eerily resembled Tessa, with catlike eyes and heavy dark hair . . .

Eleanor.

I want this forever, she said, her voice haunting and melancholy. *I want you forever. I'll die if I marry him. I swear to you, Augustus, if I can't be with you, I'll steal a knife from the supper table and slash my own wrists with it . . .*

Who are you, boy? Augustus Noble seethed inside Rene's skull, his dark eyes spearing out from the reflection in the mirror. His voice was low and resonant, velveteen but menacing.

In his mind, Rene could hear the woman, Eleanor whispering to him, *There is only one way. You know what to do. There's only one way to change the will of the Tomes.*

Rene saw fire; a bright, furious inferno whipping against the black, icy backdrop of a winter's night. He saw the dim outline of walls, windows and chimneys against the ferocious blaze and realized it was a house burning. He could hear glass shattering, timbers crumbling, but above all of this, something horrific and shrill.

Screaming, he thought, as he simultaneously realized he could see the silhouetted forms of people through the windows, burning bodies dancing and flailing, throwing themselves past the heat-shattered panes in desperate attempts to escape. *Because the doors are all blocked,* he thought, even though there was no way he could have known this; no way at all. *Jesus Christ, they blocked all the doors, trapped them inside. They're burning them alive!*

How did you get inside my head? Augustus snapped, and as the older Brethren sealed off his mind from Rene's prying eyes, it felt like hundreds of doors flying shut all at once right in his face.

"*Viens m'enculer!*" Rene gasped sharply as he sat up

in bed, his eyes flown wide. It took him a long, alarmed moment to realize where he was—*who* he was—and at last, he ran his fingers through his disheveled hair, pushing it back from his face. "Jesus," he whispered, his voice shaky.

Tessa groaned softly. He looked down and stroked his hand against her shoulder to soothe her, hoping she stayed asleep. *I'll be hard pressed to explain to her why the hell I'm dreaming of her granddaddy otherwise,* he thought. *Because frankly, I don't even know myself.*

Once assured that Tessa was undisturbed, Rene eased himself out of bed. He drew a glass of water for himself at the sink and swallowed it in a single gulp. This was followed by another cup and then another, until at last he ran the side of his hand against his bottom lip to catch dribbles creeping down his chin. He looked at himself in the vanity mirror, his reflection in the dim glow of light from the adjacent bathroom.

Who are you, boy? Augustus Noble's voice echoed in his mind, the images the house engulfed in flames, the terrified, agonized shrieks permeating the night replaying simultaneously. *How did you get inside my head?*

"*Juste un rêve,*" Rene told himself, closing his eyes and again shoving his hand through his hair. *Just a dream.*

He sat down heavily in an armchair in the corner of the small room. While here, he rolled up the leg of his jeans, fished his portable recharging cables from his bag and plugged his prosthetic knee into the nearest wall outlet. He glanced around the room uneasily, as much to convince himself that he was alone there, no Elders within sight or to be sensed, as to make sure Tessa was asleep. Yes, they'd made love, and yes, she'd seen not only the leg, but him without it, but still, that incessant insecurity remained.

He leaned over the side of the chair and grabbed the TV remote off the bedside table. Thumbing the volume nearly to silence, he turned on the television

and channel-surfed until he found CNN. He didn't
plan on paying any attention to the persistent drone of
the newscaster, but the chatter would fill the vacant silence in the room and soothe the lingering unease he
still felt following the dream. However, the news item
up for discussion caught his attention immediately.

". . . a bizarre incident in which a flock of birds apparently attacked a crowd of patrons in a riverfront
nightclub . . ." the anchorwoman was saying. Rene
held out the remote, leaning forward as he turned up
the volume. "Police in that city are still looking for suspects after two men were found dead at the scene following this same incident. The body of local attorney
Jude Hannam was discovered mutilated and partially
drained of blood . . ."

"Viens m'enculer," Rene whispered, the dream of Augustus Noble all but forgotten. He knew who Jude
Hannam was—Lina's ex-boyfriend. He'd been murdered by Tessa and Brandon's lunatic older brother,
Caine Noble, on the same night that Lina had shot
and killed Caine.

"Police are also seeking the public's help in identi-
fying another man dead at the same scene. Described
as a white male in his mid- to late twenties, the victim
was approximately five feet, nine inches tall and one
hundred and ninety pounds. He had been badly
beaten and shot four times, including once to the
head. While there are currently no suspects in either
death, investigators are actively looking for one of
their own, a missing officer named Angelina Jones,
who apparently visited the club while on duty just
prior to the bird attack."

An image of Lina in uniform flashed on screen. *Oh,
shit,* Rene thought.

"Jones disappeared after entering Apathy, a series
of neighboring nightclubs built inside three river
barges. She was once romantically linked to Hannam

and the two had been seen arguing the day before the incident at a wedding reception. Ballistic tests are ongoing to see if Jones's gun fired the fatal shots in the second Apathy slaying."

Oh, shit, he thought again.

The broadcast went on to the next news item, something about a mother of four from rural Wisconsin who had been reported missing earlier in the week. Rene thumbed the remote again, switching the television off.

"Oh, my God," Tessa said from the bed, and he turned in surprise to find her sitting up, blinking sleepily at the darkened TV. She turned to Rene, her expression stricken. "It made the news way out here?"

"Sure looks that way, *oui, pischouette,*" he replied, adding to himself, *We might be in big fucking trouble.*

"What are we going to do?" Tessa asked, all wide and frightened eyes as she crawled out of bed, reaching for her nearby socks and shoes. "We need to go and wake up Brandon and Lina. We need to tell them about this. We should—"

"No, *pischouette.*" He held up his hand. "Hold the reins. Let's not panic here."

"Not panic?" She blinked at him like he'd just pulled off the cap of his skull and flashed her a peek at his gray matter. "The police are looking for Lina!"

"Police halfway across the country from here are looking for Lina. It's nothing we need to worry about until the morning, I'm telling you. Let them sleep."

"That was the *national* news, not something from halfway across the country," Tessa argued. "We—"

"Tessa, listen to me. Those cable news outlets pick up shit like that all the time, little bits to fill the dead air in the middle of the night," Rene said. "Nobody saw it besides us night owls and chronic insomniacs and hell, even we don't pay much attention to that kind of thing."

At least here's hoping no one else does, he thought.

"I'm sorry I woke you and got you all upset," he said. "Go back to sleep. I'll leave it off."

"No." She glanced around the room almost uncertainly, rubbing her hands against her arms as if chilled. "I had a bad dream, anyway. I think I'll sit up for a while, too, if you don't mind."

"Not at all." *Looks like bad dreams are going around tonight,* he thought, adding aloud, "You want to talk about it?"

She seemed to at last take notice of the fact that his pant leg was rolled up, his prosthetic exposed, and she studied it curiously for a moment. "No. Not really." She glanced away, back to his face. "Probably just something left over from what happened with Brandon." Another glance at his knee. "What are you doing?"

"Charging my battery," he replied. "I have to do this every once in a while, otherwise it locks up on me."

She walked over to the chair, kneeling on the floor between his legs, then rested her cheek against the inside of his left thigh. When he tensed somewhat at this, feeling absurdly self-conscious with his prosthetic now directly in her face, she glanced up. "Do you mind?"

How the hell was he supposed to say no, with her gazing at him, all sweet brown eyes and a coy, slight smile? Not to mention with her mouth suddenly within kissing distance of his crotch? The idea of that alone was enough to make him relax. "No, *pischouette*. Make yourself at home."

At this invitation, she settled herself in comfortably. "I still think we should go and tell Lina and Brandon."

He caressed the top of her head. "First thing in the morning. It's going to be all right until then. I promise."

"We're going to have to leave now. Where are we going to go?"

She said this last with an anxious note in her voice,

and he understood completely. He'd hoped that by taking such a roundabout path to California—south first to Louisiana and then across the west—it might buy them some time, a few months perhaps, to elude the Elders. But she was right, and no matter how hard he tried to play nonchalant about it, he knew it, too. If someone recognized Lina's picture from TV and called the police, they would be in deep shit.

And if the dream he'd had of Augustus Noble wasn't really a dream after all, then the Elders might have been as close behind them as Thibodaux—only a matter of days. Which meant they'd be in even deeper shit.

It has to have been a dream, he tried to tell himself, even though deep down in the pit of his gut, he knew somehow it hadn't been; somehow he had been inside of Augustus Noble's head.

And oh, mon Dieu, *he was inside of mine, too.*

Chapter Twenty-three

They had made the news. Police all over the country would be looking for Lina—looking for *them*.

Oh, God, Tessa thought, shivering, and no matter Rene's reassurances, she still found herself glancing around the room or over her shoulder, as if she somehow expected to find armed SWAT members standing there in the shadows, waiting and ready to attack them.

Part of the problem was she was still on edge from her nightmare. Her mind had been troubled, tormented after what Brandon had told her that night, but she'd found some fleeting comfort in Rene's company, wrapped in his arms. Enough so that she'd thought she could take refuge at least for a little while in sleep. But her mind had other ideas.

She'd dreamed that she was outside in the night; the air was crisp and almost wintry and her breath had fogged about her face in a dim, hazy halo set aglow by the light of the moon. She hid among some tangled shrubs, a dense line of bushes marking the rear perimeter of a yard behind a small one-story bungalow. Most of the windows save one were darkened; from the way the light bounced and skittered through the one that remained illuminated, she could tell someone was awake, watching TV.

It was a small house in a small neighborhood full of cookie-cutter homes, each one squat and box-shaped with stucco exteriors painted in southwestern-inspired colors. The backyard had a sparse lawn of mostly crab-grass and weeds, with plastic children's toys left scattered about—a picnic table here, a pint-sized playhouse there, to the left, a rust-spotted swing set and to the right, a red tricycle with yellow plastic streamers protruding from each handlebar.

She dreamed of creeping close to the house, crouching alongside the back wall beneath one of the darkened windows. Here, she raised onto her tiptoes and sniffed, drawing the scents from inside the house, faint but discernable, against her nose. Pork chops for dinner, breaded and fried, with some kind of cheesy casserole baked in the oven. Laundry detergent, fabric softener, cat urine and something else—something sweet. Something that had drawn her out of the shadows and to that place, that house, that window.

Blood.

It hadn't taken much effort to pry the screen away from the window, or to hook her fingertips against the sill and pull herself up. She caught a glimpse of herself reflected in the glass and drew back in start, because it hadn't been her face she'd seen. It had been Monica Davenant's—Martin's first wife, her eyes rolled over black, her fangs extended, her jaw dislocated from the full effects of the bloodlust.

Somehow Tessa had dreamed of being Monica, of slipping her fingernails between the window pane and frame and, with the strength of the bloodlust, giving a sharp, swift enough jerk to snap the metal locking mechanisms like they'd been made from spun sugar. The window slid obligingly open and Monica had wriggled her long, narrow frame through, shimmying on her belly like an enormous snake, her extended pupils drowning her eyes but filling her sight with a nearly photo-negative view of the room beyond, one in which every scrap or hint of light, no matter how slim or meager, was detected.

She saw toys everywhere—on bookshelves and a small tabletop, a dresser, overflowing from an over-sized laundry basket in one corner. Posters of Dora the Explorer and the Disney princesses lined the walls, along with a "Grow-with-me-Elmo!" height chart. To her right was a toddler's daybed, with a painted white and faux brass metal frame and frilly, pink and white covers. A little girl lay tucked beneath the sheets, her dark hair spilled about her head against the pillow, her thumb tucked in her mouth as she slept.

Oh, God, Tessa had thought, because she'd realized what was going to happen, what she meant to do. She could smell the little girl's blood—to her keen nose, it was as thick and sweet as vanilla, the irresistible, warm fragrance of cookies baking on a cold after-noon. *Oh, God, no, don't!*

But even though she'd tried to stop herself from moving, she'd crept forward, slithering in the dark-ness, the sound of her own breath growing rapid and sodden, choked with eager slobber. She'd watched in helpless horror as her shadow had grown long, spilling across the little girl's bedsheets, and then the child had stirred, her eyes blinking open dazedly. There had been one moment of bewilderment that had shifted quickly, almost instantaneously to stark terror as the girl had realized what was at her beside, and then Tessa had heard Monica's voice in her mind, her words hissing with icy malice as she'd reached out, forcing herself into the child's head and stifling her mentally.

How sweet, Monica said, closing her hand against

the girl's nightgown and jerking her out of the bed. *Fresh meat.*

And then Tessa had awoke, her eyes wide, a scream poised in her throat. She'd found herself staring up at the ceiling of their motel room in Tahoe, the low sound of voices and the dancing play of light against the plaster from the TV set filling the room.

As she knelt on the floor, her head against Rene's leg while he charged the battery in his prosthetic knee, memories of the dream returned to her. This was probably because of her proximity to Rene's thigh, the femoral artery that lay nestled deep beneath the meat of his muscles there. She could sense it through his flesh and clothes, the heat of his blood, the fervent rush that waxed and waned with every pounding measure of his heartbeat. He'd been right when he'd rescued her from Martin. She needed to feed. The longing to had stirred even before that—the morning Rene had fallen in the bathtub and cut his lip. It had remained with her ever since even though she'd tried to repress and ignore it, a little whispering, scraping voice in the back of her head. The bloodlust.

Giving in to her sexual desires for Rene hadn't helped, either. Every time she grew aroused physically for him, the bloodlust became likewise aroused. He was half human—he felt like another of the Brethren to her in her mind when she'd sense him, but his body— his blood—smelled human to her, and there had been moments in which she'd grown so tantalized by the fragrance of him, the awareness of his blood coursing through him, that it had been a nearly painful struggle to hold herself in any semblance of restraint.

Like right now.

"No offense, *pischouette,* but if you keep doing that, I'm going to have to haul you up here into my lap and rip those pants off you."

She glanced up, snapping out of a reverie at the

sound of Rene's voice. She'd been nearly mesmerized by the rhythmic flow of blood within his thigh, so much so, she'd drifted into a nearly fuguelike state, the bloodlust within her stoking. She realized that she'd been stroking Rene's inner thigh, sliding her hand against the weathered denim of his jeans, less than half an inch away from his crotch. And, to judge by the considerable swell she could see there, straining against the zipper fly, he hadn't minded.

"I'm sorry," she whispered.

It also didn't help that whenever Rene was sexually aroused—like right now—the rate of his blood flow increased exponentially. His heartbeat quickened, his respirations sharpened, and his body released a cocktail of adrenaline and other hormones into his system that, for a Brethren, made him absolutely intoxicating.

"Don't be." He reached for her, his voice low, growing gravelly with need. "Come here, *pischouette*."

She wanted to tell him no, because she could already feel her gums begin to swell and throb, the tips of her canine teeth beginning a slight but inexorable descent. She let him draw her to her feet. He cupped his hands against her face and drew her toward him, kissing her. He tasted sweet, the rush of blood infusing his skin, his tongue, and she pressed herself against him, kissing him fiercely, wanting to slake even an iota of that desperate urge with the taste of him.

"*Mon Dieu*, woman," he whispered, nearly muffled by her mouth as she reached between them, jerking against his shirt, yanking it up from the waistband of his jeans. She caught the panels of cloth in her hands and ripped it open wide, popping buttons and seams loose, leaving his bare chest exposed.

God, I want him, she thought, leaning back long enough to shrug her way out of her own shirt, to cast it over her shoulder. She splayed her fingers against his chest, drawing them firmly along the contours of his muscles, following the plane of his abdomen until she reached the button of his fly. She kissed him again, tangling her tongue against his, helping shove his jeans down as he raised his hips from the chair. He moved to unbutton her pants, but she pushed his hands away to do it herself. She had to hurry; she was desperate for him now, her body caught in some strained limbo between the bloodlust and physical need. If she didn't take him, if she didn't grind herself to one hell of a massive orgasm against him, she was afraid of what she'd do, of where her desires would take her next.

"I don't want to hurt you," she breathed, her voice hoarse and trembling. She'd shoved her pants down and kicked them across the room. Now she straddled him, shoving her knees down between the arms of the chair and his hips, and crouched with him poised to enter her. He strained to kiss her, craning his head back.

"You're not going to hurt me," he said, and as his hands draped against her hips to guide her, she fell against him, impaling herself along his hot, hard length. His voice dissolved in a moan that she muffled with a kiss as she moved into a quick, grinding rhythm against him.

"Tu es étonnant, femme," he gasped, over and over. *You are amazing, woman.* "Goddamn, *tu es étonnant!"*

He moved his head to kiss her shoulder, but as he did, it left the side of his throat exposed to her. God, she could smell the blood pounding through his carotid artery, she could damn near hear the resonant rush of it, and she caught him by the hair, curling her fingers tightly and holding his head pinned at that angle. Her gums ached now, sharp and distinct pain as her teeth dropped, and she leaned toward him, feeling her breath flutter against his sweat-glossed skin.

"Rene, stop," she whispered, but as she spoke her lips danced against his flesh, and the blood was so tantalizingly within her reach, she salivated unconsciously.

Rene drove her harder and harder against him, digging his fingers fiercely into her buttocks. He was nearing climax; she could feel it in the tension that had suddenly steeled the muscles bridging his neck and shoulders. She could hear it in the way he gasped for breath; she could sense it in the jack-hammering of his heartbeat and smell it in the ambrosia of adrenaline, hormones and blood that his body radiated in thick, hot waves.

She opened her mouth, letting her lips settle against his throat as she might have to feed; letting her tongue press against the frantic point of his pulse, the tips of her teeth just barely nipping his flesh.

"Tessa!" he gasped, and when he came, he hit that spot deep within that always sent shudders of pleasure almost instantaneously through her. She dug her nails into his shoulders and writhed, grinding against him, keeping him at that glorious place as the bloodlust within her was obliterated—drowned in the sudden, wondrous throes of release.

As they subsided, she huddled against him, wide-eyed with the horrified realization of what she'd done—of just how close she'd come. *Oh, God!*

She could feel her teeth withdrawing, her canines sliding back into her gums, and she pressed her lips together in a thin line.

Oh, my God. She closed her eyes, stricken and ashamed. *Oh, God, I . . . I almost hurt him . . . I nearly bit into his neck!*

"*Mon Dieu,*" Rene said with a breathless, shaky laugh. "Another time or two like that, *pischouette*, and you're going to kill me."

He kissed her shoulder, running his hands up and down the length of her spine, caressing her. *God help me,* she thought, clutching his shoulder, keeping her face turned away. *God help us both, you're more right than you know, Rene.*

Chapter Twenty-four

"You want the good news or the bad news first, *chère?*" Rene asked Lina. It was shortly after six in the morning; the sun was only a rosy hint outlining the mountains along the horizon. Lina had answered her motel room door wearing only a thin T-shirt that fell to her hips and a pair of leopard-print panties, her long legs bare beneath. Lina ran more than ten miles every day, come rain, snow, sleet or hail. He loved her like a sister, but he had to admit, the girl had a hell of a set of gams.

"Rene?" She blinked at him, scowling groggily, then tucked her hair behind her ears. He could see goose bumps that had raised almost immediately on her arms, the bullet points of her nipples pushing out from beneath her T-shirt. "Jesus Christ, it's cold. Get in here."

She sidestepped and shut the door behind him as he walked into the room. It was deliciously warm inside, a toasty contrast to the crisp morning air. He shuddered slightly like a dog shaking off a splash of water, adjusting to the sudden, dramatic difference. Brandon lay on his stomach, asleep on the bed, his head turned away from the door.

"Sorry to come so early, *chère,*" Rene said, unzipping the front of his ski jacket.

"What time is it anyway?" Lina growled, squinting at

the digital bedside clock. When she made note of the hour, she groaned. "Rene, what the hell do you want? I'm sorry about last night, but please don't tell me you've been up all this time stewing over it."

"I haven't been, no. And your apology is accepted." He gave her a smacking, playful kiss on the lips, leaving her to sputter while he unfolded his laptop computer on a nearby table. "The good news, *chère,* is that between you, Brandon, me and Tessa, we've got about fifteen thousand dollars cash in our hands we can use to live on."

"Yeah?" Lina said somewhat suspiciously. When he sat down in a chair facing the table, she plopped down opposite him, drawing her knees together to sit in a clumsy, tomboyish posture he found amusing and sort of cute. "What's the bad news?"

"We're going to have to make that last awhile, I'm afraid," he replied, cuing his wi-fi internet connection. He spared her a glance. "My bank accounts have been frozen."

Lina's eyes flew wide. "What?"

He nodded once, grim. "*Oui.* I was online this morning checking on some investments and found out. All of my primary accounts—checking, savings, CDs, IRAs, my stock portfolios—everything I have in my name is on hold."

"On hold? By who?"

He typed something into the Google search bar, hit a couple of links, and spun the computer around to face her. "By our dear old Uncle Sam, *chère.* Seems like you and me, we're now officially *les gens d'intérêt* in the murder investigation for Jude Hannam and his girlfriend."

Her eyes widened all the more. "*What?*" She leaned forward, incredulous, pulling the laptop closer. "Let me see that."

It was an online copy of an article that had run in the *Metropolitan Courier* two days earlier. As startled as he'd been to discover he'd been locked out of his own bank accounts, he hadn't needed to call his accounting firm to find out why. The news piece had explained it all.

FORMER POLICE PARTNERS SOUGHT IN GRISLY SLAYINGS, the headline declared.

> Two former police partners are being sought for questioning in the ritualistic murder of local personal-injury attorney Jude Hannam and his girlfriend earlier this month. Angelina Jones and Rene Morin served on the Metropolitan Police Force together and were assigned as partners until last year, when Morin was left hospitalized and Jones on paid administrative leave following a shootout with a suspected drug dealer and gang member.
>
> Jude Hannam's body was one of two found following a bizarre, late-night incident aboard the river-barge nightclub complex, Apathy, in which patrons reported an attack by a flock of birds. More than two dozen people were injured in that incident. In the aftermath, Hannam was discovered in the Catacombs, a gothic-themed bar at Apathy that is reportedly popular among the city's growing "vampire" subculture.
>
> Hannam's girlfriend, Ashlee Ferris, was found slain in the Victorian-district apartment the two shared. Both had suffered massive injuries to their upper torsos and throats and the state medical examiner has ruled that both died from blood loss as a result of this trauma. Police would not speculate as to whether or not the manners of death were related to the alternative lifestyle practiced by many patrons of the Catacombs, including the wearing of vampirelike dental prosthetics and the recreational consumption of animal and human blood.
>
> According to the ongoing police investigation into Hannam's death, he and Officer Jones had dated until recently. Days before the killing, witnesses reported seeing Hannam and Jones arguing loudly during a wedding reception both had attended. Jones was on duty on the night of Hannam's murder and had entered the Apathy

nightclub complex, but police officials now say she was not on any documented police business.

She disappeared after the bird attack and local cab driver Abdul Aziz ben Malik reported that he drove her and an as-yet unidentified white male later that same night to an address listed as the residence of Rene Morin, Jones's former police partner. According to Ben Malik, both Jones and her male companion had blood on them and appeared to have been in some kind of physical altercation.

Morin retired from his duties following an incident in which he was shot in the knee. His leg was subsequently amputated. The suspect in that case, Reginald White, was killed at the scene when Jones returned fire. Morin is also a stockholder for Artois Oil, one of the largest independent drillers and producers of crude oil in the United States. Police have been unable to contact him for questioning related to the whereabouts of Jones and her male companion.

A second victim at Apathy was discovered beaten and shot to death on the night Hannam's body was found. Forensic tests have yet to conclude whether or not those shots came from Jones's service pistol.

Although Hannam and Ferris's deaths are being linked, along with the shooting victim who has yet to be identified, at this time, neither Jones nor Morin are considered suspects. Because neither can be reached by police, they are considered persons of interest, and anyone with information on their whereabouts are asked to contact the Homicide Division of the Metropolitan police.

"This is bullshit," Lina said, after she'd finished reading.

"Hey, it gets better," Rene said. "The story was picked up online by Fark. We got a 'weird' label."

"This isn't funny, Rene," Lina said with a frown. "We're in some serious shit here."

"It gets better," he assured. "I saw a piece on CNN

last night. I thought it was just a filler thing until this morning, but no. And I doubt this is the last we're going to hear about it."

"Terrific," Lina said, her expression clearly imparting she considered the news anything but. She folded her arms across her chest and leaned back in her chair, pressing her lips together in a thin line. She glanced at Brandon, then back to Rene. "What are we going to do?"

He shrugged, mimicking her posture. "Not much we can do, *chère*. At least not for the moment, other than keep a low profile and try not to burn our way through our operating capital too quickly."

He reached over and squeezed her shoulder gently. "I've got that place out by Emerald Bay where we've stashed *Monsieur* Davenant. It's not much, but it's a roof over our heads. Nobody's going to think to look for us there, at least not for a while. It's not high on my dossier of real estate, if anyone thinks to try and look. We can stick with my original plan—use Martin to try and call off the Elders for good. And in the meantime, you and I can try to throw anyone else off our tails a bit more."

"How?" Lina asked.

He nodded toward the window, the parking lot beyond. "I had to rent that Jeep out there on a credit card. If my bank accounts are frozen, they're looking at shit like that, too, so they'll see I used it here."

Lina's brows narrowed, but before she could say anything, he cut her off. "How the hell was I supposed to know the police would put everything together like this? Anyway, it doesn't matter. I can take the Jeep this morning and drive it out to San Francisco, drop it off at the airport there. You can follow along in the Mercedes and give me a lift back. Hopefully that will throw the police off our scents for a while until I can iron out at least part of this mess, get our cash flow restored."

"Oh, really?" Lina raised her brow. "How are you going to do that?"

"I haven't thought it out that far yet." Rene smiled

wanly at her and dropped a wink. "But don't worry. I'm rich, *chère*. And I retain a lot of very good lawyers and accountants who help keep me that way."

He disconnected from the Internet and folded the laptop. "We need to get moving if we're going to do this," he said. "I'm just going to leave Tessa a note. No sense in waking her only to argue about whether or not she can come. You want to do the same for Brandon? We can tell them to just lay low, that we'll be back sometime later this afternoon."

"All right," she said after an uncertain moment.

"Good. Can you be ready to leave in about fifteen minutes? I'll meet you out in the parking lot." He winked again. "It'll be just like old times, no? You and me against the world."

She watched him rise to his feet and looked up at him. "Rene," she said, her voice and expression uncharacteristically abashed and meek. When he glanced down, she reached out and hooked her fingertips against his. "I'm sorry about last night. I didn't mean to hurt you. You've done so much to help me and Brandon . . ." She cut her gaze down to her lap, her dark eyes glossy with sudden tears, her voice growing strained. "It's my fault you're in this mess to begin with, and I . . . the last thing I ever want is to hurt you."

He caressed her cheek with the cuff of his fingers. "*Il est bien, chère,*" he said, leaning over to kiss her nose. *It's all right.* "I told you, apology accepted."

Lina smiled, stroking her hand against his face as he pulled away. "Thanks, Rene."

"Anytime, *chère*," he replied with a smile. "Wouldn't have missed it for the world."

Chapter Twenty-five

Tessa woke to find herself blinking at the barrel of a gun.

Rene had left it for her on the bedside table, the .45-caliber revolver he'd picked up from the dead would-be bandit at the roadside rest area. That morning, Rene had apparently intended it to be as much a paperweight as an item of personal protection, judging by the note he'd pinned beneath it.

Bon jour, the note opened, and it occurred to her as she sat somewhat propped up in bed, resting on her elbows, her hair sleepily tumbled in her face, that this was the first time she'd ever seen his handwriting. For a man whose appearance was often anything but, his penmanship was remarkably neat.

> *Something weird has come up, and Lina and I have gone to San Francisco to take care of it. Will be back late this afternoon and will explain more then. Don't kill your brother in the meantime.—R.*

She glanced at the bedside clock; it was only shortly before eight in the morning. She and Rene had been up late, well past midnight. *What could have come up*

*between now and then that was "weird" enough to send him
all of the way to San Francisco?*

A knock at the door drew her attention and she
frowned, crawling out of bed. She hadn't bothered to
put on her gown the night before, or redress after
making love to Rene in the armchair outside of slipping his T-shirt over her head. Her jeans lay in a pile
on the floor and she stepped into them, drawing them
up to her hips before crossing to answer the door. In
that brief amount of time, whoever was there knocked
again and again, louder and more insistent each time.

"Jesus," she growled, unlocking the turn-bolt. "All
right already." She opened the door to find Brandon
on the stoop. "What do you want?" she asked with a
scowl, wishing she'd thought to grab the pistol off the
nightstand.

Lina's gone, he said, holding out a piece of paper
that she didn't need to see.

"I know. She and Rene went to San Francisco. He
left me a note, too."

He raised his brow. *He tell you what was going on?*

"Not really," she replied. "But I sort of know." When
his expression grew quizzical, she said, "The police think
Lina is involved in what happened at that nightclub."

What? Brandon's eyes flown wide, his mouth
slightly agape. *How do you know that?*

She stepped aside, flapping her hand in unspoken
invitation and he walked into the room. It was cold
out; his breath had been frosting the air around his
head, and chill bumps had risen all along her arms
just from standing in the doorway.

"We saw it on TV," Tessa said. "There was a little
news bit about it on CNN. They were talking about
what had happened with the birds, and how the
police had found Caine's body . . . and Jude's."

Jude Hannam? Brandon said, and she nodded. *Her ex-
boyfriend?* He paused for a moment, then his expression

grew stricken. *Jesus, Tessa, the police don't think Lina had something to do with what happened to Jude, do they?*

He looked so distraught, so immediately guilt-ridden that she couldn't stay angry with him. *Brandon, it's all right,* she said.

It's my fault, he said. *They'll want to arrest her now because of what happened.*

"No, they won't," she said. "Lina didn't kill Jude. They can't arrest her for something she didn't do."

No, but she killed Caine, he replied. *She shot him. They can sure as hell arrest her for that.*

He was going to kill her. Tessa knelt in front of him, meeting his gaze. *He would have killed you, too, Brandon. You know it—you know how he was. It was self-defense. Lina didn't have a choice. Neither of you did.*

How is she supposed to explain that? Brandon stood, his hands balled into fists. *What is she supposed to say— that her boyfriend is a vampire who was being hunted down by his crazy vampire brother, who also happened to have killed her ex-boyfriend? They'll think she's nuts. They'll lock her up and throw away the goddamn key.*

He began to pace, restless and alarmed. *This is all my fault.*

"Don't say that, Brandon," she said, standing.

He wheeled to her, his brows furrowed. *It's true, Tessa. All of this is my fault! Lina and Rene have gone to San Francisco to try and make things right somehow. And it's not their place to. It's mine.*

"What do you mean?" she asked, and when he shook his head, she caught him by the sleeve. "What are you going to do, Brandon?"

I don't know, he replied, his expression still grim. *But I got us all into this fucking mess, Tessa. Now I've got to get us out of it somehow.*

* * *

They went to breakfast, riding together in Martin's Jaguar.

Why do you think Rene and Lina took two cars? Brandon had asked in the motel parking lot.

I don't know, Tessa had replied, curious about this herself. It didn't make sense that Rene would have taken the rented Jeep all the way to San Francisco anyway; not when he had to pay for mileage on it, and they had two other cars he could have used for free. He'd picked up the Jeep locally and she couldn't fathom any reason why he'd take it clear to San Francisco to return if he was finished with it.

At a nearby diner, she ordered for Brandon and he blinked in surprise when instead of her customary oatmeal for herself, she ordered three slices of cherry pie.

Why? he asked when the waitress was gone.

"Pie's good for breakfast," Tessa said, unfolding her napkin and placing it primly in her lap. "It's not that much different than a danish or doughnut if you think about it. And cherry's the best. Not too sweet. Sort of tart." When he still looked at her like she'd just thrown her shirt wide open and sat there in front of God, the other patrons and the whole of South Lake Tahoe with her breasts hanging out, she laughed. "Really. You should try it some time."

Why three pieces? he asked.

"Because," Tessa replied. "I like pie."

After ordering, the twins sat for a long time, Brandon nursing a cup of black coffee and Tessa, a glass of milk. He was still deeply troubled. She could tell from his posture, the distant, melancholy cast to his eyes as he gazed aimlessly out the window. She tried several times to talk to him, offering idle chitchat, but he didn't fall for it.

The waitress delivered their food, and as Tessa scooped up her first heaping forkful of pie, she watched as Brandon carefully folded his fingers around the handle of his fork and speared a bite of scrambled eggs off his plate.

How are your hands? she asked, trying yet again to get his mind off Lina and the news story.

This time, Brandon seemed to take the bait, smiling for the first time since he'd come to her motel room door that morning. *Almost back to normal.* He set his fork down, chewing his eggs, and picked up a strip of bacon between his forefinger and thumb. *There's still some soreness. Not much, but a little, and everything feels pretty stiff when I try to move, but otherwise good.*

She didn't miss the way his gaze swept across her face, or how his smile faltered. *Your face is almost back to normal, too,* he observed as he took a bite of bacon.

She'd noticed it, too, that morning; the bruising in her face had faded enough so that a light layer of makeup had nearly disguised it completely from view. Around her neck, the contusions had been bad enough to still remain, faded gray handprints encircling her throat. She'd worn a turtleneck to breakfast, but Brandon had undoubtedly seen them that morning at the motel. As Rene had pointed out to her once, he was deaf, not blind. If she were to feed, they would be gone almost instantaneously, but all she had to do to dispel any urge was think back to her horrifying nightmare in which she'd somehow been Monica Davenant creeping into a little girl's bedroom with the intent to gorge herself—or remind herself of just how close she'd come to doing the exact same thing while making love to Rene only the night before.

Suddenly it was her turn to stiffen, and she wished she'd just kept her mouth shut and eaten her pie. *I don't want to talk about that anymore, Brandon.* She struggled to smile. *Let's talk about something fun. Something that has nothing to do with Martin or Caine or Grandmother Eleanor or the Brethren.*

At the mention of Eleanor, his expression shifted,

growing nearly ashamed. He watched her scrape the side of her fork tines against her plate, gathering the last traces of cherry pie filling. *Tessa,* he began at length, sounding hesitant and uncertain. *About last night . . . I didn't mean—*

"I said let's talk about something fun, Brandon," she said, drawing a peculiar look from the waitress as she leaned over the table to refill Brandon's mug. Tessa managed a polite smile as the woman walked away, then looked at her brother again. "Look, we've got the day to ourselves and I say we make the most of it."

Brandon raised his brows, curious. *What do you mean?*

Tessa smiled again, unforced this time. "You'll see."

Several hours later, the twins stood along the shores of Emerald Bay, their feet in the damp, graveled sand of a wide beach. Behind them, a stone-walled mansion called Vikingsholm stood sentry over the smooth, tranquil plane of water that was broken only by a small, knobby outcropping called Fannette Island. Part of a state park, Vikingsholm had been the last stop in a sightseeing tour that had taken them around the southernmost edge of Lake Tahoe. The day had proven flawless; a cloudless sky overhead, the air cool but pleasant all around them. They had bought disposable cameras and packed a picnic lunch, playing tourists for the first time in their lives and enjoying themselves the entire time.

Tessa watched Brandon walk ahead of her, almost to the lip of the water. He stood with a light breeze rustling his dark hair, his head tilted back slightly, and as she moved to stand beside him, she saw his eyes were closed, the corners of his mouth lifted in a soft smile.

God, it's beautiful here, he thought to her. When a car drove by on the road behind them along a steep mountainside slope, he turned, his brow raised slightly, as if he'd somehow—impossibly—heard the growl of its engine carried by the wind and water.

Rene owns property nearby, she telegraphed, pointing north. *Somewhere that way. He took me there yesterday. Twenty-five acres, I think he said, and some kind of little house he thinks was once used to watch for forest fires. It had all belonged to his father.*

She didn't add that this was where Martin was being held. Brandon knew this on his own, but more important, she didn't want to spoil what had turned out to be a perfect day by thinking about or mentioning Martin Davenant.

Vikingsholm was closed for seasonal tours until later in the spring, but they'd been able to read about the building's history from an informational display. It had been built in the late 1920s by a wealthy family named the Knights. They'd once hosted elaborate parties at the house and traveled by boat out to Fannette Island, where a little castlelike building had been constructed, and where they would continue with festivities started on the mainland.

I would love to live out here, Brandon remarked, closing his eyes again. *There's something peaceful about this place, don't you think? I feel like . . . I don't know. Like I belong here.*

"Rene said he's always felt the same way." Tessa looked out across the water, listening to the soft slap of low-lying waves against the pebbled beach. She could smell the rich fragrance of pine sap in the wind and hear the low, comforting murmur as it rustled through tens of thousands of spindly needles in the boughs all around them. Every once in a while, the tranquil stillness was broken by the rustle and snap of a pinecone crashing down. There were no other visitors, no tourists; she and Brandon had the breadth of the beach and its wondrous view all to themselves. "Like he'd come home, he said."

She thought of what it would be like to live there,

as well, imagining Rene's father coming to spend his summers at the lakeshore. Had he been acquainted with his neighbors, the Knights, who had built Vikingsholm? Had Rene's family once picnicked on the shores of Emerald Bay with them, attended their lavish parties or sailed out to Fannette Island for cocktails and cards? The placard outside of the mansion said that the Knight family had helped to fund Charles Lindburgh's famous flight around the world. Had Rene's family helped as well, due to some association or friendship with the Knights?

It's funny, Brandon said. *I used to feel so trapped at the farm. All of that land, and I still felt like it was a cage. But here . . .* He breathed in deeply, filling his lungs with air as if he couldn't get enough, and stretched his arms out wide like he meant to embrace the horizon. *Here, I feel free.*

She smiled. It had been too long since she'd seen Brandon look so genuinely happy. For years at the great house, her twin had lived under a shadow of pervasive melancholia. To watch him now, it was like a heavy burden had been lifted off his shoulders; for the first time in as long as she could remember, Brandon looked free, happy and comfortable in his own skin.

You know, a few years ago, I overheard Dad thinking, he said. He opened his eyes and glanced to his right, meeting her gaze. *He'd been drinking, so his mind was open, unguarded,* he said. *He didn't know I could overhear him. He never meant for me to know.*

"Know what?" Tessa asked.

Brandon smiled, somewhat wistful and sad. *That he wished I'd died the night I was attacked,* he said. *That he'd prayed for it. He didn't want me to suffer, to live my life like this.*

"Brandon, that's not true," Tessa whispered.

Yes, it is, he replied. *I told you—I saw it in his mind.* He turned his eyes back to the water. *I was so hurt, Tessa. I couldn't even move. I just sat there, frozen solid,*

*thinking at any moment, I was going to bust into tears like
some dumb fucking baby and bawl all over the place.*

"Brandon . . ." She touched his sleeve, heartbroken
for him. As close as she'd always believed herself to be
with Eleanor, Brandon had likewise been endeared
with their father. Brandon had pretty much been Sebastian's shadow as a child, finding comfort and com-
panionship, somebody with whom he felt safe and
loved in a house filled with other family members with
whom he felt anything but.

He never meant for me to know, he said again. *And it
would have killed him to realize that I did. I could sense that,
too.* He smiled again, still mournful. *Sometimes you can't
help how you feel. And sometimes you feel all different kinds
of things for different people. Like Dad did for me.*

His eyes had grown misty, clouded with a light sheen
of tears, but he shoved his hands into the hip pockets of
his jeans and blinked furiously, as if wanting to hide
them from her. *Maybe that's how it was for Grandmother
Eleanor and you, too.*

"Brandon," she began. "I told you—"

I know what you said, he cut in. *But I'm sorry about
what happened last night. I never wanted you to know about
that. And I'm sure Grandmother Eleanor didn't, either.*

"It doesn't matter," Tessa said.

Yes, it does. Brandon turned to her. *Dad never meant
for me to know how he felt because he loved me. Just like
Grandmother Eleanor loved you, too. I know because she
gave you that green sapphire pendant.*

"That?" Tessa uttered a sharp bark of laughter.
"That necklace was a joke, Brandon. She probably lied
to me about the whole thing, that the Grandfather had
given it to her—his first gift, she'd told me. All of it was
just a sick, cruel joke." Her voice grew strained, her
eyes stinging with tears and she looked away, pressing
her lips together. *Goddamn it, I'm not going to cry,* she
thought. *Not this time. Not anymore—not about this!*

Things were different for us, Brandon said. *We had things differently in the great house—you, me, Grandmother Eleanor, all of us because of the Grandfather, because the Nobles were dominant. But you saw how things were in the Davenant house. You always knew how things were in the other clans. Grandmother Eleanor knew, too. She grew up like that, Tessa. That was all she'd ever known until she became a Noble.*

He reached out, touching her shoulder. *I don't know why she said those things to me,* he said. *I don't know what she felt. But I think she loved you. I don't think she lied to you about that necklace. I think it was one of the things in this world that meant the most to her, and she gave it to you because she loved you. Because once you were married, once you were part of the Davenant house, she knew how things would be for you and wanted to make it better somehow— because she remembered how it was before she married the Grandfather. Hell, maybe you're right—maybe he wasn't always such a son of a bitch. Maybe they were in love.*

"If he loved her, why would he kill her?" Tessa shrugged away from him. "Martin told me the Grandfather strangled her."

Yeah, but you don't know that, Brandon said. *Not for sure. You—*

"You're right. I don't know that. I don't know anything for sure. Not anymore." She turned, walking back toward the mansion. As she tromped across the beach, her tears spilled, leaving hot, damp streaks against her cold cheeks. She pulled her hands from her pockets one at a time to mop them away. The part of her that had loved Eleanor wanted so desperately for what Brandon had said to be true. The other part, which had been wounded to the core, was left torn and bewildered, unsure of how or what to think, feel or believe.

It doesn't matter anyway, she told herself. *Not what she said or what she meant or why she gave me that goddamn necklace. Monica took it. It's gone now and I'll never get it back.*

Tessa . . . Brandon thought and she heard the

crunch of his shoes in the sandy gravel as he followed her. *Tessa, wait.*

But she didn't want to wait. She'd told him over breakfast she didn't want to talk about it anymore, but he'd pushed the subject anyway. *Damn it, Brandon,* she thought, closing her mind to him, her brows furrowing with the conscientious effort to block him. *It was turning out to be such a nice day, too. Couldn't you have just left it alone?*

Tessa—stop! Brandon snapped, his voice punching into her mind despite her best attempts to keep him out, sharp enough with concern that she paused.

"What is it?" All at once, she felt what had so alarmed her brother—a creeping, prickling sensation within her mind, raising the hairs along the nape of her neck.

Someone is here, Brandon said, but she already knew. She could sense it, too.

She turned and her breath cut abruptly short as she caught sight of a woman on the beach, striding briskly from the direction of a fishing pier jutting out over the water to the north. She was tall and reed-slender, dressed head to toe in a cream-colored blouse and slacks. There was no mistaking the fine sheaf of auburn hair that fluttered about her face in the wind, no mistaking *her,* but because there was no way Monica Davenant could be in California, much less on the same scrap of earth as the twins, Tessa simply stood there for a shocked, bewildered moment, frozen in place.

Oh, God, it wasn't just a dream, she thought in horror. *Last night when I saw her climbing through that window . . . grabbing that little girl . . . it wasn't a dream at all! Oh, God, I was sensing her somehow!*

Tessa, run! Brandon apparently didn't need any introductions to Martin's first wife. If he didn't recognize her face, given what had been their limited acquaintance in Kentucky, he knew her by sensation

alone—and knew she wasn't there to extend either of
them the welcome wagon. He turned to face Monica,
positioning his body deliberately between her and
Tessa. His hands folded into light, wary fists and Tessa
watched his entire body tense.

Monica didn't slow her pace in the least. "Where is
Martin?" she asked, directing the question to Tessa,
speaking as though Brandon wasn't even there at all,
like she was oblivious to his presence. She'd glutted
herself on the little girl Tessa had dreamed about, and
her body was still endowed from this, her strength
heightened, her reflexes superhuman, nearly to the
point where she would be impervious to pain. Her
eyes were black and featureless beneath her furrowed
brows, in stark and ghoulish contrast to her alabaster
skin. Her fangs had almost fully descended. "You fucking bitch, what have you done to my husband?"

Tessa, run, Brandon said again, shooting her an urgent, frantic glance over his shoulder. *Get out of here! Go!*

When he stepped directly in Monica's path, as if he
meant to run into her headlong, she cut her icy glare
in his direction. "*You!*" she spat, as if noticing who he
was for the first time.

She might have said something else, more than
this, but Brandon hooked his left fist around, smashing his knuckles into the side of her face. The force of
the blow snapped her head toward her shoulder and
nearly knocked her off her feet. She stumbled, regain-
ing her footing, and pressed her hand to her cheek.
"Bastard," she hissed, her brows furrowing more
deeply. Blood dribbled in a thin line from her left nostril as she spoke; she turned her head and spat more
out against the grass. "You little bastard!"

She marched toward him and Brandon swung at her
again, a swift punch aimed expertly for her nose.
Monica whipped her head to one side, raising her
hand, catching Brandon's fist squarely against her

palm. Tessa heard the sharp, startled intake of his breath and then Monica threw him by the arm, wrenching him off his feet and sending him sailing like a rag doll tossed by a toddler in the throes of a tantrum.

"Brandon!" Tessa cried.

He landed hard, slamming to the ground and tumbling down to the water's edge, where he lay facedown and still for a long, breathless, stunned moment. *Tessa . . .* He raised his head, his dazed eyes finding hers. *For God's sake . . . run!*

Tessa turned and bolted toward the house. She had no intention of abandoning her brother, especially not with Monica fully imbued with the power of the bloodlust. But she knew she had to get the woman away from Brandon. *She'll kill him—kill us both. My only chance is to lose her in the woods, double back, grab Brandon and get to the car.*

Rene had kept his Sig Sauer in the glove box of the Audi. Had he moved it to the Jaguar or was it back at the motel? She didn't know, and cursed herself now for not having grabbed the other pistol he'd left out on the nightstand that morning.

She heard Monica following, her footsteps quick in the grass. At a loud, unexpected crash and a grunt for breath, she wheeled about. Brandon had clambered to his feet and given chase; he'd tackled Monica and pinned her against the lawn by straddling her waist, holding her wrists in his hands. Monica thrashed wildly beneath him and as he struggled to hold her down, he looked up at Tessa again.

Go! he yelled in her mind.

Not without you! she cried back, rushing toward him. She didn't know what she meant to do, but she couldn't—wouldn't—leave him.

Tessa, goddamn it, I said—! Brandon began, and then Monica rammed her knee brutally into his crotch.

"Brandon!" Tessa cried. He uttered a choked gasp,

the wind and fight effectively plowed from him. He
collapsed helplessly onto his side, his face was twisted
and flushed with pain, his entire body shuddering as
Monica wiggled out from beneath him. She stumbled
to her feet and kicked him hard, driving the pointed
toe of her shoe into the small of his back.

Brandon had only fed twice before; he was still unfamiliar with the bloodlust, uncertain of how to use
it, but it had been years since Tessa's bloodletting and
she had fed many, many times. At the sight of her
brother writhing in pain against the grass, Tessa felt it
surge within her like something alive and electric. The
world grew bright, dazzling and glaring as her pupils
expanded, flooding her corneas. She tasted a coppery
rush of saliva in her mouth, felt a sudden, throbbing
ache as her canine teeth dropped. As she marched
across the lawn toward Monica and Brandon, her
hands closed into fierce fists, her stride broad and
brisk, and she shook her head, listening to the dull,
moist *pop* as her lower jaw snapped loose of its hinges.

"Keep your"—she caught Monica by the shoulder
as the older woman reached down, meaning to grab
Brandon by the scruff of his collar and haul him to his
feet.—"fucking hands off him."

Monica's eyes flew wide as Tessa wheeled her about.
She grabbed Monica by the throat and heaved mightily, hurling her skyward. Monica flew ass over elbows
across the beach, slamming facefirst into the broad
trunk of a pine tree and crashing in a heap to the
ground. Tessa didn't give her a moment to recover;
she crouched low to the ground, then sprang into the
air, her long legs unfurling as she leapt, catlike. For a
moment, she seemed to hang suspended in the air,
the way a hummingbird will be caught in limbo between momentum and stillness as it hovers at a feeder,
and then, just as Monica began to sit up, her red hair

tangled in her face, Tessa plowed into her, knocking her back into the dirt.

"Gunnnnnngh!" Tessa landed hard against Monica's back and grunted as Monica snapped her elbow back, smashing into her chin, stunning her. Monica bucked, heaving herself onto her hands and knees, and Tessa pitched sideways, sprawling against a heavy carpet of fallen pine needles.

"You bitch—" Monica began, her brows furrowed, then Tessa drove the heel of her shoe into her face, mashing her lips into her teeth and rocking her head back on her neck.

"Go fuck yourself, Monica," Tessa seethed, but when she drew her leg back to punt again, Monica grabbed her suddenly, furiously by the ankle.

"I'm going to enjoy making you bleed, you little cunt," Monica said, and Tessa yelped as she flung her, hoisting her effortlessly from the ground and sending her careening across the yard. Low-hanging pine boughs slapped against her face, tugging at her hair, and then she crashed to the ground.

The baby! Tessa thought in bright alarm, curling herself into a ball the split second before impact, trying to shield her belly from the brunt of the blow. She rolled against the grass, barking her hip and shoulder painfully, knocking the wind momentarily from herself.

She struggled to rise, forcing herself to move, to get her feet beneath her. She couldn't fight Monica, not face-to-face or hand to hand, not if she meant to protect the baby. There was no way. *She fed just last night—she's too strong,* she realized.

Brandon, get to the car, she thought, stumbling upright. *We have to get out of here. I'm going to try and lose her in the woods. Meet me at the—*

She felt a hand close suddenly, firmly against her sleeve, jerking her about, and she balled her hand into a fist and let it fly, using the momentum as she pivoted to her advantage. Her knuckles plowed into Monica's cheek, snapping her head to the side and sent her stumbling, her fingers loosening from Tessa's coat. She cut her eyes to Tessa, her black, featureless, furious gaze, and when Tessa moved to backhand her, she caught her by the fist. "You"—she seethed, reaching out with her free hand and seizing Tessa by the collar of her ski parka.—"aren't going . . . anywhere!"

Tessa yelped as Monica threw her again, sending her sailing into the air. Her voice ripped up into a scream as she crashed through one of the large picture windows on the second story of the house. Glass exploded all around her, slicing into her face, scalp and hands as she desperately tried to shield herself from the stinging spray. She sailed across the breadth of the room, smashing into a doorway and slamming to the floor, splintering a decorative wooden beam hanging above the threshold as she went. The impact knocked the breath from her and she lay crumpled against the floor, surrounded by thousands of glass shards, gulping for air.

Oh, God . . . the baby!

Her hand darted for her stomach and she opened her mind, straining to feel the soft glow of the child's presence within her. After a long, seemingly endless moment in which she couldn't seem to breathe, she felt it, dim but apparent, still nestled safely inside of her womb. *For now, anyway,* she thought, closing her eyes and heaving a relieved sigh. *I've got to get out of here, away from Monica.*

Tessa! she heard Brandon cry, his voice shrill with frantic alarm.

Brandon, get to the car, she thought again. Blood streamed down her face in countless thin rivulets and a rainfall of glass pieces spilled from her hair and shoulders as she sat up. *Run toward the trees and . . . and*

double back . . . lose Monica if you can. She looked
around, pressing the heel of her hand to her aching
head, struggling dazedly to find the nearest doorway.
She . . . she's too strong . . . don't try to fight her. Just run.
I'll meet you at the car.

Vikingsholm had been built with classical Norse ar-
chitecture in mind, and she found herself blinking
down at the remnants of the crossbeam she'd
smashed into; a Nordic-inspired carved wooden snake
or dragon of some sort that had been suspended by
two iron chains from the exposed beams of the ceiling, its mouth agape, its tongue protruding to form
the shape of a rudimentary trident.

She looked back toward the shattered window and
shrank in surprise as Monica crawled into view, hauling herself up and over the broken windowsill. She'd
climbed up the exterior of the house as nimbly as any
squirrel, by hooking her fingertips and the pointed
toes of her Jimmy Choo stiletto heels into the mortar
nooks and crannies along the mansion's stone façade.
Now her French manicured nails were ragged, her
fingers scraped or torn raw and bloody in places.

She shambled toward Tessa, teetering on her
spiked heels, splinters of glass crunching beneath her.
"Tell me where Martin is!" Her words lisped around
the unhinged maw of her mouth.

Tessa snatched the nearest weapon she could
find—a heavy, sharp-tipped fireplace poker from a
stand beside a nearby fireplace—and whirled, grasping the handle between her palms, swinging it like a
baseball bat. The iron hook caught Monica squarely
in the cheek, snapping her head sideways toward her
shoulder and ripping back a broad flap of skin and
meat from her face. There was a sickening, moist
crunch as bone splintered at the impact and Monica
crumpled to her hands and knees.

"Bitch . . . !" she wheezed, glaring up at Tessa, her

flesh flapping freely against her face like some kind of grisly, half-assed mask. There was blood in her hair now, blood in her teeth, smeared into her scalp and down the front of her shirt.

Tessa reared the poker back in her hands like a golf club to swing again, but Monica leaped up, surprising her with a forceful tackle that sent them both crashing to the floor. The poker flew from Tessa's fingers; Monica landed heavily against her, crushing the air from her lungs. They grappled together, struggling and thrashing, and Monica coiled her fingers in Tessa's hair, grasping her above either ear.

"I'll kill you!" she screamed, slamming Tessa's head against the floor once, twice, three violent, furious times, until Tessa tasted blood in her mouth and her line of sight danced with a dizzying array of lights. "You and your goddamn brother! I'll tear you both apart with my goddamn hands—now *you tell me where my husband is!*"

"Get off me!" Tessa cried, wedging her foot between them, planting her heel against Monica's midriff. She punted mightily, kicking Monica away, sending her across the room and plowing into laden bookshelves. Heavy, leather-bound volumes tumbled to the floor as Monica crumpled. She moved slowly, her hands first, then her legs, groaning.

Tessa scrambled to her feet, bleeding and limping, and tried to reach the remaining fireplace tools. Her fingers groped for frantic purchase against the handle of a coal shovel, and when Monica grabbed her from behind, Tessa whirled, sending the iron shovel blade smashing into the side of Monica's head, knocking her sideways and to the ground again.

"You want Martin?" Tessa said, hoisting the shovel again, driving the blade down in a forceful arc into the back of Monica's skull. "Go and find him, you fucking bitch." She reared the shovel back and swung

it down again, the iron spade dented now from the repeated, brutal impacts. "Go outside and hunt him
down, you nasty piece of shit Davenant whore!"

Again and again, she beat Monica, until the other
woman lay facedown on the floor, struggling vainly to
cover her head with her hands. All the while, images
flashed in her mind—of Martin dragging her down to
the laundry room and whipping her with his belt because she hadn't starched his shirts to his liking; of
Monica snatching the green sapphire pendant from
around her neck, her voice cold and mocking. *It's
mine now.*

"How do you like it, Monica?" Tessa cried, smashing her head with the shovel. All of the times Martin
had beaten her black and blue, all of the times he'd
hurt her, shamed her, bullied her, frightened her, and
all the while he'd treated Monica like a queen;
Monica had never known a moment's hardship or suffering under his roof.

"How do you like it?" Tessa screamed, and she
didn't even realize she was weeping, her body racked
with sobs, as again and again, she swung the shovel.
"How does it feel, you bitch?"

Finally, she stumbled backward, hiccuping for
breath, the shovel dropping from her hands. Monica
lay motionless, facedown against the floor, her auburn
hair matted and stained with blood. Tessa stood there
for a long, stunned moment as the bloodlust drained
from her, the adrenaline that had infused her waning,
leaving her with nothing but shock and horror at the
realization of what she'd done.

"Oh . . ." she whispered, shuddering. "Oh . . . oh,
God . . ."

Tessa! Brandon screamed. She could hear a heavy,
desperate pounding from somewhere downstairs as he
tried to batter down one of the doors. He was trapped
down on the beach, unable to climb up the wall as

Monica had done because without the bloodlust he was, for all intents and purposes, little better than a human. *Tessa! I'm coming!*

"It's too late," Tessa whispered even though he couldn't hear her. She turned around and went to push her hair back from her face. Her hands were blood-smeared and she blinked in aghast horror at her palms. "Oh, God, I killed her."

Although the Brethren thought nothing of killing humans, it was forbidden that any of them kill another of their own kind. Only the Elders could demand or deliver the death of a fellow Brethren, and only then, by the most extreme of circumstances or offenses. Murder was a human sin; a failing suffered by those beneath the Brethren race, and more than that, it was considered a travesty, an abhorrence punishable by death.

"Oh, God," Tessa whispered again, because until that moment, she would have only been punished had the Elders found her again for leaving the farm, defying her husband and the rules of the Brethren. She would have suffered considerably, of that she had no doubt . . .

. . . *but now?* she thought in horror. Now there would be no mercy for her; nothing anyone could say or do to protect her. *Or my baby.* She pressed her hands against her belly and closed her eyes. *Oh, God, they'll take my baby and kill me now.*

She heard a soft sound from behind her, a faint scratching and started to turn. Monica leaped up—very much alive and very much pissed off—and her hand clamped against Tessa's throat. Tessa yelped, breathless and startled, as Monica slammed her back against the nearest bookcase, pinning her with her feet off the ground.

"You . . . fucking bitch!" Monica screeched, blood and spittle flying from her lips, the bones of her jaw, her teeth standing out in stark, gruesome contrast to

the red, spongy meat beneath her torn, ruined skin.
Tessa saw a blur of movement out of the corner of her
eye, then Monica rammed the business-end of the
cast-iron fireplace poker through her midriff.

Tessa cried out, choked and strained, as the barbed
end punched through her belly, spearing through the
meat of her gut and thrusting out of her back just shy
of her spine. The pain was immediate and indescrib-
able, more excruciating than anything she might have
ever even imagined possible.

Oh, God! she thought, as Monica turned loose of her
throat, leaving her to stagger clumsily sideways, the
strength in her legs abandoning her. She blinked in
stunned, aghast horror at the shaft of the poker protruding from her belly, the handle blood-smeared and
jutting less than a few inches beneath the edge of her
breastbone. Already a bright, scarlet stain had started
to spread at the point of impact, seeping through the
heavy down filling of her ski coat and soaking the pale
pink nylon exterior. *Oh, God . . . my baby!*

"I'll kill you!" Monica seethed, her lips smeared
with bloody froth. She wrapped her hands around the
handle of the poker and Tessa screamed, her voice
ripping shrilly as Monica jerked her off her feet,
swinging her by the poker, throwing her the length of
the room. Tessa could feel the hooked tip of the im-
plement ripping through flesh as it was wrenched
back out of her body; it flew free just as Monica threw
her, sending a trail of blood slapping up against the
ceiling, spraying Tessa in the face.

Tessa smashed against another bookshelf and collapsed into a shuddering heap against the floor. The
pain was too much, too great; she couldn't move save
to press her hand against her belly. The front of her
coat was soaked now with blood; she stared down at it
in shock, watching as it dribbled down the contours
of her knuckles, streamed along her fingers in steady,

thickening rivulets. She couldn't sense the baby; there
was nothing but the pain and a terrible, leaden cold-
ness that seemed to have filled her, swallowing that
fragile corner of light and warmth where once she'd
been able to feel her child growing.

Oh . . . oh, God . . . oh, no, please!

She looked up, her eyes flooded with tears, her
mind fading rapidly to shadows and saw Monica leap
at her. It was almost like watching something out of a
movie; Monica moved as if in slow motion, her footsteps plodding and clumsy. When she sprang forward,
hands outstretched, her fingers blood-smeared and
hooked into claws, Tessa shrank, cowering.

Oh, God, no, please not my baby, she thought, and out
of the corner of her eye, lying among broken glass
shards, fallen books and splintered wood, she spied the
broken end of the shattered decorative dragon beam.

At this, she felt something in her galvanized, some
fire she might have once attributed to her grandmother Eleanor but now realized was her own—her
own strength and determination—reigniting in full,
furious force. She shrieked in agonized protest, and
curled her fingers around the shaft of wood.

"Not my baby!" she screamed, swinging her arm up
just as Monica began to tackle her, smashing the
dragon's head—gape-mouthed and fork-tongued—
directly into Monica's. The trident of sharp points at
its lips, the spear of its tongue punched into the side
of Monica's skull, crushing bone and mashing brain
matter, burying clear to the delta of its wooden jaws.

She uttered a startled squawk; Tessa realized she
could see the dragon's bottom jaw bisecting the roof of
Monica's mouth in a grim, gruesome plane and then a
thin stream of blood suddenly dripped down from
Monica's right nostril, spattering against her face.
Monica blinked in dazed fascination at the glistening

droplets as they rolled down Tessa's cheek, then her gaze cut to Tessa's.

"You . . . you can't . . ." she began, then her eyes rolled back into her skull, black yielding to white, and she crashed sideways, falling to the rug in a still and sudden heap.

Oh, God! Tessa kicked Monica's legs and hips, knocking her away. The shaft of the broken crossbeam jutted skyward at a listing angle from Monica's head; beneath her, blood pooled against the Oriental rug, spilling from her mouth and nose, the grisly wounds to her face and skull.

Tessa pressed her hands to her stomach and rolled onto her side, curling up into a fetal coil as her tears spilled. She didn't even hear Brandon come rushing into the room, his footsteps heavy and frantic. When he collapsed to his knees beside her, trying to touch her, she recoiled and screamed, punching at him, trying to punt him away.

Tessa, it's me! It's Brandon! he said in her mind. *Tessa, I'm sorry! I couldn't get inside! I had to break a window! I couldn't find you . . . I could hear you screaming but I . . . I couldn't . . .*

His hands stopped fluttering about her when he caught sight of the blood. *Oh, Jesus, you're bleeding!* he cried, his voice shrill and panicked. *What happened? Oh . . . oh, Christ, are you all right? Tessa! Tessa, please, answer me!*

"Oh . . . oh, God . . . !" she wept as her twin clutched at her. She clapped her hands over her face and shuddered against the floor. "My baby," she gasped. "Oh . . . oh, God, Brandon . . . she killed my baby!"

Chapter Twenty-six

"What are we doing, Rene?" Lina asked as she pulled the Mercedes to a stop across the street from a towering three-story Victorian mansion. Complete with lushly landscaped flower beds and shrubberies, a steeply pitched, slate-tiled mansard roof, ornate stained-glass windows and granite stairs leading to a stately, sprawling front porch, the house looked like something out of *Better Homes & Gardens* magazine. Without question, it was one of the crown jewels in the overflowing architectural coffer that was Pacific Heights.

Lina sat behind the wheel, her hand draped against the gearshift as the engine idled and she looked at him expectantly. Her expression grew even more quizzical as he unbuckled his seat belt and opened the passenger-side door.

"You're going to sit here for just a moment, *ma chère*," he told her with a wink as he used his hands to help swing his prosthetic foot from the car to the sidewalk. "And I'm going to get out and stretch my legs a wee bit."

He closed the door, but as he rounded the hood, she rolled down her window, shielding her eyes with the blade of her hand against the bright afternoon sky and squinting at the houses. "No, I mean, what are we doing here?"

She'd gawked almost nonstop since he'd directed her to the neighborhood, having dropped the Jeep off at the airport rental car terminal earlier. "Do you know someone who lives here?"

"Not really, *chère*," he murmured, crossing the street and mounting the broad, steep risers leading up to the mansion's front porch. "Not anymore."

You could take the girl out of the bayou, but you couldn't take the bayou out of the girl. While any other woman in the neighborhood with a husband whose net worth was roughly the equivalent of a small country's annual operating budget probably had a slew of household staff on duty to tend to such menial tasks as answering the doorbell, Irene opened the door herself, dressed with a lavender silk robe lashed around her waist and a steaming, oversized cup of coffee in one hand. He didn't know if she recognized him or not, if something in his face had seemed, at least from initial glance familiar enough to make her unafraid, or if she simply answered her door fearlessly at every knock or ring. But she opened it wide without a moment's hesitation, and looked at him for a curious moment. "Yes? May I help you?"

The years had touched her, thickening and softening what had once been a reed-slender figure. Age had graced her face with delicately etched lines framing her mouth and eyes. Her hair was short, a youthful spiky cut dyed a lighter shade of blond than he remembered. Her skin was olive-toned and tanned; she smelled lightly of faded perfume, cocoa cappuccino and raspberry lotion.

Mon Dieu, *you're still beautiful*, he thought.

Her blue eyes cut down the length of his form as if searching for something, but when they settled again on his face, he watched her expression shift—first perplexed, then startled, then utter disbelief. The coffee cup dropped from her hand, shattering against the stone tile of the front porch.

"Oh, my God!" she whispered. They were the first words she'd ever said to him and as she offered them again now, a tremor worked its way from her hands to her shoulders, shuddering through her. Her voice sounding strangled for breath, stunned and strained. "Oh, my God. *Rene?*"

"Hello, *chère,*" he said with a smile, his own voice choked, his eyes burning with the sharp sting of tears.

The last words he'd said to her had been callous and cold, hateful things shouted as she'd fled his mother's house in Thibodaux. He wouldn't have blamed her one bit if she still hated him for that, even all of those years later, but instead she stepped toward him, hands outstretched, oblivious to the broken cup, the spilled coffee at her feet. She threw her arms around his neck and hugged him fiercely, rising onto her tiptoes and gasping against his ear.

"Oh, my God, it's you! It's really you!" She stepped back, cupping his face in her hands, her eyes swimming with tears. Her brows were lifted with visible, dumb-struck wonder. "I can't believe it. You . . . you look just the same. You haven't aged a day! How is that possible?"

"Never mind," Rene whispered, touching her face, brushing his fingertips against her features, still so poignantly familiar to him. "It doesn't matter."

In that moment, as she looked into his eyes, he opened his mind and reached out to her. Her voice faded even as she began to speak, her gaze growing distant and dreamy, just like with the young couple he'd inadvertently stopped along the New Mexico highway.

"Forgive me, *chère.*" He leaned toward her and kissed her mouth, letting his lips settle softly, briefly. As he closed his eyes, treasuring that fleeting moment of her breath against him, a single tear spilled. "For everything."

He stepped away, letting his hand linger against her cheek for one last moment before pulling back completely. Irene stood motionless on her front porch, a soft breeze fluttering the hem of her robe against her calves as she blinked sleepily at him. She watched him walk away without being aware of it; he'd turned off her mind and she wouldn't remember that he'd ever been there. He'd erased her memories of that horrific last day in Louisiana, and all of the painful, terrible days that had preceded it. In less time than it took to bat an eye, he had rewritten history for Irene, giving her something kinder and more gentle to look back upon—a boy named Rene LaCroix whom she had loved in the folly of her youth, a boy she might have once married, but who had been killed in Vietnam; a boy she could think of in fond recall, and maybe weep for every once in a while; a boy who had never broken her heart or let her down. The boy he'd once been, and the man he always wished he could have been for her.

"Good-bye, Irene," Rene whispered, and turned, walking away.

Lina met him halfway across the street, her pace brisk, her cell phone in her hand, her expression as anxious as a toddler in need of the toilet. "We have to go."

"*Je sais,*" he replied. *I know.* She hadn't felt comfortable leaving Tessa and especially Brandon alone in Tahoe to begin with, and figured she'd found his detour an aggravation. "I'll make it up to you, *chère.* I'll buy you lunch on the way back east. Any place you'd—"

"No, Rene." She caught his arm as he started to walk past her, her fingers closing fiercely enough to give him pause. For the first time, he realized she didn't just seem anxious. She looked stricken. "Brandon just sent me a text message. We have to go *now*. He said something's happened to Tessa and the baby."

"He said Monica and Martin Davenant must have been in Anthony, New Mexico, together," Lina said once they'd returned to the motel. It took a lot to position his prosthetic so that he could use it to work a clutch pedal, which is why Rene seldom did it, but there had been no way in hell he'd have sat riding shotgun in his own goddamn sports car when Tessa needed him. He'd made the little Mercedes scream as he'd thrown it in gear and turned its V-6 engine wide open and loose on the highway.

I'm coming, Tessa, he'd thought, gripping the steering wheel so tightly, he'd caused the gunshot wound to his left palm to seep blood again. There was no way she could have heard him, not from such a distance, but he hadn't given a shit. He'd opened his mind to her anyway, straining desperately, searching for her. *I'm coming home to you,* pischouette. *I'm on my way.*

Rene wasn't a praying man. His grandmother Odette had forced him as a child to accompany her to church each Sunday, dressing him up in suffocating button-down shirts and hand-me-down dress pants and wetting his hair to comb it into some semblance of order. When she'd been diagnosed with stomach cancer one year after Arnaud Morin's suicide, Rene had flirted with the idea of religion again for the first time in ages. The cancer had been caught too late and the best they might have hoped for was that Odette would die without suffering too badly. At least that's what Rene had prayed for. It hadn't turned out that way, despite the best efforts of prayer, hospice and all of the morphine Rene's newfound and considerable wealth had been able to afford. Odette had died incoherent from pain, without knowing Rene or anyone else around her, crying out in garbled French for family members and friends who had long ago preceded her.

He hadn't prayed ever since, but he did on the long drive back from San Francisco, pleading with God or whoever the hell was out there, all-knowing and omnipotent. *Please let them be all right,* he'd thought. *Tessa and the baby—I'm begging you. Take whatever you want from me—my other goddamn leg, my life. Whatever you want, anything, but not Tessa. Not the baby.*

Brandon had met them in the parking lot as soon as Rene had pulled the silver Mercedes into a vacant parking slot. By then, the afternoon had begun to wane into evening, and dusky shadows drooped down from the mountains.

"Tessa remembers Martin calling her in the car, telling her to stay put," Lina said, as Brandon's fingers flew and darted in the air in front of him. She was translating for Brandon, who was still frantic and had forgotten himself, lapsing into sign language rather than psi-speech, just as Rene himself was sometimes apt to slip into French without thinking about it.

"She'd thought he meant at the farm in Kentucky, but he must have meant stay put there in Anthony, only she didn't listen," Lina said. "Martin told Monica where they were going—to Tahoe to find Brandon. She had a credit card to access the money he's been stealing from Bloodhorse all of these years. She must have used it to rent a car and follow."

Rene didn't give a shit how Monica Davenant had found them. All he cared about was Tessa. He strode briskly toward the motel room, leaving Brandon and Lina behind. He threw open the door and stood on the threshold for a long, anguished moment, his heart, breath and voice all caught in a choking, strangling knot in his throat.

"Tessa," he breathed.

She lay facing the door, curled onto her side atop the bed, with her knees drawn to her chest like a small child. The room was dark, save for the slight circumference of orange-yellow light offered by the bedside lamp, but he could still see tears glistening in her large eyes. There were new bruises marring her pale skin; dozens of scrapes and cuts on her face. She looked small and frail, vulnerable and hurting and it broke his heart.

"It hurts . . ." she whispered as he leaned over her, stricken.

"I know," he whispered back. He hooked the sheet with his hand and drew it carefully away from her. Brandon had tried to help with her wound, the gruesome point in which a fireplace poker had apparently run her through, but the younger man obviously didn't know shit for triage. He'd managed to do little more than get Tessa's blood-soaked clothes off her and try to cover the wound with one of the motel's white terry cloth towels. Tessa held that towel in place now with one hand, but it was stained bright red, as was the bedspread beneath her.

"Let me see, *pischouette*," he said quietly, easing the towel away from her grasp. He sucked in an aghast breath when he saw her stomach, the bloody, ragged hole torn just slightly below the vertex of her rib cage. "*Merde.*"

He crossed the room to his duffel bag and dug out the first-aid supplies they'd bought to tend to his hand. Grabbing a handful of fresh linens, some hand towels and washcloths from the nearby sink vanity, he returned to the bedside.

"I can't feel the baby, Rene," Tessa whimpered, watching as he upturned the bottle of hydrogen peroxide, soaking one of the washcloths. "Not like before . . . not like . . ."

"Hush now," he said, shaking his head. "That baby is going to be just fine."

When he pressed the washcloth to her stomach, he tried to be as gentle as possible, but she still cried out softly, jerking against the bed. "*Je suis désolé,* Tessa," he said softly. *I'm sorry.*

"It hurts, Rene," she gasped again, tears spilling. She began to shudder, hiccuping for breath. "It hurts . . . so bad!"

"I know." His eyes flooded with tears, his throat felt strangled with them and stroked her hair back from her brow. "*Je suis désolé.*" *I'm sorry.*

She kept her eyes closed as he dressed her wounds, using fabric tape to secure matching squares of thick gauze over the points of impact. Had the poker caught her low enough to pierce her womb? He didn't know enough about anatomy to be able to tell. She needed a hospital; that much he did know, because it sure as hell didn't take a genius. But he also knew they couldn't take that risk. Not now.

"I . . . I can't feel the baby," Tessa told him again, trembling as he finished binding her wounds. "Not now. Not like before. It comes and goes, like someone turning a light switch on and off. Only . . . it's not bright anymore. It's not bright at all."

Fresh tears spilled down her cheeks and he enfolded her in his arms. She huddled against him, clinging to him fiercely. "It's dying, Rene!" she cried, hoarse and pained. "Oh, God, my baby is dying and there's nothing I can do!"

"You're wrong," he said softly. He tucked his fingertips beneath her chin, lifting her tearful gaze to him. "There is something you can do, *pischouette.* Something we both can do. Something that will save your baby."

She shook her head, confused. "What? I . . . no, Rene, I don't . . ."

"Tessa," he said. "Feed from me."

Her body stiffened against him and she drew back, her eyes widening. "No." She shook her head. "No, don't say that, Rene. Don't ask me to do that. Not now. I just . . . I couldn't . . . I . . . I can't!"

"Tessa . . ." He reached for her, but she slapped his hand away. She tried to sit up, but the effort hurt her, and she grimaced, gritting her teeth.

"That . . . that's not fair to make me choose," she gasped. When she looked up at him, her brows were furrowed, but her eyes were frightened. "How can you ask that of me? You've seen me feed! You know what happens—you know what happens to *me!* I . . . I become a monster! I can't control myself, and I can't lose you! Not now, not you, too!" She pressed her hands against her belly and stared at him, wide-eyed and anguished. "Don't you understand? I can't lose you, too!"

Even as she tried to shrug him off, he caressed her face, drawing the pad of his thumb lightly against her tear-dampened cheek. "You're not going to lose me, *pischouette*. Not now, not ever."

She tried to shake her head, to pull away, but he wouldn't let her. "I can't!"

"Yes, you can," he said, and she blinked at him as new tears spilled.

"Please, Rene," she whimpered. "I don't want to hurt you."

He smiled at her gently and kissed her lips. "You're not going to hurt me, *pischouette*. I promise."

Chapter Twenty-seven

Tessa felt trapped, torn between her unborn child and Rene, both of whom she loved and neither of whom she wanted to lose.

Before Rene had arrived, she had closed her eyes, lying on the bed with her arms wrapped around her midriff, as if she could somehow cradle her baby that way, hold it and comfort it deep inside her womb. She'd kept her mind open as the fluttering glow of its fragile life force had grown weaker by the moment. Her entire body hurt, but nowhere more so than within her heart, where it felt like a piece of her was fading along with her child, crumbling in upon some great and terrible darkness, a cold and hollow chasm that would eventually engulf her, swallow her whole.

My baby.

She'd closed her eyes, ignoring her brother's attempts to comfort her. She hadn't wanted Brandon; for once, not even her twin could make things better. She'd wanted Rene, and in his absence, she'd turned inward for solace. She imagined her baby. In her mind, she held the child—a plump, pink and beautiful cherub with bright, dark eyes, round cheeks and downy fuzz for hair. She imagined the smell of the baby—baby oil and powder and lotion, something warm and wondrous and impossibly sweet; she dreamed of its voice, a soft, melodic babble of happy, gurgling sounds.

She imagined her child, at one moment a little girl, in another, a little boy, each around four years old, like her brother Daniel, holding her hand and walking alongside her in Kentucky, back at the farm. It was the same dream she'd had at least a million times since she'd found out she was pregnant, one that she knew by heart.

She imagined the sensation of miniscule fingers intertwined with hers, of looking down into a pair of chocolate-colored eyes that were the mirror image of her own. "Do you know how much I love you?" she dreamed of asking her child.

"To the moon and back again," the little son in her mind would reply.

"More than all of the fishes in the sea," the little daughter would chirp.

Oh, God, please, she'd prayed, holding herself tightly, tears squeezing out from between her lashes. *Please don't take my baby.*

She didn't want to lose the child, but she didn't want this, either—the prospect of hurting Rene, of bleeding him dry in the throes of the bloodlust, in her desperation to save the life of her baby. *How can I choose?* she thought, clutching at Rene, tucking her cheek against his shoulder. *Oh, God, what can I do? If I don't feed, then I'll lose my baby, but if I do . . .*

An image flashed in her mind—Rene lying sprawled on the bed, his throat torn open, his shirt soaked in blood, and her grandmother's words, Eleanor's voice echoing in her mind: *Fresh meat for the celebration of slaughter.*

Oh, God, how can I choose?

I can help you, Tessa, Brandon said in her mind, drawing her gaze to where he had come to stand beside Lina in the doorway. *I can help you feed from Rene. I can show you when to stop, just like he did for me when I fed from Lina.*

"No, *petit*," Rene said aloud, shaking his head, drawing a surprised glance from Brandon. "You and Lina leave us alone for a while. Me and Tessa, we're going to be fine."

He met her eyes as he said this, offering a wink and a gentle smile. When neither Brandon nor Lina immediately moved, he turned to them again. "Go on now," he said with a nod toward the door. "*Il est bien.*" *It's all right.*

"Rene . . ." Lina said, her face drawn, her eyes round with worry. She cut a glance at Tessa, then back again. Clearly, she, too, thought it was a lousy idea. "Are you sure about this?"

He smiled at Tessa again, brushing the cuff of his fingers against her cheek. "I'm positive, *chère.*"

When Brandon and Lina were gone and they were alone, he stood and locked the deadbolt on the door. As he turned and walked back to the bed, Tessa shied against the headboard, wincing as the movement sent pain spearing through her.

"I can't do this, Rene."

"Yes, you can." He unbuttoned the front of his shirt, tugging the tails loose from his jeans. He shrugged his way out of the sleeves and dropped the shirt onto the foot of the bed. The amber lamplight played against the contours of his chest as he walked toward her and there was no place for her to go, nowhere else she could hide.

He sat against the edge of the bed, cradled her face between both hands and leaned toward her, letting the tip of his nose brush hers. "I love you, Tessa," he whispered. "*Mon Dieu*, woman, don't you know that? Let me help you. Let me help your baby."

He lifted his hand between them, his left hand, the

one in which he'd been shot. As she watched, he began to peel back the bandages covering the wound. "What are you doing?" she asked.

He didn't answer, merely let the swaddling gauze drop in a pile to the floor beside the bed. She could see that the wound through his hand had healed considerably; it remained open and sore looking at both the points of entry and exit, but no longer seemed to hurt him enough to impede his movement. When he shoved the thumb of his opposite hand into the center of his palm—gouging open the wound—she cried out in startled horror.

"Rene! What are you doing?"

He'd buckled slightly in pain, drawing his injured hand reflexively against his belly and gasping for breath. When he looked up at her, his eyes were smarting with tears, but he struggled to smile. "Getting you a wake-up call," he said in a hoarse, strained voice.

She blinked, bewildered, and he held up his hand. The wound had begun to bleed, but she realized she hadn't needed to see this to know. The scent of his blood, a thick, heady fragrance, had already reached her nose, and her body's instinctive reaction to it had almost instantaneously begun.

"Here." Rene held out his right hand, the tip of his thumb smeared with his own blood. He brought it toward her mouth, and though she tried to shy, she froze, paralyzed and breathless when he drew it across her bottom lip. When he touched her again, tracing blood against the contour of her mouth, she let him delve between her lips, the tantalizing hint of his blood tangy against her tongue. "I love you, Tessa. Take it."

I love you. No man had ever said that to her before; no man had ever made her feel as safe and wanted, welcome and needed as Rene did. She had always listened to Eleanor's tales of love and romance with the Grandfather like something out of a storybook; beautiful and

wondrous, too much so, to ever be real. And yet it was
possible; it was indeed real. She'd found it for herself.
She'd found it in Rene.

"Take my blood, Tessa," he breathed. "Whatever
you want—anything you need. Heal yourself. Heal
the baby."

She touched his face, looking up into his eyes. Her
gums felt swollen and sore; her canine teeth had begun
to drop, sliding out of the recesses of her mouth. She
could sense the pounding rhythm of his heart pushing
blood through his body in a forceful, fervent tide. She
could see his earnest, desperate sincerity in his eyes,
hear it in his words, feel it in his mind.

"Please, Tessa," Rene said, and he leaned toward
her, turning his head so that he pressed his left cheek
against her right shoulder. By doing this, he left his
neck open and utterly exposed, directly in front of
her, the side of his throat—his carotid artery—less
than an inch from her mouth.

Oh, God, she thought, her eyes welling with tears.
Her lips were parting; she felt the slight, uncomfortable popping of her jaw reflexively dislocating, her
fangs sliding downward to their full, curved lengths.
Oh, Rene, please forgive me . . .

The world shifted to stark contrasts of shadow and
glare as her pupils opened wide, bathing everything in
the glow of the bloodlust. She pressed her lips against
the warmth of his flesh, letting her teeth first pierce
him, then sink deeply through underlying muscles and
tendons. She felt the soft, sharp intake of his breath
against her, his shoulders stiffening reflexively. Blood
suddenly spurted into her mouth, her fangs hitting
home against the thick, pulsing carotid. She drank
greedily, gulping to keep pace as his heart sent a rhythmic flow coursing down her throat. It was like nothing
she had ever tasted before; he wasn't fully human, and
his blood had a flavor uniquely his own, something

coppery, bittersweet, thick like molten chocolate and impossibly hot.

All at once, she could feel the baby again; with every pounding measure of Rene's heart, she could sense it growing stronger, her awareness of it in her mind strengthening. The more she swallowed, the more thready Rene's pulse became, but the brighter that precious golden glow grew. After several moments, Rene uttered a low, breathless sound, nearly a moan and she closed her fist in his hair, keeping her lips clamped against his throat. His hands drooped away from her, trailing limply against her shoulders and torso before slumping to the mattress.

An image flashed through Tessa's mind: walking along at the farm again, following the narrow road through grazing pastures and bluegrass fields, looking down into the upturned face of a child—a little boy, with dark eyes and hair and no hint of Martin whatsoever in his face. Only this time, they weren't alone. Rene walked with them, holding on to one of the boy's hands while Tessa clasped the other. The child beamed as he looked up at Rene.

"Guess how much I love you, Daddy?" he asked.

At this, at the word *Daddy*, Tessa was shocked from the fugue of the bloodlust and her mouth faltered, her lips slipping from Rene's throat.

Daddy.

As many times as she'd had the daydream of walking with her child, playing that long-remembered game Eleanor had once taught them, Tessa had never envisioned a father. Martin didn't know how to love anyone, much less a child; he might have provided the seed for the baby nestled in Tessa's womb, but he was not now, nor would he ever be *Daddy*.

He gave the seed, but it's Rene who's giving the baby life.

Tessa let go of Rene's hair. She drew back, sliding

her teeth free from his throat, sending a dribble of blood spilling down her chin.

Guess how much I love you, Daddy? the little boy in her dream had asked, the son she now realized with sudden but unwavering certainty was growing inside of her. *A son,* she thought. *Oh, God . . . my son . . .* our son, mine and Rene's.

"To . . . to the moon . . ." Rene murmured, his eyelids fluttering closed as she lay him gently back against the bed, cradling his head with her hands, ". . . and back again."

"Rene?" She stroked his face, pushing his hair back. "Rene, can you hear me?"

He opened his eyes, blinked dazedly up at her. "There was a boy . . ." he said, sounding groggy and hoarse. "*Où est-il allé?*" *Where did he go?*

When he tried to sit up, wincing, she eased him back again. "It's all right."

"Did it work?" he asked, brushing his fingers clumsily against her face, smearing blood along her chin. "The *bébé . . . ?*"

"I think so," she replied. "It may be too early yet, too soon to know for sure . . ."

But I can feel it, she thought. *And I dreamed of it, too— I dreamed of our son, Rene.*

She didn't mean for him to overhear her thoughts, but she hadn't meant for him to share in her dream, as well. But somehow now, as then, he seemed to, and now, as then, he drew comfort from it. He nodded once, his eyelids drooping closed, his breath huffing out in a long, deep sigh. "*Bon, puis,*" he murmured. *Good, then.*

Tessa lay down beside him, tucking her head against the nook of his shoulder. She'd taken enough from him to probably have proven fatal had he been fully human. His Brethren birthright would help him recover, but he was weak now and exhausted.

"*Sie tu plais . . . séjour avec moi,*" he breathed to her, more unconscious than awake. *Please . . . stay with me.*

She closed her eyes, listening to the comforting cadence of his heartbeat, feeling the soft but steady golden glow of life within her belly. "I will, Rene," she whispered, reaching for his hand, slipping her fingers through his. "Always."

Chapter Twenty-eight

To Tessa, everything that happened after that seemed to be a blur. Rene had given her pain medicine, powerful prescription narcotics that had left her mind swimming, submerged in a murky state between unconsciousness and awake. When her head finally cleared enough to allow her some lucidity, she found herself blinking up at the motel ceiling, a swirling mass of miniature stalactites in plaster dripping down at her. There was light, the pale glow of new sunlight as it seeped through the nearby window drapes.

Her entire body felt stiff, like the hinges in her hips, knees and shoulders had all rusted in place. When she moved, trying to stretch her legs slowly beneath the blankets, a dim tremor of pain shooting through her midriff reminded her of why she was bedridden in the first place.

She groaned softly, pressing her palm to her belly. With her free hand, she pulled aside the blankets. She was naked beneath the covers, save for bra, panties and a large square of gauze taped in place just below the edge of her underwire cups.

"Well, good morning, sunshine," Rene said, coming out of the bathroom and blinking at her in surprise. This was the first time she could remember coming to and not finding him at her bedside. No matter how many times she had opened her eyes, no matter the quality of light in the room to indicate the passage of day or night, she had found him sitting in a chair next to the bed, his fingers laced through hers.

His hair was wet, his face freshly shaved, his body nude except for a white towel worn swathed around his waist. She could see the skeletal frame of his prosthetic beneath the bottom hem of terry cloth. He'd been swatting at the nape of his neck with another towel, drying his hair, but set it aside now as he walked toward the bed. "Are you hurting, *pischouette?* I can get you another pill . . ."

She shook her head, wincing as she propped herself slowly onto her elbows, a somewhat seated position. "No," she said, the sound of her voice—croaking and hoarse—startling her. She tried to summon enough spit with which to clear her throat and settled for coughing dryly. "No more pills. I'm tired of sleeping. How long was I out, anyway?"

"Three days," he said, making her groan again. He went to her side, slipping his arm around her as she swung her legs from the bed and sat up. "You shouldn't . . ." he began but she shook her head again.

"Stop telling me what to do," she growled, shoving her hand against his chest and using him to help steady herself as she rose to her feet. It hurt like hell, as much from having been flat on her back for so long as from the wound. That, at least, was healing; she could tell just by moving. Not to mention the fact she and the baby were both still alive.

"I'm not telling you what to do," he replied. "I'm trying to help you."

"Good." She stumbled, feeling momentarily dizzy and having to lean against him. "Then help me to the bathroom so I can take a shower."

"You shouldn't be out of bed yet. Not until you're feeling better."

"I *am* feeling better." Tessa snagged the towel from his waist, snapping it loose as she limped into the bathroom. As she closed the door, she heard him laugh behind her.

"I can see that, *oui*."

When she came out again, he dressed her wounds, tending to her with a remarkable and gentle ease. "You're healing well," he observed as she sat against the side of the bed with her bare back to him. He'd put his jeans on, but remained bare-chested, while she sat nude against the bedspread, holding a towel demurely over her chest. There was a little soreness as his fingers prodded carefully against her, taping a fresh gauze square in place, but nothing unbearable.

"We both are," she said, smiling at him over her shoulder, touching her stomach. "Thanks to you."

He glanced up from his work and dropped her a wink. "It was my pleasure, *pischouette*," he said, adding after a slight pause, "Don't ask me to do that again anytime soon or anything, but . . ."

She laughed. "You seem to have recovered none the worse for wear."

He canted his head slightly, awarding her a brief peek at the side of his neck, where she could see the fading imprints of her teeth still against his skin. "Not too shabbily," he said. The playful edge to his voice faltered. "And the *bébé*? It's still all right, too, no? I've felt for it a time or two while you were sleeping, but I didn't want to too much or anything. Not my right and all."

She pivoted on the bed, turning to face him. "Not your right? You saved his life. You have every right in the world."

She touched his face and he smiled, looking uncharacteristically shy and moved. After a moment, however, his expression shifted as her words sank in and he blinked at her in sudden, wide-eyed surprise. "Saved *his* life?" he repeated. "*C'est un garcon?*" *It's a boy?*

She laughed and nodded. "Can't you tell now? I don't know how or why, but I can. I feel it inside. It's a boy."

"That's fantastic, Tessa," he said, laughing against her mouth as he kissed her. "*Saint merde,* congratulations, *pischouette!* I'm so happy for you."

"Us," she said, and he raised a puzzled brow. "Be happy for *us,* Rene. There'd be no reason to celebrate, nothing to feel happy about if it wasn't for you."

When he kissed her this time, he let his mouth linger against hers, his tongue slipping between her lips to brush her own. She lifted her head, touching his face to draw him near and the kiss deepened. His mouth lingered against hers, and as his heartbeat quickened with arousal, it sent a rush of aromatic chemicals through his body, infusing the air around him.

She turned to face him fully, scooting her hips on the bed, but at a twinge of pain in her abdomen, she winced, sucking in a sharp breath against his mouth, giving him immediate pause. "Stop, *pischouette,*" he said, resting his hands against her shoulders and drawing back from her. "It's too soon, and you're—"

"Healing," she said, pressing her fingertips to his lips to quiet him. When his brows lifted and she felt the intake of his breath against her hand in protest, she smiled. "Really, Rene. What is it you told me after that kid shot you in the hand? There's hope for me yet. I promise."

"Don't." He caught her hand as she reached for his fly. When she blinked at him, somewhat hurt now, he reached up, brushing his hand against her face. "If we're going to do this, *pischouette,* then we're going to do it right."

Rene hadn't made love with a woman beneath him since Irene. Having Tessa astride him, making love to her face-to-face had been an emotional breakthrough for him, something that had required unprecedented trust from him, not just because he'd wanted to hide his leg but because he'd likewise wanted to hide his heart. Now there was nothing he wanted to hide from her, not any longer, and he wanted to face her with all of his insecurities pushed aside. He wanted to make love to her like any other man; he wanted to watch her move beneath him, look down at her face as she climaxed.

"Here, *pischouette*," he breathed, laying her back against the bed. He pushed his jeans down, kicking his feet to rid himself of them, then fumbled along the head of the bed before hooking a pair of pillows. He removed his prosthetic, sliding the silicone sleeve away from the stump of his thigh.

Tessa understood what he was doing, what he meant to do, and moved her thighs apart as he positioned the pillows carefully between them.

"Can you do this?" she asked as he lay down, settling his weight atop her.

He raised a speculative brow. "It's not me I'm worried about."

She smiled, stroking her hands against his arms. "I'm fine, Rene. I promise. I want this. I want you."

I want you. She meant more than just in a sexual way; she meant in her life, a part of her world—a part of her baby's world. He knew this without opening his mind. It was apparent in her eyes, evident in her touch. She wanted him, needed him. *Just like I need her.*

He could have left the prosthetic on and made love to Tessa, but he wanted to experience her, enjoy her on his own, no props. Tessa wrapped her legs around him as he used his arms, balancing his weight between his hands, knee and stump, with the pillows to support him on the right side. He could bear at least some of his weight on his stump, he discovered; not as much as he might have had he still had his leg, but enough and without a lot of immediate discomfort.

He pressed himself against her threshold and slipped inside. Tessa gasped, tightening about his waist with her thighs. Immediately concerned about hurting her—her wounds had begun to heal but still had a long way yet to go—he froze, wide-eyed with alarm. "Tessa . . ." he began uncertainly.

"Don't stop," she whispered, hooking her fingertips against his forearms, urging him. "Please, Rene . . . don't stop."

He leaned down, kissing her, feeling her ragged breath against his mouth as he slowly, deliberately withdrew from her, only to plunge down again, filling her once more. Again and again he did this, taking her long, slow and deep, savoring the slick, velveteen friction, the rhythmic undulations of her hips as she rose to meet him.

For the first time since he'd lost his leg, he felt whole. He could look the woman he loved in the eye and make love to her on his own terms—not in a way that made him feel safe or that spared his ego. He made love to Tessa the way that he wanted to, and for the better part of the next half hour, he marked a strident, steady rhythm inside of her, until her voice had dissolved into moans and she writhed beneath him, her body glossed with a light sheen of perspiration. All of that time, he'd been building toward release and when he saw she could no longer stand it, when she clutched at him, pleading in soft, breathless whimpers, he gave it to her.

Tessa tightened against him inside and out. Her hair was swept about her face, clinging to her brightly flushed cheeks in sweat-dampened strands; her eyes were closed, her brows lifted, her mouth ajar as she cried out.

My God, you're beautiful, he thought, and then he

came, a powerful shudder of pleasure wrenching through him, plowing the senses momentarily from him.

He crumpled against her, resting his weight on his arms, relieving his sore stump of the burden. "Are you all right?" he whispered as he pushed himself up, propping himself somewhat on his left side so he could look down at her. "I didn't hurt you?"

"No." She raised her head and kissed him softly on the mouth. "I love you, Rene."

A man could never get tired of hearing those words, he decided, as he lay back against the bed and she snuggled up to him once more, pressing her cheek against his heart and letting her hand rest against the flat plane of his stomach.

"I love you, too, Tessa," he said, because a man could never get tired of saying those words, either, as he was rapidly learning.

"It's never going to be over, is it?"

He'd only meant to close his eyes for a moment, maybe two, but when he opened them again, he could see the quality of sunlight against the motel room ceiling had shifted, brightening. Time had passed, maybe an hour or so, and Tessa had apparently been lying there all the while, awake and thinking.

"What?" he asked, groggy and bewildered.

Tessa sat up, looking down at him, her dark eyes round and troubled. "It's never going to be over, is it?" she asked again. "The Brethren, I mean. Not until they hunt us down, me and Brandon. They won't kill him now, you know. The Grandfather needs Brandon if he wants to stay dominant, especially once he finds out Caine is dead. But as for me . . . ?"

Her voice faded and she cut her eyes away, her hand drawing unconsciously to her stomach. She didn't have to say more; she'd explained the harsh ways of the Brethren to him, their brutal and un-flinching methods, and he understood.

They'll kill her now, but not until she has the bébé, he thought. *She's carrying a boy—a son. They'll keep her alive long enough to deliver, then they'll punish her for what happened to Monica. They'll kill her.*

He watched as her eyes grew clouded. "I'm scared, Rene," she whispered. "How can we live like this? Always running, always looking over our shoulders, jumping at every shadow? We may have escaped the farm, left Kentucky behind us, but we're still just as trapped as we ever were." A tear spilled, rolling slowly down her cheek in a thin, glistening trail. "We'll never be free, Rene. Any of us—Brandon, Lina, you or me . . . the baby."

"Hush now," he said, wiping away her teardrop with his fingertips.

"I'm scared, Rene," she said again, and he cupped his hand against her nape, drawing her to his shoulder in an embrace.

"Hush," he said again, pressing his lips against her hair. He could look down the graceful length of her spine and see the bandage covering her wound, the place where Monica Davenant had run her through, trying to kill her. *She's right,* he realized in dismay. *They're never going to stop trying now, never going to give up the hunt.*

"No one's going to hurt you—or the baby," he whispered. "I promise you, *pischouette*. With everything I have, no matter what it takes, I'll make sure of that."

She drifted back to sleep. Even though she'd fed, her body had gone through so much in such a little amount of time and she was still fairly fragile—despite her stubborn insistence to the contrary. This time it was Rene's turn to lie awake in bed while she slept, but once her breathing had slowed, growing rhythmic and deep, he slipped carefully away from her.

He hauled himself onto the bed and sat against the mattress to put his prosthetic back in place, then dressed once more. He put a clean shirt on, shrugging his ski jacket over top. His car keys were still in his coat pocket; he heard their muffled jangle as he pulled up the zipper. Martin Davenant's ledger, all of the invoices Tessa had inadvertently stolen from him were stowed away together in Rene's duffel bag; he crossed the room and fished them out, along with the Sig Sauer P228 pistol he'd brought in from the car. A quick check of the clip revealed a full thirteen shots. Not that he was planning on using that many.

"One ought to do the trick," he murmured to himself as he gave one last sweep of the room with his gaze from the doorway. He let his eyes linger on Tessa's sleeping form, still curled peacefully on the bed. Some of the severity that had knitted his brows, cleaving a deep furrow at the bridge of his nose, softened. Then he turned and stepped out into the early dawn, closing the door behind him.

A Jaguar sure as hell wasn't as nimble along the rutted mountain roads as the four-wheel-drive Jeep had been, but Rene figured it wasn't his goddamn transmission or suspension to worry about fucking up, so he made do. He drove around the basin of Emerald Bay, then cut up into the hills, past the locked gate that marked the perimeter of his property, and from there, deep into the lush pine-covered slopes.

For three days now, they'd topped the news all around Lake Tahoe. A historic landmark like Vikingsholm had pretty reliable security systems in place, and between Monica Davenant tossing Tessa through an upstairs window and Brandon battering one in on the ground floor, alarms aplenty had apparently been sounded. Rene was frankly astonished that Brandon had managed to get Tessa out of the house and both of them clear of the area before the police had arrived. What had probably started out as nothing more than a simple vandalism investigation had quickly shifted to full-blown murder with the grisly discovery of Monica's body. Rene listened as a local morning radio personality recapped viewers with all of the gory details as he pulled the Jaguar to a halt beside his vacant watch house.

". . . and I have a friend down at the local precinct who tells me—hand to God here, gang—that this dead woman's got one of those carved dragon crossbeams sticking out of her head. I'm not kidding. Someone rammed one of those big old things—have you seen them over there at Vikingsholm?—clear through this lady's skull. Now I don't know about you, but in my book, that's some weird sh—"

Rene turned off the engine, killing the radio. As he got out of the car, he paused, looking over his shoulder into the trees. He felt inexplicably like he was being watched. It was a sensation he'd come to expect from this place; usually it was a comforting, welcome sort—like he was home, he'd told Tessa, and that had been the honest to Christ's truth—but it felt different that morning. The air felt heavy and still to him, the pervasive cold seeping through the insulating layer of his down coat and permeating clear down to his bones.

He mounted the stairs leading up to the wraparound porch and fished his keys from his pocket. Before unlocking the door or stepping foot into the house, he unlatched several of the window padlocks and propped open the shutters, sending a spill of pale sunlight across the interior floor. There was no promise of making love to Tessa that morning to distract him from his claustrophobia, and he needed to be at the top of his game for what was about to come.

He could see Martin Davenant inside, still bound to the post and gagged; he squinted, baring his teeth in a grimace around the washcloth in his mouth at the sudden, blinding glare.

"*Bon jour,*" Rene said, opening the front door and walking inside.

Martin didn't say anything. He glared at Rene from over the edge of his gag, keeping his teeth clenched deeply into the fabric. The scratches on his face had all but healed, but there was still dried blood crusted around his nostrils, caked on his upper lip and the corners of his mouth. When Rene leaned over, jerking it sharply, freeing the washcloth from his mouth, he turned his head to the side, gulping and gagging loudly for breath.

"You . . . you son of a bitch . . ." he spat at Rene. "What are you?" Without Tessa there, he could clearly sense Rene now, the Brethren component of his nature without mistaking it for hers. "Who are you, you . . . you bastard fuck?"

"I'm the guy with your ledger, shit for brains." Rene pulled the little leather-bound volume out from the inside pocket of his coat, waggled it just beneath Martin's nose, then tossed it on the floor.

He had Martin Davenant's attention now, whole and undivided, and he smirked, shaking his fingertip at the other man. "I know what all of that is, *mon ami.* You've been a naughty boy, helping yourself off the top of the till all of these years. It sure would be a shame if Tessa's granddaddy found out what you've been up to, no? Especially since from what I understand, Augustus Noble isn't the sort of man one crosses . . . unless of course you like the idea of being introduced headfirst to your own ass."

Martin cut his eyes to the ledger, then back to

Rene. He took a moment to wheeze some more for breath, then wisely decided not to play dumb. "What do you want?" he asked in a croak.

Rene smiled, reaching beneath his coat again, pulling out the Sig Sauer from the waistband of his jeans. Martin's eyes widened at the sight of the pistol and he shrank against the pole, suddenly, frantically twisting his hands against his bonds.

Rene dropped him a wink. "I thought you'd never ask."

Chapter Twenty-nine

Someone knocked loudly enough at the door to rouse Tessa from a sound and dreamless sleep. "Rene?" she called, her voice hoarse and sleepy. She looked around the empty room, bewildered. "Rene? Are you here?"

The knocking continued and Tessa stumbled to her feet. Rene was apparently gone, his clothes along with him, and she frowned as she pulled on a T-shirt and wiggled her way into her jeans.

She opened the door and found Brandon on the stoop. "Hey," she said with a smile, tucking her disheveled hair behind her ears. "Good morning."

What are you doing out of bed? Brandon's eyes had widened in alarm and he reached for her as she stepped aside, letting him into the room. *You shouldn't be on your feet. You need to be resting! Where's Rene?*

She shrugged. "I'm not sure. He was here earlier. Maybe he went to get some breakfast."

Rene had told her that Brandon and Lina had taken turns coming to check on her over the last few days. Tessa had been touched by their concern, moved by Brandon's obvious guilt and shame over her attack, and the fact she'd nearly lost the baby.

Blaming himself for even those things furthest from his control was just a part of her twin's gentle nature.

He shouldn't have left you alone. Brandon tried to steer her toward the bed and she laughed, ducking away from him.

"Of course he should have. I'm fine, Brandon. Jesus, you're as bad as he is!"

Fine, huh? he asked, because when she twisted to sidestep out of his reach, she'd felt a slight shudder of pain that had made her wince visibly.

"Mostly fine, then." She touched her stomach, feeling that comforting glow of the baby's mind and her smile widened. "I'm really, really good, in fact."

When he cocked his head and brow in tandem, curious, she blushed. "I think it's a boy. I mean, I'm pretty sure it's a boy. I can really feel it now. It's like Rene's blood made it stronger—made both of us stronger somehow." She rubbed her tummy again. "It's a little boy."

Brandon's face lit up and he smiled broadly. *Holy shit, Tessa!* he exclaimed. *That's fantastic! Congratulations!*

He moved to hug her, then hesitated, his expression growing uncertain. She laughed. "I'm not going to break, Brandon," she said, stepping against him, wrapping her arms around his neck. He relaxed against her, returning the embrace, holding her snugly.

I thought I lost you, he whispered in her mind, and when she stepped back, she saw his dark eyes glistening with tears. He averted his gaze to the floor. *I just . . . when I saw all of that blood . . . realized what had happened, I just . . . I thought . . .*

Don't cry, Tessa said as a tear rolled down his cheek. She felt her own throat constrict, her eyes suddenly sting. *Oh, Brandon, you're going to make me cry, too. Stop it.*

He glanced up, his eyes still swimming and she

hugged him again, even more fiercely. *It's all my fault,* he said, clinging to her.

No, it's not, she said.

He trembled. *I was so scared, Tessa. I . . . I thought I lost you.*

I'm fine, Brandon, she said to him. *I promise. Please don't cry.* As she stroked her hand against his hair, she thought of all the years she'd lost with him, four long years trapped in Martin Davenant's house, years in which the twins had each been tormented in their own ways, suffered their own abuses—suffering that had only been compounded because they hadn't had each other to turn to for comfort or support. *You'll never lose me again, Brandon,* she thought. *I promise that, too.*

She drew away from him and he reached into the hip pocket of his jeans. He sniffled, his brows furrowed slightly as he struggled to compose himself. *Here,* he said, pulling his hand out, his fingers folded into a fist as he offered something to her. With his free hand, he swatted at his face, wiping away tears. *I . . . I thought you'd like to have this.*

Curious, she looked down as he opened his hand. To her surprise, she saw the green sapphire pendant resting in the basin of his palm, the filigree gold chain coiled beneath it in a small pile.

Monica Davenant had it around her neck, he said. *I found it before we left Vikingsholm, when I checked to make sure she was dead.*

When Tessa didn't immediately move to take the necklace, instead gazing at it for a long, uncertain moment, his brows lifted. *Tessa, come on. Don't let one stupid, shitty memory from me spoil all of the countless wonderful ones you have of Grandmother Eleanor. I don't know how she felt or what she meant that day, but I know that I love you, even if she didn't. So let this pendant stand for that, if nothing else.* He smiled feebly. *That's got to be worth something, doesn't it?*

She looked into his dark eyes, nearly mirror images of her own, and couldn't help but smile. "It's worth a lot, Brandon," she said, slipping the necklace from his hand. She dropped him a wink, then mouthed the words *olive oil*, making him laugh. "That makes it priceless, in fact."

Chapter Thirty

Little more than an hour later, Brandon opened his motel room door, his eyes flying wide when he saw Rene leaning heavily against the door frame.

Jesus! What happened? the younger man exclaimed.

"Je suis bien," Rene said as Brandon got an arm around his middle and led him, stumbling and dizzy, into the room. "I'm all right, *petit.*"

That's bullshit, Rene—you're bleeding! Brandon eased him down into an armchair and squatted beside him, visibly stricken. He reached for Rene, the shallow but messy laceration that cleaved a crooked path from his left temple to his cheekbone. *What happened?*

Rene shook his head. "Nothing I didn't bring on myself," he said, squinting against the sting of blood in his eye. Brandon stood, rushing to the sink vanity and soaking a washcloth under the cold tap. "I did something really fucking stupid, *petit.* And I need you to help me fix it."

What are you talking about? Brandon brought the washcloth to him, then knelt again, leaning forward to press the wet rag against his brow. When Rene jerked, sucking in a quick, hissing breath, Brandon winced. *I'm sorry.*

"That's all right. I got it," Rene said, taking the washcloth from Brandon and holding it gingerly against his face. He glanced around the room. "Where's Lina?"

She went for her morning run, Brandon replied. *She just left a little while ago, but she's got her cell with her. I can call—*

He started to rise again, but Rene caught his arm. "That's all right, *petit*. I'd just . . ." He sighed, glancing toward the window somewhat sheepishly. "I'd just as soon she not find out about this, if at all possible. Her or Tessa. We can just tell them I had car trouble or something, cracked my head on the hood when I popped it. The Jaguar is gone anyway. They won't know the difference."

What do you mean, gone? Brandon asked. *Rene, what the hell happened?*

"Martin got away," Rene said after a long, shamed moment. Brandon's eyes widened and he grimaced, nodding. "I know. I know, *petit*. I went out there to try and get him to help us, you know, like I'd told you before. I thought I could use that ledger Tessa found, all of those bank account records, to blackmail him into contacting the Elders, calling them off somehow. And if that didn't work . . ." He gasped as he inadvertently touched a particularly painful place on his head with the washcloth. "If that didn't work, I brought my pistol along. Figured I'd cut our losses if he wasn't willing to play ball."

What happened? Brandon asked.

Rene shook his head. "The son of a bitch clubbed me. I untied him long enough so he could take a piss— you know, making nice with him to get him on our side of things, and he slammed me back against the wall. Grabbed my goddamn gun and pistol-whipped me upside the head."

Jesus Christ! Brandon exclaimed and Rene nodded grimly.

"*Oui*. Tell me about it, *petit*. He got my car keys, too. Took the Jag and tore out of there. I had to fucking hitchhike back here and used my telepathy afterward to wipe out the memory of the driver who gave me a lift. It was too much, too soon." He winced again, drawing the washcloth back to find the terry cloth stained with blood. "I'm still weak from where Tessa fed from me. Damn near wiped myself out."

Why did you go up there all by yourself? Brandon asked. He took the rag from Rene and went back to the sink, rinsing it out. *You should have grabbed me or Lina, at least. Martin Davenant is next in line to be an Elder—he's strong and he's dangerous. He could have killed you.*

"He tried awful damn hard, *petit*," Rene said, as Brandon returned with the washcloth. "Trust me." He looked up at the younger man, his expression drawn and grim. "We've got to find him, Brandon. He knows where we are. He can lead the Elders right to us."

If he hasn't called them already, Brandon said, glancing suddenly, anxiously at the window and door.

Rene shook his head. "He hasn't. He doesn't have the balls. Not with that ledger in his hands. If your grandfather finds out about that book, he'll string Martin up. Martin took it from me and I know where he's going—back to Kentucky. Back to the farm. Then he'll call his daddy and the Elders, tell them all about us."

How do you know that? Brandon asked, raising his brow.

"Because, *petit*," Rene replied with a wink and a humorless smile. "A little birdie told me. I sent the birds out to look for him—just like I did to find Tessa. I saw through their eyes; I watched his car get on highway 58 heading north."

North? Brandon frowned. *Where the hell is he going?*

"My guess is Reno. He can ditch the car there and get a plane ticket for Kentucky. Be home by dark." He met Brandon's gaze. "Which means the Elders can be here by the morning, *petit,* unless we stop him."

Brandon nodded once. *Tell me what we need to do.*

"Did Lina take the Mercedes keys with her?" Rene asked, and when Brandon shook his head, he said, "Good. Toss them here." He set the washcloth aside, wincing as he rose slowly, stiffly to his feet. "I'm driving."

They drove north, diverting onto Highway 395 toward Reno and heading into the arid, high desert countryside of Nevada north of Carson City. They'd been on the road for little more than a half hour, when Rene suddenly veered the Mercedes off course, turning damn near one hundred and eighty degrees around onto the southbound Highway 429.

What is it? Brandon thought, leaning forward, frowning as he peered out the windshield.

"What the fuck is he doing?" Rene murmured, also frowning. When Brandon glanced at him, curious, he said, "I'm trying to track him in my mind, using the birds. He's up ahead here a little ways. He's pulled off the road, turned into some kind of parking lot. Looks like warehouses or something."

He stopped the car, pulling the Mercedes off onto the soft shoulder of the highway and closed his eyes, pressing his fingertips against his brow. "Not warehouses," he said after a moment. "Hangars. Airport hangars." He looked over at Brandon. "He's not going to the Reno airport. He's going to some pissant little mom-and-pop one. He must mean to charter a plane." He closed his eyes again, his brows narrowed, but after a moment, he shook his head, uttering a quiet, frustrated cry. "Goddamn it! I lost him. I can't seem to keep focused. I'm still too weak."

I don't think it's you. Brandon studied the road ahead of them, still frowning. *I'm having trouble, too.*

I'm getting all kinds of weird sensations. I know he's near us, just up ahead somewhere. I can feel him. But it's different. He, too, touched his head, his frown deepening. *I feel like he's blocking me somehow. Maybe blocking us both.*

"Can he do that, *petit?*" Rene asked when Brandon turned his way. "He's strong enough?"

I don't know, Brandon replied. *I told you—he's the oldest Davenant son, next in line to be named an Elder. That means he's pretty damn strong. And if he stopped along the way to feed off someone, then it means his powers are even stronger, at least for the moment.*

His expression grew apprehensive. *I don't know if we can take him, Rene. If he's strong enough to block our telepathy . . .*

"I know we can," Rene cut in, leaning forward and pulling the Sig Sauer from the waistband of his jeans, where he'd tucked it at the small of his back. He showed it to Brandon with a thin smile. "I don't need telepathy."

They drove again, following the two-lane highway south until they saw the airport ahead of them on the left, little more than an outdated control tower and a couple of blacktopped runways crisscrossing a broad expanse of sagebrush-dusted plain. Three large hangars, each Quonset hut–shaped and constructed of corrugated metal, flanked one another along the far side of a small adjacent parking lot. Here, even from a distance, Rene and Brandon could see Martin's maroon Jaguar parked in the midmorning sun.

"I don't see him anywhere." Rene had again stopped the car along the highway, and they had both climbed out. They stood side by side next to the Mercedes, shielding their eyes with their hands and surveying the landscape. "You got a feel for him, *petit?*"

Brandon had been watching Rene as he spoke, reading his lips, and shook his head, averting his gaze back to the trio of hangars. *Nothing. It's like I've run into a brick wall. Can you send a bird or two down there to scope things out?*

Rene shook his head. *No. I'm with you—nothing but a wall. Goddamn it, he's blocking us somehow. He must have known we'd find a way to follow him, track his sorry ass down.*

So what do we do now? Brandon asked, and Rene glanced at him with a wry smile.

"Offhand, I say we go down there and you use a little of that aikido shit to start things off. Then, whenever you get tired, I'll introduce him to ol' Betsy here." Again, he pulled out the pistol, giving it a demonstrative little waggle. "How does that sound, *petit?*"

Brandon grinned. *Fine by me.*

Rene parked the Mercedes in the airport parking lot, observing a modest, wary distance from the Jaguar. There was still no sign of Martin; no sign of anyone, in fact. There were small propeller planes parked here and there with wheel blocks to hold them fast. A bright orange windsock flapped and waved in the breeze, but otherwise there was nothing; not a sound, not a hint of anything stirring. All of the hangar doors were closed, the tower windows dark.

Rene looked around, turning in an uneasy circle, the nine millimeter gripped lightly in his hand. "This place is a goddamn ghost town," he muttered.

Over there. Brandon pointed to one of the hangars. *Look, Rene. There's a sign on that side door that says "office." You think that's where he went?*

Rene thumbed the safety off on the pistol. *I think it's as good a place as any to start,* petit. *Let's go.*

They walked together into the shadow-draped hangar. Although there were light fixtures dangling from the rafters, none had been turned on and the narrow windows close to the ceiling provided only dim hints of illumination. Seven planes were parked inside the broad belly of the building, six smaller, propeller-powered charter planes and one large,

sleek, glistening private jet parked at the far end of
the room.

Do you see anything? Brandon asked, frowning as he
glanced around. *I have a really weird feeling about this,
Rene. I—*

Rene caught him sharply by the arm, drawing his
mental voice short. When Brandon looked at him, his
brows raised, Rene nodded to indicate the jet. *Voices,*
he said in his mind. *I hear people talking. They're inside
that plane.*

He moved forward, striding briskly but quietly
across the room, ducking and weaving in and among
the planes.

Rene, wait. Brandon followed, his footsteps nearly
silent against the smooth concrete floor.

No way, petit, Rene replied, his brows furrowed, his
mouth turned down in a frown. *That son of a bitch isn't
getting away. Not again. Not this time, goddamn it.*

Rene, wait, Brandon said again. *Something's not right.
I can feel it. I just—*

As the younger man thought this, they rounded the
tail of one of the charter prop planes, just in time to
see Martin Davenant emerging from the jet. He
started to walk down the steel steps while speaking to
someone, a man who stepped out of the plane almost
immediately behind him.

Rene froze and heard Brandon skitter to a halt
behind him, his breath cutting abruptly, sharply short.
Another man stepped onto the stairs leading down
from the jet behind Martin, then another and another and another—ten of them altogether, all men
in their late forties or early fifties dressed nearly iden-
tically in dark, well-tailored, crisply pressed suits.

Oh, Jesus, Brandon gasped inside of Rene's head,
his voice shrill and panicked. *Oh, Christ, oh, fuck me,
Rene—it's the Elders! For Christ's sake, run!*

Rene whirled just in time to see Brandon take off,

racing across the hangar floor away from the jet. He followed, hoping like hell his prosthetic knee didn't fail him now as his feet slapped a heavy, hurried cadence against the floor.

Rene, come on! Brandon reached the door first and shoved against the bar, spilling a broad beam of daylight in as he pushed it open. *Jesus Christ, Rene, we've got to—*

He turned around and Rene shot him.

The nine-millimeter slug caught him in the right shoulder—almost exactly where he'd been shot only weeks earlier—and knocked him a good foot and a half backward, if not more. Brandon floundered, his knees buckling, his hand darting to his chest, and he blinked at Rene in wide-eyed, openmouthed bewilderment and shock.

"I'm sorry, *petit,*" Rene whispered.

Brandon gasped soundlessly, crumpling to the ground, and then the Elders were upon him, moving impossibly fast as they whipped past Rene, all of them grabbing hold of Brandon, tussling with him from all sides.

Brandon tried to fight them, but it was useless. Rene watched as one of them hauled him up, clamping a hand about his throat, and slammed him back against the wall, pinning him with his feet off the floor.

One of the Elders had lagged behind the others, standing with Martin Davenant at the base of the stairs leading from the jet while his fellows had pounced on Brandon. Now he walked forward, the soles of his polished leather shoes scraping softly against the ground, his pace almost leisurely. He watched Brandon's struggle with cool detachment, as if the young man whose blood was splashed all over the concrete was nothing to him, less than a stranger.

He had long, pale hair that hung past the middle of his back in a smooth, heavy sheaf. His face was strikingly handsome, similar in features to Brandon, but colder, harder, as if etched out of a block of granite. Rene knew him; had seen him once before in what at the time had seemed like a dream.

"You and me, we're square, no?" he said to Augustus Noble, drawing the man's gaze. How his grandson and granddaughter could have such warm, wonderfully expressive eyes while his own—the same color, same shape, nearly identical in every way—could be so icy, almost dead, was beyond Rene's understanding.

"*Oui.*" Augustus nodded once, watching as Brandon gargled helplessly for breath, slapping vainly, feebly against the hand that strangled him.

"You got what you came for," Rene said, cutting a painful glance at Brandon. "You'll leave them alone— Tessa and the *bébé?* They're free now. For always."

"You're going to call Augustus Noble," Rene had instructed Martin after untying him in the watch house. "You're going to tell him his grandson Caine is dead. Then you're going to broker a little deal for me."

Martin had been thumbing through the stack of incriminating invoices and bank statements Rene had given him. "And why the fuck am I going to do that?" he'd asked, to which Rene had smiled wanly.

"Because if you don't, mon ami, *I'm going to send the rest of the shit you kept tucked in that ledger directly to his goddamn front door, certified and hand delivered," Rene had replied, tossing him a cell phone. "Do you think I'm really fucking stupid enough to just hand it all over to you and trust you won't screw me? Now make the goddamn call."*

Martin had taken a little too much pleasure in the part of Rene's plan that had him clubbing Rene in the head with the pistol. He'd knocked the senses momentarily from Rene, sending him crashing to his knees, his scalp split open, his ears ringing.

"Nice doing business with you, mon ami," *Martin had sneered, lending particularly snide emphasis on the French words as he'd tossed the Sig Sauer on the floor beside Rene.*

*"You fuck with me on your end of this, and I'll come back
and bleed you dry. You and that goddamn cunt I married."*

He didn't know Tessa's baby was a boy—none of
them did—and Rene sure as hell wasn't about to tell
them. He was going to force Augustus Noble to his
goddamn word and keep him there, no matter what.

Augustus cut those black, fathomless eyes his way
and it felt for all the world as if he'd physically reached
out, clamping his hand against Rene's throat. "We had
an agreement, boy," he said, his voice low and even, yet
still tinged with a brittle undertone of malice. "And
you've kept your part. Now I'll keep mine."

Rene thought of the dream he'd had, when he'd
somehow been inside of Augustus's mind, when he'd
seen the images of two young boys—Augustus and
Rene's own grandfather—sealing their friendship in a
bond of blood, juxtaposed with the horrific sight of an
enormous house ablaze, the people trapped inside
shrieking.

"You know me," Rene had told him on the cell phone from
the watch house in the woods. *"You know my name—Morin."*

*"The world is full of names, boy, and yours—like you—
means nothing to me,"* Augustus had replied.

But as Rene looked now, he could see that wasn't
true; he could see the thin pale strip of scar cutting a
diagonal path across the older man's right palm. Augustus Noble had lied; he'd indeed known Michel
Morin. Even if the other Elders hadn't somehow realized who Rene was—*what* he was—Augustus Noble
did. *And oh, Christ, I think he killed them—killed them all.
He burned my family alive.*

Augustus nodded once to the Elders, and they released Brandon. The young man collapsed to the
floor in a shuddering, bleeding heap, nearly unconscious. Rene turned away, his stomach knotted, his
heart feeling as if he'd just shoved the business end of
a meat cleaver clear through his sternum. *I'm sorry!* he

wanted to cry to Brandon. *I had no choice! I did it to protect Tessa and the baby! There was no other way!*

"What . . . what are you going to do with him now?"
he asked, his voice choked and strained.

"The question is not what I'm going to do *with*
him," Augustus said as two of the other Elders hauled
Brandon up, seizing him beneath the arms. They
began to drag him toward the jet, leaving a glistening trail of blood smeared on the concrete behind
them, "but what I'm going to do *to* him. And that,
boy, is none of your concern."

"But you're not going to kill him," Rene said. "You
need him, no? I told you—Caine is dead. You need
Brandon now so the Nobles will stay dominant."

Augustus studied him for a long moment, those dark
eyes impaling him. "That, too, is none of your concern."

Rene watched as he turned, walking away, the diffused
light seeping down from the windows pale and aglow in
his hair. He waited until they were gone, disappearing
from view among the shadows and airplanes before he
wheeled about, stumbling clumsily for the door.

Oh, God, he thought, raking his fingers through his
hair and staggering about in the glaring sunshine
beyond the hangar. *Oh, viens m'enculer, what have I
done? What have I fucking done?*

He could hear the steel door of the hangar rum-
bling, screeching on its tracks as it rolled open. There
was a low whine as the jet's engines fired up, readying
the sleek plane to taxi out onto a runway. The Elders
meant business; there'd be no side trips to Reno to
take in a little gambling or a show, no visits to nearby
Virginia City to down a cold, frosty one at the Bucket
of Blood Saloon or to pay an amorous call to the
Bunny Ranch brothel. They were heading back to
Kentucky and they were bringing Brandon with them.

God help him, they're taking him home, Rene thought,
then his stomach heaved and he doubled over, vomit-
ing against the tarmac.

Epilogue

Rene returned to South Lake Tahoe in a fugue-like state, his mind and body both on autopilot, his gaze fixed on the road ahead of him without any real awareness. He drove by reflex only, his palms tacky with sweat against the steering wheel, his mouth dry and cottony, his tongue leaden.

I need a drink.

He stopped at a liquor store near the motel and sat behind the wheel for a long time, watching a neon sign for Budweiser in the front window flicker and blink at him in alternating shades of red and blue.

I need a drink, he thought again, because he could still taste vomit in his mouth, and his brain kept wanting to think about things, to return to that goddamn airport hangar in the middle of the desert, and that, in turn, was causing his heart to break.

I'm sorry, petit, he thought, closing his eyes, forking his fingers through his hair. His breath escaped in a shaky, choked sigh. He knew he would never forget that look on Brandon's face, the confusion and pain, the stunned realization of Rene's betrayal. As long as he lived, it would haunt him, burned indelibly into the landscape of his mind.

I did what I had to do. He grasped the steering wheel again, folding his fingers so fiercely, it made his injured palm ache. *Goddamn it, I did what needed to be done to protect Tessa and the baby. There was no other way.*

He opened his eyes, relaxing his grip on the steering wheel. After studying the blinking beer sign for another brief moment, he reached for the door handle. A fifth of Bloodhorse would help numb his mind, ease his memory. Or maybe some vodka, a nice bottle of Grey Goose to anesthetize his heart.

But he couldn't bring himself to open the door, get out of the car, even though the liquor was his old and familiar friend, the escape he'd always sought whenever he'd needed refuge from thinking too much, caring too deeply.

Because there's Tessa now, he thought. *And the baby.*

He turned the key in the ignition, firing up the engine again. Dropping the car in reverse, he pulled out of the parking lot and back on the road, leaving the store behind. He returned to the motel and ducked quietly into his room.

The curtains were drawn, the room enveloped in shadows. Tessa lay sleeping in the bed, blankets draped in graceful folds to outline her slim figure beneath. He crossed the room and went to her, easing himself into bed, spooning his body against hers in the darkness.

Forgive me, he thought as he drew his arm across her waist, closing his eyes against the sting of tears. He could never tell her what had happened, never let her learn the truth. She wouldn't forgive him and he knew it. There would be no explaining it, no undoing it, nothing to make her understand. *I love you, Tessa. They'll never bother you, never come for you, never hurt you again. I love you, and I made sure of that for you. It was the only way, the only choice I had. Because nothing else matters to me in the world. Only you and the* bébé—*our son.*

Tessa murmured softly in her sleep and he felt her

hand slip against his, holding his hand gently against her stomach. He could open his mind and sense the baby inside of her, the golden glow that had nearly waned, the life his blood had helped to restore.

Our son. A tear slipped from the corner of his eye, trailing down his cheek toward the pillow. *I'll spend the rest of my life making things right for you somehow, Tessa. You and our* bébé. *With all that I have—everything I call my own, I swear it,* pischouette.

"I swear it," he breathed against her hair.

ABOUT THE AUTHOR

Sara Reinke lives with her family in Kentucky. The first in her Brethren series, *Dark Thirst,* has been called "a great, keep-you-up-all-night read" by *New York Time* bestselling author Karen Robards as well as "a new twist on the vampire legend" and a "fascinating and unique romance" by *Romantic Times Book Reviews* magazine. Reinke is a member of the Louisville Romance Writers Chapter of Romance Writers of America. Visi her online at www.sarareinke.com.